MONTROSE MANOR | BOOK ONE

BETWEEN SUNRISE AND SUNSET

A. R. TALLEY

Black Rose Writing | Texas

ISBN: 978-1-68513-689-5
LIBRARY OF CONGRESS CONTROL NUMBER: 2025941482
PUBLISHED BY BLACK ROSE WRITING
www.blackrosewriting.com

Printed in the United States of America
Suggested Retail Price (SRP) $21.95

Between Sunrise and Sunset is printed in Bookerly

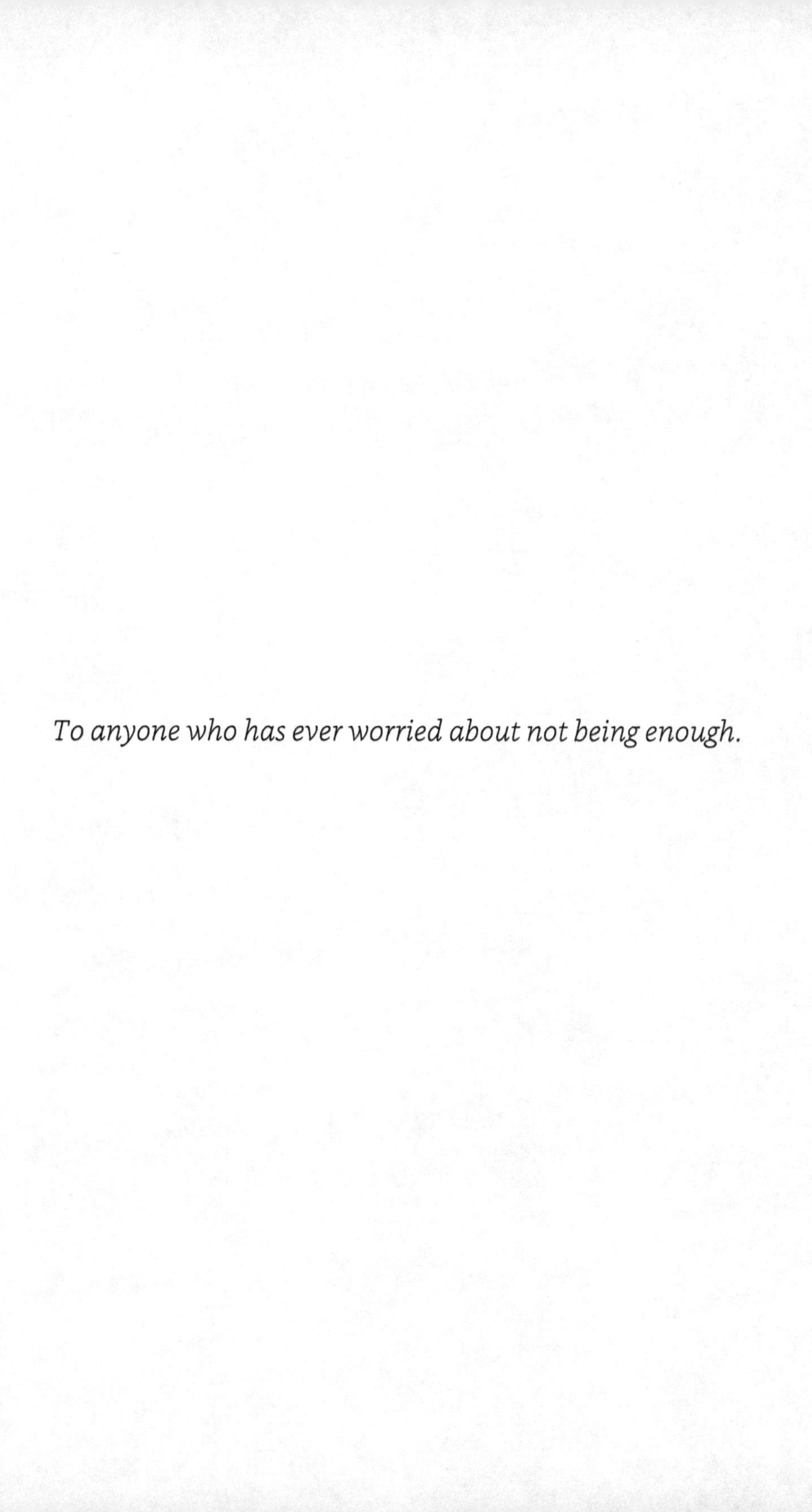

To anyone who has ever worried about not being enough.

BETWEEN SUNRISE AND SUNSET

CHAPTER ONE

"Accuse not a servant unto his master."
–Proverbs 30:10

Lainey had never been summoned to Lady Warrington's chambers before. And of course, it had to be at the most inconvenient time of day. She had three more bedchambers to dust and sweep and bed linens to change. Her shoes clacked against the wood flooring and echoed through the vast hallway, but it was the hammering pulse in her head that eclipsed all other household noises. In her haste, she passed open doorways, the heat from stoked fires briefly warming her legs. Threads of smoke and the sweet smell of honey floated in the air from recently snuffed candles.

Stopping at the massive walnut door leading to Lady Warrington's quarters, Lainey reached up and tucked a few stray hairs into her bonnet. How she wished she could leave the homes of gentry behind and join her brother Robert in Barbados. She would recover what was left of her family and accomplish what her mother wanted. But not today.

She smoothed her skirt and apron, took a deep breath, and blew it out slowly. Squaring her shoulders, she lifted her hand and knocked.

"Come in."

The stern voice warned her of trouble to come—not that she didn't expect it. One more time, she ran her hands down her apron, then reached for the brass handle and pushed the heavy door open. Stepping inside, she was surprised. Lady Warrington sat at her desk. Her odious son, Harold, Mr. Hobbs the butler, and Mrs. Crowthers, the head housekeeper had lined up behind the mistress of Harlsburg Manor, each wearing a severe frown—with the exception of Harold. Lainey was in deeper trouble than she'd imagined. Not one friendly face greeted her, not even Mrs. Crowthers, who'd been Lainey's advocate since she arrived.

"You asked to meet with me?" Lainey said, dipping into a small curtsey. She purposely ignored Master Harold and the ugly scratch that ran down one cheek and across his neck. She hadn't meant to harm him, but she couldn't deny he deserved what he got.

"A serious charge has been brought against you," Lady Warrington said.

Lainey's breath caught in her chest. "A charge?"

Without a word, Lady Warrington lifted a small, jewel-studded tiara from her lap and placed it on the desk in front of her. "Do you recognize this?"

"Yes, ma'am. That's Miss Lucinda's tiara."

"Can you explain why it was discovered in your quarters among your belongings?"

Lainey's eyes grew wide at the accusation. She glanced toward Master Harold, his expression now a derisive smirk. If it weren't for the scratch, Lainey might have thought he was smiling.

"Alaina?" Lady Warrington's use of Lainey's formal name drew back her attention.

"No, Ma'am."

"She obviously stole it," Master Harold said.

"I did not!" Her eyes met his and she knew. In retribution, Harold planted the tiara in her room.

"Is this your answer?" his mother asked.

Her heartbeat and breathing increased. "I swear, Lady Warrington, I did not steal the tiara. Possibly Miss Lucinda was in my room, or…"

"A member of the family in the servants' quarters?" Mr. Hobbs asked. A preposterous notion, Lainey agreed. But she couldn't accuse Harold of the deed, just as she couldn't confess to the reason for his injury, or his need for retaliation.

She turned her attention back to the lady of the house, silently praying for mercy.

"I'm afraid your answer is unsatisfactory," Lady Warrington said.

"A common thief," Harold added, shaking his head.

"We will not tolerate such behavior in this house. Lord Warrington is a man of honor and respect. How would it reflect upon his lordship, if while a guest was staying with us, some of their belongings disappeared? We will not employ anyone with the least taint of thievery about them."

She was being dismissed.

"I took you on as a favor to Mrs. Crowthers." Lady Warrington nodded in the head housekeeper's direction. "And as a favor to Mrs. Crowthers, we will not turn you over to the constable. However, you will leave this house immediately. You will take nothing with you but what you came with. Is that understood? And it goes without saying, you shall have no reference from this house."

Lainey swallowed, an attempt to keep her emotions in check. She turned a pleading gaze on the housekeeper. If anyone could save her, Mrs. Crowthers was that person.

With sympathy in her eyes, Mrs. Crowthers spoke. "Excuse me, ma'am. Perhaps if I asked around, I might be able to discover how the tiara was misplaced."

Exhaling a breath of annoyance, Lady Warrington waved a hand in Mrs. Crowthers' direction. "I appreciate your attachment to the girl, but I will not have a thief in my home. Please ensure that she collects her belongings and leaves immediately." She reached into a desk drawer, extracted a piece of paper, and picked up her quill. When no one moved, Lady Warrington turned a stern eye on Lainey. "You are dismissed."

Lainey's lower lip quivered. Was there no mercy? No clemency? This was the first time Lainey had been the cause of any concern, and yet the punishment was swift and harsh. She turned back to Harold. His mouth had pulled up at the corner, a half grin of sorts, and revenge glimmered in his eyes.

Mrs. Crowthers moved from behind the desk. Gently, she took Lainey by the arm and led her from the room.

When they stepped into the hall, Lainey took a shuddered breath. "I didn't take it," she said through tears she barely restrained. She had to maintain control. She couldn't let Harold see he had won.

Without a word, Mrs. Crowthers led her down the paneled hallway, through the kitchen to the servants' staircase. As they climbed, Lainey's mind jumped from one thought to another. Where would she go? How would she find work? It wouldn't take long before word of her dismissal would be all over the county. No one would hire her. How would she get to Robert?

As Lainey packed, Mrs. Crowthers observed from the doorway.

"What happened with Master Harold?" she asked, breaking the silence.

Lainey glanced down at the small satchel that contained her few personal belongings, a faded likeness of her mother in a frame, the two letters she'd received from Robert, a few undergarments, and a blouse and skirt she wore on her personal days.

"I'm sure you can guess," Lainey said as she clutched at her beloved locket, the one she habitually wore about her neck. There was something reassuring about the smooth, cool metal.

"Was it the first time?"

Lainey let out a derisive laugh. "Hardly. But certainly the most persistent. He was into his cups."

"Not enough to forget what happened."

"No, not enough." Lainey pushed the past night's memory back to the place where she kept all unpleasant thoughts—her mother's death, her older brother's accident, her father's drinking. If only she'd been able to escape without scratching Harold. It could be he would have left her alone.

Mrs. Crowthers smiled sympathetically. "Where will you go?" the woman asked.

Lainey shook her head. "I don't know." That's what concerned her the most.

"Let me write to my sister. She has a position in London. Surely, she'll be able to find you employment there. Especially after I explain…you know, about Master Harold."

Lainey pulled herself a little taller. "No. I will go my own way. I think now is the time I locate Robert." She scanned her satchel to reassure herself his letters were there. "His last letter was from Barbados. I can go there."

"But how?"

"I don't know. But it's what I must do. I will find a way." She hoped she sounded more confident than she felt.

Lainey fastened the clasp on the satchel, then with feigned stoicism, she descended the three flights of stairs and walked out the servants' door. She didn't stop for sentimental farewells with the other servants at the manor, nor did she shed a tear. Truth was, she never enjoyed working for the Warrington family—had never felt accepted by the staff or the family. Only Mrs. Crowthers had been a friend, but even she couldn't save Lainey from Harold Warrington's groping hands or his unjust accusation.

With the large sandstone manor house now behind her, Lainey marched down the gravel path toward the columns that marked the entrance to the estate, her footfall the only sound in her ears. Moments before she reached her freedom, Harold stepped out from behind a tree and sneered.

"You'll be sorry you didn't take me up on my offer. You think you'll have any better luck out on the road? A girl...traveling alone? You'll be prey to the worst kind of men."

"I've already been that." She raised her chin. "And I managed to fend him off."

Harold absently touched the scratch on his cheek. "I should have had you whipped for this."

"In that case you would have to explain where it came from." She shook her head. "Coward you are, you wouldn't take the chance that someone might believe my account."

"So, what if they did? Do you think anyone would care? You wouldn't be the first plaything in my father's employ."

"No. Simply the first who refused to play."

"And what good did that do you?"

"I'll make my way. You'll see. And someday, you will be unveiled as the devil you are."

She took an unwavering step forward, hoping—no, praying—that Harold would not detain her. With a sinister expression, he watched, but did not advance as she moved past him. Without looking back, she walked past the tan-colored columns and out into the Essex countryside, nervous to be on her own. This wasn't the first time she'd been left to make her own way. Just the first time she had no family to help her.

"Don't expect any assistance from me if you're found on the side of the road," Harold called after her.

She continued on as if she hadn't heard him.

"I'd rather die on the side of the road," she said to herself, "than be left to your mercy."

~~*

Leaving Harlsburg Manor turned out to be the easy part of Lainey's journey. She walked through three straight days of bone-chilling rain, only gaining shelter under trees—if that counted as shelter. After days of being cold and hungry, she traded her satchel and clothing for a night in a barn, a stale piece of bread, and a tattered blanket.

Morning number four, she awoke stiff and cold. The sun was up, promising a warmer day. Leaves overhead showed signs of gold they'd hidden all summer long. Smells from a nearby farmhouse—woodsmoke, manure, and hay—drifted on the air, giving a small measure of assurance. She started walking, ignoring the growl in her belly. She had to keep going. She had to reach Liverpool. Hopefully, she traveled in the right direction.

After walking for some time, Lainey heard the lazy clop of horse hooves behind her. As the sound drew closer, she moved to the side of the road, giving the rider easy passage. It wasn't a rider, however. When the horse pulled up beside her, she realized the animal was an old nag pulling a milk float. Stepping further into the grass, she waited for the cart to pass.

But it didn't pass. The farmer sitting atop the wood seat, tipped his hat. A skinny fellow with a full beard and longish hair smiled at her.

"You headed to Montville?" he asked.

It seemed days since Lainey had heard another voice. It was as if the man had spoken in a foreign tongue. She could only manage to stare and gape.

"Are you okay, miss?"

She blinked. "Yes." She wasn't sure which question she answered.

"I'm headed there myself. Do you want to ride along? You appear as if you've been on the road a while."

Lainey glanced down at her clothing. Mud lined the bottom of her skirt. Leaves and pieces of straw seemed stitched into the rest of her clothing. She must be a sight. Humbled by his kindness, tears stung at the back of her throat.

"Thank you, sir."

He reached out to help her into the cart. Lainey scrambled to take his hand and within moments was settled next to him, her tired legs relishing the rest.

He extended his hand again. "Emmett Johnson, miss. Pleased to meet you."

"Alaina Clarkson," she said. She took his hand and gave it a sure shake.

"Do you have acquaintances in Montville?" he asked after he had signaled the nag to move along. The horse barely moved faster than Lainey walked, but Lainey nearly giggled at the relief she felt—at least the horse was doing the walking.

"No, sir. I'm on my way to meet up with my brother."

"And where is he?"

"Last I heard, he was in the Caribbean."

"The Caribbean?"

"Yes."

"You planning to walk there?"

She laughed. "No, sir. I was hoping to make it into Liverpool and obtain employment, so I could buy passage."

"Ambitious plan for a young girl on her own."

She squared her shoulders. "I've been on my own for some time. I am not as young as you think."

The man chuckled.

After a period of silence, Emmett asked, "Do you know how far Liverpool is from here?"

"I understand it's some distance," she said, trying to hide that she really had no idea exactly where Liverpool was or how to get to there.

Emmett scanned the countryside, taking his time to answer.

"Well," he eventually said, "depending on how fast you walk…I'd say you have near on three weeks by foot."

Lainey's heart dropped into her stomach. Three more weeks? She'd die of starvation first.

"With the weather changin'," the man continued, "you might think about holdin' up somewhere…maybe work some place. You got skills?"

"I've been in domestic service."

"That's good. Perchance you might find a house needin' some help. You could check up at Montrose. Nice house. Nice family. They employ domestics. I'm headed right there. Have a delivery to make." He nodded toward the back of the cart. "I could introduce you to Mrs. Hollingsworth. She's the housekeeper."

"Thank you. But I really think I should keep moving."

He shrugged. "Suit yourself. But with winter comin' on, you best make good time."

They spent the rest of the trip talking about the weather and the countryside. As they drew close to Montville, Emmett told Lainey about the village, the people he knew there, and all about the Montgomery family.

"Had a bad spell there about three years ago. The young Mistress Montgomery passed in childbirth. Babe died shortly thereafter. Sad affair. Shows livin' in a big, ole house doesn't spare you the heartache."

They pulled around a tree-lined bend, and the village came into view. A main street lined with shops—some brick, some Tudor—all with slate roofs. The street itself was muddy and full of ruts from carts and carriages. Several people milled about, shopping for the day's vegetables.

Emmett tugged on the reins, bringing the float to a halt.

"Don't suppose you've changed your mind? Want to come up to the house and meet with Mrs. Hollingsworth?"

"No," Lainey said, coming to herself. "No, thank you. I'll get off here and see what I can make of the village." She gathered her dirty, tattered skirt about her and paused. Turning to Emmett, she fought the urge to give him a hug. "I can't thank you enough," she said. "May the Lord bless you for your kindness."

His smile revealed yellowed teeth. "I can always use blessings from the Lord." He patted her hand. "You take care. And think about what I said. Walking through the countryside by yourself…it's a dangerous business. You never can tell who you'll meet out on the open road. And the weather is changing. Find yourself some work. Your brother will wait for you."

Lainey wished more than believed that sentiment to be true. Taking in a deep breath, she climbed down from the cart and paused as Emmett pulled the nag in the direction of the stone bridge leading to Montrose. She waited until the cart was well down the road then turned to the town of Montville.

CHAPTER TWO

"Is not marriage an open question…?"
–Ralph Waldo Emerson

A frigid wind whipped across the expansive terrace of Montrose Manor. Phillip pulled his coat tight, folding his arms to keep it closed. As chilled as he felt, it was nothing compared to the ice in his bones. The afternoon had soured with the simple mention of the word "marriage." Not that Phillip minded the idea of marriage, if it were intended for someone else—his sister, Charlotte, or Kenton, his younger brother. But for him? He'd already fulfilled that duty, not that Katherine had ever been a duty.

Katherine.

The thought of her brought a different kind of pain, sharp and searing. He could remember her smile, full of charm and mischief, her long hair the color of bittersweet chocolate, soft and feathery as a fern, and those eyes, those beautiful copper-colored eyes, haunting him forever.

Phillip lifted his face heavenward. Surely Katherine would save him from a loveless marriage. If he thought of her long enough, hard enough, she would give him the answer, the argument he needed to deter his father. For now, he'd settle for weeding the earlier conversation from his mind.

Walking often settled his soul. With a deep breath, he stepped off the terrace and down the cobblestone path that led to the edge of the manicured park, but the memory of his father's request persisted.

~~*

The afternoon had been quiet until Lord Montgomery joined them in the parlor.

"Tell me, Phillip, what do you think of Miss Hilton?"

Phillip raised his head, using a finger to mark his place in the book he'd been reading. He hadn't heard his father enter. His mother sat across the room, near a window, working on her latest embroidery. A fire crackled in the hearth near the chair where he sat.

"Miss Hilton?" Phillip repeated.

"Yes," his father said as he moved toward the fireplace, lording over the very air of the room.

Phillip shrugged. He'd not given the girl much thought. "I guess, if asked…"

"Which you are."

"I'd say she was a bright, intelligent girl. If not a little quiet."

"Would you say she's attractive?"

Phillip glanced toward his mother. Was she paying attention? Did she have any interest in the conversation? She maintained her work, not meeting Phillip's eyes.

"I suppose she's a comely girl. Why do you ask?"

"She's the same age as your sister, Charlotte, is she not?"

His father knew the answer to that. Charlotte and Marianne Hilton had been playmates since they learned to walk. "She is."

Lord Montgomery walked across the room to his desk and picked up a worn brown pipe. He tapped it on the edge of a waste basket emptying the remaining ash. Philip glanced at his mother. He knew she hated the smell of smoke. She stared at Lord Montgomery, her nose wrinkled in disgust. She would react to a pipe but appeared indifferent to the direction of the conversation. Phillip sighed. She would offer no support.

"I've been speaking with Chester Markhall about a union with Charlotte," Lord Montgomery said, redirecting the conversation back to Phillip's sister and regaining Phillip's attention.

"Marriage?" Phillip turned toward his mother. Her embroidery rested in her lap as she gazed out the window. She appeared disinterested, but that was a trick she often used when, in truth, she was listening intently. "Isn't Markhall a little old for Charlotte?" Phillip asked.

"Age is not an issue when the match is a good one."

"I appreciate that, Father. But he's closer to your age than mine, and Charlotte's only seventeen."

Lord Montgomery flashed a disgruntled smirk at his wife. The subject of Markhall's age must be a source of contention between them. Could be his mother had used the same words. That wouldn't be surprising, Phillip thought. Why would any mother want to marry her only daughter off to a man more than twice her age?

"How old are you, Phillip?" his father asked.

"Twenty and eight, sir."

"And you've already had yourself a wife and would have a child or two as well, if misfortune had not intervened."

Phillip swallowed hard, opening his book for a diversion, but he couldn't read the words. They brought no comfort— no relief from the customary stab to his heart at the mention of Katherine's passing. This was typical of his father, consistently reminding Phillip of his loss. At times, he wished he were in the grave as well. Death sounded like a better alternative than his father's constant harping.

His father continued. "Do you not think Markhall could be anxious to find a bride? It's been years since his wife passed away."

"God rest her soul," Phillip's mother said from across the room.

"I cannot say what Markhall's intentions are," Phillip replied. "I am not in his confidence. Some gentlemen make a sport of avoiding marriage."

"I can assure you, Markhall does not. He is most eager to find a wife."

"Is Charlotte eager? Does she have some affection for the man?"

"What difference does affection make? She recognizes what her responsibilities are. She knows she must make a good match, which is exactly what Markhall is. And since Markhall's wife died without producing an heir, he realizes what must be done as well. *Herein lies wisdom, beauty and increase; without this, folly, age and cold decay.*"

Phillip stifled a groan. Once his father started quoting the Bard, it was only a matter of time before he reminded Phillip of his own responsibilities.

"Charles Hilton is also seeking a suitable match for Marianne," Lord Montgomery continued. "I have consented to help him. It's possible the girls could have a double wedding since they've been as close as sisters."

"Utterly reminiscent of sisters," Phillip said, taking guard. "Father, this is all somewhat interesting, but I don't understand why you are discussing the matter with me."

Phillip glanced at his mother again. Certainly, two weddings at the same time would be too much to endure. Lady Montgomery had abandoned her interests outside the window and focused her attentions on her son. *Help me, Mother, please*, he silently begged. They held eye contact as Lord Montgomery continued.

"Trying to find another viewpoint is all," Lord Montgomery said. "Perchance you are aware of a suitable gentleman who would consider Miss Hilton as a wife. Of course, she doesn't come with much of a dowry, but that is not to say she doesn't have other compensating charms. What about Hal? He hasn't married yet, has he?"

Phillip scoffed. "He has not. Nor is he likely to. And while he might be my friend, I wouldn't let Hal within three counties of any young woman of my acquaintance."

"Well, perhaps there are others? Possibly even yourself."

There it was.

Lord Montgomery leaned against the front of his desk with his unlit pipe propped in his mouth.

"Our families have been well connected for years. Charles is one of my most trusted friends, and his advice in legal matters has been unparalleled. He's spared no expense in raising Marianne as a lady even though they are not wholly in the same standing as our family. I've often viewed her as I do Charlotte. I wish her to make a good match."

"Well, Father," Phillip said, totally grasping his father's duplicity. "I can ask among my associates if anyone desires to marry. But other than that, I don't have anything else to offer."

"Phillip," his mother said, her voice filled with deep tenderness. "Your father is being overly obtuse. He does not want you asking among your associates. He wants you to offer for Marianne."

He sighed. Why must his mother be so direct? She rose from her seat and walked over to him. Reaching down, she laid a soft hand on his cheek. The gesture made him feel young, childish.

"We know your heart was wounded when Katherine and the baby died."

He blinked. *Wounded?* He was desolate. His heart lay in ruins, his life stripped of meaning.

"But dear, it is time to consider not only your future but the future of the estate as well. You need a wife. The estate needs an heir."

Phillip scowled. "I understand my duties to the estate, Mother."

"Do you?" his father asked. "Kenton will be leaving for Cambridge. Charlotte will be married. Your mother and I want to retire to the house in London. That will leave you alone here at the estate."

"I am aware of many men who manage estates without the assistance of a wife."

"We do not want that lonely existence for you," his mother said.

"*Look in the glass,*" his father recited, "*and tell the face thou viewest now is the time that face should form another.*"

"Dearest, I don't think this is the time to be quoting sonnets," Phillip's mother said. She turned back to Phillip and took both his hands in hers. "Marianne is a lovely young woman. She comes from good stock, would be able to provide you with beautiful children—many of them."

Phillip bolted to his feet, pushing his mother's hands aside and dropping his book to the floor with a thud. He walked to the window, as far from his parents as the room would allow. "Mother. Father," he said, trying to control his anger. "As fond as I am of Marianne, I do not love her."

"Sentimentality," Lord Montgomery barked. "What you had with Katherine was unusual, Phillip. Men marry for many reasons, position, wealth, seldom for love. If a woman is agreeable in both temperament and appearance, we count ourselves lucky. All this talk of love—it's a result of Victoria and that German she married."

"Dearest," Lady Montgomery gently scolded.

"It's unfortunate, is all I can say," he said in his defense.

"Unfortunate?" Phillip said, turning on his father. "You find love unfortunate?"

"Your father doesn't mean that. He simply means that love often grows between a man and a woman when they share a life together."

"You must forgive me. I am inclined to want it to develop before the banns are read."

"You are fond of the girl," his father pointed out. "You said so yourself. Fondness is as good as love in the beginning."

"She's akin to a sister is what I said. I'm fond of her the way I am of Charlotte." Phillip glanced between his parents. "Tell me you have not spoken to Mr. Hilton about this." Lord Montgomery diverted his eyes. "Do you not think a man of my age can arrange his own nuptials?"

"I would expect it!" his father nearly shouted. "But, Phillip, you have not demonstrated any inclination in that direction. It's been three years! It's time to move forward."

"That's easy for you to say."

"Phillip. Dear, dear Phillip," his mother said, coming to stand next to him. She reached for his hands again. He took a step back. He would not be treated as a child. He knew his rebuff caused her pain for which he was sorry, but he would not, could not capitulate in the slightest.

His mother pulled herself a little taller and said, "Spend some time with Miss Hilton. See if affection doesn't bloom in her company. You simply need some time—with her and to get used to the idea." She paused. "At least give it a try for your father and me."

As he walked in the cold and reflected on the conversation, he couldn't imagine feeling true affection for any other woman. What a ludicrous idea—spend time with the girl. He'd loved Katherine from the first time they danced. It was a cruel fate that had taken her life and that of the child's. It appeared fate was once more taking control of his life. Why couldn't his father leave him in peace—allow him his grief?

Although chilled, he kept walking until he found himself standing outside the family cemetery plot. It was quiet there, and the promise of snow hung heavy along with the fresh scent of Scotch pine. Phillip stared at the family tombstones, lined like leaden bells of mourning across the ground.

Marianne Hilton was an attractive girl. She had her mother's features, petite and well-defined facial structure, hair the color of spun gold, and eyes as blue as a springtime sky. She had blossomed of late—turning from Charlotte's gawky little friend into a graceful young lady. But that didn't mean he wanted to marry her. Phillip scowled. He had no more desire for the girl than he did for his own sister.

He reached out and laid a hand on the cemetery gate. It was cold to the touch and groaned as he pulled it open. Ever since childhood, Phillip felt a rueful reverence when he entered these grounds. His great-grandparents, grandparents, and two of his siblings who had died in infancy rested here, along with Katherine and the baby. Phillip stepped lightly across the frost-covered grass until he stood directly in front of the headstone—Katherine's name engraved in the granite.

Katherine Rebecca Waller Montgomery
April 4, 1818 —November 21,1839
Directly underneath hers, was the infant's.

Donald Phillip Montgomery
November 20, 1839 — November 21, 1839

They had died within hours of each other, both in the dark early hours of morning. Phillip hadn't even had a chance to ask Katherine what to name the child. He'd decided upon his own father's name, although the man hadn't seemed flattered at the honor. In retrospect, Phillip wished he'd named the child after Katherine's father instead.

As he stared at their names, the same empty, cold ache clutched at his chest. The feeling had not faded over time.

"Katherine," he said, his voice husky, "they're pressuring me to remarry. Father's actually chosen the girl for me. Miss Hilton. Do you remember her? She's Charlotte's friend. The one you teased me about. The one you said was enamored with me. I can't imagine marrying her. Being…" he couldn't say the word. The thought of being intimate…he cringed at the idea.

"What would you have me do?" Closing his eyes, he remembered gazing into hers—the hint of teasing ever present.

"The girl is infatuated! Don't you remember how she blushed when you complimented her dress?" Katherine's voice filled his ears.

He opened his eyes and sensed her standing before him, her head tilted just so, her dark hair falling over her shoulder as it had on the day he asked her to be his wife.

"The dress had a nice color."

"Of course it did. And the handsome Phillip Montgomery took notice. The poor girl, you stole her heart and didn't care."

"I never stole a thing."

She smiled. "Not true. You stole my affections."

"I thought you gave them to me."

"Why would I do something as foolish as that? Next thing I know, you'll be offering for my hand in marriage."

He wrinkled his brow. "We are married, dear Katherine. Did you forget?"

She reached up to stroke his cheek, teasing him toward her own lips. "Prove it," she whispered.

A deep chill ran down his spine as he leaned toward her, but the illusion disappeared. Vanished. He threw his head back in frustration. "You didn't answer me. What do I do about my father's plans!" He surveyed the empty graveyard, feeling forsaken. Not an unfamiliar feeling.

Closing his eyes, he called out, "Little Donald would be three now." Perchance if he talked about the child, he could conjure her anew. Instead, the air filled with a stifling silence. He often wondered about the child. He'd been born with a mop of dark hair, identical to his mother's. Who would he favor now? Would he be a miniature of Katherine? Or would the child have favored him?

The ache was unbearable. He turned from the cemetery, wondering if his parents were right. If he spent time with Marianne, would he grow fond of her? Could she lessen the pain?

"It doesn't seem fair," he said aloud as he walked back through the cemetery gate, "to ask anyone to follow you. I can't love anyone as I loved you. Any woman would be a pale replacement for what I've lost."

Resignation was his only recourse. His fate was cast. Montrose needed an heir. His parents had spoken. Being the oldest male, the estate controlled his life—regardless of his personal wishes, regardless of his happiness.

CHAPTER THREE

*"If you give to a thief he cannot steal from you,
And he is then no longer a thief."*
–William Saroyan

How long Lainey stood at the mouth of the town, she did not know. It was quaint. Unlike London with its busy, carriage-filled streets. And not at all similar to the small village that had been closest to Harlsburg Manor. Montville, with buildings that stood shoulder to shoulder, had charm and warmth. The townsfolk appeared friendly and welcoming. Lainey could imagine living in such a place if she didn't have other plans.

Down the main thoroughfare, she spotted a cart, loaded with fruits and vegetables, parked next to a brown and tan Tudor store. From the flock of ladies standing around, probably haggling over a price, Lainey concluded this must be the local market. Her stomach grumbled at the sight of fresh food. How long had it been since she'd had anything better to eat than wild berries?

She started in the direction of the cart, keeping her distance, but trying to imagine how wonderful a real meal would taste. Her mouth watered as she thought of a thick and savory stew. Eyeing the cart from across the way, she knew she had no money to purchase a morsel. If she wanted a bit to eat, she'd have to steal it. Oh, the irony of it. Harold Warrington had falsely accused her of being a thief and now she was forced to be one. The thought unsettled her, but starving unsettled her more. One apple, or one potato…it's not as if one piece of missing produce would harm the vendor—if he somehow noticed it missing.

Two ladies, house servants Lainey guessed by their dark-colored skirts, chatted with another woman, probably the wife of the owner. She wore a cap and apron, her girth suggesting a full larder at home. Somehow that thought made pilfering less offensive.

Lainey peered over the shoulder of one of the women. Apples, plums, black berries and elderberries were piled to one side, while the other held acorn squash, pumpkin, carrots, mushrooms, and potatoes. Lainey inhaled deeply, reveling in the scent of berries, apples, and the musky smell of earth from the root vegetables. Her mouth watered. One apple. They were conveniently located, so that she could walk past and slip one in her pocket. She'd walk down the street and duck behind another store, or go back to the bridge, or possibly to the church, whose steeple she could view over the roof of the buildings across the street. There, she would sit and eat slowly, enjoying each bite.

She glanced over her shoulder, surveying the area. When one of the women nearby began to haggle over the outrageous price for a sack of potatoes, Lainey made her move. She stepped to the side of the cart, reached out and grabbed a red, luscious apple from the top of the pile. As she slipped the fruit into her pocket, a heavy hand came down on her wrist. Lainey stared up into the grizzled face of a man twice her age.

"Where ya goin' with tha, missy?"

"With what?" she said. Her mouth went dry.

"Tha apple."

Lainey tried to pull away. "Unhand me!"

"Nora! Send the boy for the constable!"

Lainey tugged and pulled and begged. "Please, please, I'll put it back. I promise. And I won't return."

"You certainly won't," the man said with a sneer as he tightened his grip. "Nora! Urry up!"

"May I offer some assistance?"

Lainey and the grizzled man both turned at the sound of a stranger's voice.

"Oh…Oh! Mr. Montgomery, 'ow nice to see you. Can I offer you some fresh produce? Nora!" he hollered again.

"I already sent Marcus," Nora replied, coming to stand next to the man.

Lainey glanced at the woman who, moments before, had been serving the other ladies. Everyone present turned to take in the spectacle. She wanted to crawl under the cart and disappear. How much more humiliating could this be? She found out in a matter of seconds.

"Oh! Mr. Montgomery! May I 'elp you?" Nora said as she caught sight of the new arrival. Lainey's attention turned to the gentleman, and he was a gentleman no doubt, dressed in pressed trousers and a double-breasted coat of the finest wool. Lainey had seen similar fashions on Harold Warrington. This man was tall, a good head taller than Lainey, and he held himself with such comportment—such grace. Under a black top hat, a peek of warm, golden blond hair curled around his ears. His mouth was flat…no smile, no frown, just empty, as were his russet brown eyes.

"Here, woman, hold this girl while I 'elp his lordship," the man said, passing Lainey's wrist to Nora.

"I'm not a Lord yet," the gentleman said. "And I apologize, Mr. Walker, but I didn't come to make a purchase." He hesitated for a heartbeat, then added, "I meant, make a purchase for myself. I wanted to pay for the item in question for the young lady." The gentleman glanced toward Lainey, who should have been pulling against Nora's grip, but found herself mesmerized by the man's offer.

"She's no lady, sir," Mr. Walker said.

It was then that the gentleman first observed Lainey. His eyes flashed in a recognition of sorts. But Lainey had never seen the man before. How could he have recognized her? His eyes narrowed as he studied her face. She reached up with her free hand and tried to smooth her hair, following his gaze as he measured her appearance. Instantly, her tattered, mud-stained skirt and blouse with specks of hay from places she'd slept made her feel small, insignificant…and yet, it appeared as if he was there to help.

"She was stealin' from us," Mr. Walker explained.

"She must be hungry," the man said without taking his eyes off of her.

"In that case, she should get a job like the rest 'o us an pay for wha she needs. I don run no charity."

The gentleman forced himself to turn his attention back to Mr. Walker. "I understand. That's why I am offering to cover the cost of the items she needs."

"Mr. Montgomery, you can't do that," Nora said. "You start payin' for one 'o 'ese urchins and you'll be payin' for 'em all!"

The man offered a watered-down smile. "Mrs. Walker, I am not offering to pay for every urchin on the street. But as you can discern…" He motioned to Lainey, "she is obviously hungry. Maybe if we feed her, she could seek some employment and be able to pay for herself next time."

"Mr. Montgomery, yo' generosity is verra magnanimous. But certainly, we can't allow thievery to go unpunished," Mr. Walker argued.

"The constable's already on 'is way," Mrs. Walker added.

"Mr. Walker," the gentleman held out a hand, inviting Mr. Walker aside, as if taking him in great confidence. Mr. Walker puffed his chest at the honor. Together they took one step away. *Hardly a private audience*, Lainey thought.

"Please, allow the girl to select a few items and add it to my family's account. When the constable comes, ask him— as a personal favor to me," he laid his hand across his heart, "if he would be able to find a place for her to stay. And possibly he could help her locate some employment. I'm certain he will be more than willing to help if you mention my name."

Mr. Walker stood speechless, uncertain how to respond. It was clear he wanted to please a Montgomery…but what about the punishment due?

"And please accept this," Mr. Montgomery said, passing a coin into Mr. Walker's hand. "For your troubles."

Mr. Walker took the coin without hesitation, slipping it into an apron pocket. Lainey shook her head. Funny how a coin managed to satisfy the man's need for justice.

"Certainly, sir. I'm sure the constable will be mos' accomodatin'."

"I'm sure he will be." Mr. Montgomery turned to Lainey and offered her a bow.

"Thank you," she whispered.

Without another word, he walked away. Lainey watched him cross the street and meet up with another young man, equally well-dressed, and a lovely young woman wearing a well-adorned hat. The two men talked for a moment, then, with the lady, proceeded down the lane.

Lainey frowned, torn between gratitude and censure. It was her observation that the wealthy often tried to ease their guilt by giving to charity...or charity cases in this instance. And what was with his scrutiny of her? So, she wasn't as clean, and well-dressed as the lady friend he escorted down the street. She was about to build a case against the man, but before she could really get going, the constable arrived. Mr. Walker was good to his word. He told the man of Mr. Montgomery's request and, moments later, Lainey followed the constable down the lane and toward the church.

CHAPTER FOUR

"Where there's marriage without love,
There will be love without marriage."
–Poor Richard's Almanac, May

Eyes downcast, Phillip turned from the Walker's cart and started across the street where his brother waited, stepping carefully, observing to avoid muddy puddles and ruts, and the occasional pile of horse droppings. Stopping and helping that young woman was merely a stall tactic. Whatever it took to keep from making a call to the Hilton's.

Katherine's teasing voice filled his ears. *"Extremely philanthropic of you."*

He glanced to his side, pleased to find her there. He started to lift his arm to assist her in crossing the street but caught himself before anyone would notice.

"Extremely advantageous of me," he replied, lowering his voice so that no one would hear him talking. "You know why I'm here."

"To rescue damsels in distress?"

"If that's what you want to call Miss Marianne."

"I saw your attraction to the waif."

"I don't know what you're talking about."

"Of course, you don't. Let me explain...her eyes captivated you."

"They were so similar to yours. The same copper color. It felt so familiar, it was as if I knew her."

"You should go back and take her to Montrose."

"Whatever for?" He again glanced in Katherine's imagined direction.

She smiled. *"You can impress your father with your generous spirit."*

Phillip laughed. "I think the only event that will impress my father is to hear I'm providing an heir."

"You don't have to marry the girl."

"Tell that to my father."

"Tell Father what?" Kenton asked, snapping Phillip back to the real world.

He cast a wary glance to his side, hoping to discover Katherine had remained with him. She was gone. Abandoned once more.

"The village appears to be attracting vagrants," Phillip replied. He turned from his brother gave a curt bow to the woman, if you could call a seventeen-year-old a woman, at Kenton's side. "Miss Hilton. How are you today?"

She dipped into a small curtsy and with her eyes focused on Phillip's brown and black Wellingtons said, "Very well, sir. Thank you for asking." Her voice was so soft that both Phillip and Kenton leaned a bit forward to hear her reply. Phillip remembered her voice being shrill and loud as she ran around the house with his sister. How life had changed.

"And your parents? Are they in good health as well?"

"Yes, sir."

"I was just telling Miss Hilton that we were on our way to her house," Kenton offered. "What good fortune it was for us to meet up with her."

Phillip forced a smile. "Yes, good fortune, indeed." Regrettably, his distraction with the vagrant had proved unfortunate. If they'd gone straight to Mr. Hilton's and found Miss Marianne away—perchance he could have escaped the inevitable. "May we escort you home, Miss Hilton?"

Again, she curtsied. "Thank you, sir. That is most kind of you."

Phillip waved his arm forward, inviting Kenton and the lady to start ahead of him. He needed time to think—to prepare—and Kenton was doing a splendid job at keeping a conversation going with the girl as they walked.

In the past few weeks, the pressure to marry had been unbearable. Not one day, one meal, went by without his mother and father addressing the subject. Kenton was fed up with the boorish turn of conversation. The previous night, he threw his napkin to the table, stood and declared, "If all we're going to talk about is a marriage that Phillip doesn't want, I'll start eating at the village pub." Before their father could order the boy to sit, he was already out the door, muttering to himself how welcome the beginning of the school term would be. Phillip was required to sit through the rest of the meal listening to the presumed advantages he would have as soon as he did remarry.

At breakfast that same morning, Phillip received word that his father needed to speak to him—immediately. Suspecting what the meeting was about, Phillip regarded his bowl of porridge and decided he would take his time finishing. The weather was so fine that Phillip had considered a ride about the estate before meeting with his father. Thinking better of it, Phillip steeled himself for another discussion of marriage and entered his father's office.

The fire was lit, the room warm—not that this room ever felt cold. With its dark paneling and heavy brocade curtains, on the chilliest of days the room tended to be warmer than the rest of the manor. At first the conversation centered on matters concerning the estate. Phillip relaxed, hoping that the meeting would be all about business. But after a few remarks regarding improvements needed to the south end of the property, Lord Montgomery asked when Phillip planned to make his offer to Miss Hilton.

"What are you waiting for?" His father bellowed when Phillip said he did not know. "She's not growing any younger!"

"I thought you'd granted me time to spend with her...to give my feelings time to change."

"Have you spent time with her?" Lord Montgomery marched around his desk taking the chair across from Phillip. What appeared to be a tactic to invite conversation, was Lord Montgomery's way of strong-arming his children. He sat on the seat's edge, leaning forward, a hard, driving expression in his eyes.

"Some. It's been difficult to find time."

"Poppycock. You manage to make time for your daily walks around the park."

"You have a problem with daily constitutionals?" He intended to keep his daily walks to the cemetery, married or not.

"Don't play innocent with me. We all know where you go. We also recognize that you need to put Katherine behind you."

"*We* does not include me," Phillip muttered under his breath.

"Today," his father said, using the tone of voice that brooked no argument, "when you take your daily constitutional, you will use it to visit the Hiltons. I've already sent word that you would be arriving mid-day."

"Father...really..."

"If you won't step up to your responsibilities on your own, I will ensure that you do."

A tense moment passed between father and son, each holding the eye of the other. Phillip wanted...needed to stand up to his father—to be his own man. But what good would that do?

He rose to his feet. "I wish you could show some confidence in me."

Lord Montgomery sat back in his chair, softening. "Phillip...I can't wait any longer. I've tried to be patient. But from my vantage point, you are not moving on."

"Forcing me to marry someone I do not love will not take away my loss."

"And neither will moping about the estate. You must take a step. Marianne Hilton is that step. I'm counting on you."

Don't. Phillip would do as his father asked. He would visit with the Hiltons, but that did not mean he would marry their daughter. With any luck, he might be able to persuade Mr. Hilton that his daughter deserved better.

Kenton had volunteered to walk with Phillip—a gesture Phillip suspected was at their father's urging, a way to ensure the deed got done. Phillip pushed aside the thought, instead trying to enjoy the exercise and the weather. The walk into town had proved pleasant enough. A slight breeze rustled the leaves, and bright sunshine made the last days of autumn beautiful instead of melancholy. The season had made Katherine blue. She loved spring and rebirth, and cloudless summer days.

Phillip's enjoyment had derailed when in the near distance, Miss Hilton had exited the milliner's shop.

"The fates are with you, Phillip," Kenton said.

Fortunately, the fates had other ideas. Phillip heard commotion at the Walker's shop. The perfect diversion, if short lived.

While in this reverie, the Hilton residence came into view—a stately brick home on a small patch of grass, surrounded by a vine-covered stone wall with an ornate wrought iron gate that gave the impression of a house being held prisoner. Phillip sympathized. Marriage to Miss Hilton felt exactly the same.

Kenton walked up, opened the gate and stepped to the side, allowing Miss Hilton and Phillip to proceed ahead of him.

Miss Hilton stepped up to the thick wooden door with a heavy iron knocker and pushed it open.

"Mother! Father! Look who I ran into in town!" The quiet, mousy voice had disappeared.

Phillip planned to stay only long enough to pay his respects. After that he and Kenton could be on their way—duty fulfilled.

Charles Hilton emerged to greet them, followed by his stout wife, who bubbled in delight.

"Hello! Hello! How nice of you to pay us a call. Larkin, please, take their coats," Mr. Hilton instructed their man servant.

Phillip and Kenton slid out of their coats, handing them off to the servant, and followed with their hats. Phillip wished he had remained outside in the soothing sunshine.

Mr. Hilton, a portly man, balding at the back of his head, reached out to shake hands with the brothers. He had a warm smile to offer any member of the Montgomery family.

"Marianne, would you please have cook provide some tea and refreshment for our guests."

"Please, do not go to any trouble on our account," Phillip said. "We really can only stay for a short time."

"A little tea won't hurt," Kenton said as he rubbed his hands together. "And…" he smiled impishly in Mrs. Hilton's direction. "If there are some scones available—it would be perfect!"

"Cook made some delicious cranberry scones this morning," Mrs. Hilton said. Turning to her daughter she added, "Marianne, be sure to include some on the tray."

"Certainly," Marianne replied, then hurried down the hall.

"Master Phillip. Kenton. Please, won't you come in and be seated." Mrs. Hilton held her hand out toward the parlor door.

Kenton followed Mrs. Hilton. As Phillip was about to step forward, Mr. Hilton laid a hand on Phillip's arm.

"Phillip, since you are here, may I have a word with you. In private." Mr. Hilton gestured toward another door on the opposite side of the hall. Phillip knew this to be Mr. Hilton's office. He'd sat in the room with Lord Montgomery on several occasions as legal matters were discussed.

Phillip managed a weak smile. "Certainly, sir."

He followed Mr. Hilton into the small, stuffy office that smelled of wood smoke and earthy cigars. Bookshelves lined one wall, overflowing with one sort of volume or another. Phillip wished he had opportunity to peruse all those books. There was a wealth of learning on Mr. Hilton's shelves.

"I see you have an edition of Izaak Walton's, *The Compleat Angler*," Phillip said.

Mr. Hilton smiled. "Yes, yes…Here, please be seated." He waved toward a comfortable chair near the fire. "I was able to purchase that edition not long ago. Has wonderful, wonderful advice on reeling in your catch."

Phillip caught himself on the arms of the chair. The man's comment made it sound as if Phillip was about to be caught and fileted.

"Can I offer you a little?" Hilton stepped over to a sideboard and held up a heavy glass decanter with grape vines etched on the side. Phillip declined with a shake of the head as he settled into his seat. Hilton poured a thumb's width into a glass tumbler then sat in the chair across from Phillip.

He raised his glass as if toasting Phillip and swallowed.

"I can't tell you, Phillip, how pleased Mrs. Hilton and I are," he said. "To have you and Marianne joined in marriage has been one of my fondest dreams. Mrs. Hilton cannot contain her joy over the upcoming union."

"Excuse me?" Phillip said, the air in the room thickening.

"Your father told me of your intentions. I could not have arranged a more perfect match for Marianne."

"Mr. Hilton, I believe there's…"

"I understand, Phillip," Hilton said with a pleasant chuckle and wave of the hand. "I suppose you're surprised that your father mentioned the matter to me already."

"Actually, I'm not. But that's not what…"

"It's fine. It's fine. A little unconventional, I know."

"No, sir. Please." Phillip sat forward in his seat. "I have not offered for your daughter. Not that…"

"Oh, I know. But I don't think we need to stand on ceremony. You have my blessing to ask for her hand."

Phillip scratched his head, staring into the fire as he formed what he would say next.

"I know she will accept," Mr. Hilton added.

Phillip rose to his feet, wishing now that he had accepted the offer of a drink. "Does she expect an offer? Has someone mentioned this to your daughter?"

"Mrs. Hilton and I discussed the matter recently. I suppose Marianne might have overheard, I cannot say for sure." The older man waved for Phillip to take his seat again. Reluctantly, Phillip sank back into the chair. "Your father suggested, and I concurred, that a double wedding with your sister and Mr. Markhall would be most appropriate. You were aware of that arrangement, were you not?"

Phillip nodded. "Father did mention it." He wiped a hand over his mouth. "Mr. Hilton, to be honest, I had not decided..."

"If you don't wish to have a double ceremony, that is all right as well. We have the means to celebrate the union in a manner suitable to your station."

"That was not my concern."

"Of course not. You're much to gracious to ever presume."

"No. You misunderstand, Mr. Hilton. I am aware our families have been friends for many years. My father has mentioned how grateful he is for the association many times. But I have not chosen Miss Hilton to be my wife."

"Yes. Yes," Mr. Hilton offered a dismissive wave. "Your father mentioned that you were a bit reluctant to remarry—and for good reason."

For good reason? How could he think that Katherine's death...the baby's death... would be good at all? Did he not understand? Phillip choked back the words that wanted to burst out. He wanted to inform Mr. Hilton of the constant ache he felt, how simply the mention of Katherine's name made his chest hurt, the hollowness crippling.

Mr. Hilton leaned forward, placing a comforting hand on Phillip's knee. "It is time to do what is expedient for the estate. Marianne will be a loving and devoted wife. You will not be able to acquire better in that regard. She's adored you for years."

"But, Mr. Hilton, I haven't adored…"

"You will come to. I know it." The man leaned back in his chair. "Marianne doesn't want to replace Katherine." *No one could ever replace Katherine.* "She's aware that Katherine will always hold a special place in your heart. But I can tell you from experience, it is hard to resist the affections of a woman who adores you."

"And you would wish her to marry someone whose heart lies elsewhere?"

"Well…not if that elsewhere were another living woman. But given the circumstances, I believe that Marianne's affection will help you heal."

Why did everyone think that?

"Just ask her, my boy." He waved his hand in a grand gesture. "Put all that concern aside and ask for her hand. After the decision is made, you'll feel more settled, more at peace, better able to move on."

Phillip could hardly breathe. The room had become hot. He tugged at his cravat.

Was this what happened when a man marries a second time? Were all matters of protocol tossed aside? Good heavens, Mr. Hilton had given his permission before Phillip had raised the topic. In fact, he told Phillip to ask, that the girl's answer was assured. This was unconscionable.

"Mr. Hilton, this arrangement is…is…" How did he express his dismay without being guilty of disregarding social mores himself? "It's unprincipled, so contrary to social…"

"Yes, yes," Mr. Hilton said, again waving his hand as if to brush away an annoying insect. "Come." The man rose from his seat, placing his unfinished drink on the desk. "Let's join the others in the parlor."

Extending his hand to show the way, he escorted Phillip out into the hall, quickly moving in front of Phillip to open the parlor door.

"Now's the time. Go ahead, Phillip," he whispered, and added more loudly, "Marianne, Master Phillip wishes to ask you a question."

Phillip's chest went hollow. He glanced around the room. Mrs. Hilton sat across from Kenton and Marianne who sat on a love seat near the fire. All had turned an expectant gaze toward Phillip. At her husband's announcement, Mrs. Hilton began to bounce lightly in her seat, a bright smile trying to break free.

"Kenton, we need to get back," Phillip said. He turned to Mr. Hilton. "May we have our coats, please."

Mr. Hilton worked unsuccessfully to hide his dismay. "Certainly." He turned to call for Larkin.

Kenton rose to his feet, also appearing confused by the unexpected change in plans.

"Phillip," Mrs. Hilton said, "The tea has just arrived. Can't you stay for one cup?" Sitting on the table to her side was a lovely china tea set, complete with cranberry scones.

"I'm afraid not, Mrs. Hilton. We must be going." He turned from the disappointment that simultaneously appeared on Marianne's face and her mother's.

Phillip and Kenton stepped into the entrance hall, followed by the women. Mr. Hilton was already there, standing with his manservant.

"Phillip," he said, a one-word rebuke.

Phillip turned back towards the ladies, intending to offer a sincere apology but was thwarted by the crestfallen expression in Marianne's eyes. He regarded the girl for a moment, recognizing the distress he was causing her entire family, and the repercussion he would face back at the manor when his father heard of his abrupt and rude departure. Larkin stood ready to help Phillip with his coat. He slipped it on and reached for the door, not wanting to wait for Larkin to help Kenton with his coat.

"Wait!" Mrs. Hilton called. "Please, let me send some scones home with you."

Kenton's eyes lit with delight at the prospect at the same time as Phillip stifled a groan of frustration. His brother stepped close.

"What is the matter with you?" he whispered.

Phillip glanced at his brother, then at Mr. Hilton and Marianne who stood at his side. His eyes met Marianne's. Quiet resignation and sadness filled her eyes.

Mrs. Hilton returned with a napkin carefully wrapped around the promised treat. She handed it to Kenton who gratefully took it, offering his thanks.

Phillip swallowed. He clenched his fists as his breathing became short and rapid. He closed his eyes, wishing the palpitations would stop. It was all too much. Was he really required to sacrifice his happiness, his freedom for the sake of the estate? Was there no choice in the matter? His resolve crumbled before him like an ancient ruin.

"Miss Hilton," Phillip blurted. "Would you do me the honor of becoming my wife?"

A moment of stunned silence ensued, followed by her quiet reply.

"I would be honored."

"Well…good…fine…that's settled," Phillip said. He shot one last glance at Mr. Hilton, and before anything more could be said, pulled the door open and stepped out into the welcoming sunshine. The fine weather mocked his misery.

~~*

Overnight, a steady rain began. That sound, and some brandy, had lulled Phillip into sleep and made it hard for him to face the world the next morning. His head ached. What had he done? Groaning, he pulled the heavy blanket over his head. Visions of the awkward proposal replayed in his mind. Obviously, he'd not imbibed enough to make him forget the fiasco of the previous day. Chimes from a clock in the hallway forced him from his hideaway. There was no choice but to face the day.

After dressing, Phillip made his way to the morning room, stopping in the doorway. This was one of Phillip's favorite rooms. Pentagonal in shape, three of the five walls were large, floor-to-ceiling, leaded glass windows. On cloudy days similar to this one, where water ran down the glass in rivulets, the room continued to be filled with light. The room typically soothed his soul with the aroma of cooked meats and fresh breads, and the tradition of joining his family here to start the day. If only today he weren't entering it as an engaged man.

The last time he'd done that, the world was a blank slate filled with possibilities. He could hardly contain his happiness. Katherine had accepted his offer of marriage the night before. Of course, Phillip had to talk to her father. But what worry was there in that? Lord Waller had already expressed his pleasure in Phillip's interest in Katherine. And Phillip knew that he would bring Katherine to a wonderful home and future. Lord Montgomery was a genius when it came to estate business, and he was teaching Phillip all he knew.

Charlotte and his parents were seated at the round pedestal table discussing the day's plans.

"Lady Ackerley and her daughter Fiona are calling this afternoon," Lady Montgomery said.

"Whatever for?" Lord Montgomery said without losing focus on the missive in his hand.

"A social call is all."

Charlotte sighed. "Fiona is so annoying."

"Be kind," her mother said.

"I hope you're not expecting me to attend, I have…"

"Of course not, dear, I am aware you find such visits intolerable." Lady Montgomery noticed Phillip lingering in the doorway and staring out the windows. "Good morning, Phillip. Quite a bit of rain, isn't it?"

"Good morning, Mother," he said, stepping into the room. "And yes, it's been raining steadily since last evening."

"Such a shame. Yesterday was such a beautiful day."

Depends on how you view it, Phillip thought as he moved to the sideboard to fix a plate of meats, breads, and eggs, avoiding the beans that always graced the breakfast menu. He detested beans and from childhood refused to eat them. He poured a cup of tea, then moved to the table.

"Phillip, can you escort me to the Hilton's today?" Charlotte said before he had a chance to get settled. "I haven't seen Marianne in nearly week."

"I already have plans for the afternoon."

"And you need to be here to entertain Fiona." Lady Montgomery turned to her son. "Didn't you visit the Hiltons yesterday?"

"He certainly did," Kenton said as he entered the room. Phillip shot his brother a warning glance. Their parents did not yet know of the proposal.

Lord Montgomery laid his letter aside. "And how did you find the Hiltons?"

"They were well." Phillip busied himself buttering his toast. He could feel his father's eyes upon him.

"Is there any news to share?"

Phillip stopped and stared at the plate in front of him.

"An announcement, perchance?" his father prodded.

"There is," Kenton said before Phillip could reply.

"Oh?" Charlotte and her mother both said at the same time.

Slowly, Phillip stared at Kenton over at the sideboard and imagined dumping a plate of beans over his brother's head. He hid a smile at the thought.

"You made your offer?" A statement more than a question.

Swallowing hard, Phillip turned and faced his father. "I did." He paused. "And she accepted." The words were difficult to choke out.

Glancing around the table, the reactions varied. His father broke into a grin...practically a smirk, as if to say, "See...I told you it would all work out." His mother also appeared pleased, but her expression held a hint of sympathy...or pity...as if she understood what this cost her son. Kenton had no reaction, too busy with his food. Charlotte bubbled with excitement.

"How did you propose?" she asked. "Was it romantic?"

Kenton snorted as he joined the family at the table. Reaching out, he took Charlotte's hand. "I have never witnessed any event so astounding," he told her. "It saddens me to think that Sir Markhall's proposal of marriage to you simply won't compare."

Charlotte yanked her hand away, averting her eyes.

"He's teasing you," Phillip said, hoping to relieve some of her discomfort. "It was an offer, that's all."

Another scoff from Kenton.

"Offers of marriage are always romantic," Lady Montgomery added. "Why don't you share the story with us, Phillip?"

"It was nothing, really."

"He's not kidding," Kenton said. "It was over and done in seconds. She deserved better," he added under his breath. Phillip didn't think anyone else heard the comment. At least he hoped not.

"That is true," Phillip said, trying to make the event sound a bit better than it actually was. "I asked if she would give me the honor, and she said she would."

"Did you get down on one knee?" Charlotte asked.

"Was she pleased with the offer?" their mother asked at the same time.

"I did not get on one knee." He didn't add that he ran out the door immediately afterwards. "And…I guess she was pleased." He didn't stay long enough to find out.

"Did you set a date?" Lord Montgomery asked. "I think as soon as possible would be good. What say you, Helena?"

"If we're to make this a double ceremony, don't we need to wait on Sir Markhall?"

"No need for that," Charlotte said. "I think Marianne deserves her own day. Don't you, Phillip?"

How should he answer? If he said yes, he would be rushed to the altar at his father's insistence. If he said, no, he risked his father's disapproval and a chance that the arrangement with Markhall would be rushed, leaving both he and Charlotte to their misery.

"I suppose it's up to Marianne," he hedged.

"We can announce Phillip's engagement at a dinner to honor the couple," Lady Montgomery said, rising from the table. "Charlotte, why don't you come with me. We'll talk to cook and plan a date and menu for the event. I'll send a note to the Hiltons regarding a visit—possibly as early as tomorrow."

Charlotte scooped the last bit of toast into her mouth, brushed crumbs from her hands and followed her mother. Phillip heard their delighted chatter over the clacking shoes on the stone flooring that led to the kitchen. At least his engagement brought joy to someone in the house.

"I'm glad this is finally settled," Lord Montgomery said. "You'll see, Phillip, that this is the right move. You will be able to move on. You need a distraction, someone different to focus on."

"Can I add my thoughts?" Kenton asked.

"Will they be helpful?" Lord Montgomery replied.

"You probably will not think so. But I feel I must speak my peace, not that anyone will listen."

"I'll listen," Phillip said, while he focused on his breakfast. The sooner he could finish, the sooner he would escape this conversation and talk of a future he did not want.

"Father, I think you're being unfair," Kenton said.

"Unfair?"

"Yes. To Phillip, but more toward Miss Hilton. You are consigning her to be second best for the rest of her life. By not allowing Phillip to choose to marry someone he loves, you are dooming them to a loveless marriage and years of malcontent."

Lord Montgomery leaned forward, not hiding his irritation. "And what would you know of love or marriage? You have experienced neither. Your brother is using his loss to escape his responsibilities..."

"That's not fair," Phillip said, but was ignored.

"Montrose needs an heir. The world is changing, Kenton. We have to move quickly, or we could lose more than a house."

"The world is changing, Father. Starting with these archaic ideas about arranged marriages. You're forcing two of your children into marriages they don't want."

Lord Montgomery slammed his hands on the table causing both Phillip and Kenton to flinch. "Enough of this!"

He paused, taking a deep breath. When he spoke again, his voice reflected a measure of control, but also finality. "I understand what needs to be done to protect this family. Your sister will be well cared for. Your brother, though truly marrying beneath his station, will open the family to a new day and age. And you…you will go to school. You will learn, get good marks, and seek your future. One that will be secured by your brother's actions." He stood. "Phillip, I will be reviewing accounts later. Be in my office in an hour to go over them with me."

Phillip and Kenton kept their eyes lowered as Lord Montgomery marched from the room, hearing his heavy footfall move in the direction of his office. The brothers sat in silence, using their forks to play with the remnants of their breakfast.

Phillip spoke first. "Thank you for trying to speak some sense to him."

Kenton pushed back from the table, his chair scraping loudly against the wood floors. "I didn't do it for you." He, too, marched out of the room, his footfall sounding similar to their father's. Puzzled, Phillip sat alone. How had he made half the family glad and the other half angry? He did what he was told. That was his duty—to his father as well as to the estate. If he went through with this, it could be their father would back off from Charlotte's match with Markhall. There was no need for his sister to be miserable as well.

He closed his eyes, pushing his fists into them, wishing to escape.

"Phillip." The sound of Katherine's voice had him reaching desperately for her. She'd come. She came when he needed her most.

"Katherine," he replied.

"You're discouraged."

He envisioned her across the table—her hair loose, down around her shoulders, soft and thick. Her copper-colored eyes sparkled at him.

"I'm trying to do what's right."

"You always do."

"But how can I do this? How can I marry someone I do not love? How can I do this to our memory?"

"Nothing will change what we have."

"I'm not sure I can do what is needed...you know...to produce an heir—not with her."

She laughed. It was not the throaty laugh he remembered, but a light, amused sound that echoed around the room. *"You will have an heir,"* she said, *"Mark my words. He will be beautiful, just as little Donald is beautiful."*

"You can see my future?"

"I can see your heart."

A stifled giggle caught his attention. Phillip glanced at the door in time to catch the flash of a black sleeve disappearing from view. He groaned. Desperate to be in Katherine's presence, he'd ignored where he was and had spoken aloud. He knew the servants talked about him—said he was touched. Catching him in the act only made the rumors run faster. Phillip understood what would happen if the staff thought him incompetent—unable to run the estate. As long as he was living, the estate fell to him—not Kenton. No one of worth would work for a man they believed unhinged. And was his father aware of how the servants gossiped? With this wedding, was Lord Montgomery simply trying to stop the chatter?

He'd have to be more careful—more observant. Folding his napkin, he laid it neatly beside his plate, rising to his feet. As he moved to leave the room, he took one last glance at the table, at the spot where Katherine had been. No longer there, he wondered—could he be a bit unbalanced? If so—there were worse things—losing Katherine again would be one of them.

CHAPTER FIVE

"Fortune leaves always some door open..."
–Miguel de Cervantes

Three weeks had passed since the day in the market, when the constable had delivered Lainey into the capable hands of the good Reverend Porter. The weather had turned colder, the rains had increased, and nightfall came earlier. Lainey had settled in well at the Porter's home and was coming to much appreciate the Reverend and his wife. Mrs. Porter tried hard to be stern. But after learning about Lainey's experience with Master Harold, she developed sympathies for the girl.

"It's a hard matter having a pretty face," she'd say randomly. Or, "With beauty such as yours, you'd be the talk of the season if circumstances were different."

Lainey laughed when Mrs. Porter first said that. If circumstances were different, Lainey wouldn't be living in their home, sleeping on a cot in the corner of the kitchen. If circumstances were different, her family would be together—her parents and oldest brother wouldn't be in the grave, and Robert wouldn't be halfway across the world serving the Queen. If circumstances were different, why...Lainey herself could be the queen of England. She really would be the talk of the season. And men similar to Prince Albert would be kissing her hand and seeking her favor and approval.

But circumstances were not different. Instead, Lainey cooked for the Porters. She stood in the chilling rain cutting back plants and turning the soil, priming the garden for winter. And all the while, she dreamed of Robert and his letters about turquoise oceans and warm breezes. Those descriptions, and the thought of seeing her brother, drove her on and kept her focused.

That afternoon, she sat near a window repairing a tear in Reverend Porter's breeches. Frequently when the man mounted a horse, a seam gave way. Rain, mixed with an occasional snowflake, made her glad that she had finished the garden preparations. She was warm. And a delightful fragrance of herbs, carrots, onions, celery, and rabbit wafted from the kitchen. She hadn't been hungry in nearly a month now. Almost long enough to forget what her life had been …almost.

"Mrs. Porter!" the Reverend called as he walked in the door. "Mrs. Porter, I have news!"

The stout woman emerged from the kitchen. "What is it, Mr. Porter?"

He shook droplets off his coat and hung it on a spindly coat tree near the door. "Good fortune has come."

"What? What is it?"

"I have news from Montrose." The Reverend walked over and warmed his hands near the fire. "Master Montgomery is engaged to be married. And you will never guess who the lucky young woman is. You'll never guess."

"Well…if I'll never guess, why don't you just tell me?" Mrs. Porter landed her hands on her hips. Lainey smiled. She'd seen the same gesture a number of times whenever Mrs. Porter was agitated with her husband.

"Miss Marianne Hilton," he said in triumph, as if he'd arranged the marriage himself.

"Well, I'll be…" Mrs. Porter took one of the armchairs near the fire. "I never thought he'd find love again…after Lady Katherine."

"It's to be a marvelous affair. But more…if they have such a celebration coming, of course they will need help." He turned to Lainey. "I believe we have found you some employment. I've sent word to Lady Montgomery that I have a matter to discuss with her. We will go tomorrow afternoon."

Lainey laid the sewing in her lap.

"Mrs. Porter, will you write a letter for her ladyship explaining all of Miss Clarkson's skills and how valuable you've found her."

With a frown, Mrs. Porter turned to Lainey. "This would be a wonderful opportunity for you. But I must say, I have enjoyed your company and will miss having you here."

Lainey swallowed hard. While she, too, had become fond of Mrs. Porter, she knew she wouldn't stay long. She needed to be in Liverpool by spring. The Porters had paid her in room and board—nothing more. Working for the Montgomery family—well, hopefully in a matter of months she might find her way. She clasped a hand around her locket—this was good news. It would take her to her family.

~~*

Lainey pulled her shawl tighter, fighting off the chilled air, sitting beside Reverend Porter, as they made their way to Montrose Manor. Mrs. Porter spent the morning telling Lainey all about the Montgomery family, at least what she knew. They appeared to be decent folk, but the Warringtons seemed like decent folks, too. That is, until they weren't.

Lainey fidgeted with her locket, a habit when she was nervous. The Reverend was presenting her without knowing if the Montgomerys were in need of any additional household staff. Between the Reverend and his wife, they hoped to convince Lady Montgomery to take Lainey on even if there wasn't a need.

As they rode toward the manor, Lainey ran proper conversation through her mind, remembering the lessons she'd been taught by Mrs. Crowthers while serving at Harlsburg Manor. They turned onto a stone bridge and the stately home came into view.

Somehow, when estates were planned, the designers had to make some grand show of the first appearance from the road. Montrose Manor was no exception. The house appeared in all its resplendent beauty. And a beauty it was, one of the grandest Lainey had ever seen. Unlike Harlsburg, which was made of stone and more stone giving it the feeling of a castle, Montrose was a grand Tudor mansion sprawled out over a lush, green lawn with manicured gardens to one side. Of course, this time of year, the gardens were barren, but Lainey could imagine their glory and hoped there were more behind the house that she could not see.

As the carriage pulled up to the entrance, a liveried footman approached, taking control of the horses. Reverend Porter hopped down from the wooden seat, coming to aid Lainey from the carriage. It was a gallant gesture for a man to offer a servant girl, reminding Lainey of the good fortune she'd had in being placed with the Porters.

Together they walked to the heavy, mahogany door that stood in a brick alcove. Reverend Porter with an iron knocker, rapped on the door. A few minutes passed before they heard the latches being lifted and the door swung open revealing a portly butler, dressed in a dark suit.

"Ah, Reverend Porter. Lady Montgomery is expecting you. Please..." He stretched out an arm, welcoming the Reverend into the home. As Lainey followed, she felt the man's scrutiny. She was only being allowed to enter because she was with the Reverend.

"How does the day find you, Mr. Hollingsworth?" The Reverend asked, using the butler's name for Lainey's benefit. The Porters had reviewed important names with Lainey before bringing her to meet with Lady Montgomery. She repeated this name in her mind, associating it with the butler's round face.

"I am well, sir." Mr. Hollingsworth motioned to his left. "If you will wait here, I will notify her Ladyship of your arrival."

"He's a bit imposing," The Reverend whispered as the man walked out of the parlor. "But truthfully, he's a good man. A trusted employee. His wife is the housekeeper."

Lainey raised her eyebrows.

"I know. I know, unusual," the Reverend said in response.

Standing in place, Lainey took in the room as they waited. For a parlor, it was small. Or it felt small because of the dark paneling that covered the walls. Reverend Porter took a seat on an upholstered chair with ornately carved armrests. Across from him, there was a lovely settee and a few odd chairs with tables nearby. Sconces hung about the room, which at night would add light and ambiance. During the day, the large leaded glass window allowed plenty of light.

As Lainey was about to take a step toward the fireplace to get a closer view of the art hanging above the mantel, the door opened, and Mr. Hollingsworth returned.

"Her Ladyship is ready for you."

The Reverend rose to his feet. Lainey followed behind watching for other staff members as they went. After a short walk down another darkly paneled hallway, Mr. Hollingsworth stopped before a small alcove that surrounded a beautiful, beveled walnut door. He knocked, opening the door without waiting for a response.

Entering the room, he turned to the side to allow the Reverend a clear path into what appeared to be a bright and warm office. "Reverend Porter and guest, ma'am."

Over the Reverend's shoulder, Lainey saw two women standing behind a mahogany desk, studying what appeared to be a ledger. At the sound of Mr. Hollingsworth's voice, they both looked up. *Mother and daughter*, Lainey thought, catching the resemblance between them.

"Reverend Porter," the older woman said as she floated out from behind the desk, hands outstretched. "It's so lovely to see you." With both hands she grasped his as he leaned into a formal bow.

"Lady Montgomery. Thank you for meeting me today. Miss Montgomery," he added with an acknowledging bow in the young woman's direction.

"Yes. Yes. Well, it is a bit inconvenient. You'll notice," she waved a hand toward the younger woman, "Charlotte and I are planning a dinner party." She leaned in. "Young Master Montgomery is engaged."

"Congratulations, Madame. That is happy news."

"It is, it is," she said, turning to take her place behind the desk.

"Lady Montgomery, Miss Charlotte, may I please present Miss Alaina Clarkson."

Lainey curtsied as both women turned in her direction. The younger woman's expression brightened.

"She is actually why I asked to meet with you today," Reverend Porter continued.

"Oh?"

"This is a bit awkward, your Ladyship, but Master Montgomery has put me in a delicate position, and I was hoping that you might offer some assistance."

Miss Montgomery smiled while her mother frowned. Apparently, this was not the first time Master Montgomery had put someone in a delicate position.

"What is it you desire?"

The Reverend took a few steps closer to the women. Lainey remained where she was, afraid to move lest she draw attention to herself too soon. And besides, where she stood, she had the heat from the fire to ward off any chill.

"Well, some weeks ago, while in town, Master Montgomery gave some assistance to Miss Clarkson. She had traveled a long distance and was hungry and fatigued. He purchased some food for her…"

"That was generous of him."

"Yes, ma'am. He is forever kind and generous."

Lainey had to agree. Master Montgomery had been nothing short of a savior that day. But experience had taught her that few rescues were offered freely. She wondered what this Master Montgomery might require from her in payment. The thought made her shiver despite the warmth of the fire.

The Reverend paused for a moment, clearing his throat. "Afterwards, he requested that I take the girl in and try to find her some employment."

Lady Montgomery's eyes narrowed.

"I have tried to locate some useful employ for her. She is skilled and has worked as a domestic before. But alas, I have had little luck."

"You are questioning if I might take her on."

"Yes, Ma'am."

"Does she have references?"

Lainey held her breath as Reverend Porter pulled his wife's letter from his breast coat pocket, passing it quickly to her Ladyship. Lainey wanted this job desperately. What would Lady Montgomery think of a reference given by Mrs. Porter alone?

Lady Montgomery opened the letter, never taking her eye off Lainey.

Lainey stood tall and straight and, unable to contain her nerves, palmed the front of her skirt hoping to make it more respectable. Unfortunately, the action drew the lady's eyes to the skirt, which led to the tattered bottom. It was a fleeting examination, but Lainey was sure the woman took in everything. On first impressions, Lady Montgomery was not a flighty or ignorant woman.

Her Ladyship glanced down at the paper in her hand. "Mr. Porter...this letter is from Mrs. Porter." Lainey's heart wilted, what little hope she had slipping away.

"Yes, Ma'am. Miss Clarkson has been earning her room and board at the rectory by working for us. We can attest to her skills."

"This is most unusual," Lady Montgomery muttered as she returned her attention to the letter. After reading through, she raised her eyes and while she addressed the Reverend, she sized up Lainey. "Are there no other references?"

"I'm afraid not. Her first employer is no longer in a position to grant any references."

"You said her first. That implies a second or third. Where are those references?"

"If I may, ma'am," Lainey said, stepping forward and dipping into a deep curtsy.

Lady Montgomery waved her hand. "Get up. I'm not royalty."

Lainey straightened and waited for permission to speak, hoping she showed the manners and training needed for household staff.

"Go on, please." Lady Montgomery said.

Nervous, Lainey reached for her locket. All hope of being with her brother seemed to evaporate as quickly as a morning mist. If she were ever to be with him again, she somehow had to convince Lady Montgomery to take her on.

"My last employer…"

"Miss Clarkson had to leave her last employer for safety reasons," Reverend Porter said. Lainey glanced between the Reverend and her Ladyship, mortified at the blunt explanation.

"Safety reasons?" Lady Montgomery repeated with a frown. She glanced from the Reverend to Lainey. After a moment's thought, her eyes grew wide in understanding. "That being as it may," she said, "I can't in good…"

"I'll take her," Charlotte burst in, surprising both her mother and Lainey.

"Charlotte."

"She can be my lady's maid."

"You have a lady's maid."

"Who has one foot in the grave. Please, Mother…Mrs. James is so old!"

Lady Montgomery sighed, giving her daughter a stern scowl. She turned back to Lainey. "Do you have any experience as a lady's maid?"

She wanted to lie, to make up a grand story of a great lady she had served. But, alas, her shoulders slumped.

"No, ma'am," Lainey answered, certain she'd lost her chance.

"Well, then I'm afraid Reverend…"

"How difficult can it be, Mother? Certainly, she can lace up a corset."

"Charlotte! A lady does not discuss her personal garments in front of a…"

"For heaven's sake…the Reverend knows all about corsets." Charlotte waved a hand in Lainey's direction. "I'm sure she is capable of helping me dress. And…do you know how to do hair?" Charlotte asked, directing her question to Lainey.

"What I don't know, I can figure out," Lainey replied.

"There. See? She will do marvelously. And it will be such a joy to have someone closer to my age instead of Grandmother's. Really, Mother, she will do splendidly. And I can take her with me when I marry."

Lainey bit her lip—no need to divulge future plans. Hiding her hand in her skirts, she crossed her fingers.

Lady Montgomery sighed, her eyes darting between her daughter and Lainey. Both Lainey and the Reverend held their breaths. Lainey knew she was unproven. While she hoped Mrs. Porter's recommendation would sway Lady Montgomery, she knew the job would be uncomfortable. She'd be serving in an area she had few skills for. But Miss Charlotte appeared hopeful and eager. Certainly, her Ladyship wouldn't deny her daughter what she truly wanted

"Very well," Lady Montgomery said. "We will take her on, Reverend Porter. But if there are any troubles, we will have no problem in sending her right back to your doorstep."

If Lainey could have, she would have thrown her arms around Miss Charlotte and cried in gratitude. As it was, she fought to keep an overexuberant smile from her lips.

The Reverend bowed. "I assure you, Lady Montgomery, you will not be sorry. Miss Clarkson is a quick learner and a hard worker. It will not take long for you to be satisfied with your decision."

Lady Montgomery walked around her desk and took a seat. She did not appear satisfied. "Mr. Hollingsworth," she said to the butler who had been waiting quietly in a far corner of the room. He stepped forward at the sound of his name. "Please take Miss Clarkson to meet with Mrs. Hollingsworth. Have her show the girl around, give her a bed and..." She again examined Lainey's dress. "...get her an appropriate dress. Charlotte, you will stay here to help with the dinner plans and afterwards you may start training Miss Clarkson in her new responsibilities. I hope you appreciate what you've done."

Mr. Hollingsworth extended an arm to direct Lainey and The Reverend from the room. Before stepping through the door, Lainey glanced back, catching Miss Charlotte's eye. Charlotte winked at her. Lainey lowered her head and smiled. Montrose may turn out to be a fine place to work as she waited to make her journey to her brother Robert.

CHAPTER SIX

"Happy is the house that shelters a friend"
–Ralph Waldo Emerson

Mrs. Hollingsworth, a tall, thin, severe-looking woman, who wore her graying hair in a tight bun and spoke in short, sharp sentences, passed Lainey off to one of the other housemaids as quickly as she could. Jane smiled and curtsied slightly as Lainey was introduced.

As Mrs. Hollingsworth walked away, she muttered, "I don't have time for this. A lady's maid for Charlotte. Hardly seems necessary."

Jane stifled a laugh, turning to Lainey. "I'm Jane," the girl said. "And don't worry about her." She nodded in the housekeeper's direction. "She's frequently grumbling about one matter or another. What was your name?"

"Alaina. Alaina Clarkson, but most people call me Lainey."

"Welcome to Montrose," she said, ignoring Lainey's reply. "Come on, follow me, I'll show you around."

Jane turned and started up the stairs, chattering as they climbed a full three flights. Why was it that servants' quarters were either in a dark, dank basement or up several flights of stairs? Didn't the owners ever think about how tiring it was at the end of the day to climb all those stairs?

As Lainey had the thought, she heard Jane say, "I believe we should have the rooms on the second floor. Don't they realize how tired we are at the end of the day?

Lainey smiled, taking an instant liking to the girl. She was rather plain to look at, average height, skinny, brown hair and eyes, but those same eyes sparkled with life, making her prettier than she may have appeared without them.

Slightly out of breath, the two girls stopped at the landing on the third floor. Lainey scanned the area. The walls were painted white, appearing rather sterile. The comforting scent of beeswax candles had disappeared, along with smoke from the fires. Lainey hoped that extra blankets would be provided in the winter months. And although the house was new to Lainey, it somehow felt familiar as well. All the homes she had worked in held this same feeling—stately, old, as if it held a myriad of secrets.

The stair landing was between two hallways sectioned off by white painted doors, one hallway being longer than the other. Jane pointed down the shorter.

"The men's quarters," she explained. "The family is quite insistent that these doors are closed at night." She gave a wicked grin. "Keeps the men from joining us."

"Or us from joining the men," Lainey replied, causing Jane to laugh.

"I think I'm going to like you."

Down at the end of the women's hallway was a floor-to-ceiling window that allowed light to filter through. Jane led Lainey to a door at the end of the hallway. Inside was a plain room with a small, solitary window, and several large wardrobes. Jane opened the wardrobe next to the window revealing shelves of bedding: sheets, pillows and pillowcases, wool blankets, and bath towels. Jane pulled out the pillow first and handed it to Lainey, who cradled it across her arms, so Jane could pass off the other items. After stacking the bedding and towels in Lainey's arms, Jane walked over to another wardrobe. Pulling it open, she revealed several servant dresses. The entire time, she kept up a steady stream of chatter.

"Where are you from?" she asked Lainey, as she pulled a black dress from the wardrobe and measured it across Lainey's back.

Lainey hesitated for a moment, unsure whether the girl meant where Lainey was born or last worked. She decided on the former.

"I grew up in London."

Jane leaned against the wardrobe door, a dreamy expression on her face. "Oh. You're from London?"

"I grew up there."

"I've dreamed of going to London."

"It's not as glamorous as it sounds. Especially not for the likes of us. It's crowded and dirty…"

"But if you went with a family it would be different." Jane rehung the first dress and pulled out another. "If only poor Charlotte wasn't being married off to that old man. She won't get a season if this marriage arrangement goes forward."

Lainey hadn't realized that Charlotte's comment about taking a maid with her when she married was an approaching event.

"You don't happen to be good with a needle, do you?" Jane asked.

"I am. My mother taught me how to sew before she died."

"If this dress doesn't fit, you can alter it later. Mrs. Hollingsworth will be happy to know you can use a needle."

Jane draped the black dress over her arm, selected a cap and collar, and headed for the door. Lainey followed.

Down the hall, three doors to the left, Jane opened another door and stood aside for Lainey to enter. The room was small, the only light came in from the hallway. The only furnishings were a bed and dresser with a small, dirty mirror that had several black spots close to the edges. Jane laid the dress she carried across the bed.

"Let me get you a lantern," she said, stepping back into the hallway.

Lainey hugged the bedding in her arms. As she suspected, the room was chilly. There was little space between the bed on the left and the dresser on the right— just enough to open the drawers. With the door closed and a candle or lantern burning, the quarters were going to feel close. A concern, but nothing that couldn't be overcome. *And...*she thought, *at least I don't have to share it with anyone.*

Jane returned with a lit lantern. Setting it on the dresser, she turned about and took a sheet from Lainey's arms, opening it with a flourish.

"I can help you get set up," she said. "And fill you in on a few protocols. You should be out of bed by five in the morning to take care of preparing the house for the family. Of course, Charlotte will let you know what time she'll need your assistance. We have breakfast in the servants' room off the kitchen. I can show you that later. We're paid one time a month. Mr. Hollingsworth distributes wages on the last day. We're expected to attend church on the Sabbath."

"I already am acquainted with Reverend Porter," Lainey said.

"And you'll be given one afternoon off a week to take care of personal matters," Jane continued as if Lainey had not spoken. "Do you have any questions about that?"

Lainey shook her head.

"Good," Jane said as she finished tucking the wool blanket around the mattress. "I'll give you a moment to change. Afterwards I can show you around the house and tell you about the family and staff." Jane was a gossip. Every household had at least one, usually there were many more.

When the girl had slipped from the room, Lainey welcomed the immediate quiet. Since arriving at Montrose, Lainey had been a mixture of emotions. She was going to miss the Porters. They were kind and treated her well. But this was a chance to earn money to buy passage to Barbados. And Jane was friendly enough. More so than anyone at Harlsburg Manor.

When she'd first arrived at Harlsburg, she'd overheard a footman mention that Lainey was too pretty to be household staff—she'd soon have other duties to fulfill. A shudder ran down her spine. He must have known about Master Warrington. A warning would have been nice.

Quietly, she sighed. Hopefully, here at Montrose, the staff would be similar to Jane and less subject to petty jealousies. Certainly, those at Harlsburg had to know she'd never wanted the advances of any male in the household. But if Montrose was the same, she figured she could put up with most discomforts for a few months.

Slipping out of her skirt and blouse, she laid the garments across the foot of her bed. Standing in her undergarments, she saw her reflection in the mirror, her gold locket shining against her skin. She unclasped it, and taking it in hand, rubbed her finger across the engraved letter 'D.' Ivy scrolled in and through the letter, adding to its beauty. She popped the locket open and gazed at the images of her mother and grandmother. Lainey never knew her grandmother but had heard stories of the lady. Kind stories of how her grandmother taught Lainey's mother how to read and sew—talents that she'd passed on to her daughter.

Memories of her father surfaced as well—the night he'd presented the locket to Lainey.

"This was your mother's," he'd said. "She'd want you to have it." He'd laid the locket with its long gold chain in her hand. Lainey was sure she'd never seen such a beautiful piece of jewelry. The locket had to be special. Her father could have sold it for much-needed monies, but he never had, deciding to deliver it to Lainey at just the right moment. And it had been the right moment, for the next morning he died. She flattened her mouth as she fought the urge to kick the corner of the bed. What good would that do? She'd be left with a sore foot and no justice. And her father would still be gone.

Life after her father's death had been cruel, but Lainey knew it could have been worse, much worse. The neighbor, Mrs. Pruitt, took her and Robert in, although she could scarce afford to. Lainey was forever grateful to the woman.

Realizing she'd spent too much time dawdling, Lainey quickly slipped on the black dress—yes, it would need to be taken in later. But she must not keep Jane waiting.

When Lainey stepped out into the hallway, she found Jane talking with another member of the household staff— a small girl wearing a cap and apron.

"Lainey, this is Mary. She's one of the chamber maids. Mary, this is Miss Charlotte's new abigale, Alaina."

The woman clapped her hands together. "Oh, Mrs. James will be happy. She's often said she's much too old to be chasing after Miss Montgomery."

So, it was mutual, Lainey thought.

"You will love the Montgomerys," Mary gushed. "They are a great family to work for. Lady Montgomery runs a tight household, but she's fair, and astute. Not much goes on without her notice. You can count on her to handle matters quietly, even if she is displeased with your work. I've never seen her let anyone go. Most have left of their own accord."

"Silly to leave, in my mind," Jane added. "I've been here near on five years. My mother hired me out at fourteen. It was the best thing that ever happened to me. I live much better now than I ever did at home. I had to share with seven other siblings. Here, I have my own bed, and meals that are more than thin soup and stale bread. I'll never go back. Ever," she added, mostly to herself.

"Did Jane explain the rules?" Mary asked as the three girls walked toward the staircase. "There are supposed to be no romantic attachments between staff members. But I'm not aware of how much mind the Montgomerys pay to what actually goes on. Ruth, who works in the kitchen, and Everette, one of the stable hands, have had an attachment for some time now. If anyone has noticed—and I can't imagine how they could have missed it—no one has said a word. Leonard knows all about it, so I suspect that Master Phillip knows as well. Leonard is his valet," she said. "And honestly, I think Leonard has had a romantic interest in Charlotte for a long time."

"Really?" Lainey was amazed that such an attraction hadn't led to the man's dismissal.

"Miss Charlotte is as much as engaged to Sir Markhall." Jane took Lainey by the arm and added in a low voice, "After having seen Sir Markhall, if I were Charlotte, I'd be begging for a different match. A servant would be better than Markhall."

"Sir Markhall is an old coot—older than Master Phillip," Mary said.

"And how old is that?" Lainey asked.

"Master Phillip is at least eight and twenty. Mistress Charlotte is barely seventeen." Jane shivered. The three women exited the stairway, emptying out on the second floor of the manor.

Mary stopped Jane with a touch on her arm. "Have you told her about Master Phillip?" She spoke so quietly that Lainey had to strain to hear.

Jane's eyes widened. "Not yet." She glanced toward Lainey who swallowed hard. *Oh no, not another philanderer.* "But I will. I'll warn her."

"Good," Mary said. "She needs to know." The girl stood a bit straighter and smoothed her skirt. "I need to get busy. Nice to have you with us, Lainey. I'll see you at dinner."

"I look forward to it," Lainey replied. Mary quickly walked toward other rooms needing attention. After she was gone, Lainey turned to Jane with an expression that said, "What was that about?"

Jane offered an apologetic smile. "I'll explain later. Here...let me show you Miss Charlotte's chambers." She opened a dark wood door that creaked. Jane stepped inside, Lainey following immediately behind. It was a lovely room with a wood dressing table topped with a tri-fold mirror. The four-poster bed was directly across from a fireplace with glowing embers making the room comfortable at present. In size, the room was similar to the rooms at Harlsburg, but it held none of the foreboding that she'd experienced there. In fact, the colors and furniture arrangement were welcoming.

Jane pointed toward a door in the corner. "Her dressing area is in there. She has the most exquisite mirror—floor to ceiling." Before Lainey had a chance to peek behind the door, Jane was already escorting her away.

"This is Master Kenton's room." Jane said, opening another door.

"Is Master Kenton a brother?"

"Yes, between Master Phillip and Lady Charlotte. He's headed off to Cambridge soon."

They stepped inside. There was nothing to recommend the room. Another four-poster bed covered in thick down coverlets stood as the centerpiece. A large fireplace adorned an adjacent wall as it had in Charlotte's room.

"Master Kenton is everyone's favorite," Jane said. "And…he's as handsome as a king!"

Lainey chuckled. "I never supposed kings to be handsome simply because they were kings."

"Of course they are! Being queen would be thoroughly dull if the king were not handsome."

The reasoning was a bit faulty, but it made Lainey smile, nonetheless. Jane was going to be delightful to work with.

They walked a little further down the hallway, stopping outside another dark wood door.

"This is Master Phillip's room." Jane said, laying a hand on Lainey's arm. She glanced up and down the hallway, then leaned close to Lainey. "He's an odd one," she said just above a whisper. "A bit daft since his wife died, if you ask me. He talks to ghosts."

So that's what Mary had meant. Better to talk to ghosts than ravish servants.

And yet. "Ghosts?" A chill ran up Lainey's spine.

"You'll hear him from time to time. He talks to Lady Katherine—his departed wife. She must continue to walk these halls." Both girls peeked up and down the hallway as if they might catch sight of the apparition. "I think Lord and Lady Montgomery fear for his sanity as well. They've arranged a marriage for him with Miss Marianne Hilton. I think they secretly hope it will lay Lady Katherine's ghost to rest."

"Who is this Miss Hilton?"

"Marianne Hilton," Jane said, her voice returning to normal volume. "She's a favorite friend of Miss Charlotte's. They've been thick as thieves since they were children. There's a dinner plan in the works to announce the engagement...possibly two if Lord Montgomery has his way."

"I'd heard about one marriage when I met with Lady Montgomery."

"The engagement is big news. We were all a bit surprised. He's never shown any interest in remarrying or in Miss Hilton."

"Certainly, he wouldn't marry her if he had no affection for the lady."

Jane shrugged as she pushed open the door. "Lady Katherine redid this room soon after they were wed. Master Phillip hasn't moved a single trinket since her passing. When we dust, we are sure to replace each item exactly where we found it."

"Is he that meticulous?" Lainey asked as she stepped into the room, promptly forgetting the question. "Oh." She surveyed the room. The walls were burnt sienna in color, a large, canopied bed with red curtains draped from the top stood between two windows. A chandelier with glass globes hung from the ceiling with matching sconces on three of the four walls. But all of that was secondary to the portrait that hung over the fireplace.

"Is this Lady Katherine?" Lainey asked as she approached the painting. The woman in the picture had penetrating copper eyes and glossy dark hair. The expression on her face was mystifying, as if she were hiding a great secret. Also, plainly evident in the portrait was the exceptional amount of love that radiated from her eyes. If that love had been for Master Phillip, no doubt he'd had a difficult time in letting her go.

"Yes," Jane answered with a sense of reverence.

"She was beautiful."

"She was. And as kind as she was beautiful. She made Master Phillip beautiful as well. They shared an unqualified love. Everyone remarked on how unusual it was. I've certainly never seen two people share such affection. I can only hope to have such a love one day." Jane's voice had gone wistful.

"My parents were like that," Lainey whispered.

Jane stepped up beside her to admire the painting. "I pity Miss Hilton. I doubt that Master Phillip will ever love her as he loved Lady Katherine."

"Maybe he will learn to love her."

Jane scoffed. "It's an arranged marriage—all Lord Montgomery's doing. He's rather concerned that there be an heir for the estate."

"It will be a pity if the younger master cannot learn to love Miss Hilton. If he doesn't, there's not much hope of exorcising the ghost, is there?"

"True," Jane said with a shake of the head. "But…it is not our problem to worry over or repair. We need to move on. There is so much more house to show you."

CHAPTER SEVEN

*"If there is anybody here I have not offended,
I apologize."*
–Johannes Brahms

Phillip's mind replayed his most recent conversation with Katherine as he approached the parlor. Together, they'd concocted a plan. He hoped it worked. If he could dodge this wedding and at the same time manage to reassure his parents and the staff that he was in full control of his faculties, then maybe…maybe he could marry when he was ready. Of course, his parents wanted to believe that he had not lost his mind to grief, therefore they would be easy to convince—the staff on the other hand could prove more difficult.

After Katherine's death, when his visions of Katherine began in earnest, to the point of his talking with her, his parents had scrutinized him at every turn, looking for signs that he'd lost touch with reality, or that he might do something to harm himself. Phillip's parents never understood that Katherine was his lifeline. If he could keep on talking to her it would make him strong, capable of moving on. But when they decided that Phillip might harm himself, they insisted that he stop the playacting. He learned to keep the visits, real or imagined, to himself. Occasionally, a member of the household staff would happen upon him as he talked with Katherine. Those moments kept the servants gossiping about Phillip's sanity and, suspicious as they were, that ghosts might be haunting the manor house.

He wasn't crazy. His deceased wife had not deserted him, as she'd promised. He found great comfort in that. There was the problem of Charlotte's new maid, however. He dreaded the thought that a new hire, especially one closely connected to his sister, would repeat the rumors that ran rampant in the kitchen.

At the parlor door, he paused, took a deep breath and released it slowly. With what he wanted to propose to his father, he needed to be calm—have his wits about him. With another steadying breath, he entered the room.

His parents sat chatting with the Hiltons as they waited for other guests to arrive. Katherine's parents had been invited, but Lady Montgomery received no word of their attendance. Phillip hoped they would. He found Lord and Lady Waller comforting without fail. They fawned over Phillip, especially after losing the baby and Katherine. He often wondered if they also received visits from Katherine. She loved her parents, and it only made sense that she'd spend time with them as well.

"Phillip," his mother said, stretching out her hand toward him. She sat primly in a straight-backed chair, not appearing the least bit comfortable. He walked to her side, taking her hand in his.

"Mother." He turned to the Hiltons. "Mr. and Mrs. Hilton, welcome to Montrose."

Lord Montgomery laughed. "Listen to the formality," he said. "You'd think that you'd never dined with us before."

"There's nothing wrong with good manners," Mrs. Hilton said. She smiled at Phillip. "Thank you, Phillip. It is a pleasure to be here this evening—especially with such a happy occasion to celebrate."

At her mention of the occasion, Phillip's smile fell. What he was about to say was not going to be met well by anyone present. But it's what he and Katherine had decided would be the best course of action.

"I wanted to discuss the occasion, if I may," he said.

"What about it?" his father asked with narrowed eyes.

As Phillip observed those in the room, their expressions ranged from curious to cautious.

He lifted his chin a bit and squared his shoulders. He could not appear weak. "I was thinking that, conceivably, we might forgo the engagement announcement this evening."

As his father barked, "Absolutely not!" and his mother cried out, "Whatever for?" Phillip kept his eyes on the Hiltons, both of whom said nothing, but their concern was undeniable.

The parlor door opened allowing for a momentary reprieve in the tension. Kenton took a few steps into the room. He stopped. "What did I interrupt?"

"Your brother wants to call off his engagement!" their father said.

"That's not what I suggested," Phillip protested. "I only want to postpone the engagement announcement."

"So he can call off the wedding!"

"Father. Please. That's not my intention."

"What is your intention?" Mr. Hilton asked.

Phillip sighed. He knew this wouldn't be easy, but now he had the notion that this was comparable to facing an unfriendly judge and jury. "I simply want to buy some time."

"For what!?" his father bellowed. "So you can weasel your way out of the marriage?"

"No! Father! I simply want some time. I want to ease into this. Spend more time with Marianne. I don't understand why we have to make it public."

"To make sure you go through with it!"

Phillip threw his hands up in the air. "For heaven's sake—are you not listening to me?"

"Phillip," his mother said, her voice soothing, "what would be the purpose for this dinner party if we don't make the announcement?"

"Purpose? Can't you hold a dinner party to hold a dinner party? Why does there have to be a purpose?" Phillip scanned the room wishing that at least one person would take his side. He wasn't asking to call off the engagement— why didn't they understand that?

"We planned all of this as a celebration for you and Marianne," his mother said. "She'll be disappointed."

"I can explain it to her."

"You'll break her heart," Kenton said. He hadn't moved from his spot near the door.

"I'm not calling off the wedding! Just the announcement of it! Why is this so difficult for all of you to understand?" He paced in front of the fireplace, heat radiating against his legs, frustration filling in his chest.

"Of course, Marianne will be most disappointed," Mrs. Hilton said. "But if you're not comfortable..."

"Don't baby him," Lord Montgomery said. "He's a man. He's made a commitment."

"I committed to marry her, not announce the engagement tonight. That was all yours and mother's doing."

"Seems to me," Kenton said, walking over to stand near the Hiltons, "That you're forgetting the bride-to-be's feeling in all of this, Phillip. Marianne has been in love with you since she was twelve! Now you're going to make her wait? Why? Because you're having a difficult time—*three years later*—letting go of Katherine?"

"This has nothing to do with Katherine."

"Oh, please," Kenton moaned. "Everything you do has to do with Katherine. Marianne was in tears the day you married Katherine. Now you're going to deny the girl the only love she's ever wanted! And for what? Time?"

"I don't love her!" Phillip shouted.

The room fell quiet except for the crackling of the fire. He hadn't meant to blurt that out…at least not in front of the Hiltons. No one spoke for a long moment. It was Kenton who broke the silence. "I think we all knew that." His voice was low and accusatory.

"I didn't mean that like it sounded." Phillip dropped into a straight-backed chair and rubbed a hand over his forehead.

"The announcement will be made as planned," his father decreed. "And as most of us have done—you will learn to love your new wife."

Phillip stared at his boots, too embarrassed to face the Hiltons or his family. His plans to put off the wedding indefinitely were foiled. At the dinner tonight, he would have to smile, act happy, accept graciously all the congratulations, and pretend this conversation never happened. He glanced at Charles Hilton. Did the man still think marrying his daughter to Phillip Montgomery was such a grand idea? If only Katherine were here.

~~*

It was close to midnight when all the guests departed. The dinner had proceeded pretty much as Phillip thought it would. His father made a grand toast to honor the newly engaged couple. As the men had drinks and puffed on their cigars afterwards, they made bawdy comments and joked about Phillip's short-lived freedom. Mr. Hilton said little, Phillip even less. On the positive side, all through dinner, Marianne had smiled and blushed as attractively as a girl could. It actually pained Phillip to find her so happy. It wasn't that he didn't like Marianne—it's, well…she wasn't Katherine. As the house quieted for the night, Phillip stole into the library with a bottle and glass in hand. He'd developed a devil of a headache. A stiff drink and some solitude would serve him well.

~~*

Lainey hadn't intended to nap. While Miss Charlotte and Miss Marianne were at dinner, Lainey had planned to take care of some needed mending, and straightening Miss Charlotte's chambers. Clothing was scattered about from their efforts to dress for the occasion. After tending to the room, Lainey had only gone to her room to fetch a sewing kit. While rummaging in a drawer, she'd come across the two letters her brother had sent from Barbados.

She'd frowned. It had been so long since she'd heard from him.

With nothing more pressing than the mending, she sat on the edge of her bed and opened the first letter. He wrote of white sand beaches, turquoise water, a place where the sun shone nearly every day. Sugar plantations covered the island. He teased that between the sugar and the British, the island couldn't be sweeter. She reread the missives, laid back on her bed, and fantasized of life on the exotic island. Smiling, she closed her eyes and dreamed of all the soldiers, of their attentions to her. There she would be able to work for herself—make her own way, instead of catering to the rich and spoiled. There, with her brother, they could have a home and could enjoy all that sunshine and beautiful water. Who knew? It's possible they could have a little sugar plantation of their own? Not that she knew much of running a plantation. But she could learn. She'd learned to do many things. She'd spent her life managing for herself. Learning was a matter of survival.

She lay on the bed musing and before she knew it, she was asleep. A rap on her door awakened her in time to rush to Miss Charlotte's chambers.

Charlotte and Marianne chattered about the evening's events. The engagement had been announced, and now the girls talked of wedding dresses and parties and future children—including some inappropriate comments about the origins of children that kept them giggling until Charlotte dismissed Lainey sometime after midnight. Though it was late, Lainey was not tired. She'd returned to her room and dressed for bed but found it difficult to sleep. The room had chilled, the bed felt lumpy, and because of her nap, she couldn't drift into her usual solid sleep. She would pay for it when 5a.m. arrived and she'd be expected to help get the morning started. A lady's maid shouldn't have to rise before her charge. Charlotte and Marianne were unlikely to be roused before noon.

Lainey tossed and turned, and tossed some more. Sitting up, she fumbled for a match to light a candle. What to do with herself? The mending she needed to attend to was in Miss Charlotte's room. She couldn't retrieve it now. But after a moment's consideration, she grabbed her shawl, the candle, and tiptoed out of her room. The chill in the hall made her room feel balmy. Tightening her shawl, she headed for the servant's staircase.

She tiptoed down the stairs, hoping to avoid the ones that creaked. When she landed on the main level, the stone floor was cold. She glanced down at her bare feet. House slippers would have been nice. Lifting the candle higher, Lainey was greeted with dark silence. A chill, not from the temperature, ran down her spine. Supposedly, this house held at least one ghost. She wondered how many more might roam the halls. Could be this wasn't the best of ideas.

Earlier that day, the manor buzzed with activity. Servants attending to their duties flitted in and out of rooms. At night, did ghosts flit about? Now, with fires banked and readied for the morning, the house held nothing but shadows and the uncomfortable feeling that someone was watching her. But, the beautiful library several steps past Lady Montgomery's office called to Lainey. If she were going to meet her brother in Barbados, help him set up a business or better yet, that plantation, she needed to practice her reading.

As she passed the dining hall, the house, eerily quiet, no longer felt friendly. Lainey was sure at any moment she would meet the ghost of Lady Katherine. And even if she was as kind and lovely as everyone believed, Lainey wasn't interested in running into any apparitions. She hurried past the breakfast room, and the great hall, imagining something in every corner, alcove, and doorway. Her candle didn't help. With its limited range, it only created more shadows and pricked her imagination.

Mr. Hollingsworth was known to wander about the house after the family and servants were in bed to make sure that all had been buttoned up for the night. While she didn't want to meet his disapproval, it would be nice to have another live person about. She glanced down at her attire. He would not think highly of a nightdress and a shawl—they were not an authorized uniform. The thought brought a smile to her lips and helped her relax—but only a little. Focusing on her mission, which should take no more than a few minutes, get a book and get out, Lainey pressed forward.

The double library doors stood wide open, the only light in the room, a patch of patterned moonlight that fell in a rectangle across the floor. A faint odor from the banked fire filled the room. Lainey held the candlestick a little higher as she entered, marveling at the number of books this one room held. Her mother would have loved a library such as this. Bookcases lined two walls. Smaller bookcases stood in the middle and served as desks or tables if someone wanted to lay a book open for study. Lainey bypassed those and went straight to the shelves that lined the far end of the room. There were books to cover a multitude of subjects, from mathematics to herbalism. She ran a finger over the edge of a shelf as she studied titles. *The Fall of Robespierre*, two volumes of *The Life of Nelson*, *Poems of Byron*. There were art books, atlases, and scientific journals.

Atlases. She set her candle on a nearby table, circling back to search for an atlas that might include the Caribbean. Discovering a thin volume labeled *Antilles, Virgin Islands, Caribbean*, she pulled the book from the shelf.

"Pilfering books now?"

Startled, she dropped the volume to the floor as she spun around, expecting to find Mr. Hollingsworth in the doorway. She narrowed her eyes, forcing them to adjust to the darkened side of the room. The banked fire, with its eerie orange glow, allowed enough light for Lainey to make out a faint shadow sitting in a chair close to the fireplace. *Not a ghost.*

"Who's there?" she asked.

"Once a thief always a thief?"

The voice was not one she'd heard often but sounded a bit familiar.

"I'm not a thief."

"You stole food in the market."

"I was hungry."

He chuckled, a sardonic sound. "And now you have an appetite for books."

"I'm not stealing. I'm borrowing."

"Oh, same as you were *borrowing* the food?"

Three people knew of that day in the market. One was Miss Marianne—it was obviously not her. Another was the young Master Kenton. But he had no reason to hold Lainey's bad judgement that day against her. That only left Master Phillip.

She curtsied. "I beg your pardon, Master Montgomery. I did not mean to disturb you. I couldn't sleep and thought I might borrow a book until I became sleepy."

"I am disturbed frequently. It's difficult to believe it's never intended."

His words were slurred. She furrowed her brow. "Truly, I do not mean to be a bother. But if you should need some help, I could summon…"

At that he laughed. Lainey heard the clank of a glass hitting a table.

"Is that why you are here? At this hour? To summon help? As if there is any," he added under his breath.

"No, sir. I believe my arrival was simply coincidence."

"Coincidence," he repeated, "I don't believe in coincidences."

Lainey, frozen in her spot, painfully conscious of her attire and with whom she was speaking, realized the tenuousness of her position.

"I suppose…Miss…Miss…Ha! I didn't learn your name," Master Montgomery said, suddenly amused.

"Alaina…Alaina Clarkson."

"Well, Clarkson, are you telling me you actually read?"

"A little, sir."

"And where did you learn this skill?" Liquid poured into a glass.

"My mother, sir." She wished the room were lighter, that she could see the man. It was uncomfortable that he could see her.

"Your mother could read?"

"Yes, sir. Otherwise, she couldn't teach me."

He chuckled. "And where did she learn to read?"

Lainey paused. Her mother had been guarded with information she gave her children. Lainey reached up and fingered her locket.

"I'm not sure, sir. But I promise you—she knew how to read."

Once more, he laughed, a cynical, harsh sound. "And why should I believe a promise of yours."

She swallowed. "Sir, you sound as if you've had quite the celebration. Can I call your valet to help you to bed?"

"Celebration. I certainly was not celebrating."

Lainey pulled her shawl tighter around her, afraid to move, but certain that she should find some help.

"Where is your mother now?" Master Phillip asked.

"My mother passed away when I was twelve, sir."

"Oh." He sounded sympathetic—less accusatory. "It's horrible to lose the people you love."

"Yes, sir. It is. May I call your valet?"

"Come closer."

"What?" She glanced down at her state of dress, cursing herself for coming out of her quarters in nothing but her nightdress. But who would think the young master of the house would be sitting in the dark in the same room she wanted to visit?

"I said...come closer."

She stood her ground.

"I'm not going to hurt you. I simply want a better view of you. That candle behind you, doesn't allow me to view your face."

Instead of stepping closer, she picked up the candlestick and held it in front of her, the soft light illuminating not only her face but her state of dress. Her cheeks burned with embarrassment. And the added light made it more difficult for her to see Master Phillip and what his reaction might be.

"Why are you here?" he asked.

Her mouth dropped open. He must be more inebriated than she thought. Hadn't they just covered why she was there?

"I...I came to get a book."

"No, no, no. Why are you here? Why are you at Montrose?"

"I was hired to be your sister's maid."

"Charlotte needs a maid? Oh...I suppose she's old enough."

"Sir... can I please call someone for you?"

"Do you like it here?"

The hairs on the back of her neck lifted. She had sudden visions of being out on her own with nowhere to sleep, nowhere to take shelter. The words of the kind man who brought her into Montville repeated in her head...*You won't last out in the elements.*

"Pardon me?"

"I said, do you like it here."

"Yes, sir. Very much, sir." She braced for a dismissal.

"I wish I did."

"Excuse me?"

He laughed. "Does that surprise you? Does it surprise you that someone should not enjoy being in their home?" In the shadow, Lainey saw him raise the glass to his lips. "Why should I?" he said. Lainey wasn't sure if he was talking to her or himself. "I am not a person," he said. "I am nothing more than a way to keep the estate in the family. My wishes are nothing more than empty words. I have no control, no say, no life." Again, he raised his glass, appearing to drain its contents. "I don't know who I am anymore."

Lainey clamped her mouth shut. The rich. They never appreciated what they had. They never considered how it was to have no home, no family. His self-pity was a waste of energy. But at least he wasn't dismissing her. And...with any luck he wouldn't remember the encounter in the morning. She knew her father often spoke of what he thought, but never voiced, until he was into his cups. He never remembered what he'd said the following day. She could only hope that Master Phillip would be the same.

For now, her best course was to return to her room, slip away from him before he came to his senses and dismissed her for stealing a book...or for witnessing his unfortunate state.

As she was about to seek permission to leave, Mr. Hollingsworth entered the room.

He stopped abruptly and scowled at the sight of Lainey in her nightdress.

"Hollingsworth!" Master Phillip called out. "Have you come to join our little party?"

Startled at Phillip's presence, Mr. Hollingsworth turned to face the young master. Lainey blew out a breath of relief. At least she wasn't the only one surprised.

"I beg your pardon, Sir," Hollingsworth said. "I did not know you were here."

With the added light from Mr. Hollingsworth's lamp, Lainey had a better view of Master Phillip. His cravat was undone, his hair mussed as if he had run his hands through it a hundred times. If she hadn't figured it out from his slurred speech and erratic conversation, it was plain the man was drunk and extremely unhappy.

"I was assisting Miss…Miss…Clarkson," he said, sounding pleased that he had remembered her name, "in choosing some appropriate reading material. Did you know she could read?"

Hollingsworth glanced in Lainey's direction. "I did not."

"What's going to happen when all the help can read? There won't be need for lords and ladies anymore."

"I don't think you need to worry over that," Hollingsworth said as he set his lamp on a nearby table. "Come, sir. Let me help you to your chambers." He walked over to Master Phillip, placing a hand under his arm.

Phillip waved the man away. "I can walk." Pushing on the chair arm, he started to rise. Hollingsworth was there to catch him when he stumbled.

"Allow me," the butler said. He pulled Phillip's arm over his shoulder and indicated to Lainey to take up the lamp. She quickly tied her shawl about her shoulders and retrieved both her candle and Hollingsworth's lamp. Walking out into the hall, she led the way toward the main staircase as Mr. Hollingsworth helped the young master to walk. Phillip mumbled the entire way, about marriage, about Lady Katherine, about responsibilities and duty. Hollingsworth acknowledged the ramblings, adding that Master Phillip would feel differently in the morning. Lainey stifled a laugh. In the morning, Master Phillip might feel differently, but it wouldn't be better. She waited at the top of the stairs for the two men to pass her, following them into Master Phillip's chambers. She stayed long enough to set the lamp on a table near the bed. Without a word she slipped back into the hallway. It was unlikely that Mr. Hollingsworth would forget her late-night wanderings, but she hoped Master Phillip would. One ill encounter with the heir to Montrose was enough to last her for many a day. She would avoid him, stay happily tucked away in Miss Charlotte's chambers or down in the servant's area.

She turned toward the servant's staircase when Mr. Hollingsworth stepped into the hallway and called her name. She cringed, expecting the worst.

"Wandering the manor after midnight. Wandering the manor inappropriately dressed. And what were you doing in the library? I should have you dismissed for this."

Lainey held her breath.

Hollingsworth paused. "No word of this tomorrow. No one need hear about Master Phillip's condition."

"Condition?" she asked. "I have no idea what you could be referring to."

Hollingsworth smiled. "In the future, if you want to read, ask Mrs. Hollingsworth. She has a small library that I'm sure she'd be happy to show you."

"Yes, sir. Thank you, sir." She curtsied.

At the sound of Master Phillip retching, Mr. Hollingsworth hurried back into the chambers. Lainey waited a moment debating whether to offer help, instead she headed quickly down the hall. As she started up the staircase, she realized she didn't have a book.

CHAPTER EIGHT

"An old saying and a true,
Much drinking, little thinking."
–Jonathon Swift

Talk in the kitchen the next morning was all about the dinner party the night before. The two footmen, Henry and Martin, told stories of strained relations between the families unlike any they had ever seen before.

"Master Phillip looked as if he'd eaten a bucket of lemons," Henry said. "He scowled the entire night. Poor Miss Hilton, who was as lovely as I'd ever seen her, didn't know what to say to him to bring him out of such a dour mood."

"She's a fool to marry him," Jane said loud enough for only Lainey to hear.

"I think she might be especially fond of him," Lainey replied.

"There is rumor that Master Phillip tried to get out of the engagement right before the dinner," Mary, the housemaid said.

"Says who?" asked Mrs. Crawford, the cook.

"I do," Martin said. "I was walking by the parlor, I was, when I heard voices. Master Phillip himself saying he did not love the girl."

Mrs. Crawford sighed as she threw a towel on the table. "That doesn't mean he was trying to call off the wedding."

"And it's common knowledge that he remains in love with poor Lady Katherine," Henry added.

Lainey remained quiet as speculation increased over Master Phillip, whether he would go through with the wedding, and whether that would chase Lady Katherine's ghost away. While the gossip was entertaining, Lainey just hoped that after the events of the previous evening, Phillip wouldn't dismiss her.

Mr. Hollingsworth stepped into the room. "Master Phillip has every intention of marrying Miss Hilton," he said, setting the record straight. "Any speculation otherwise is improper and cause for discipline." The room fell silent. "Any talk of Master Phillip being anything but of sound mind and body is also inappropriate, and if I hear of one person spreading such malicious gossip, I will dismiss that person without further inquiry."

Mr. Hollingsworth glanced about the room, meeting the eye of each person present. To Lainey, it felt as if his gaze rested on her a bit longer than the rest. She nodded imperceptibly in acknowledgment. She understood.

"Now, if the lot of you don't have enough to do, maybe we should start a deep clean of the manor so that it will be ready when the wedding occurs."

A chorus of "That won't be necessary" rang through the room as maids and footmen scurried from the table.

Jane leaned close to Lainey. "Cleaning is scarcely necessary. The likelihood of the wedding going forward is as likely as goats taking up residence in the music room."

Lainey smiled. After what she had witnessed in the library, Jane could well be correct.

As Mr. Hollingsworth left the kitchen, Henry lowered his voice and said, "I say we should wager on it."

"I heard that," Mr. Hollingsworth called from down the hall. After a moment of mortification, everyone laughed.

The family slept later, as expected. Lainey wasn't called to Miss Charlotte's room until nearly the noon hour. She brought a tray with apple pastries and tea to get Miss Charlotte started for the day. Charlotte squinted when Lainey pulled the curtains open. Unusual for the time of year, the skies were clear, and the sun shone brightly and directly into the room. But it was chilly. Lainey stoked the fire to get it started again, laying a few coals down to warm the room. Charlotte sat up in bed and perused the tray before her.

"Ooh. This looks yummy," she said, lifting a turnover to her mouth. "It is," she said after the first bite. "Mrs. Crawford is amazing. You should have had a taste of the roast lamb she made for the party last night. It was divine."

Since Miss Charlotte had broached the subject, Lainey had no reservation in asking about the party. "Did you enjoy yourself?" she asked.

"I did. I may have been the only one. Mother and Father seemed distracted, though they had guests to entertain. And Phillip...Oh...he was the picture of discontent. You know, when my father announced the engagement, I thought for a moment that Phillip wouldn't acknowledge Marianne. I think Kenton actually kicked Phillip under the table before Phillip turned to her. He smiled oddly, as if he'd sipped some pickle juice, then took Marianne's hand and kissed it. I think that was the only time he paid her any mind. He spent most of the evening talking about land management with Lord Mason. Can you imagine anything more tedious?" She took another large bite of her turnover continuing to speak as she chewed. Lainey hid her smile. Watching Miss Charlotte ignore all the rules of polite society was the most delightful sight Lainey had had since arriving at Montrose.

"When Phillip had to line up with Marianne…" Charlotte finally swallowed, "He had to stand by her side and accept everyone's congratulations. He looked positively ill." Charlotte shook her head. "Poor Phillip. He simply doesn't realize it yet. I think he and Marianne will make a splendid couple!"

"I'm sure they will, Miss," Lainey said. Life regularly turned out in a splendid manner for the wealthy.

Lainey went about her responsibilities in helping Miss Charlotte wash and dress. After her charge had left the room, Lainey tidied up a bit—hanging clothing and straightening the dressing table. Jane, who usually cleaned the room for Miss Charlotte, had remarked how much she appreciated that Lainey did some of the cleaning. If Lainey could make herself useful, she would. Time passed more quickly that way.

"It's one room I can bustle through without much trouble. Master Kenton's room is the worst!" Jane told her one day after Lainey started. Apparently, Mrs. James didn't help with Charlotte's room at all.

Lainey actually enjoyed tidying up. She didn't have to touch the chamber pot, which was a blessing. And she never dusted or washed down walls. But often, she would pull the covers straight on the bed, fluff the pillows, and later in the day she'd add greenery and any flowers continuing to bloom in the gardens to the room. If she had a room similar to this, she would never leave it. She would spend her time doing whatever it was that entertained her, whether that be music, or reading, or sewing, sitting by the window to enjoy a view of the grounds.

After finishing, Lainey gathered together a few items for the wash. With tray in hand and laundry over her arm, she used her foot to open the door wider and stepped into the hall.

"Clarkson, do you have a moment?"

~~*

Phillip couldn't believe his luck—to run into Clarkson so quickly and in a deserted hallway. He had the opportunity and the privacy he desired. When she turned to face him, her eyes were as round and wide as the teacup she held on her tray. *She's imagining the worst,* he thought. But it was he who needed to beg forgiveness for his ill behavior the night before. It pained him to apologize because the cause of that apology pained him.

The girl waited near Charlotte's door, apparently not wanting this conversation any more than he did, but it must be done. In a few short strides, he was down the hall standing face to face with the girl. Since her arrival at Montrose, he'd not paid her much mind, he supposed in an attempt to forget how she came to be there. As he approached, her expression grew more guarded.

"Clarkson, I feel the need…" he couldn't finish. This was the first real opportunity he'd had to get close to the girl since their meeting on the street. And it was a repeat of the breathlessness that he'd experienced at the market. Something about her…something in her eyes…something in the shape of her face. She was attractive, as attractive as a household servant could be, he guessed. She had light brown hair, the color of wet river stone, sleek and shaded with reds and gold, pulled into a tight bun at the nape of her neck. Her eyes, those eyes that managed to steal his breath each time he gazed into them, were copper-colored, but haunted—as if she'd also experienced great sadness in her life. And their shape, round and evenly set…they were so similar to Katherine's. He felt his brow furrow.

"Did you need some assistance?" she asked, bringing Phillip out of his stupor

He shook off his daze and raised his chin. "I feel the need to apologize for my behavior last evening. I hope I did not frighten you. I should have announced myself when you entered the room."

"Oh." She lowered her eyes. "It was not your fault, sir. I had no business wandering about the house at that time of night. I should be asking for your forgiveness."

"There is no crime in walking about the manor. And," he paused, feeling sheepish, "I accused you of stealing. That was uncalled for."

Her shoulders dropped. "Considering how we became acquaintances, I do not think your accusation was inappropriate. I…I've never been able to truly thank you for your help that day."

Her eyes remained downcast. To Phillip, she had the countenance of a trampled flower. It could be his own trampled spirits were making him sentimental, but he felt for the girl and felt an uncanny desire to protect her.

"Were you really only looking for a book to read?" he asked.

"At first, sir."

His eyebrows raised at the admission. "At first?"

"At first, I wanted a book to read until I became sleepy. But I noticed the atlases and became distracted." She dropped her gaze.

"Where did you learn to read?"

"From my mother."

"Do you write as well?"

"Some. My mother taught me enough letters to write my name."

Phillip let out an incredulous laugh. "Did she think you'd be signing contracts?"

Clarkson lifted her head and glared at him. The expression was so unexpected that Phillip took a step back.

"My mother was an intelligent, kind, talented woman. She could do many tasks. If she had lived longer, I may have had more skills than to read and write a bit."

This girl had spirit. It was as if she forgot who she was talking to. But Phillip could overlook her impertinence. She was reacting out of loyalty and sadness. She had lost her mother.

"How old were you when your mother passed?" Loss was an emotion Phillip could well relate to.

The girl's expression softened. "I was twelve. She died in childbirth."

Phillip flinched. He truly knew that pain. "I'm sorry."

She stared at him as if he'd somehow grown antlers about his head. Could it be so surprising that someone in his station could offer sympathy to someone of her station?

"Thank you," she said with a slight curtsy. "It is kind of you to say so."

"Well, as you are probably already aware, I've had my own losses."

"Yes, sir." She paused, chewing on her lip as if she considered saying more. "I've seen her portrait. She was very beautiful."

The familiar ache swelled in Phillip's chest. "Yes," he said swallowing down the sudden knot in his throat. "And she was as kind as she was beautiful."

"I'm sorry for your loss as well, sir."

This was too much, Phillip thought. Before they knew it, they would both be sobbing like children and what good would that do? Phillip reserved those moments for private, when no one would call his emotions into question. With all the talk circulating about the manor, he needn't add more.

Clarkson eyed him with a bit of suspicion. *She's heard the rumors already*, he thought.

"Your tray must be getting heavy," he said, nodding at her hands. "Please, accept my apology and continue on with your duties."

She offered a timid smile. "I don't believe an apology was necessary, but I will accept, if you will accept mine, and my thanks for your help." Again, she lowered her eyes. He wished she would stop doing that. He welcomed peering into her eyes.

"Consider both accepted. Good day, Clarkson."

"Good day, sir." She curtsied and turned to make her way to the back staircase.

As he watched her go, Phillip felt the corner of his mouth turn slightly upward. If he had done nothing in his life worthy of praise, at least he had helped that young girl. She had a sweetness and a deportment that defied her station in life. Perhaps, when he became Lord of the house, he would give her a different position so that she could stay on instead of following Charlotte. Realizing he was wishing his father into the grave, he caught himself with a shake of the head. Enough death had visited this house. There was no need for more.

CHAPTER NINE

"Blessed are they that mourn: for they shall be comforted"
–Matthew 5:4 - Bible

Four weeks ago, no one would have convinced Lainey that she would spend her morning in the large and ornate music room of Montrose Manor, not as a servant but as an invited guest, at least that's how Charlotte explained it, for an impromptu music performance.

"You must come be our audience," Charlotte said that morning as Lainey lay a tray of sweets on a table and opened the curtains in the girl's room. "What fun is it to perform with no audience?"

So, Lainey observed. Charlotte and Marianne, who had been a daily visitor lately, presumably to spend time with Master Phillip but in reality, spending all her time with Charlotte, sang and played the piano. Lainey understood her job was solely to clap and encourage them. Not that she minded. Next to the library, the music room was Lainey's favorite room in the house with its massive fireplace that had an opening as tall as she was, and the beautiful grand piano centered on a raised platform where Charlotte sat on the piano bench. The room carried the faint aroma of wood polish and a hint of evergreen from the boughs of white pine brought in for decoration. The room felt surprisingly cozy, mostly due to the red damask curtains that hung by every window from ceiling to floor.

Of the two girls, Miss Charlotte was the more accomplished, although both were far more skilled than Lainey. Lainey's mother had had a lovely voice and often sang to Lainey and her brothers. As she listened to Marianne sing while Charlotte played the piano, Lainey smiled. She remembered lullabies her mother sang when Lainey and her brothers were small—she reached for her locket.

"And what's going on in here?" said Kenton.

"We're practicing," Charlotte replied.

"Wasting your time," Kenton teased. His shoes clacked across the polished, hardwood floor as he entered the music room, his hands clasped behind his back, eyeing the girls as if he were a music master ready to critique their abilities. "You should come play Whist. I'm in the mood for some sport and playing you girls would satisfy me sufficiently."

"We're busy," Charlotte said.

"I love Whist," Marianne said. She turned an imploring look on Charlotte. "It would be great fun to play."

Charlotte frowned and glanced between her friend and her brother. Lainey watched on hopefully; if the girls went to play cards, she could retreat to the servant's quarters and spend time with people she more readily related to. If they chose to continue with their makeshift recital, Lainey would be stuck in her role of indentured enthusiast, clapping and complimenting. Life could be worse, she supposed.

"We were suitably occupied, Kenton." Charlotte appeared to want to say more, but one more glance at Marianne and her shoulders fell. "Oh…all right. We can play your silly game." She stood and gathered her music. "Lead the way."

Kenton grinned and turned toward the large oak-framed archway that opened to the rest of the house, Marianne close on his heels. Kenton stopped and glanced toward Lainey. "Bring your maid. Phillip refuses to play."

"Ugh…he's so dreary," Charlotte said. "Come, Alaina. We need four people for Whist."

Lainey didn't move. It was one thing to sit with the girls while they practiced their music. It was another to sit with the family at a table playing card games. If Mr. Hollingsworth caught wind of it, she'd be reprimanded for sure. Charlotte had started treating Lainey more as a poor relation than a maid. And while in private, Lainey enjoyed the inclusion, the reality was she was nothing more than a servant and she had to remember her place when Charlotte did not.

"I'm not sure…" Lainey protested.

"Nonsense," Charlotte said. "We need you. You must come."

"I don't know how to play," Lainey said, which was a lie. It had been a favorite game in her family as well. Her mother often encouraged a game after the late meal even if it meant she stayed up long past when the streetlamps had been snuffed. Lainey often stayed up with her mother to clean and prepare dishes for the next morning. Precious time she longed for now.

"Good. We'll make you Kenton's partner." Charlotte smiled and flounced out of the room. Kenton and Marianne waited with raised brows. Feeling outnumbered, Lainey sighed and followed along.

~~*

Sitting at a table with three people, far beyond her station, with Phillip overseeing the game was more uncomfortable than Lainey had words to express. And on top of that, she had to pretend she didn't know how to play...the entire situation was unbearable. Master Kenton was patient, reminding her on several occasions which card suit was trump. Charlotte and Marianne won the first few hands, much to Kenton's dismay. Having pity on the poor man, Lainey acted as if she'd caught on to the rules and helped him win the next three rounds. By the last round, the table had become so animated they'd caught Phillip's attention. Although he tried to appear disinterested, Lainey caught him watching, making eye contact with her on a few occasions.

He nodded the first time their eyes met—she was unsure of its meaning. The second time, she raised her cards slightly as if asking him if he wanted to play. He shook his head and returned to his book. He was an intriguing man if not a bit distracting. She couldn't help noticing his sad brown eyes or how his dark blond hair curled around the nape of his neck. Glancing back at her cards, she imagined the feel of those curls winding through her fingers. Alarmed at her thoughts, she concentrated on the cards before her. Charlotte was the next to play. They went around the table, each laying a card down. Kenton gave a little whoop when he took the trick, offering Lainey an approving grin.

Lainey peeked over her cards, back to Phillip. His brow furrowed as he read. She smiled. Her brother, Robert, used to have that expression when he tried to read. Reading didn't come as easily for him as it had for her. Robert's talent lay in numbers. Of course, Phillip wasn't frowning because he was having difficulty—that was absurd. A man such as Phillip only frowned when displeased. His eyes rose and met Lainey's anew. The crease disappeared. He nearly smiled. Her cheeks warmed. She'd never reacted to Robert's smile in such a manner. Well, that wasn't completely true. The last time she'd seen Robert, right before he sailed off on his great adventures, he had made her blush.

~~*

They stood on the street outside a lovely white brick home. It towered above Lainey and Robert, three stories high. With its double red doors and wrought iron gate and fencing, the home loomed like a giant aristocrat. Lainey, a scared and nervous fourteen-year-old girl, trembled from head to foot.

"Don't worry," Robert said. "You will feel at home quickly."

"Robert," she whispered, afraid of disturbing anyone inside. "We've never lived anyplace so fine."

"Well, our fortunes are changing now, are they not?"

She knew his fortunes were changing. Look at him in his white navy uniform. Large blue collar and cuffs. Her future remained questionable.

"What if they don't like me?"

He cuffed her on the chin. "Everybody adores you, Lainey."

"What if I can't do the work?"

Robert laughed. "You've been doing the work since Mum passed. They will most likely increase your pay immediately when they notice how skilled you are." He pushed open the gate.

Lainey hesitated. Turning her head from side to side, she wished she were anyplace else. Somewhere other than being left on a stranger's doorstep to become part of a household staff.

"Come, Lainey. I need to get you settled before I sail. And I should have already been on board. You don't want to have me flogged the first day, do you?"

"Of course not." She picked up her skirts and marched through the gate, up the short walk and to the door. Robert followed closely behind.

"Let me look at you," he said. She stood straight waiting for his assessment. He tugged at her collar, then wiggled her skirt to and fro. "Yes, that will do." Reaching up, he used the rapper to knock on the door. And they waited.

Lainey took several deep breaths, trying to quell her nerves. A trick her mother had taught her. How she wished her mother was with her now. She was moments away from a new home, a new work, and losing her brother to the seas. Tears burned in her eyes. She must be strong...strong for Robert. It's what her mother would expect.

She raised her eyes to his. A flash of uncertainty appeared but was quickly replaced by tenderness as he reached out and took her locket in hand. "You are a beautiful young lady," he said, weighing the locket. She blushed at the compliment. "Don't let anyone take..."

The door opened to a man with a stern demeaner, dressed in fine livery. He scowled. "Yes?"

Robert took a step back, forcing Lainey to take charge.

She curtsied. "My name is Alaina Clarkson. Mrs. Hall has hired me." She tried to make that sound like a statement and not a question. "I am here to start work."

The man's expression relaxed. "Ah...yes. Mrs. Hall did tell me you would report today. Please, come in." He stepped aside to make room for Lainey.

Panicked, she turned to Robert. This was it...this was their goodbye.

"What were you saying?" she asked.

He swallowed. "You take care, Lainey. Work hard. I'll be in touch." He bowed as if that were the end. Lainey scurried down the stairs and threw her arms about his neck. He returned a quick hug, afterwards he pushed her away, toward the open door.

"I love you, Robert," she said.

A genuine smile lit his face. "I love you, too..."

~~*

"Alaina? Alaina…it's your turn."

Lainey blinked. Everyone around the table was staring at her.

"Oh, I'm sorry." Quickly studying the cards on the table, she pulled one from her hand and tossed it to the center.

"I think you're a natural at this. We won…again," Kenton gloated, as he scooped up the cards. "Brother, do you want to play this round?"

He'd invited Phillip to join them after each round. Each time Phillip declined, this time much to Lainey's disappointment. With fresh memories of Robert, she was ready to busy herself with work—distract herself. But now it was her turn to deal the cards. As she began, Lord Montgomery blustered into the room.

"What the deuce?" he said, staring at Lainey and his children at the table. Within seconds he'd assessed the situation—Phillip sitting across the room while the others were engaged at the card table. Releasing a frustrated sigh, he said, "Charlotte. Kenton. I need to speak with both of you in my office. Immediately, please."

Miss Charlotte and Master Kenton traded glances, laid their cards on the table and stood. Lainey took the opportunity to leave as well. She followed Charlotte out of the room. Once in the hallway, it was Master Kenton who glanced back and saw Marianne staring hopelessly at the cards in front of her, alone in the room with Phillip.

"Father," Kenton said, "Is it appropriate for us to leave the couple unchaperoned?"

Lord Montgomery's face twisted into a scowl. "Bah! Dash it all." He surveyed the people present, his eyes resting on

Lainey. She took a cautious step back. "You—girl—go sit in the room but make yourself invisible."

"Yes, sir," Lainey said with a curtsy. Ill at the thought, she stepped back into the room and found an inconspicuous chair in the corner near a window where she could look outside, but carry on as a chaperone. Could this day get any worse?

Marianne remained seated at the table, turning cards over one by one. This was not the girl Lainey had come to know. Yes, at first, she was a bit shy, but on further acquaintance, she became a chatty young lady, frequently peppering Charlotte with questions about Phillip. Lainey never understood why the girl didn't spend more time with her intended. But more perplexing now, noticing how painfully shy Marianne became in Phillip's presence, was why she agreed to marry him in the first place.

Phillip sat in the same spot he'd been in all morning, engaged in his book. Lainey could tell he was only pretending to read, as if decorum were warring with his better judgment. He'd glance down at the book, then raise his eyes to Marianne. She never turned in his direction, but kept flipping her cards, and sighing. Lainey fought a smile. Several times Phillip went to close his book. But he'd quickly reopen it. At last, he stood, laid the book aside and took a seat at the table with Marianne. Lainey turned to the window. Be invisible, she told herself.

"Your game became quite lively," Phillip said.

"Yes, it did."

"You enjoy playing games?"

"I do like card games."

"And which is your favorite?"

Lainey gave Phillip credit for at least trying to engage Marianne in conversation. But his attempts gave him no advantage. Her answers remained quiet and clipped.

"Whist." And before he could ask another question she added, "And Hearts. I like Hearts."

"Oh. Yes, both games can be diverting."

An awkward silence ensued. Lainey stole a glance in the couple's direction. Marianne continued to turn her cards, picking up the deck when the cards ran out and starting over. Phillip gazed about as if searching for a topic to converse about. He caught Lainey's eye and shrugged. She offered a sympathetic smile before again turning toward the window.

"Are your parents well?" he asked.

"Yes."

"And your younger brother?"

"He's well."

Lainey heard the scrape of a chair against the floor and looked over in time to catch Marianne rising from her seat. Phillip followed suit. The girl curtsied.

"Excuse me. I must be going." Without another word, she bolted from the room.

Master Phillip remained, his expression dumbfounded. He let out an amused snicker as he turned to Lainey.

"You'd think I'd suddenly grown horns, the way she ran from the room."

"I see no horns, sir," Lainey replied with a slight smile.

He chuckled. "Thank you. I was beginning to wonder." He glanced toward the door where Marianne had fled. "She's become a flighty girl. She never used to behave that way."

"I wouldn't know, sir." Now that Marianne had gone, Lainey wasn't sure whether she was required to stay but was afraid to move.

Phillip walked back to the chair he'd previously occupied and picked up his book and flipped casually through its pages.

Holding it up, he said, "Have you read this one?"

Lainey's eyes opened wide. "Most likely not, sir."

"It's poetry. Do you enjoy poetry?" He examined Lainey with such intensity that she shied back into her seat.

"I've not much chance to read it."

"No. No, of course not." He turned the book over in his hand. "I thought since you were searching for Shakespeare in the library that you were familiar with some of the other poets."

"I was not looking for Shakespeare," she corrected.

"Were you not?"

"Not particularly. I hoped to find a book to read. But I discovered an atlas." Why had she told him that?

"Ah. Yes. You did mention that. Why were you seeking an atlas?"

She lowered her eyes. "I was curious about Barbados."

"Barbados?" Amusement laced his voice.

She nodded toward the book in his hand, and asked, "What was that you were reading?"

Phillip lifted the book and flipped through the pages. Stopping on a page, he smiled.

"This is Alfred Tennyson. Some of it I thoroughly enjoy. Some of it is a bit long, but others are timely, like this one…" he held the book open for Lainey to read the title of the poem, "*The Charge of the Light Brigade*—dreadful folly that was." He flipped through a few more pages. "And there is this one, *Requiescat*, it was read at Kath….at a funeral I attended." He closed the book and turned away from her.

Lainey felt for the man. "Did it bring comfort?"

"No."

"When my oldest brother died, there was nothing that could bring my father comfort."

Master Phillip glanced over his shoulder.

"He'd already buried my mother. To lose his oldest son, I think, contributed to my father's passing as well."

"You've lost both your parents and a brother?"

The familiar ache tugged in her chest. "Yes, sir."

"How did your brother die?"

"An accident, sir. He was working on the railroad, some supports collapsed—not sure how—but he fell a great distance. His neck broke in the fall."

Master Phillip grimaced. "And your father?"

"Weakened by the drink, I believe. After Allan's death, my father drowned his sorrows until he became ill and never recovered."

"You have no family?" His brow furrowed as he clutched the poetry book to his chest.

"I have another brother." She lowered her eyes, and out of habit when she talked of her family, reached up and fingered her locket. "He's with the navy. He left for Barbados after I'd found a place in service. He didn't want to leave until he knew I would be cared for."

"Hence your interest in Barbados."

"Yes, sir."

"What about aunts, uncles, or cousins?"

"I have an uncle on my father's side—and a few cousins. Most are in London. I never knew my mother's family."

Charlotte appeared in the doorway. "Here you are," she said to Lainey. "I thought you'd gone downstairs."

"She was chaperoning, as Father charged her to do...not that I need a chaperone."

"The chaperone wasn't for you, Phillip, it was for Marianne. A girl can't be too careful with her reputation."

Phillip chuckled. "What threat am I to the young lady?"

"Well…the two of you are engaged to be married. We wouldn't want you to think you can take liberties…yet."

Phillip laughed. "I can assure you, Charlotte, your friend was in no danger from me. Your maid can tell you I was the perfect gentleman."

"No doubt you were. Shame that is."

"Charlotte!"

"Phillip, I only want to detect some life in you. Be a rogue…at least then you're being something!"

"I'm plenty of things, Charlotte." His voice hardened. "But compromising young girls, whether engaged to them or not, is not anything I'd consider. Now…if you'll excuse me, I'm sure Father will have some words for me."

"Yes…yes, he will," Charlotte said as he pushed past her. "Come Alaina, Marianne has decided to go home. We need to talk her out of it."

Charlotte turned and pranced from the room. Hesitating only a minute, Lainey followed.

CHAPTER TEN

"Noble be man, helpful and good!
For that alone sets him apart"
–Johann Wolfgang von Goethe

Convincing Marianne to stay hadn't been all that difficult—once Charlotte assured her friend that she hadn't made a fool of herself in front of Phillip.

"He's challenging to talk to on a good day," Charlotte said. "And today wasn't one of his better days."

Marianne lay across the bed while Lainey brushed Charlotte's hair.

"If you say so. I'm so tongue-tied around Phillip. Whatever will we talk about when we're married?" Marianne mused.

Glancing up at the reflection in the mirror, Lainey saw Marianne throw her arms out wide in exasperation.

Charlotte chuckled. "From what I understand about marriage, you don't have to worry about talking. Ouch! Alaina, don't pull so hard."

"Sorry."

Marianne rolled onto her stomach, viewing Charlotte in the mirror. "And that's another thing. He…well…he knows all about…that. I know nothing."

"It's better to have an experienced lover than not," Charlotte said. "Isn't that right, Alaina?"

Lainey fought a smile. "I wouldn't know, miss."

"Besides, Marianne, you are exactly what Phillip needs—a way to forget his loss."

Lainey quietly scoffed, but not quietly enough.

"You don't agree?" Charlotte turned in her chair to face Lainey. At the same time, Marianne scrambled to the edge of the bed, her blue eyes wide.

Taking a step back, Lainey glanced between the two girls. Although she was only a few years older than they, at times it could have been decades. Lainey envied their naivete, their sheltered, privileged lives. What did they understand of loss? Of loneliness? Of the heartbreak that comes with death? The wealthy appeared to have no sympathy for what the rest of the world suffered.

"Well?" Charlotte prodded.

"I think you do your brother a disservice." Lainey's voice held no authority, but Charlotte considered the observation.

"How so?"

"You're assuming all he needs to do is to forget. I don't believe he will ever forget." Lainey lowered her eyes.

There was a moment of silence before Marianne threw herself back on the bed. "I'm doomed!"

"No, no, no." Charlotte rose to her feet and rushed to her friend's aid. "You can make him forget. He needs someone like you. Someone young. Someone sweet. Someone he has to protect."

Marianne looked to Lainey for confirmation.

"She'll haunt us all our married lives!" Marianne cried. "I never should have agreed. I'll never measure up. I'll never be able to make him forget Lady Katherine."

Charlotte turned pleading eyes to Lainey. "Surely," she said to Marianne while staring down Lainey, "Alaina didn't mean that."

Surely, she did, just as surely as Charlotte wanted her to console Marianne.

Lainey walked to the bed, taking hold of the wood post. "What I meant, Miss Hilton, was that when people lose someone they love, they don't want to forget that person. In the case of Master Phillip, I don't think he wants to forget his first wife and child. But that doesn't mean he can't love someone else." She didn't add *when he's ready*. Which in Lainey's mind wasn't going to be anytime soon—especially if the woman's ghost followed him around.

Marianne took hope. "Really? You think he might love me?"

Lainey hesitated. One glimpse of Miss Charlotte's warning glare and Lainey knew what she had to say. "I think it's a real possibility."

Turning to Charlotte, Marianne's shoulders relaxed as her smile blossomed. Charlotte gave the girl a hug, then winked at Lainey. Her eyes reflected exactly what Lainey was thinking. Phillip really falling in love with Marianne was as likely as his falling in love with Lainey.

~~*

Waning daylight filtered through the windows of the library. Phillip had spent most of the afternoon there, hiding from his sister and fiancé. He sorely wished the girl would return to her parent's home. Montrose was not her home…not yet.

"What is troubling you?" Katherine said, appearing in his mind's eye at the exact moment Phillip realized he wanted to talk to her. She made a habit of that.

"I can't stop thinking about her."

"*Charlotte's maid.*" It was a statement, not a question. But of course, that's how it would be. Katherine knew all of his thoughts and every emotion without a word. She'd been that way in life, but in death, her gift was enhanced. "*And this troubles you.*" Phillip envisioned Katherine in the chair across from him, her hair falling delicately around her shoulders, her expression gentle and not the least concerned.

"She's lost so much," he said. "She's an orphan. She only has the one living brother. I can't imagine how awful that would be. What would I have done without the family when you..."

"*Your family has been a great comfort to you.*"

Phillip bolted from his chair by the fire and walked to the window. While he'd been in the library, much of the time pacing back and forth, he'd been trying to make sense of this new obsession with a house servant.

"It isn't proper," Phillip said after peering out the window for a long moment.

"*What isn't proper?*" Her voice held a hint of humor. "*That she's lost her family, or that you're thinking about her?*"

"She's a maid!"

"*Yes. She is.*" Katherine smiled. "*Does that mean you can't sympathize with her? That's what you're doing...if a little obsessively.*"

"Am I?" He stared out into the approaching night. Several days had passed since his conversation with Clarkson in the garden room. She haunted him. Could it be his parents were right? Should his sanity be questioned? It made little sense that his sister's maid should be any of his concern. Why couldn't he get her out of his thoughts? Though he'd been drunk that night in the library, he couldn't forget the sight of her in nothing but a night dress.

What had she been thinking? Coming out in the house in such attire? He could have her dismissed for less. But he wouldn't. Something about her...unsettled him. The moment he'd laid eyes on her in the market—something told him they shared a connection. He'd never imagined it would be loss.

"*Phillip.*" He imagined Katherine stood closer now, the sound of his name wrapping him in comfort, easing the ache in his heart. "*You feel the girl's sadness. There is nothing wrong with that. I would think you heartless if you didn't.*"

He groaned. "I wish I didn't have a heart."

"*Nonsense. I wouldn't love you if you weren't compassionate. Remember how you consoled me when Pippy died? And you hadn't even had a dog of your own.*"

"Dogs are meant to work, not lay around the house."

She laughed. Phillip closed his eyes to enjoy the sound. "*And yet you comforted me. Phillip, that's what you do. This girl is haunting your thoughts because you want to comfort her.*"

He opened his eyes, surveying the dark yard. "That's not proper."

"*Not in the way you comforted me, no, it is not. But is there a way you might help the girl?*"

His brow furrowed. Could he find a way to help her?

"The atlas," he said, his thoughts cascading like dominoes. The atlas. Barbados. Only living brother. No other living relatives. She wanted to be with her brother. Of course she would! She was working as a servant because she had no other choice. Her brother would support her. He could arrange a good match for her. It's possible being with her brother would remove her from service and allow her to use her abilities to read and write.

"*Help her,*" Katherine's voice whispered. She knew him so well. She knew he needed a purpose, a way to distract himself from the impending marriage he loathed. Helping this girl reunite with her beloved brother was a worthy cause. And in doing so, maybe…possibly…he could find a measure of peace.

He walked to the bookshelf that lined the far side of the room. Running his finger over the spine of several volumes, he searched.

"Where is it?" he muttered.

"Are you searching for something specific, sir?" Hollingsworth stepped up beside him. He smelled of coffee and pipe smoke. The scent often lingered on him after he'd been with Lord Montgomery.

"An atlas."

"Any particular one?"

"Yes." Returning to his search, he moved his hand down to a lower shelf. "This is where reference books are supposed to be. You don't suppose someone has moved it, do you?"

"Which one, sir?"

"Barbados."

"Barbados. That would be with the Caribbean," Hollingsworth muttered as he also dragged a finger along the books. "Ah…here." He pulled a thin volume from the shelf and handed it to Phillip.

Phillip smiled as he flipped through the pages.

"Are you planning a trip?" Hollingsworth asked.

"Just curious."

"I see."

The butler hovered while Phillip searched. It was similar to having an overgrown bulldog breathing down his neck. After a few cursory glances and no conversation, Phillip stood to his full height and turned to the man. "Is there anything else?"

"Yes, sir. Your father asked me to find you. He wishes to speak with you."

Icy fingers wrapped around Phillip's stomach. Not again. Daily recounting of interactions with Miss Hilton made Phillip want to spend the day riding where he wouldn't have to face his father or the girl. Why didn't she go home?!

"Very well. Tell him I'll be there shortly." His definition of shortly and his father's were bound to be completely different.

Offering a slight bow, Mr. Hollingsworth turned and left the room.

Phillip laid the book down on the top of a smaller shelf and began the search. When he found Barbados, he calculated the distance...3,650 nautical miles. His brow furrowed. With favorable winds, the sailing would take at least a month. Did Clarkson know that? Could it be she'd only been curious how far away her brother really was? Maybe she had no intention of joining him? But if it was her intention to join him...he could help. In good conscience, Phillip couldn't let her travel all that distance without some measure of safety. He could make sure she arrived at the correct destination—after all, there was a chance her bother was no longer in Barbados. Once the brother's location was established, Phillip would pay her passage leaving any money she might have saved while in their employ to help her establish herself. And in return? In return, he might feel as if the biblical adage were true, "whosoever will lose his life...the same shall save it."

First, he needed to face his father. Afterwards he would prepare a letter for his friend, Hal—he had connections in the Royal Navy. And lastly, he would talk to Clarkson.

But...responsibilities first. Steeling himself, he headed toward his father's office.

CHAPTER ELEVEN

"So haunt thy days and chill thy dreaming nights"
–John Keats

Lainey sat patiently as mail was delivered to the rest of the household staff. Of course, there would be nothing for her. Robert had no idea where to find her, and she had no one else who would think to write. Busying herself with some mending, she tamped down her envy. Jane, excited to have received two letters that week, sat down next to her.

"My mum, and my cousin." She held up the two missives and leaned in closer to Lainey. "This one's from my cousin." She showed a letter to Lainey. "He's been courting me for some time now, but I keep him at a distance. He don't make as much money as I make here. Why would I give up a fine place to live and such riches for a man, the idea is absurd." She threw her head back and laughed.

Lainey smiled. "Yes, indeed. Such riches." At the rate servants around the manor sunset were paid, Lainey was afraid her plans to sail in the spring were a simple fantasy.

"Listen to this," Jane said. *"My dearest Jane. My days have been long and lonely without word from you."* She laughed. "I never answer his letters. You'd think he would take a hint."

"Isn't that kind of cruel?"

"It would be worse to give him hope, don't you think?"

"Yes, you're probably right." Sometimes hope was the cruelest emotion of all.

The bell from Miss Charlotte's room rang.

Jane looked up in surprise. "I thought the mistress was gone for the afternoon."

Lainey rose from the table. "I hope nothing has gone wrong."

"I'll save the rest of this for later," Jane said, waving the missive in the air. But Lainey paid her no mind, too concerned about what happened to Charlotte's plans.

Lainey made her way through the tight hallways and up the staircase. Winded, and a bit perplexed at Charlotte's early return, Lainey appeared in the doorway and stopped. It was not Charlotte who waited for her, but Master Phillip. He stood with his back to the door, gazing out the window. Surely, he hadn't called Lainey here.

"Eh-hem." Lainey waited immediately outside the room as he turned to the sound.

"Miss Clarkson." He bowed slightly. Such gentlemanly behavior being offered to a household servant set Lainey on high alert.

"Master Phillip." She curtsied. Her eyes darted about the room. "Does Miss Charlotte need me?"

"I rang for you."

She took a step back.

"Please, come in. I want to talk to you without an audience."

She remained rooted in place. Was it possible to refuse? What if he'd been drinking? What if after discovering she had no family to protect her, he thought her easy prey? She shuddered at the idea of fighting off another spoiled estate heir.

"Please," he said again, motioning for her to come and be seated at Miss Charlotte's dressing table. He turned the chair so it would face the room.

"Sir," her voice cracked, "this is not proper."

"I know. I know. But I have a proposition I'd like to discuss with you."

Her eyes grew wide.

"Oh, no...that did not sound...that was not what I intended. Please, please come in and talk with me."

She hesitated, then inched her way into the room, keeping as much distance from the man as she could. Perhaps sensing her unease, he moved away from the dressing table to stand across the room. Lainey sat on the edge of the chair, alert, ready to run. Hints of Charlotte's floral perfume, the one from Paris she had bragged about, lingered in the chilly room. The fire had died down, and the drizzly weather seemed to crawl its way into the chambers. None of this alleviated Lainey's concerns.

"You need not be worried, Clarkson." He paced across the floor. "It has occurred to me, you may not be intending to stay in our employ for long."

Lainey remained silent, her eyes following him as he moved about the room.

"After our conversation in the Garden Room, and your attempt to steal the atlas—"

"I was not trying to steal."

Master Phillip smiled at her reaction. "Of course not. But, do you deny that your intention is to leave Montrose and join your brother in Barbados?"

How did he know? She lowered her eyes. "No, sir."

"I thought not." He moved to Charlotte's bed and sat on the edge. "So, I have a deal I wish to make with you."

"A deal?" Her skin crawled as the memory rushed back of Harold Warrington grabbing her shoulders and pushing her against a wall.

The way Phillip watched her, studied her, made her vulnerable. "I will not ask anything improper from you," he said, appearing as if he might laugh. "I would like to help you."

Tingling ran up her spine as she let out a soft gasp. "Help me? How?"

Phillip chuckled. "Well, I guess you could say I find myself moved at the harsh circumstances life has handed you. I know how it feels to lose someone you love deeply. And you have lost nearly your entire family. I suspect you would want to be with your brother."

"I would. But why...why would you help...me?" She reached up and clutched her locket. Could this really be true?

"Do you know exactly where your brother is?"

Her heart shrank. "The last letter I received from Robert was over a year ago. He was in Barbados. I'm assuming he's still there. Do you think he may not be?"

"It's difficult to tell. The English fleet has a presence on several of the islands in the Caribbean. He could have been reassigned. I'd hate to think that you would sail all that way and not find him when you arrived. What would you do?"

She hadn't considered that. "I have no idea, sir." The possibility of arriving on the island and her brother being stationed elsewhere was more discouraging than she could comprehend. "But he could be there," she added, not wanting to lose heart.

Master Phillip nodded. "He could be. What I am proposing is that I write a letter to make sure. I would be amiss if I sent you off not knowing he was there to meet you."

"But why would you…"

He waved her off. "I will locate your brother, and pay your passage to be with him."

She rose to her feet. "Sir, there is no way I can possibly accept—"

"This isn't a gift, Clarkson. There is something I wish from you in return."

Her shoulders fell. Here it comes, she thought. He wouldn't *take* favors from her, as that devil Master Warrington tried. Master Phillip was a gentleman; he would demand payment for his perceived kindness. That would make her no better than a harlot. She shook her head and moved toward the door. She would not allow this to happen again.

"Hear me out," he said, reaching out as if to stop her. "What I would like…" his face screwed up as he sought for words. He licked his lips, a brief pause, before continuing. "What I would like is for you to help me forget…no…that's not the right word. I want you to help me move on. I need to—if I'm to marry Miss Hilton—I need to find a way to put Katherine behind me."

"And…how would you propose I do that?" She didn't hide her contempt at the idea.

His eyes filled with pleading. "I need someone to talk to. Someone who will let me talk about Katherine. I don't know why, but my family, my parents, they change the subject whenever I bring up her name. You understand loss."

She studied him, her eyes raking him from head to toe looking for any signs of duplicity. She found none. But this was too much to believe. Would he offer to locate her brother, pay her passage, all that assistance for simply listening? "You want me to listen to you?" Even to her own ears she sounded skeptical.

He looked her in the eye, his expression tortured. *The poor man.*

"If it wouldn't be too much trouble."

"Your family will frown on the association."

"More than likely."

"I could be dismissed."

"I won't let that happen."

"They...your family, the other household staff will think..." She didn't need to elaborate. He understood. She could detect it in his eyes.

"I will be discreet. I have no intention of ruining anyone's reputation."

"And you'll buy me passage?"

"I will."

Keeping a fixed eye on Phillip, she considered. What did she have to lose? Well...plenty if she thought too deeply about it. But thoughts of being with her brother, walking on a white sand beach next to turquoise waters, the sun on her back, the freedom would be so delightful—a dream come true. Could be it wasn't the smartest deal she would ever make, but how could she resist?

She curtsied. "I accept."

CHAPTER TWELVE

"I cannot tell why this imagined
Despair has fallen upon me
The Ghost…that will not let me be."
–Heinrich Heine

Near the morning room, at the end of the hall, a door emptied to a tree-lined stone path that the Montgomery family fondly called "Birch Alley." Lainey walked down the path, admiring long, white willowed branches heavy with yellow leaves that spread overhead in a canopy of gold. The air felt cool, but the sun shining through the leaves made the day feel warmer. Lainey tugged at her shawl, adjusting it about her shoulders, as she strode toward the end of the alley where Master Phillip waited for her.

The previous evening, Lainey had encountered Phillip in the hallway. He asked after her plans for the next day and requested that she meet him at the overlook at the end of "Birch Alley." Charlotte was to be gone for the afternoon, making visits with her mother, and when they returned, Marianne Hilton would be in their company. As Lainey approached the gentleman standing with his back to her, she imagined he wanted to meet with her for that exact reason—he was going to have to entertain Marianne for a few days.

Having had time to think about Master Phillip's dilemma, Lainey's sympathy had waned. Miss Marianne, an attractive girl, with lovely blond hair the color of sunshine, and sharp, vivid blue eyes, was sweet, almost sickeningly so, with a quiet voice and demure manner. So what if she didn't match Phillip's beloved Katherine? Was it fair to ask her to? Was it fair that Phillip thought every woman should attain his impossible standard? The moment the thought crossed her mind, she regretted it. How fair was it to judge harshly a man in the throes of grief?

As she moved closer, her regret grew.

"I heard from Hal. He's on his way to France, but assures me he'll be here for the wedding," Phillip said to no one, as he leaned his hands on a gray stone wall that surrounded the overlook. He paused for a moment, then chuckled. "What's he doing in France? Chasing the ladies, I'm sure."

Lainey stopped. She glanced about to determine if she was missing someone, or if, perhaps, there was...she shuddered as if she'd just walked through an invisible spider's web.

With resignation in his voice, Phillip said. "I imagine he'll gloat the entire time he's here. Happy that his father has yet to insist on his marriage." Another pause. "I pity the woman if he ever does marry."

A few leaves drifted about, as Lainey listened in. Her eavesdropping should have bothered her. It didn't. But the sympathy she felt for the man did bother her. Was he really seeing a ghost or only missing his wife so desperately that he'd pretend to converse with her? Lainey's father had done that after her mother passed. But he assured Lainey that her mother was in heaven with the rest of the angels, and that he talked to her hoping that she might hear. His "talk" with her mother didn't have the same conversational quality as Phillip's did with Lady Katherine.

The thought of the lady being present brought on a rash of second thoughts. First, she didn't want to have a run-in with a ghost. Second, if he was actually talking with the woman's spirit, did she want to interrupt? And third…was it safe? Was Phillip in his right state of mind? Could be the whispered questions circulating among the household staff had merit.

Lainey took a step to the side as she weighed her options. In doing so, a twig snapped under her foot. Phillip turned.

"Clarkson," he said with a scant glimpse to his side. Was he looking at his ghost wife?

Lainey curtsied. "Master Montgomery."

"Thank you for coming. I half-suspected you wouldn't."

"I told you I would. And…I was curious. Have you made your inquiries yet?"

"I have. My friend Hal has some connections with the Royal Navy. He's making the inquiries for me."

"Is this the same Hal that is on his way to France?" Horrified that she'd divulged her eavesdropping, she lowered her head and took a step back.

An awkward moment of silence weighed between them before Phillip answered. "Yes, as a matter of fact, it is the same man."

Lainey nodded. She moved closer to the stone railing on the overlook leaving a wide berth between Phillip and herself. The view from the overlook was breathtaking. Rolling, tree-covered hills stretched as far as the eye could see, dotted occasionally by fields of grain. In the sunlight, the hardwood trees showed off their autumn finery in gold, orange, and red, while evergreens added a depth of color and stability. The change of seasons stilled the air with a sense of impending loss. How appropriate.

She rested her hands on the cold railing. A chill seeped through her threadbare gloves.

"Have you ventured across all this land?" Lainey asked, as she took in a deep breath of crisp autumn air.

"I have. As a child, riding was my favorite pastime." He surveyed the view. "Out there, on the back of a horse..." He smiled at the memory. "The world was mine. I could do whatever I pleased."

"Has that changed?"

He rubbed a hand across his jaw as he contemplated the question. "I believe so. Now, I am constrained by responsibilities."

Lainey scoffed. "I should be so constrained," she muttered.

A sly glance from Master Phillip told her he'd heard the comment and chose to ignore it.

"Come," he said instead. "Let's walk."

Taking the lead, he descended the stone staircase from the overlook into the gardens immediately below. A small lagoon, green in color, housed lily pads void of flowers this time of the year. Quickthorn shrubs, field roses, and service trees, heavy with autumn berries, surrounded one side of the water. A wrought iron bench sat on the other side. The space was lovely and serene, and Lainey briefly imagined sitting in a muslin dress, dawdling, free from chores and uniforms.

They walked in silence over a wooden bridge that straddled a stream feeding into the lagoon and through a small, ivy covered, peaked-roof gate house that led into a walled garden. The walls, made of a light-colored stone, rose in height well over Lainey's head. Oak and maple tree branches draped over the sides, dropping their colored leaves in a lazy dance. Another small pond, with a greenish, bronze statue of a little boy stood on a podium in the middle. Scattered among the dead and dying vegetation, were wood benches. Phillip motioned toward one, inviting Lainey to be seated.

As she sat, she arranged her black skirts about her legs as if she were more than a servant.

Phillip remained standing, keeping an appropriate distance.

"This was another place I used to play as a child."

Lainey surveyed the area, recalling pirate games she played with her brothers when they were all small. Oh, how they would have loved such a place to play, instead of the grimy, waste-ridden streets of Devil's Acre near Westminster Abbey. To have the perfume of roses, lilac, and peonies, instead of the stench of sewers, rotting food, and unwashed bodies.

"What did you play?"

He smiled. "Kenton and I would play knights of the Round Table. Charlotte would play the damsel in distress. We fought off dragons and villainous Scotsmen. And later, when Katherine and I were courting, we'd sneak here to…"

When Lainey drew up her eyebrows, Phillip blushed.

"It was never completely inappropriate."

"Only somewhat inappropriate?" She did nothing to hide her amusement.

"She was a difficult woman to resist." His eyes glazed over as he relived one of those moments.

"What about after you were married?"

"What?"

She'd clearly brought him back to the present.

"After you were married…did this continue to be a special spot?"

He took a seat at the opposite end of the bench.

"Yes. We always came here when we wanted to escape the family." He scanned the garden, motioning toward a pocket of rose bushes, currently bare of leaves. "I planted her favorite yellow rose in her memory."

"What a lovely gesture."

"I never come to view it when it blooms."

"Why not?"

"Can't."

"My papa used to take us to the cemetery every Sunday after my mum passed. I hated it. One time, after my brother Allen was killed, I refused to go. Papa insisted I walk with him. We had a huge row about it. Later that night, right as I was going to bed, he asked me why I no longer wanted to visit my mum at the cemetery."

"What did you say?"

"I told him that I refused to believe she was there. If she was, she was a decaying heap of flesh and bones, and I didn't want to envision her that way." She looked down to her hands, twisting them about. "After that, he never insisted."

"Did you ever go back?"

She nodded. "On special occasions. Her birthday. Papa's birthday. Christmas. Easter. And of course, when my father passed, they were buried close together."

"How did your family afford such burials?"

"I don't know. Robert believes it was my mum's family that provided for the burials. But no one from my mum's family came to the funeral. At least not that I remember."

"Your mother was estranged from her family?"

"She was." Lainey glanced over at Phillip. He had shifted to face her. "The only thing I ever heard, and this only from my father, was that her family thought she married beneath herself—famously beneath herself. Mum never told me about her family. That's why I think it unlikely that they paid for the burial, especially for Papa, but otherwise there is no explanation for it."

"What about your brother?"

"Allen is buried somewhere up north. The railroad took care of his remains."

"You've never been there?"

"No. And since my father's death, I haven't been back to that cemetery either."

Phillip scanned the garden. "Katherine is buried here on the estate. We have a small family cemetery on the property." He extended his hand presumably in the direction of the family plot. "I'm afraid I visit it frequently. Sometimes it is pure torture."

"Then why go?"

He frowned, as if he'd never thought about not going. "I can't seem to help myself."

A sympathetic silence fell between them, and for that Lainey was glad. She didn't like thinking of her parents, cold and alone in separate caskets, decaying. She'd wager that Phillip felt the same.

"Are you religious?" Phillip asked, bringing Lainey out of thought.

"I consider myself so. Although I don't know if I prescribe to one faith over another."

"Do you believe there is a life beyond this one?"

"With fire and brimstone where we all pay for our transgressions? I'm not sure what I believe in that regard. I only know what I've been taught."

"Did your parents teach you?"

"My parents and the most holy Pastor Reynolds. He could deliver a fiery sermon." She sighed. "Scared me silly when I was a child."

Phillip smiled. A nice sight, Lainey thought. His eyes crinkled up at the corners giving Lainey a glimpse of how he must have appeared in happier days.

"Obviously you believe in life after death." At her words, his smile instantly disappeared.

"Why would you say that?"

She studied her hands. "I've heard rumors, sir."

"Rumors. Of course you have." He said nothing more.

After a moment, she lowered her head and asked, "Are they true? Does she haunt the manor?"

Phillip rose to his feet, taking several deliberate steps away. Surprised, Lainey looked up. His brow was furrowed, as his eyes darted about. He frowned.

"No," he said, his voice deep and somber. "She does not haunt the manor house." He met Lainey's gaze. "She only haunts me." And with that he turned and walked straight out of the garden.

On her way back to the manor house, Lainey scanned the heavens. The skies had clouded over, and a damp chill filled the air—matching her mood. She pulled her shawl tight around her shoulders and, though she knew she shouldn't waste time, roamed about Montrose's formal gardens. A rich, earthy aroma blew with the breeze, another reminder of the waning season. In the spring, these gardens would be filled with color and fragrant blossoms. But she would never see them. She had no intention of being here in the spring.

At her feet a small round stone named a withered plant. All along the path, markers laid in even spacing, indicated where plants long now dormant had grown. None of these names made sense.

"Lava...lavan...dula," she said aloud, trying to sound out a word. Her mother used to name the flowers they passed at the market—delphinium, foxglove, larkspur—nothing sounded like Lavandula. She wrinkled her nose and moved on to the next marker.

She couldn't make out the first word, so she moved to the second. "By…byzan…tina." She shook her head. Could this be one of the beautiful flowers her mother had talked about?

Lainey gazed about the garden. Dark green hedges, each neatly trimmed, separated one area from another. Had her mother grown up with such gardens? Is that how she had known the names of so many blooms? Clutching her shawl tighter, Lainey turned about wondering what her mother's childhood must have been. Had she lived somewhere as grand as Montrose?

"Mother, why did you never tell me your story? Did you miss it after you were married, stuck with us in London?"

The memory of her mother placing three wilted dandelions in a tin cup with water caught Lainey by surprise. She hadn't thought of that moment in years.

"These are lovely," her mother had said, as she placed the cup in the middle of their worn table. "You have brought sunshine into our home, Lainey. I have never seen such beautiful flowers."

"They aren't as bootiful as the flowers at the market," Lainey had said, disheartened by the droopy weeds.

Her mother stood before her, cupping Lainey's small face in her warm hands.

"They are more beautiful because they came from you. Gifts from the heart are the best." Her mother leaned down and planted a small kiss on Lainey's forehead.

Lainey sucked in a staggered breath. How old had she been? Four, maybe five? Tears tugged at her eyes. What would her mother think of her now? She shook off the thought, certain that her mother had hoped for a better life for her daughter.

Talking with Phillip about his wife—that's what had brought this on. Lainey needed to stay focused, think of

Robert's letters and his descriptions of the blue waters and palm trees in Barbados. Lainey started toward the manor imagining that instead of walking through rows of browning vegetation, she walked sand-covered beaches with the sun warm on her face.

With Robert she belonged—she'd have a home and a family. She wouldn't answer to housekeepers or butlers. She wouldn't have to fight off men who thought to take advantage of her. That type of freedom was worth any price of passage. After all, there were worse jobs than talking to a handsome, wealthy, grieving widower.

But back to the matters at hand—she needed to return to her duties. She picked up her skirts and made her way to the house.

The moment Lainey entered through the door, Jane grabbed her by the arm and pulled her down the hallway.

"You were seen," she said in a tone for only Lainey to hear.

"What?"

Jane glanced over her shoulder. "You were seen. With Master Phillip. Charlie came in from the stables and told Mary and me that he saw you and the master entering the walled garden. What were you doing? If Lady Montgomery gets word of this, you'll be dismissed—immediately."

Lainey held up her hands. "You don't understand. Master Phillip asked to speak to me."

"That won't matter." Jane shook her head. "Lady Montgomery has strong views about our place. And it isn't with her children. I've already heard talk about Charlotte and how she has taken you under her wing."

Lainey fell against the wall. "I didn't ask for this." She couldn't lose this job...for any reason. "I'll simply tell him...I can't talk to him." Although if she did, would he help her get to Barbados?

"And tell Miss Charlotte, too. She can't treat you as her friend. You need to keep your distance."

Lainey wasn't sure she could keep a distance. But she must. She pushed her shoulders back. "Thank you, Jane. I will take care of this. I know my place."

Jane smiled, visibly relaxing. "I like you, Alaina. And don't worry. Charlie won't say a word. He was careful when he mentioned it to me. If the wrong people found out…" She didn't need to continue. Lainey knew if Hollingsworth found out—servants were easily replaced.

Jane slipped her arm through Lainey's and leaned closer. "It's odd that Master Phillip is showing interest in you. He normally doesn't behave in such a manner."

"I wouldn't say it's interest. He wanted someone to talk to—that's all."

"It is odd that he would choose a maid. Be careful around him. He's not been the same since his wife passed. He drinks a lot, and…well, you know. We told you about his ghost."

"Maybe I should be more worried about the ghost than Master Phillip. Was she the jealous sort?"

Jane laughed. "Not to my recollection, but you are right. No one needs an angry ghost chasing them about."

Arm in arm, Jane led Lainey into the servant's room. Several other servants sat at a table taking advantage of Lady Montgomery's absence for the day. Mrs. Crawford placed a plate of warm pastries in the middle of the dining table. Lainey's mouth watered at the warm sugar and cinnamon scent.

"You're just in time!" Charlie said on seeing Jane and Lainey.

Dropping Lainey's arm, Jane moved quickly to the table, snatching a pastry for herself.

Lainey surveyed the room. What was everyone thinking? How many knew of her meeting with Phillip? Did Charlie tell anyone else? What would they think of her? Unsettled, she sank into a seat at the far end of the table.

Charlie waved her closer. "Alaina, come. Have you had one of Mrs. Crawford's cakes? No one makes Welsh cakes like our own Mrs. Crawford." Taking a large bite of his, he groaned in pleasure.

"Yes," Jane agreed. "Why are you sitting down there? Come get a cake. They won't last long."

Truer words were never spoken. Everyone who entered the kitchen helped themselves to the plate of pastries. If she was going to try one, and they did look and smell delicious, she needed to move quickly.

Lainey took a seat next to Jane and reached for a cake. Charlie was right, they were exquisite. Sweet gooiness melted in her mouth. It reminded her of pastries her mother used to make. She shook off the memory as quickly as it came—it only made her sad.

As she ate, she listened to the others talk. They gossiped a bit about the Montgomery family—nothing Lainey hadn't heard before. They talked of work they should have been doing, their own families, and, of course, the delicious cakes. Lainey offered little. But as she sat with Jane and Charlie and the others, an unfamiliar but not unwelcome sensation warmed her. She liked these people. She had never felt that at Harlsburg Manor.

The feeling was short-lived, however. Miss Charlotte's bell rang, bringing the entire room to attention. If Charlotte was home, so was Lady Montgomery. Chairs scraped along the floor as everyone stood and went back to work.

CHAPTER THIRTEEN

"What fates impose, that men must abide"
–Shakespeare

Phillip stopped immediately outside the garden room door listening to Marianne's voice carry out into the hallway. He groaned. She'd finally gone home the week before, and now she was back. Once more, he would be expected to make entreaties, be attentive, and make the girl feel welcome. Conversations with his father would no longer be about the estate, but about how well he and Marianne were getting along, when they would exchange vows. Didn't she have some sewing or flower-arranging to do that would keep her home?

At the sound of her laugh, he closed his eyes. He really did not want to talk to her.

"You're cheating," Kenton said.

Phillip peeked in the door to find out what his brother was referring to. Kenton and Marianne sat across from each other, a backgammon board on the table in between them.

"It's not cheating. I'm allowed to fill all these spaces." She waved a hand over the game. "It's not my fault you can't get back on the board."

"Of course, it's your fault! You're the one I'm playing with."

She giggled. "What's the matter, Kenton? Am I too clever for you?"

"Clever, yes. Too clever, no. You've thwarted me for the moment, but not for long."

Phillip watched, intrigued. Marianne's countenance was bright, animated. Was this simply a good mood? Perhaps, if he joined them, she might actually have a conversation with him. He stepped into the room.

"Phillip!" Kenton said. "Come see the predicament I find myself in."

Phillip approached the table and perused the game board. When he saw that she'd blocked all of the spaces with her pieces, Phillip knew she'd outwitted his brother.

"Well played, Marianne," he said. "You've proven my brother is not nearly as skilled as he pretends to be." As soon as his eyes met hers, she dropped her gaze.

"Kenton is exceptionally skilled," she said, so softly that Phillip barely heard her. "I have only been lucky."

Phillip and Kenton exchanged glances.

"She's being modest," Kenton said.

"I think you're right." Phillip couldn't believe he was saying this. "After you've beaten my brother, might I have a chance?"

She moved her hands from the table to her lap. "If you would like."

"Please. Continue." He took a step back from the table to watch the game and especially to study Marianne. The bright, animated girl he'd witnessed moments before had disappeared. Even Kenton could barely draw a word from her. And her exceptional play rapidly fell apart as she made several ill-calculated moves. She did win the game but did not deliver the trouncing that appeared inevitable.

Kenton pushed back from the table. "Your turn, Phillip. I do believe you'll fare better than I. She's not thinking as clearly as she did before. Perhaps you've put a spell on our friend. Good luck, Miss Hilton." He offered Marianne a slight bow, before walking out of the room.

She lifted a hand as if to stop him. It was a small move that Kenton didn't notice, but Phillip did. She wanted Kenton to stay. Did he provide her with a measure of security? Or was it a bit more?

As she watched Kenton leave, Phillip took his seat, pulling in the chair to be more comfortable.

"You wanted him to stay."

"I thought he might want to."

Phillip chuckled. "Do you plan to obliterate me as you did my brother?" He hoped she heard the teasing in his voice.

She made no reply, leaving her eyes focused on the game board. It was as if she hadn't heard him speak.

"Which color would you prefer?" he asked.

"It does not matter. You choose." She kept her eyes fixed on the board.

"Okay." Phillip pulled a pile of markers toward him. "I will take black, if you don't mind."

"I don't mind."

Phillip began setting up the board, placing his pieces in order. When he was finished, he realized Marianne had not placed one piece, nor had she made any attempt to collect the tan markers that would be hers.

He sat back, trying to come up with some repartee that would put the girl at ease. Nothing came. After a long moment, she scooped pieces into her hand. She had yet to even peek at him.

"Do you not wish to play?" he asked.

"If you want to, I am willing."

He wiped a hand over his mouth. Did she not notice his side of the board ready for play?

"Marianne, may I ask you a question?"

She glanced over at him and quickly lowered her eyes. "Of course."

"Why do you not look at me?"

She lifted her head. Her expression nearly made Phillip laugh. Her eyes were wide and unblinking as if she had been scolded by a school master.

"Is this better?"

Phillip scowled. "Not really." Instantly she lowered her head. "I only meant...if we are to marry—" He nearly choked on the words. "Shouldn't we be able to look at each other...have conversations?"

She nodded. "Yes."

"Don't you think we should start before the wedding?"

"Yes."

Did she have nothing but one-word answers? "Is there a topic you particularly enjoy talking about?"

She shook her head.

"Okay." Phillip glanced about the room, hoping to find something to discuss. His eyes rested on a book lying on the table near the door. "Have you read an interesting book recently?"

Again, she shook her head. How was he ever going to tolerate this marriage—constantly trying to pull words from the girl? He should never have given into his father's wishes.

"We went to London last week," she said, her voice so quiet he nearly missed it.

"London! Splendid! And what did you do in London?"

She glanced up at him with those wide, stunned eyes before pushing back her chair. "My father had a business engagement. Mother and I went shopping." She stood. "We had tea with some relatives and did nothing that would be of interest to you. It was all frivolous." The words tumbled out of her in a rush, as if she didn't get them out, they would choke her.

"How do you know it wouldn't be of interest to me?"

"I just know!" And with that, she turned and scurried from the room.

Phillip buried his head in his hands. *She's five years old*, he thought. No, even five-year-olds can carry a conversation. He couldn't breathe. With one swift move, he wiped all the game pieces to the floor, got to his feet and marched from the room.

Lainey didn't notice Phillip arrive but knew the moment he had. Chairs scraped over the stone flooring and the few who were in the servant's dining area stood at attention, murmuring his name. She laid her sewing in her lap. Seeing Phillip in the doorway, knowing he was there for her, was akin to being force fed another bowl of gruel.

"Clarkson, do you have a moment?" He asked the question, but there was little need for an answer. From his intonation, his expression, she would make a moment. Glancing about the room, she saw the questions in her fellow servants' eyes. How would she explain this? And after Jane had been so kind to warn her. The others stood with pursed lips, their eyes darting from her to Phillip. She let out a heavy sigh and stood.

"Of course, sir. What do you need?"

He nodded his head to the side, indicating she should follow him. Laying her sewing on the table, she quietly obliged, feeling the others watch as she left the room. When they were out of sight, Phillip grabbed her by the wrist and pulled her toward the nearest door.

"I need to talk."

Fuming at his lack of consideration, Lainey followed Phillip into the walled garden. Though more than a week had passed, Jane's warning remained fresh in Lainey's mind. She couldn't imagine what could be so important that Phillip couldn't have waited for a more discreet moment to talk. Surely, if his job were at risk, he would be more careful.

Lainey found the entire situation frustrating. Meeting with him jeopardized all she hoped for, and yet, not meeting with him risked ever making those hopes come true. How happy she'd be when she heard from Robert and would be set free.

Before entering through the gate, she took a moment to pull her emotions into check. No need to be surly with the man no matter how much he deserved it. Phillip had gone inside the garden without her and when she joined him, she found him pacing with such intensity she thought the stones under his feet might wear away to nothing.

Before she could mention his inappropriate appearance in the servant's dining room, he stopped and stared at her.

"I can't do it."

"Do what?" She grimaced. Her voice reflected her annoyance.

He began his pacing anew. "I can't marry that girl. She's a child. When she's alone with me, she scarcely speaks. When Charlotte or Kenton is near, she whispers and giggles like...like..."

"A girl?"

"Exactly!"

Lainey moved from her spot near the gate to a stone bench close to where Phillip paced. Crossing her arms, she sat, shivering as a chill seeped through her skirts. A reminder of the approaching winter.

"How can she think she's ready for marriage? For running a household? She's barely out of pinafores! How could someone as quiet and withdrawn as Miss Hilton consider running an estate as large as Montrose?"

"She doesn't have to run the estate…does she?"

Phillip stopped, turned and glared at Lainey.

"I mean, yes, at some point she'll be required to run the household," Lainey continued, "but as long as your mother is alive, she has time to learn, doesn't she? And don't you and your father run the estate? That's not your mother's job, is it?"

He scowled. "You're supposed to be supportive. That was part of the agreement."

"Even if you are wrong?"

"Wrong? I am not wrong on this. She is a child! I cannot marry her."

"She is young. I won't argue with that, sir. But you can marry her. You are perfectly capable of being a husband. You are by law capable of taking a bride. You do not want to. There is a difference."

Again, he offered the wrinkled brow, the half-scowl. He turned from her. "You are not helping."

Good, Lainey thought. *Serves you right.*

Phillip let out a tired sigh, then with sagging shoulders and an air of defeat, he lumbered toward Lainey, taking a seat next to her on the stone bench. Misery radiated from him, and Lainey felt her anger subside. She didn't necessarily disagree with him. But what choice did he have? He already had asked the girl to marry. That was his fault.

Realizing she didn't have to make the situation worse for him, she added, "Miss Hilton really is a sweet girl."

"I know," he said in resignation. "It's all so different this time." He surveyed the withered garden. "I couldn't wait to marry Katherine. I never considered her incapable of running an estate or whether she even wanted to. I simply wanted to gaze into those eyes from sunrise till sunset and to note them in the candlelight."

Lainey sighed for him.

"Katherine wasn't much older than Miss Hilton is now, only eighteen when we married. My father thought I was too young to marry, but Katherine's age was tolerable."

"How old were you?"

He glanced sideways at Lainey, then turned to the garden, to the gray stone fountain a few feet from where they sat. "Four and twenty. Kenton's age." The corner of his mouth turned up. "I suppose I can understand what my father's objections were. I would say Kenton is too young to marry now as well."

"Age always looks different on someone else."

Phillip turned to her. His expression had tempered from when Lainey first entered the garden, as had her irritation. She studied his face, and he studied hers. His eyes, when not enraged at the thought of his upcoming marriage, reflected kindness, gentleness. *He will make someone a good husband.*

"How old are you, Clarkson?"

She lowered her eyes. "I am twenty, sir."

"And how long have you been on your own?"

"Since I turned fourteen."

"Have you been in service all this time?"

She nodded. "Yes, sir."

Phillip stared at her until she shifted under his gaze. "Your life has been difficult."

An inane observation. Of course, her life had been difficult. She'd not been raised in a big house. She didn't have privilege and respect. She was a child when her mother passed and not much more than that when her brother and father died. She'd been abandoned at the doorstep of strangers, left to fend for herself while Robert left to sail the world. She paused. Where had that come from? She'd never thought that before. Robert hadn't abandoned her...he would have stayed if he'd had the chance—surely, he would have.

"I envy you." Phillip's voice pulled her out of thought.

"What? Envy? Me? Whatever for?"

"You have a great adventure awaiting you. When we locate your brother...when you set off to the Caribbean...you will be your own person. You'll decide your own future."

"And you cannot?"

He let out a derisive laugh. "My birth determined my future. The male heir...the continuation of the Montgomery line, the Montgomery fortune. From the moment I was born, my education was decided. My life's vocation. The type of men and women I would associate with...all decided by the family and position I inherited."

"You speak as if that were a bad thing."

Shaking his head, he looked back to that same spot near the dry fountain. "I am simply a pawn to be moved about by the dictates of my position."

"Then you and I are not so different," she replied as she tried to decide why an old, slime-covered fountain proved so fascinating. "I, too, am defined by my station in life."

"Yes," he said, and smirked. "The difference is you will escape. I cannot."

Lainey considered his dilemma for a moment. "And yet," she said, "you can."

Her comment pulled his attention from the fountain. "Escape? How so?"

She half-smiled. "You're breaking all the rules of civility, sitting in a garden, talking to a lady's maid." She cocked an eyebrow. "How scandalous!"

Phillip smiled. His whole appearance changed. Lainey caught a glimpse of the man that Lady Katherine had fallen in love with. The man that Marianne Hilton had longed for from a distance. His eyes sparkled for a moment. Lainey swallowed.

"I'd hardly call this an escape," he said.

"Well, not only are you talking with me, but you are also helping me to break away. What will your father say when he hears you used your funds to send a servant girl halfway across the globe? You will be fodder for all the gossips in your gentleman's club."

"Ha. We do not have a gentleman's club in the country."

"But you do in London, no doubt."

He bit his bottom lip, caught. "That we do." His eyes filled with mirth. "You will not let me wallow, will you?"

She ran her hands across her black skirts, flattening out the wrinkles. "Sir, you certainly have cause to mourn. But you are correct." She looked at him, lifting her chin. "I will not allow you to wallow. You have more than I can ever dream of. And I will make certain you appreciate your blessings." She rose to her feet. "Now, if you'll excuse me, I need to return to my duties before I am missed." She curtsied, before starting toward the garden gate.

"Clarkson," Phillip called after her.

She stopped and turned.

"May I call you Alaina?"

"No, sir."

His brow rose at the sudden denial.

"We are not close acquaintances. You are the master of the house. I am your sister's maid. We do not move in the same circles and never will. I meet with you because you are the means to an end. You meet with me because…because…well, God knows why. I cannot relieve your grief because I cannot bring your beloved Katherine back. We will keep this relationship as a business arrangement just as it started."

"My request offends you?" It was a statement more than a question.

"No, sir. On the contrary. I appreciate your asking. But what you request cannot be."

"Very well," he said with a nod. "I guess…you are dismissed."

Lainey hesitated before offering a slight curtsy. She had disappointed him. But how could she let him become familiar with her? He had risked her employment, her standing as a lady's maid, and most of all, her reputation by dragging her away in front of half the household staff. Before long, he would think he could take the same liberties as Harold Warrington. Remembering her dismissal from Harlsburg, she spun on her heel and stormed through the garden gate. Insufferable nobility. They thought they could take whatever privilege crossed their minds. They had no understanding, no compassion for those who struggle to survive. As the thought crossed her mind, she wrestled to push aside the memory of a noble gentleman coming to her aid at the Montville market. No! She would not allow a moment of his weakness to color what she knew to be true. Lifting her skirts, she marched toward the manor house.

~~*

Phillip watched the girl leave the garden, perplexed and intrigued by her boldness and tenacity, but only for a moment. He turned back to the fountain, envisioning Katherine sitting at the edge.

"It's uncommon for you to linger about when other people are near."

"She's clever, is she not?"

"What makes you say so?'

Katherine smiled. *"She's convinced you to send her to her brother and managed to make you forget all manners and ask to call her by her given name. I barely recognize you."* Her eyes sparkled with merriment.

Phillip leaned back against the stone wall. "You object?"

"No. I do believe she intrigues you. And…she provides a distraction from little Marianne."

"And God knows I need that."

"In fact, around her, you appear to be lighter." She rose to her feet. *"I like seeing you this way. It's been much too long."*

He hoped she would come closer, sit with him, let him believe he could touch her, kiss her. When she moved to the far side of the fountain, the birds stopped their song. She was balm and poison at the same moment, forever just out of reach. "Are you leaving?" he asked, hoping she only wanted a stroll around the garden.

As Katherine turned, her hair fluttered as if caught by a small wind. Her countenance, ethereal and graceful, shimmered with sunlight though clouds hovered overhead. Phillip's breath stuttered at the vividness of his dreams.

"You know I cannot stay forever."

He swallowed. "But you cannot leave me, either. How would I…"

"Shhh…" He was not sure if it was her voice that quieted his soul, or a breeze cutting through the garden.

Her expression filled with tenderness. *"You will be fine, my darling."*

On unsteady legs, he rose to his feet. This couldn't be the end. He'd broken into a cold sweat. She could not leave him alone.

Cocking her head to one side, her eyes filled with concern, as if she could read his thoughts. Well, of course she could—she had that ability in life as well.

"Will you come back?" As much as he didn't want to know the answer, he had to ask the question.

Her answer was nothing more than a nod as she faded away. Phillip dropped back on the stone bench, his heart aching at the thought of never seeing Katherine again. This was the first he'd ever envisioned the possibility. Rubbing his hands roughly over his face, he worked to dismiss the notion. As often happened after her appearances, his mind labored to make sense of what he was experiencing. He wished so desperately to keep Katherine in his life, but in the same moments he knew that seeing her, talking with her, was more dream than reality. But even in moments of rationality, he couldn't let her go. His heart would not allow it.

Lainey rubbed her hands together as she approached the stone steps leading to the entrance near the kitchen. The chill in the air had not bothered her as she talked with Master Phillip, but now she shivered. Was it the cold, or was it the conversation with the man? He had a peculiar effect on her. She grieved right alongside him. She understood his pain, his loneliness. And that was a good…right? That is why he asked to speak with her in the first place. But she didn't trust the connection she felt. First, it was improper for a servant girl and a family heir to be friends, let alone close friends. She refused to admit any more relationship than that. Second, in those moments when he let the grief subside, when she saw his smile, or heard it in his voice, an unexplained resentment toward Miss Hilton arose. Why should she regret the girl having what Lainey hoped for? And third, making connections here, at Montrose Manor, with the family or the servants for that matter, only stood in the way of reaching her brother. She *must* keep her distance. But paradoxically, as she determined to do so, none of it felt altogether right.

Another shiver caused her to pick up her step. *I should have brought a wrap*, she thought as she hurried toward the kitchen door. Glancing up, she did a doubletake. There, in all her tall, thin, severe-looking glory stood Mrs. Hollingsworth.

The elderly woman opened the door. "Where have you been?" Her voice was curt, annoyed.

Lainey averted her eyes. "I stepped out for a few minutes to get some fresh air."

"Why did you not inform anyone of your whereabouts? Miss Charlotte has been ringing for you."

"I'll tend to her immediately," Lainey said. Juggling between these two grown Montgomery children had become a feat fit for a court magician.

"Clarkson." Mrs. Hollingsworth's voice brought Lainey back to the matter at hand. "We cannot have you taking liberties whenever you have a whim to! You need to be attentive to your duties."

"Yes, ma'am." She replied with a small curtsy—holding her tongue, at the moment, a heroic achievement. How she wanted to tell the old woman that she was attending to duties, because apparently, her employment extended beyond serving as Charlotte's maid, it also included serving as Master Phillip's confidant as well.

"Well...get to it. I believe Miss Charlotte is in the music room."

Another recital. Lainey made her way down the paneled hallway, through the parlor. As she approached the music room, her mind raced to find a reason not to stay.

A fire blazed, warming the room, lending a coziness to the gathering. Lainey padded across the dark red carpet toward the piano where Miss Charlotte stood next to Miss

Hilton who sat on the piano bench. Charlotte looked up at Lainey's approach—her eyes lighting up as Lainey drew near.

"You're right on time," Charlotte said. "You must hear how Marianne has improved in her rendition of *Für Elise*." She turned her attention back to her student at the piano. "Here, Marianne. Start from the beginning."

Lainey braced for missed notes and poor timing. Not that she was any expert on music performance. But she had heard enough at Harlsburg Manor to know when music was being properly performed.

Much to her surprise, Miss Hilton, biting her lower lip in concentration, and at a speed more suited to *Moonlight Sonata*, moved her fingers through the piece with only one mistake. Lainey probably would not have noticed the missed note if the girl had not stopped, scrunched up her face as if she'd sucked on a persimmon, and scrambled to discover her place in the music. After Charlotte pointed to the spot in the music, Miss Hilton continued. Though a slow performance, the song was recognizable.

As Lainey listened to the girl working intently at the piece, she thought of Master Phillip. She tried to imagine the two, Marianne and Phillip, standing side by side welcoming guests to Montrose Manor. At some point, Miss Hilton would grow into the role. But she could understand Phillip's concern. The girl lacked confidence—though she meant well and would work to succeed. But Phillip needed someone with the grace and charm of his departed Katherine. Lainey smiled sadly to herself. Was Lady Katherine as magnificent as all believed? Or had death given her a halo that no one would ever be able to remove?

The music stopped, and Lainey politely clapped. Charlotte, with a beaming smile, stepped down from her perch as instructor and came to Lainey's side.

"Phillip will be pleased, don't you think?" Charlotte said, turning to face Marianne, whose face blushed pink with pleasure.

"He should be," Lainey replied, while fighting the unreasonable tug at her conscience. "She has worked diligently."

"Now..." Charlotte took hold of Lainey's wrist, "You must come and learn to play."

"What? No! I have no experience...I can't play."

"Of course, you can. Anyone can learn...look at Marianne!"

Lainey did look at Marianne, who, from the bewildered expression on her face, either didn't want to relinquish the piano, or didn't understand what Charlotte meant by her comment. Though Lainey resisted, Charlotte refused to take "no" for an answer. She tugged until Lainey acquiesced and followed her to the instrument. Miss Hilton slid to one side of the bench when Charlotte patted the seat, an indication for Lainey to sit. Reluctantly she did.

"Now," Charlotte instructed, "Marianne, show her where to place her hands."

Marianne did as instructed, taking Lainey's hands, one at a time, and placing them along the keys.

"Good. Now, Marianne, show her how to play a scale."

And so, it began. Charlotte issued instructions, Marianne complied, and Lainey followed. After the first awkward moments, Lainey forgot her vow to keep a distance from the family, and within a short time, they played a simple, if not rustic, version of *Greensleeves*. Lainey only used her right hand, but she felt some satisfaction in creating the familiar melody. Charlotte stood near the piano, cheering the two girls on, appearing for all the world like a proud teacher. The longer they played, the faster Lainey's fingers danced over the keys. Before she knew it, she was smiling and laughing along with Charlotte and Marianne, especially when she made mistakes, or her fingers fumbled over Marianne's.

"What is going on here?" Lord Montgomery's stern voice brought instant silence from the girls. Lainey immediately rose to her feet offering the man a deep curtsy. He studied her for a moment, before turning to his daughter.

"Charlotte? What are you doing?"

She swished her skirts as she stepped down from the stage and approached her father. On tiptoe, she reached up and kissed his cheek. If she meant to temper the man's displeasure, Lainey thought, she had failed. His brow creased as he glared at his daughter.

"I was teaching them," she said.

"Why?"

"I thought it would be good for Marianne to know how to entertain guests." Charlotte glanced over her shoulder at Lainey and Miss Hilton. Lainey swallowed, sure of chastisement for her participation.

"And the maid?" Lord Montgomery asked.

For one moment, Charlotte appeared unsure of what to say. One more time she glanced to Lainey. Then, turning back, and with squared shoulders she confronted her father. "I wanted to note what kind of teacher I would be."

The Lord's expression relaxed slightly. "You are not a teacher. You are a lady—or will be one soon."

"Oh, Father. Times are changing. Women can be whatever..."

His countenance sharpened. "No. They cannot. Now...stop this foolishness and be about something constructive. Do you not have lessons?"

Charlotte sighed. "Yes. But this was so much more fun."

"Lessons." It was a one-word command that Lainey knew Charlotte would not disobey. "And Miss Hilton, I believe Phillip and his mother are in the library. I suggest you join them." The girl curtsied and immediately started toward the door.

"And you." He shifted his gaze to Lainey. She lowered her eyes. "You…isn't there a place…"

"Yes, sir," she said and without another word, scurried from the stage and followed Miss Hilton out of the room.

As she passed the threshold, she heard Charlotte say, "Father, you have no sense of adventure."

CHAPTER FOURTEEN

"And drinking largely sobers us again."
–Alexander Pope

Lainey tended to her duties for the rest of the day, staying as far from any member of the Montgomery family as she could. After the evening meal, she hid in the servant's dining room playing gin rummy with Jane, Mary, and Clair. The game reminded her of quiet evenings at home with her own family, sitting near a fire and playing with torn and tattered cards. Being with fellow servants was comfortable and easy. She didn't have to look over her shoulder to wonder who might be watching. She didn't have to worry about how she addressed someone. And she certainly didn't have to worry about Phillip and his request to be so familiar as to call her by her given name. What was he thinking? No matter how close their association grew, calling her by name was wrong on more levels than Lainey could ever consider. The fool would get her dismissed before he could ever help her get to Robert.

When Charlotte's bell rang, Lainey wanted to ignore it, but that, too, would get her dismissed. Reluctantly, she bid goodnight to her friends and made her way to the staircase.

Holding to the thick mahogany banister, she climbed the stairs and entered the hallway leading to Charlotte's bed chamber. Sconces, holding three candles each and placed evenly between family portraits, offered warmth and an inviting path down the hall. The sweet smell of honey scented the air. These were not cheap tallow or stearin candles, but beeswax—befitting the gentry—holding a much more pleasant aroma. The thought of tallow candles made her shudder. Those were the candles she was given at Harlsburg Manor to light her room. The scent resurrected the feel of Harold Warrington's hands as they clamped over her mouth, right before he attempted…she shook her head chasing away what she'd rather forget.

She glanced up and found herself standing in front of Master Phillip's portrait—one that obviously had been painted in a happier day. His eyes held life and possibility—an expression she'd not seen since knowing him. He was handsome. The portrait was a good likeness with his broad, erect shoulders, and his wavy, dark blonde hair curled about his ears. Kenton's portrait hung next to Phillip's. Side by side, Lainey found the family resemblance uncanny. Both had the same hair, same eyes, same build. Kenton smiled in his portrait, unlike his brother. It's possible Phillip thought, being the heir, he should show soberness. Lainey wished he had smiled—she loved his smile.

"There you are!" Charlotte said, standing in her doorway, hand on hip. "I was wondering what was taking you so long."

Lainey dipped into a small curtsey. "I'm sorry. I got distracted." She looked up and down the hall. "Where is your portrait?"

Charlotte scoffed. "Father waits until we are eighteen before he commissions these." She waved a hand at the wall.

Yes, as Lainey had expected, it was a happier day for Phillip, long before Lady Katherine and her death. Upon arriving in Charlotte's room, Lainey was surprised to discover the young woman alone. She'd expected Miss Hilton to be lounging on the bed, bemoaning her awkwardness around Master Phillip.

"Will Miss Hilton be joining us?" Lainey asked as Charlotte lifted her hair, allowing Lainey access to the small pearl buttons on the back of her dress.

"No. She went home," Charlotte said with a sigh. "Apparently, an afternoon in my brother's company was more than she could bear."

"Oh, certainly not."

"Certainly so!" Charlotte spun about to face Lainey. "I swear, Alaina, I don't know how Marianne thinks she will ever marry him when she can't spend more than a moment in his company. She languishes whenever he is around." Charlotte moved to a seat in front of the mirror and gazed up at Lainey. "Why do you suppose she behaves so? Phillip is not *that* intimidating." Charlotte squared her shoulders. "We must help her."

"We? How can I help?"

"It appears Phillip has taken a liking to you. Possibly you could show Marianne how easy it is to be around him."

"A liking? I'm afraid I don't know what you're referring to." At least she hoped not.

Charlotte's smile was coy, mischievous. "Come, Alaina. I know you've been meeting with him in the garden."

Lainey's blood chilled. "The garden?"

"It's really out of character for Phillip to consort with household staff." Charlotte waved a hand in dismissal. "But everyone will overlook his behavior if it helps him get rid of Katherine's ghost."

"I assure you, ma'am, I am not consorting with your brother."

"Oh?" Shifting on her chair, Charlotte motioned for Lainey to be seated on a nearby chair. "If that is true, why are you meeting with my brother in the garden?"

As much as she wanted to deny the charge and act affronted that Charlotte would make such an accusation, Lainey found her knees weakening, unable to hold her aright. She sank onto the upholstered chair.

"You can tell me, Alaina. We're friends. And unlike my parents, who may not smile on such an alliance, I'm not provincial in my thinking. The fact that Phillip has loosened his laces a bit, I find refreshing."

Lainey shook her head. "I tell you, Miss Charlotte, there is nothing untoward happening between Master Phillip and myself."

Charlotte let out a bark of a laugh, causing Lainey to flinch. "Listen to you," the young mistress said. "Untoward." She continued to laugh. "Every now and then you sound so proper, I would swear you have noble blood hiding under that plain exterior."

"Truly, Miss Charlotte..."

"We are friends, Alaina. Tell me. Tell me the truth. I will not reveal you to my parents. Although, it wouldn't surprise me if they were suspicious—with Phillip's disappearances and all. But, rest assured, I will not betray your confidence. I told you we would be good friends. I told you how I did not wish to marry Sir Markhall. Certainly, you can share your innermost thoughts with me. Especially when those thoughts involve my brother." Her eyes lit with mischief, and her grin turned a shade short of wicked. "Tell me. Are you in love with him?"

"No." Lainey's response was quick and decisive.

Charlotte's lips drew into a straight line. "Well," she said, shifting peevishly toward the mirror. "If you refuse to tell me…"

Lainey sighed. "Truly, Miss Charlotte, I have no feelings for Master Phillip." Okay, that could be a lie, but she wasn't sure what feelings she did have for the man.

"Truly?" Her voice dripped with disbelief.

Lainey's shoulders dropped. If she told Charlotte about her brother's assistance, perhaps, as Charlotte said, she could be an ally. Conceivably she could help in the process of locating Robert. Maybe Charlotte *could* keep the secret, prevent her parents from discovering the clandestine meetings. On the other hand, Charlotte could just as easily ruin everything. What would happen when she found out Lainey had no intention of remaining in her employ? What would become of this "friendship"? Would she tell her parents? Cause her dismissal?

Charlotte leaned over, placing a gentle hand on Lainey's knee. "Alaina, you are clearly troubled. Has my brother offended you?"

"No, ma'am." Lainey understood Charlotte's imploring gaze. Phillip's sister wanted to know more. She could share a few select details—but keep ultimate plans a secret. Wringing her hands, she said, "Your brother is helping me to locate my brother."

The surprise on Charlotte's face made it evident that she had suspected nothing of this nature. "Where is your brother?"

"Somewhere in the Caribbean. I believe he's in Barbados. That was the last word I had from him. Your brother wheedled from me that I had not heard from Robert in some time and was worried about him. He offered to send some letters, see if he could discover Robert's location."

Charlotte clapped her hands and bounced in her seat. "That's delightful! How kind my brother can be when he steps out of his grief. Has he made any progress?"

"Not yet."

"So, the meetings in the garden, they are about your brother?"

Lainey bit her lip, not sure she should answer the question. But, knowing Charlotte, the girl would not leave well enough alone. With a slight grimace, she said, "Mostly they are about your brother."

"What?"

"In exchange, he asked me to talk with him about Lady Katherine. He thinks I understand his grief."

"And do you?"

Lainey shook her head. "Not really. He mourns so deeply, that I'm not sure anyone can truly understand."

"That is why we must help Marianne. I know she could be a balm to his soul. In these meetings, you must discover what his feelings are towards Marianne. You must discover a way to break through—"

Loud voices in the hall interrupted their conversation. The two girls glanced at each other, then to the door. Charlotte was out of her seat and moving in an instant. The voices continued to grow. In the weeks that Lainey had been at Montrose, she had never heard such a commotion. Curiosity moved her to follow Charlotte.

Out in the hall, Mr. Hollingsworth and Master Kenton had Phillip by the arms. Phillip struggled, pulling away first from his brother, secondly from Hollingsworth.

"I don't need accompaniment," he said, his voice echoing about the hallway. Phillip took a few staggered steps in the direction of his room. He extended his hand toward the wall as if to gain his bearings.

"Don't be an ass," Kenton said, "You can't even walk straight. Where is Leonard?" He scowled at Hollingsworth, as if the butler had purposely hid Phillip's valet.

"I believe he was dismissed." Hollingsworth replied.

"Dismissed? As in relieved of duties or gone to bed?"

Hollingsworth raised his arms to say he did not know.

Lainey, hiding behind Miss Charlotte, focused on Phillip. She knew exactly how he'd been passing his time that evening. The man really should refrain from whiskey in the library. How long had he been at the drink tonight?

"I don't need a valet," Phillip said, taking a halting step forward.

Kenton stepped up to take his brother's arm. Phillip yanked away, pushing Kenton in the process.

Kenton threw his arms up. "Fine. Make your own way."

Standing in the middle of the hallway, Phillip swayed. "I…I…" he reached out to balance himself, but too far from any furniture or walls to find purchase, he started to fall. Charlotte sprinted to his side, catching him, but falling under his weight. Hollingsworth moved in to assist.

"I…I need a chamber pot," Phillip managed to say. Hollingsworth and Charlotte both furrowed their brows.

How could they not understand? Lainey turned and searched Charlotte's room. Grabbing the wash basin, she arrived in the nick of time. Lainey held the bowl, trying not to gag as Phillip wretched.

"Oh," Charlotte groaned, dropping Phillip into the arms of Mr. Hollingsworth. "Phillip, that's disgusting." She stepped back, her face contorted into a scowl. Kenton laughed.

Phillip raised his head and peered directly into Lainey's eyes. "She's going to leave," he said.

"What's he talking about?" Kenton asked. "Who's leaving?"

Lainey understood. A wash of compassion filled her chest. This poor man.

"You," Phillip added, his lip quivering. "It's you."

Tears stung at her eyes. "I'm sorry," she whispered and took a step back. Glancing around to Charlotte, Kenton, and Mr. Hollingsworth, their faces all held the same expression, heads tilted to one side or the other, eyes narrowed, with lips in matching frowns.

"I'll take care of this," Lainey said, anxious to be away. "Miss Charlotte, do you need any more assistance this evening?"

Charlotte snapped out of her stupor at the mention of her name. "No, Alaina. I need nothing till morning."

Lainey hurried down the hall feeling several sets of eyes on her back.

CHAPTER FIFTEEN

"Though it be honest, it is never good to bring bad news"
–Shakespeare

Phillip paced across the walled garden, hands firmly tucked into his coat pockets warding off the cold as he waited for Alaina to arrive. It had been three weeks since he had embarrassed himself in front of not only her, but his brother and sister, and Hollingsworth. Although that hadn't been the first time Hollingsworth had seen Phillip in such straits. And he could put that all behind him except for Katherine. He couldn't decide if it delighted him or not to be visiting with her multiple times a day. It wouldn't surprise him now if she weren't hovering somewhere beyond sight, waiting to witness his meeting with Alaina. As many times as he told Katherine that he could never have a relationship with Charlotte's maid, Katherine persevered.

"She's more than she appears," was the last conversation they'd had on the matter.

"I don't doubt that had she been born in different circumstances I might admit her attractive," he'd replied to Katherine's amusement.

"You might?" She laughed. "You are already gone."

"I am not gone," he muttered to himself just before the garden gate creaked and he saw Alaina enter. The garden was a shriveled, dry imposter of its summertime glory. The cooler weather and early nightfall had done their damage, but in spite of that, Alaina's arrival warmed him. Katherine would never let him rest if she knew.

As Alaina came closer, Phillip frowned. What was the girl thinking? She had nothing more than a flimsy wrap across her shoulders. She'd freeze out here. They would have to move to the conservatory. But again, with the news he had to deliver, having some place warm, where they could spend some time would be welcome.

She hesitated before approaching him. As she did, Katherine whispered, *"She's quite attractive."*

"She's a servant," he said under his breath.

"Don't let that stop you."

He fought the urge to look over his shoulder, afraid Katherine would notice the effect she was having on him. It was true, Alaina tantalized his imagination in a way it had not been tantalized in far too long. She approached with caution and curtsied as she came to stand in front of him. Her eyes, the amber color of the leaves that now dotted the ground, deep and rich, peered up at him, causing his breath to catch. Before he could stop himself, he wondered how that light brown hair would entice him as it cascaded down on her shoulders. This was all Katherine's fault.

Before greeting Alaina, he rubbed a rough hand over his eyes, an attempt to wipe away his improper thoughts. "Miss Clarkson," he said with a slight nod.

"Master Montgomery," she said with another slight curtsey.

"Did you not have a warmer wrap?"

She tugged the fabric snug about her shoulders. "I didn't expect this chill. Your sister's rooms were comfortably warm this morning."

"Well, you'll get chilled if we stay here. We can go to the conservatory." Her eyes widened at the suggestion. "I assure you, I only suggest the move for your comfort."

"No offense, sir. But aren't we likely to be noticed?"

He felt a smile pull at his mouth. "By whom?"

"I don't know. A gardener. One of the stable hands…"

He leaned close to her ear. "And whose reputation are you trying to protect?" Why was he flirting with her? Katherine must be completely amused.

Alaina took a quick step back and replied, "It may not have occurred to you, but meeting with you in such a manner is dangerous for me."

He'd offended her—not what he had intended. But for some reason this amused him. "So, it's your reputation you're protecting. Did you ever consider what someone might think of me if they knew of these meetings?"

Her eyes flashed. With a huff, and another distancing step, she replied, "It has been my experience, sir, that the masters of the house can do no wrong. They are protected from gossip simply because they are men and are wealthy."

He laughed. "Obviously, you pay no attention to the gossip, as you call it, that circles about my own home." He'd caught her. Those amber eyes grew startled right before she lowered her gaze. "Ah…you have. Trust me, Miss Clarkson, I am not immune to the talk of the household staff. And contrary to other wealthy men you may have had the misfortune of knowing, I do take care not to damage my own reputation any more than I already have." He waited for her reply. She made none. "Very well." He extended his hand toward the gate. "Shall we?"

He let her lead the way. Walking behind her, he couldn't miss the gentle sway of her skirts. His imagination dragged him right back to the thoughts he'd had when she first entered the garden. Katherine...he would have to speak to her about this.

The conservatory was empty, and warm, as Phillip had hoped. Although the day's cloud cover had made the glass murky, the air was heavy with green foliage, and depending on where they walked, the sweet scent of rose blossoms tickled their noses. Phillip was a boy when his grandfather insisted the estate needed a conservatory. Once built and functional, it had become one of Phillip's favorite places to hide...especially with Katherine. The memory of his wife in his arms felt so real and distracting that he almost stumbled over a small container of soil someone had left on the floor. Pulling himself together, he glanced at Alaina who eyed him suspiciously. He couldn't blame her. She'd caught him more than one time when he couldn't walk straight. Which reminded him.

"Miss Clarkson, I must apologize for the last time we saw each other. I behaved in a most ungentlemanly manner. You were kind to assist me." Phillip motioned to a bench surrounded by small trees. She sat down, wrapping her fingers over the edge of the stone seat.

"I questioned if you would remember the episode," she said.

Phillip removed his hat and drew the brim through his hands in a circular motion. "Unfortunately. And Kenton, full of brotherly love, I'm sure, is quick to remind me of the evening."

She had the graciousness to bow her head before she smiled. He saw, nonetheless.

"It is amusing, I suppose," he said, taking a seat beside her. She slid to the end of the bench, as far from him as she could get.

She fussed with her skirt, smoothing and tucking it about her legs. He looked at her hands. They were not rough or calloused as he supposed all servants' hands must be. In fact, her fingers were slender, agile, and for the smallest of moments he wondered how they might feel against his skin. He averted his eyes, unsettled by the thought.

"You said she was leaving you," Alaina said, "Do you want to explain what you meant by that?" She turned to him, trying to appear brave and wise, but not quite getting there. The expression was endearing.

Phillip, thrown by her question, hesitated. With the crazy path his thoughts wandered while sitting next to this girl, he felt too guilty to talk about his wife. "No. I don't want to talk about Katherine today."

"You don't?" She was instantly on her feet. "Please, then explain why I am here?"

"Sit down, please." He reached into his coat pocket. "I've had news of your brother." He pulled out a letter that he'd received that morning and handed it to her.

Her hand shook as she reached for the missive. Without returning to her spot on the bench, she unfolded the letter and began to read. Her face, filled with joy and anticipation, disintegrated into confusion when she read about her brother.

"What does this mean?" She shook the letter at him.

"It means we don't know where he is."

"He's in Barbados! He's serving in the Royal Navy! This must be wrong!"

Phillip fought the desire to pull her into his arms, to comfort her. "It's not wrong. He left Barbados several months ago." He pointed to the page. "It says right there. He resigned his commission and took employment with a merchant trader."

"Who? Who is this trader? Why didn't he write to tell me?"

"I cannot tell you that," he replied in as gentle a manner as he could. She wilted before his eyes. The headstrong, brave, and wise young woman, who moments before was ready to sit and listen to him talk of grief and loss, had now succumbed to the same emotions. She handed the letter back to Phillip. He folded and returned it to his pocket.

"Tell your friend, Mister Hal," she said, motioning to the letter she had relinquished, "That I am most grateful for the efforts he made on my behalf."

Phillip's brow furrowed. "What? We're not done. If your brother has joined a merchant ship, certainly they'll make port from time to time. Hal will keep looking for him if I ask."

She shook her head. "It's no use. He must be dead. Otherwise, he would have contacted me. Let me know of his change in circumstances. He's probably lost at sea."

"That's a dark thought."

"He would have contacted me." She turned to Phillip, a fierceness in her eyes. "He would have."

"Miss Clarkson." He laid a hand on her arm. It was cool and soft to the touch. She jerked away. "If a merchant ship has gone down, there would be news of it," he explained. "Hal will ask about. Someone will know. If nothing has occurred of that nature, you can rest assured he is alive. And we will locate him. In the meantime," he looked across the conservatory at the lushness of the room. "In the meantime, you will stay here, employed as Charlotte's maid. There's no need for you to go in search of your brother or to be without home or employment."

"Except."

"Except?"

"If I continue to meet with you, it will only be a matter of time before Lord and Lady Montgomery become aware and I am dismissed without reference. I have no desire to be in the situation where you first encountered me."

He sat back on the bench and smiled. "I suppose you could be right."

"Could be? I most certainly am."

He loved when her eyes flared like a newly stoked fire. "I suppose what you are saying is a possibility. But, given my behavior over the past few years, I suspect my father would be thrilled."

"Thrilled?"

"Yes, thrilled. He would assume I'm bedding you, pardon my frankness, and he would believe that a good sign. You need not look so horrified, Miss Clarkson. My father would generally frown on fraternizing with the help, but I believe where I am concerned, there are extenuating circumstances."

"And your mother?"

"She would be mortified. But, if my father approved, she would not speak against him."

"But I would."

"You need not worry. I will not let them dismiss you. Nor would Charlotte, I'm sure. She would cause such a disturbance that if they did send you away, they would quickly call you back." Thinking to himself, he grinned. "And besides, I need you here." Her surprise at the comment pleased him. "Your quest to locate your brother is a convenient distraction from my upcoming nuptials. And you're the best nursemaid we have ever had. My behavior has been inexcusable."

"Your behavior is not inexcusable." Her voice softened.

"Now you are lying, Miss Clarkson. I did not expect that of you." He studied her for a moment. She was changing. Phillip couldn't put his finger on it, but it seemed she was relaxing or accepting their situation in a way she had not before. She leaned back on the bench, losing the rigid posture she had held during their conversation thus far. Her mannerisms were most curious. She knew how to read. She held herself, conducted herself, similar to other ladies Phillip knew. And while she played the role of a house servant, she didn't cower as the others did.

"Are you sure you do not wish to talk of Lady Katherine?" she asked.

He surveyed the conservatory again, expecting to see Katherine across the way, a smug grin on her face. She was nowhere to be found.

"We used to come here," he said. "When we wanted to be alone. When you and I walked in here today…" He wanted to say he could taste Katherine's lips but wouldn't that be scandalous. "I could almost feel her here."

"Is she?"

"No." He bowed his head. "You humor me, don't you?"

"What do you mean?"

"You don't believe the gossip. You don't believe her ghost walks these grounds. You think I'm not in touch with reality."

"I really don't know. Are ghosts real?" She glanced about the conservatory, anticipation in her eyes. "If she truly appears to you, I think I may be jealous," she said.

He scoffed. "Jealous?"

"I wish daily that I could talk with my mother once more. She was so wise."

"It's a blessing and curse all at the same time."

She shifted on the bench, turning to face him. "How do you mean?"

How did he explain the ache to hold someone whose voice seemed more alive than his own. He often wondered, if Katherine were a figment of his imagination, how could he have kept her exactly as she was in life? In the three years since her passing, she'd remained vibrant, never having become a simple memory. And how did he explain his fear that one day, at some point, that person—that angel—would disappear forever, leaving a void, a cavernous pit that would swallow him whole, never to be found again.

"Her presence never lets the pain heal." He studied his hands. "But I can't let her go, either."

She nodded, as if she might genuinely understand. "It would be difficult to lose my mother all over again."

"You were a child when she died?" he asked, making it sound more a fact than question.

"I was twelve. Right on the cusp of womanhood. I could have used her guidance."

"What was her name?"

She smiled. He enjoyed that shy curve to her lips—it tempered all of her features.

"Rebecca. Papa called her Becca."

"That was Katherine's baptismal name." He chuckled. "She said it was only used by her mother when Kat was in trouble."

Alaina tilted her head to one side—so similar to how Katherine reacted when she was curious.

"I've never heard you refer to her as Kat."

"Slip of the tongue. I only called her that in private moments."

"Oh." She lowered her head.

"I didn't mean to embarrass you."

She shook her head. "No. I'm not embarrassed." She immediately stood. "I really should be returning to the house."

That was unexpected. "Did I say something wrong?"

"No. If I am away too long, Mr. or Mrs. Hollingsworth will notice."

"Ah, yes." He rose as well. "Let me offer my apologies for not delivering more promising news about your brother. But I assure you, the quest continues. He will be located."

"I appreciate your continuing the search. You're doing far more than I deserve."

She deserved so much more. A lump caught in his throat. "I am most pleased to be of service." He reached out, tucking a stray strand of hair behind her ear. Her breath caught at the motion. He quickly stepped back, clasping both hands behind his back. "I cannot express how sorry I am for all you have lost. I sincerely hope to locate your brother and facilitate your reunion."

Her eyes filled with tears. "Thank you." Keeping her eyes locked with his, she dropped into a deep curtsey, before starting toward the door. At all times she kept the servant relationship at the forefront. He wished, for a moment she would forget. But that was unlikely. He didn't forget...well, not usually. In the last hour, the class distinction for him had faded. She was a friend, a confidant.

"Oh, Katherine," he whispered. "This is not good." There was no response.

Alaina approached the door. As she laid her hand on the handle, he called to her.

"Alaina." She stopped but did not look back. "If you are not opposed, I wish to meet you again...perhaps tomorrow."

She lowered her head, thinking, he presumed. "I do not know if I can pull away."

"Yes. I understand. We will find another opportunity."

She did not answer, only offered another small curtsy and closed the door behind her. Phillip frowned. "No, this is not good at all."

CHAPTER SIXTEEN

"Very little is needed to make a happy life."
–Marcus Aurelius Antoninus

Lainey pulled her shawl tight. How was it colder now than when she'd entered the conservatory with Phillip? She glanced over her shoulder at the conservatory and slowed her step. Stones beneath her shoes crunched as she walked along, and she found herself careful with each step. The news on Robert had been disappointing, but Phillip thought they would locate him, and that was comforting. She wanted to be concerned about Robert, but she couldn't concentrate on that. More troubling were the thoughts that kept wandering to Phillip. Was his grief compromising her rationality? He was gentry! She was a servant! A friendship between them was as improbable as a friendship between a rabbit and a fox. She frowned. But today...talking with him...she felt valued. He listened and shared in her grief without demeaning her as "only" a servant. For goodness sake, he allowed that she should have real feelings. That was something she'd not encountered with gentry before. Gentry. Phillip did not behave in the manner of nobility, at least not with her. What if...no...but what if...could someone like Phillip have interest in someone like her? She half smiled, entertaining the idea that classes could disintegrate, and a commoner could love and be loved…but no…that was absurd.

"Alaina!"

So caught up in her musings, she didn't realize how close to the manor house she'd gotten. At the sound of her name, she turned and saw Charles standing outside the carriage house. In his hand, he held a basket of apples. He raised the basket as if to salute her, waving for her to come near. Confused, she hurried back to the carriage house door.

"Here," Charles said, handing the basket to her. "Cook wants to make apple pie. If that old bitty Hollingsworth is waiting for you, you can say you were in the orchard."

"But there are no apples left in the orchard," she said, reluctantly taking the basket.

"If that's true, where did these come from?" He winked at her.

"I don't understand."

Charles grinned. "We wouldn't want anyone to get suspicious of your afternoon activities."

"Oh! OH!" She'd been seen. She glanced at the basket in her hand and the pieces fell into place. Jane had alerted Charles to the nature of her meetings with Phillip. Charles, having seen her with Phillip that afternoon, had concocted a plan to keep her rendezvous a secret. Her friends were rallying behind her. She swallowed the lump in her throat.

"If needed," Charles said, his tone low and conspiratorial, "Cook will say since you didn't have to tend to Miss Charlotte, she sent you out for the apples. You know how far the orchards are."

Actually, she didn't. She knew there were orchards on the property, but if she had to locate them, she might have trouble.

"That will explain your flushed complexion as well," Charles added. "You know, rushing back to tend to the mistress."

Raising a hand to her cheek, Lainey realized she wouldn't have had an explanation for her ruddy face.

"You've thought of everything," she said. "How can I thank you?"

"Save me a piece of pie," he said, giving her another wink. "You better get going. Cook is waiting."

Without thinking, Lainey threw her arms around the rough young man, giving him a hug. He sputtered a little in surprise but returned the gesture. Though her reunion with Robert might be delayed, at least she wouldn't have to leave these people too quickly. Who knew that friends could be found in such places?

When Lainey arrived at the big house, Mrs. Hollingsworth wasn't waiting at the door, but she had noted Lainey's absence. As soon as the woman saw Lainey had returned, she followed her into the kitchen.

"Finally," Cook said upon Lainey's arrival. "I was starting to think you fell out a tree, and I was gonna have to retrieve them apples myself."

"Sorry it took so long," Lainey said, pretending she didn't feel Mrs. Hollingsworth breathing down her back. Lainey placed a hand over her heart. "I hurried as fast as I could. You know how far the orchards are."

"Mrs. Crawford," Mrs. Hollingsworth said, "could you not have had one of your assistants bring apples from the larder? It's not appropriate for Miss Clarkson to be roaming about the grounds."

Cook planted her hands on her hips. "I could have gotten apples from the larder," she said, glancing in Lainey's direction. "But I thought the family deserved a dessert with fresh apples. If you want to deny the family the best I can offer, next time I will use the softer, less flavorful apples from the larder."

With her back to the housekeeper, Lainey found it easy to hide her smile. Only Mrs. Crawford could speak to Mrs. Hollingsworth in such a manner.

"And I volunteered to go," Lainey said, once she'd regained composure. "I didn't realize the distance, or I would have let someone else take the job. But I knew Miss Charlotte was not due back for some time, and I really wished for some fresh air." She turned and offered the housekeeper a humble curtsy. "I beg your pardon, Mrs. Hollingsworth, I should have cleared the outing with you." She entreated the woman with pleading eyes.

With a 'humph' Mrs. Hollingsworth relaxed. "I guess there is no harm done. Miss Charlotte has not yet returned. There will simply be no keeping you indoors, will there?"

"On the contrary, ma'am. It was cold today. I assure you, when the snows fly, I will stay indoors."

"Enough of all this chatter," Mrs. Crawford said. "I have a meal to prepare." She waved a hand at the two women. "Shoo…I need space."

As Lainey followed Mrs. Hollingsworth out of the kitchen, she glanced over her shoulder and mouthed a "thank you" to the cook. The woman shook her head. Lainey wasn't sure what that meant, but she hoped it meant well.

After dinner that night, Mrs. Crawford promised everyone a piece of pie. She had made three. Charles came in from the stables, bathed and dressed to be in the big house, to enjoy the spoils of the day and the warmth. Although a bit dark, the kitchen radiated heat from the meal preparations and the sweet cinnamon scent of apple pie.

Chatter about the table was mostly benign, only a few questions were directed toward Lainey and her adventures in the orchards. For that, she was grateful. Only James mentioned he thought the orchards had been picked clean.

"Did you notice that Miss Hilton has returned?" Mary said as she set plates of apple pie on the table. Most of the servants were unaware. Of course, Lainey knew. She had helped both Charlotte and Marianne dress for the evening meal.

"Dinner upstairs was awkward at best," Henry said. "Lord Montgomery insisted the girl sit next to Master Phillip. Miss Charlotte was across the table, two chairs away. I don't believe the master and Miss Hilton said two words to each other. When they are Lord and Lady of the manor, dinners will be a quiet affair."

"Did you notice how frequently Master Kenton and Miss Hilton conversed?" Martin, the other footman, said.

"Can you blame her?" Henry replied. "At least Kenton paid her some mind. Master Phillip behaved as if she were not there."

Jane laughed. "She should consider marrying the brother."

"Oh no, Jane," Mary said. "You know she's loved Master Phillip since she was a tiny girl."

"That was before Lady Katherine. No woman stands a chance with the man now."

Lainey tried to ignore the gossip, but she found the increasing speculation of interest. Something about the idea of Phillip actually marrying Miss Hilton didn't sit well in her stomach. Must be because she knew Phillip would be miserable in the marriage. He would probably spend his nights drinking in the library and never give the girl any attention. She smiled. Guess his life wouldn't change too much. But she felt sorry for Miss Marianne as well. The poor girl. She didn't suit Phillip.

"What do you think, Alaina?"

Startled out of thought, Lainey looked up at the sound of her name. She wasn't sure who said it. "Think about what?"

"Do you think Master Phillip will marry Miss Hilton?" Henry asked.

She glanced about the table. Everyone waited for her opinion on the matter as if she were an expert. Was that because she was Charlotte's maid and therefore closer to Miss Hilton? Or did they suspect something else?

"He will." She hoped she sounded more certain than she felt.

"Why do you think that?" Mary asked.

Sitting a bit taller, she answered, "Because he is a gentleman and a man of honor. He will not go back on his word." As she said it, she knew the truth of it. But somehow, it did not bring her any comfort.

Before the conversation could continue, a bell rang. Everyone looked to the wall. The call came from Charlotte's room. Lainey immediately stood. As she stepped into the hallway, she nearly ran right into Mr. Hollingsworth. Had he been eavesdropping? He smiled at Lainey, gave her a cursory nod as he stepped out of her way allowing her to pass by. She hoped Mr. Hollingsworth heard her reply, saw firsthand that she wasn't spreading stories about Master Phillip. She'd sleep better thinking so.

Charlotte's door was open, and Lainey politely knocked before entering the room.

"Alaina! Come in," Charlotte said.

Charlotte and Marianne sat on Charlotte's bed, both dressed in the clothes they had worn for the evening meal. The fire had been lit, and the room was warm in both light and ambiance. Lainey noticed some wilted flowers on the dressing table and thought how Marianne resembled those same flowers.

"I've been trying to give Marianne a cheering up," Charlotte said. "She's certain she disappointed Phillip once more. I told her it was nonsense. He was as dull as dull could be tonight. He said scarcely a word to anyone, not even Father. Usually, they get into some boring discussion about the property, the horses, or the price of some goods coming from India. Tonight, he appeared unusually distracted. It was not Marianne's fault."

"I'm sure it was not," Lainey agreed. Phillip hadn't been dour when she left him in the conservatory. What could have caused the change?

"You must help me cheer up my dear friend," Charlotte said, patting the bed in invitation.

"Oh…I don't know…"

"Please," Marianne said. "I can use the company."

"Very well." Lainey sat on the edge of the bed, a piece of coal between two gems.

"Tell us," Charlotte said, "Has there been any word of your brother? I told Marianne how kind Phillip has been in assisting you with your search. If you've had news, it will divert us." What would Phillip say if either his sister or Miss Hilton said something about his pursuit? Would he be angry at her? Would he give up on the search?

Regardless, there was no good news to share. "I received word today. But I'm afraid it was not promising."

"Oh dear," Marianne said, her voice sounding as if she might burst into tears at any moment.

"Has something happened to him?" Charlotte asked, her face filled with concern.

"I do not know," Lainey answered. "He is no longer in Barbados as I had thought." Both girls gasped. "It appears he resigned his commission and has taken up employment with a merchant trader of some kind. Master Phillip was unable to identify the merchant, or where my brother is currently. He promises to continue the search, but I fear it will not end well."

"You poor girl," Marianne said, laying a hand over Lainey's. "Charlotte was telling me how you've lost so many members of your family. You can't lose your last living brother. You simply can't."

Lainey lowered her head, genuinely touched by the girl's sincerity. "I pray he will be found safe and well." She took a deep breath. "But I suppose I should prepare for the worst."

"No," Charlotte said. "You must keep up hope. You must not give up. I will talk to Phillip and have him increase his efforts."

"Please don't. He is trying his best, I'm sure."

Marianne sighed. "He is such a good man. I should not mind that he said so little to me tonight. But I do. Perchance he was preoccupied by the unfortunate news he had to deliver to you today."

"That must be it," Lainey agreed.

"Well," Charlotte said. "This is not proving helpful. We're meant to cheer Marianne, but she looks worse now than she has all night. I think we should come up with some conversation topics for Marianne to use tomorrow while conversing with Phillip."

Marianne chuckled. "Kenton said I should just kick him."

"What?" Lainey and Charlotte said together, both amused.

"He said that if Phillip behaved as an..." Marianne's cheeks bloomed in color. "He used a word...well, he said if Phillip behaved like a donkey, he deserved to be kicked like one."

There was a moment of silence before the three girls burst into laughter. Marianne's appearance brightened. "Oh my, I suppose I should not have repeated that."

According to Lainey's mother, laughter served best when nothing seemed to be going well. When they'd lost a house, or there was little food on the table, or Papa was dismissed from yet another job, Lainey's mother continually tried to discover something they could laugh about. *Laughter makes the heart lighter...no matter the circumstances*, she'd often say. Tonight, Lainey believed the saying. With news of Robert missing, and poor Miss Marianne's dismal dinner with Phillip, life felt too dark to find any joy. But as they laughed, Lainey's spirits lifted.

Afterwards the conversation changed. There was no more talk of Phillip's strange behavior around Marianne. No more talk of Lainey's missing brother, or the loss of the rest of her family. They talked of dresses and hairstyles. They gossiped about Queen Victoria and Prince Albert, each wishing for a prince of their own, which led to talk of possible suitors for Charlotte.

After an hour of girlish conversation, Lainey helped the two young women prepare for bed. Charlotte, seated at her dressing table, looked at Lainey in the mirror as Lainey brushed out her hair.

"You seem happy," Charlotte said. "Happier than I think I've seen you since you arrived at Montrose."

Lainey glanced at her own reflection, trying to detect what Charlotte saw. "Do I?"

"I will take credit for that. I knew when I saw you that you would fit in well. And I was right. The flush in your cheeks, the sparkle in your eyes...yes, you are happier."

Later, as Lainey climbed the stairs to her room, she thought about Charlotte's observation. Was it true? Was she happier? And if so, why?

Jane passed her in the hall. "G'night Lainey," she said as they each stopped at their respective doors.

"Goodnight, Jane." Before both girls entered their rooms, Lainey asked, "Jane, are you happy here?"

"More so than I've ever been. I told you about living at home. I never want to go back to those circumstances. And I believe the Montgomerys are the best of people."

"I think I agree." Lainey pushed her bedroom door open. She smiled. "And I think the household staff is the best I've ever worked with. Thank you."

Jane's eyes twinkled. "We're fond of you, too." She leaned toward Lainey, as if to reveal a great secret. "Don't let Master Phillip ruin it."

Lainey smiled, but didn't respond. She stepped into her room, placing her candle on the night table near her bed. Phillip wouldn't think of ruining her situation, would he? And if he tried, she was certain that Charlotte would come to her defense. Lainey sat at the edge of the bed, then threw herself back, stretching her arms out wide. How fun it had been to talk with Charlotte and Marianne as if they were simply friends. In fact, the affection she felt for the two girls and for Jane made her think that this was exactly what it must be to have sisters. To have another female who would watch out for you, who you could talk with about silly plans as well as heartache and hope, who treated you as someone of value, someone trustworthy and lovable. She'd been included. Having sisters felt better than any brother.

What if Robert were alive and well? What if he were found? What if…would she, could she, leave Montrose? Would she want to? She pushed herself to sitting and glanced about the room. It wasn't much to speak of—four walls, the old mirror, the lumpy bed, but…but it felt like home. More like home than any place she'd lived since her mother passed. Reaching up, she wrapped her fingers around her locket. Rubbing her thumb over the smooth, warm metal, she could almost feel her mother near, almost hear her say, "*I love you, little Lainey girl.*" And as if the veil between heaven and earth grew thin, in her mind, her mother whispered, "*Home is wherever you make it. Whenever you are with those whom you love and who love you, you are home.*" Tonight, Lainey was home.

CHAPTER SEVENTEEN

"We desire nothing so much as what we ought not have."
–Publilius Syrus

Phillip leaned his head against the back of his chair. He'd been sitting in his chambers for more than half an hour, hoping to unwind before retiring, hoping to forget about the disagreeable dinner with Miss Marianne and his family, and hoping to figure out what to do about Miss Clarkson and her missing brother. Each time he got comfortable in his chair near the fire, a cackle of giggles—coming from his sister's room—filtered down the hall. Taking another swallow of whiskey, he debated making the effort to rise and close his door. As loud as those girls were laughing, he wasn't sure that closing the door would make much difference. He released a heavy sigh. It was too much effort.

Another burst of laughter. This time his ears perked a bit. Was that Miss Clarkson he heard? How unusual for a maid to be on duty at this hour. But again, Charlotte treated the girl more as a friend than a servant.

"You do that, too." Katherine's voice drew Phillip's attention from the noise in the hall back to the chair on the other side of the fireplace.

He smiled, sensing Katherine there. His conversations with her were decreasing both in frequency and duration. But he hadn't let go of her yet.

"I do not treat her as a friend."

Katherine smirked. *"You are right. If someone saw the two of you dart into the conservatory, they would think you treat her as a playmate."*

Abashed, his eyes opened in mortification and Katherine laughed.

"You know that's not…"

"Yes, Phillip dear, I know." She looked away and smoothed her skirts across her lap. Phillip didn't understand. She appeared so real, so corporeal. If he reached out his hand, he thought he could touch her. But he'd learned from sad experience that he would feel nothing if he did, and immediately she'd disappear. He took another swallow of his drink. Katherine, tilted her head, as she frequently did when broaching a sensitive subject, and asked, *"How are the arrangements progressing for the wedding?"*

Phillip's entire body sank in despair. Why did she have to bring up the wedding?

"Miss Marianne is here for a few days," he said.

"I know. How is that going? Are you warming to the idea?"

"Not in the least." He shook his head thinking about the evening's meal. "We said not two words to each other throughout the entire meal. I intimidate the girl. How can I become comfortable with the idea of her as a wife, when she won't even speak?"

"Do you speak to her?"

Phillip frowned. "I have nothing to say to her. I can't conceive of a question to ask that might ignite some conversation."

"Then it is not all her problem, is it?"

More giggling echoed down the hall. Phillip inclined an ear trying to detect Miss Clarkson's voice. But, remembering Katherine, he quickly returned his attention to her, relieved that his momentary inattention had not driven her away.

"Phillip." Saying his name, her voice settled him like the murmur of the stream at the back of the estate. *"I agree, you cannot marry Miss Hilton. You will both be miserable. But there is someone out there who makes her blush whenever he speaks to her."*

"Who? Who is this person?"

Katherine laughed. *"Are you jealous? You sound jealous."*

"No...no, it's not jealousy." He reached up and rubbed the back of his neck. "If she is in love with someone else..." he raised his eyes to Katherine. "Why would she consent to marry me?"

"She thinks she loves you. But she does not. Talk to her, Phillip. If you talk to her, I believe she will release you from your promise of marriage."

"She might, but my father will not. He won't be satisfied until I marry. Until I provide an heir." He frowned, sitting back in his chair. For a moment, he'd entertained the hope that he would not have to marry Marianne. "I would have to marry someone. And he could arrange a prospect that I dislike more than Marianne."

"Marry the servant girl."

His head shot up. "What? I couldn't marry her. She's a servant."

"Is that your objection or your father's?"

"It's just not done," he said, questioning why Katherine would suggest the untenable.

"You don't have any trouble talking to the girl. You are interested in her life, her family. Working for the gentry, certainly she's developed the skills to run a household, and an estate."

"Do you hear yourself? She's a servant."

"Yes, Phillip, she is. But not a common servant. I think…"

"There's no reason to continue talking about this. I cannot marry a servant."

"Why not?"

"You know why! Her station is so far beneath mine." Anger welled in his chest, surprising him as much as it disturbed him. How could he be angry with Katherine? But how could she suggest something so totally objectionable?

"Well then," she said, eyeing him intently. *"I suppose, you must marry Miss Hilton."*

Phillip sprang to his feet and walked across the room. For the first time he could remember since her death, he didn't want to talk to Katherine. He wanted her to disappear, return another time when he wasn't tired, when he didn't feel so constrained by social mores. He couldn't break off the engagement to Marianne without bringing disgrace to the family. Nor could he marry a servant for the exact same reason. He ran a hand through his hair and turned to face Katherine. She had stayed, sitting in the chair she used to occupy in the evening as they reviewed their day. Her eyes riveted on him as if to tell him something her words could not.

"Katherine," he said, his voice hoarse with frustration. "How can I marry Miss Hilton? I do not love her."

She smiled, a soft, sympathy in her lips. *"Is your only objection to the servant girl her station?"*

Before he could answer, the sound of a door closing down the hall caught his attention. He glanced at his door, and back to Katherine. She was gone, but her question lingered in the air. After a moment's hesitation, Phillip walked to the entrance of his chambers and peeked into the hallway. There she was, Alaina, heading toward the back staircase that led to her quarters on the *servant's* floor. She held a candle in one hand, and as she walked, she hummed a sweet tune. A lullaby perhaps. With her free hand, she reached up and pulled a few pins from her hair, allowing her bun to fall open. She ran her fingers through it, the silky strands separating and sliding across her shoulders and down her back. Phillip clenched his fists. Oh, to be those fingers. To know the sensation of those strands as they fell, soft and sleek, across his hand. His breath shallowed, his chest hollowed with an ache he hadn't sensed in some time.

As she started up the stairs, Phillip ducked back into his room, worried that she might catch him watching her. He looked at the chair where Katherine had sat moments before. It remained empty, but her question lingered in the air.

"Is your only objection to the servant girl her station?"

"No, no, no," he muttered aloud. Falling back against the wall, repeatedly smacking his head with his hand. He could not be falling for the girl. It was unheard of! Well, not unheard of...but not acceptable—not in anyone's estimation. And yet, the desire he'd experienced a moment ago, tormented him...a sensation he'd not felt for anyone since Katherine's death. After closing his door, he turned to the fireplace, picked up his glass, tossed back the rest of the whiskey. He needed more but had left the bottle in the dining room. He couldn't fall in love. Not with a servant girl. Closing his eyes, he tried to chase the emotions away. Instead, he recalled her sadness on hearing of her brother, her tenderness when she spoke of her mother. He smiled, remembering her spunk when he accused her of impropriety, her amber eyes, her hair, long and satiny flowing down her back. He groaned as he dropped into his chair by the fire.

"Katherine," he called, "What am I doing? What am I *to* do?" She did not answer.

CHAPTER EIGHTEEN

"Death is better, a milder fate than tyranny"
–Aeschylus

Marianne stayed at Montrose for nearly a week. Charlotte entertained the girl far more than Phillip did and often included Lainey in the activities. They played card games and gave each other music recitals for which Lainey felt wholly unqualified. She would plunk out a piece on the piano with Charlotte's help and the girls would end up in fits of giggles. More than once, Lord Montgomery discovered their antics and, after scolding Charlotte for her frivolities, sent Lainey back to her place in "the kitchen or wherever you belong."

Master Phillip started lingering in the vicinity, especially if a card game was afoot. Charlotte and Lainey both agreed he was showing more interest in Marianne and that his presence was a good indication he was warming to the idea of marriage. Marianne wasn't so sure.

On the first fine day of the week, Charlotte insisted they take a stroll about the grounds.

"We won't have weather such as this much longer. And…I think we should include my brothers."

Marianne blushed. "That would be lovely."

Lainey tried to excuse herself from the outing, but Charlotte would not hear of it. As the girls wrapped up in scarves and cloaks, Lainey relished her growing love for Charlotte and Marianne, so much so, that more often than not she considered never leaving Montrose. Phillip hadn't asked to meet with her since their last encounter in the conservatory, and since they had talked little of Katherine that day, she thought it possible he might be relinquishing his grief in small, but perhaps, significant steps. If only he would talk to Miss Marianne as he talked with Lainey.

The girls stepped out onto the large porch gracing the back of the manor house and discovered Phillip and Kenton waiting for them. Charlotte immediately took Kenton's arm, leading him down the wide, stone stairs to the gardens below. After a brief hesitation, Phillip extended his arm to Marianne who obliged, leaving Lainey to follow behind in an awkward separation from the couples, neither a chaperone nor a party to their conversation, but rather like a lost, tag-a-long child.

They strolled through the gardens in silence. Lainey breathed in the fresh fall air. The gardens were far past their prime, with only a few purple chrysanthemums holding tight to their blossoms. The sun shone warm on her shoulders and, walking leisurely, she didn't regret joining the family after all.

"Tell me, Miss Hilton," Phillip said after they had walked halfway about the gardens. "Have you ever fancied yourself in love before?"

Lainey bit her lip to keep from gasping. What an inappropriate question for a man to ask a young woman! What was becoming of the Montgomery children that they include servants in their outings and ask improper questions?

Kenton must have overheard the question as well. He turned to face his brother, a wide grin on his face. "Have you taken to fishing for compliments, brother?"

"I'm simply trying to make conversation."

"Perchance you could ask something a little less revealing in mixed company," Charlotte said.

"Such as?"

"Such as, you could ask her what she's read lately."

Lainey lowered her head, hiding her amusement.

Phillip huffed and tried again. "Miss Hilton, have you read anything of interest lately?"

"Nothing that would be of interest to you, I'm afraid," Marianne answered in her usual quiet tone.

Phillip held out his free hand to his siblings, as if to say, "See? My first question was better."

Lainey wanted to jump in and lead Marianne to answer the question in a more suitable fashion. She knew the girl had read a treatise on women's suffrage, a topic Mr. Hilton was keenly interested in. Marianne and Charlotte had had a lively debate about the subject a night ago. Charlotte came to the rescue instead.

"Marianne, what about women's vote." She turned to Phillip. "We discussed this recently," she said, waving a hand about to include Lainey. Phillip looked at Lainey for the first time that day—a curious expression in his eye.

"And what do you think on the matter?" Kenton asked Marianne.

"Well," she said. "I suppose I would support it. But really, what do women grasp of politics?" She tossed a shy glance at Phillip, perchance to seek his approval.

"A woman could know a great deal if she would read about it," Phillip said, with a quick glance to Lainey.

"She's not being forthcoming," Charlotte said. "She fully supports women having a say in the elections."

"That's not true," Marianne said, shaking her head.

"Well," said Kenton, "I agree with Marianne. What do women know of such matters? Men can handle the running of the government. Let women do what they do best."

Phillip laughed. "And pray tell, what is that?"

"Running a household, hosting parties and banquets, having babies." The minute the last words were out of his mouth, Kenton realized his offense. "Brother…I didn't mean…"

Phillip waved a dismissive hand in Kenton's direction. "No. You are right. For many women…" he swallowed hard, "bearing children is…" His voice faded.

"My mother also died in childbirth," Lainey blurted to take some pressure off of Phillip. The diversion worked. Everyone turned their attention to her.

"My condolences," Kenton said without feeling.

Charlotte moved to Lainey's side and took her arm. "Yes, Kenton. It could be birthing children is not so much what women do well but do because the human race requires it."

A nearby tree creaked in the wind as if affirming the fissure among the siblings.

Phillip took a step back. "I believe I should return to the house. I have some matters of business that need attention."

"It appears I have dampened this party," Kenton commented.

"No," Phillip reassured him. "I should have taken care of this before wasting time walking in the cold."

"It wasn't a waste, Phillip," Charlotte said.

"Regardless." He took another step away, bowed stiffly toward Marianne, then turned toward the house. As he passed, his eyes met Lainey's. She couldn't stand to witness his pain. What promised to be a fruitful activity for Phillip and Marianne had rotted on the vine. Lainey watched

Phillip's dejected form walk the path leading back to the manor.

"There's no hope," Marianne whined.

"You deserve so much better," Kenton added.

At Kenton's words, Lainey looked back at the threesome, all focused on Phillip's departure. Lainey had heard a tone in Kenton's response she hadn't noticed before. Charlotte waited and fell into step with Lainey, as Kenton and Marianne began walking together. If what Lainey suspected was true, the drawbacks to Marianne and Phillip's impending marriage were more than a single ghost.

~~*

Lainey stood next to a potted plant in the garden room hoping that this time Phillip would acquiesce and play cards with his sister, brother, and Miss Hilton. Lainey served as chaperone and the extra player if needed. Phillip stood across the room, gazing out the window at the dreary rain, his hands clasped tightly behind his back. He had not as yet agreed to play.

Charlotte and Marianne set the table for the game while they waited for Kenton to appear.

"I do believe we need more light," Charlotte said. "It is dreadfully dark today."

"Makes me sleepy," Marianne replied.

Phillip turned and surveyed the room, his eyes resting on Lainey. What did he expect of her? As if reading her mind, Phillip made his way across the room, stopping next to Lainey to inspect a plant.

She wanted to laugh. His attempt at nonchalance was awkward at best.

"Are you playing?" he asked in a low voice.

"Only if you are not," she said, not taking her eyes off the commotion Charlotte and Marianne were creating. It appeared not only did they want more light, they also wanted a brighter, larger fire. "I should help them with the fire."

"Let them call for someone else. You're a lady's maid, not a house maid."

"That doesn't mean I can't stoke a fire. Or that I shouldn't."

"Charlotte," Phillip called to his sister. "Why don't you ring for someone to do that?"

Charlotte straightened, planted her fists on her hips, and turned to her brother. "That would be the easy way, wouldn't it?"

"Agreed," Phillip said, amusement in his voice.

"But why shouldn't I know how to do this myself?"

Phillip shrugged. "There's no need for you to know. You have someone to do it for you." He nodded at Lainey. "Miss Clarkson here, could assist you."

"I would be happy to," Lainey said taking a step forward. Phillip held up a hand, stopping her from moving any closer.

"No, no, Miss Clarkson. Charlotte wants to do it on her own." He turned his attention to Marianne. "And you, Miss Hilton? Do you wish to know how to stoke a fire as well?"

The poor girl's face went pale, possibly stunned that Phillip had spoken to her—she'd been in the house for three days and he'd barely addressed her at all since the walk in the garden. Lainey knew this from the bedtime conversations that occurred nightly. And the girl most certainly did not know how to answer the question. Which answer would win Phillip's favor? Yes—she would be an independent sort, or no, she would fill her role as lady of the house.

"I believe I should help," Lainey said, hoping to save Marianne from an apoplexy.

"I shall ring for some help," Phillip said, moving to the braided cord that would ring in the basement.

"Ah, Phillip, you ruin everything," Charlotte said. "You probably won't play whist with us."

"Probably not," he said.

Kenton entered the room bringing with him a well-fueled and trimmed lamp. Immediately the room brightened, enough so that no additional light would be needed.

"Charlotte, when I leave for school, who will you coerce into playing this infernal game with you?" he asked as he set the lamp on a stand next to the game table.

"I guess it will have to be me and Marianne, Alaina, and...Phillip," she said with a self-satisfied smirk.

"God, help me," Phillip muttered, returning to stand near Lainey. "Isn't there a game that three can play?"

"Why should you be so reluctant to play?" Lainey asked.

"Yes, Phillip," Charlotte said. "Tell us why."

Before Phillip could reply, Kenton answered for him. "Because he played with Katherine and playing with you would not be the same." He sat down at the table.

"That's not..." before Phillip could finish the reply, Charlotte interrupted "Kenton, that was not kind."

Kenton shrugged. "Sometimes truth is not kind."

"And what has you so sour this afternoon?" Phillip asked.

"You are not," Kenton said. "Someone in this house has to be sour...if not, it throws off the equilibrium."

Charlotte let out a delighted laugh. "Isn't that father's job?" The brothers exchanged glances.

"She has a point," Kenton said.

Charlotte took a seat at the table to Kenton's left. "Come Marianne, you must sit." Marianne did as commanded, taking the chair across from Charlotte. "Now," Charlotte said, turning her attention to Phillip and Lainey. "Which of you two will join us?"

Lainey nodded toward the table. "Please, sir, you should play." She looked up at him, surprised by his steady gaze on her. A moment of expectation filled the room as everyone waited for his decision. Lainey wondered if they could detect the focus in his eyes, the determination...although she wasn't sure what any of it meant. What would his brother and sister make of it?

Phillip offered her a slight bow, an unexpected gesture from Master to servant. In a voice that Lainey was sure only she could hear he said, "If it will please you, I shall play." Without waiting for her response, he redirected his attention to his sister. "I have changed my mind. Count me in." He strode across the room taking his seat across from Kenton. "Appears it shall be the gentleman against the ladies." He took the cards from the middle of the table and began to deal.

Lainey moved to a chair near the fire. It was warmer than near the windows and offered her a view of Phillip. She looked about, wishing for some sewing, or reading, any occupation to busy herself. A brief distraction occurred when Mary entered carrying a pail with more coal. As she added coal to the already glowing embers and poked it, encouraging a blaze, she took several swift glances at the card table. After she finished with the fire, she leaned toward Lainey and simply raised her eyebrows. Lainey understood. Master Phillip was playing cards with Miss Hilton. Gossip in the kitchen would be rich at dinner.

Lainey smoothed her skirts, examined her fingernails, enjoyed the fire. She refused to watch Phillip and the card game. As much as she worked to keep from doing just that, she couldn't stop up her ears. She heard every word spoken. The rest of the staff would be disappointed when they asked for a report, which they certainly would now that Mary knew Lainey was in the room, and she had little to reveal. Phillip kept all his remarks to the game. Miss Hilton did likewise in such a quiet and timid voice that several times Charlotte barked at the girl to speak up.

After a bored sigh escaped Lainey's mouth, one of several, Phillip rose from his chair. "Come, Miss Clarkson. Please, take my place. I am not in the mood for games at present. I have some business matters that really need my attention. I'm afraid they are keeping me distracted. And you are bored."

Before Lainey moved, she perused those around the table. Poor Miss Marianne appeared as crestfallen as a child robbed of a pastry.

"I am not bored," she protested. "And I really don't wish to ruin the game. I do not play nearly as well as you."

"Believe me, Clarkson," Kenton said. "Phillip has not been engaged in the game at all. I do believe my horse could play better."

Charlotte and Marianne both laughed. Lainey fought the smile that tugged at her mouth.

"Go ahead and laugh," Phillip said. "Kenton's horse is an extremely intelligent animal. It wouldn't surprise me if his horse plays cards better than most people."

"That's not what I meant," Kenton replied as Phillip rose from his seat, holding the chair for Lainey.

"I suppose if I don't play, the afternoon's entertainment is ruined."

"It certainly would be," Charlotte said. "Come, be my partner." She waved a hand at Marianne. "Marianne, you can take Phillip's seat and be Kenton's partner." Marianne moved to the seat Phillip vacated and graciously, he helped her sit and settle at the table. Marianne offered him a bashful smile and words of thanks. After the experience in the garden, Lainey analyzed Kenton's response with Marianne seated next to him. Sure enough, although his head was bowed, he couldn't hide his satisfaction.

Lainey stood, reluctant to leave the warmth of the fireplace, right as Phillip moved toward the door. He stopped next to her, offering the same slight bow as he had before. "Possibly you will have better luck," he said. Adding in a tone just above a whisper, "And perchance you might want to look for a book later."

"Thank you," she said, puzzled by Phillip's strange invitation. She didn't know what to make of his words. Tonight, if…when she met him in the library, she would find out.

CHAPTER NINETEEN

"Man is a prisoner who has no right to open the door of his prison and run away."
–Plato

Phillip sat in his favorite chair next to the fire. With the weather changing, the house grew darker and colder by the day. At times he wondered why his father was so keen to keep the estate in the family. Of course, it provided their income, gave them standing in the town as well as in London. At one time, he also shared his father's dreams for the family and estate. But all of that changed more rapidly than Phillip ever imagined. Over the past few days, with Miss Marianne in his presence at every turn, he found himself looking for Charlotte's maid. Parts of him he thought dead were waking with a vengeance. The maid had invaded his dreams over the past few nights. And today, in the game room, all he wanted to do was look at her, talk with her.

He reached out and poured himself a thumb's width of whiskey. He sat back, glass in hand, and stared at the fire. Hopefully, she would come. He couldn't make the invitation any clearer without Kenton catching on to his meaning. A rustle at the door, and Phillip's heart jumped.

"Master Phillip." It was Hollingsworth. As quickly as Phillip's mood had lifted, it sank back into the melancholy he'd felt since leaving the game room earlier in the day.

"Hollingsworth." Phillip said.

"Your father wishes for you to join him in his office."

Phillip's head fell forward. It never bode well when his father summoned him. If only he could escape into the night, run away, disappear. With a heavy sigh, he grabbed his glass and downed the rest of the whiskey.

"Tell him I'll be there momentarily."

"Very good, sir," Hollingsworth said with a bow.

Phillip stared at the empty doorway. He could dawdle, delay the meeting, linger long enough to make his father angry. Not a good plan. Could his father simply want to talk about estate business, or a needed trip to London? He could use the break. Blowing out his frustration, Phillip stood and headed to his father's office.

He entered the office surprised to find his mother sitting in the chair by the desk. She scarcely ever entered this room. Either something was amiss, or Phillip was up against the united front. He suspected the latter and prepared for the worst.

"Ah, Phillip, come in," his father said, motioning for Phillip to take a seat near his mother. He preferred to stand.

His mother reached out for him. "How are you this evening, dear?"

"I'm doing well, Mother. How are you?" He took her outstretched hand and leaned in to kiss her cheek.

"A bit tired," she replied. "I look forward to a good night's rest."

Phillip agreed. He could use one of those. The dreams about Charlotte's maid had made sleeping restless at best.

"Phillip," his father said as he walked around his desk and stood behind his wife, resting his hands on her shoulders. Yes. The united front, as he'd suspected. What did they want from him now? "Your mother and I have been discussing the upcoming nuptials." He paused as if waiting for Phillip to make a reply. When he didn't, his father cleared his throat and continued. "Your mother and I believe that…well…perhaps I should inquire first. Have you and Marianne decided when the wedding will take place?"

A chill ran up Phillip's spine. "We have not."

"With the Christmas holiday approaching, we thought that you and Marianne might enjoy spending it as husband and wife."

"Why would you think that?"

"Dash it all…are you going to argue with me before hearing what your mother would prefer?"

Phillip's gaze shifted to his mother. She had the decency to avert her eyes, studying a flaw in the wood of the nearby desk.

Phillip glared at his father and asked, "Mother, do you have a preference on when the wedding should be held?"

Her response delayed, Phillip turned. She sat fiddling with a string on the edge of her sleeve, her lips pursed as she decided how to answer his question.

"Well, Phillip, it would be nice to have Marianne here as our daughter for the holiday. December is such a lovely time, and the manor will already be decorated. If we held the marriage celebration mid-month, that would allow our guests time to travel back home for Christmas." She regarded him with such imploring eyes Phillip took a step back.

He ran a hand through his hair. That was only a month away. He realized instantly, nothing he wanted to say would postpone the inevitable. Why hadn't he followed Katherine's advice and talked to the girl about calling off the wedding? He didn't want to marry her now any more than he did when he initially proposed. And he suspected that, with their less than productive visits, she might wish she hadn't so readily accepted as well.

"Has this been discussed with the Hiltons?" he asked.

"As a matter of fact, it has," his father answered.

"And I suppose they are in favor." He saw his life slipping away like evening into night.

"They agreed it was excellent timing. They have family coming for the holiday. It would save them several trips down from London and, I believe, they have some relatives in Scotland who may attend."

Scotland, Phillip thought, there's a place he could hide.

His stomach turned rather nauseous. He needed a drink. He needed Katherine. He needed Alai…no…she was not an option. "I'm actually perplexed. Are you asking me or telling me that this is the way it will be?"

"If we're to hold the wedding in December, we need to send out invitations as quickly as possible. I plan to invite Lord and Lady Waller." His mother spoke Katherine's parents' name as if that should please Phillip. It didn't. It only caused more dread. How could he stand in front of Katherine's parents and make a vow to someone he did not love? How could he let his own parents control his life? When would he ever be able to claim his own happiness?

He rubbed both hands over his face, wishing to wipe away the headache that had appeared behind his eyes.

"Phillip, you will see. This is the best course for you. This is the best future for the estate."

"Stop. Stop now," Phillip barked. "This wedding has nothing to do with me. All I want is the freedom to make my own choices. This is all about the estate, about your desire to have an heir. You don't care what it may do to me, or to that poor girl you're asking me to marry." He pointed at the door as if Marianne stood on the other side.

"That poor girl," his father spat out, "will have a better life than she could possibly dream of. She will be tended to and cared for unlike at any other time in her life. She will want for nothing. And you…you will have all the freedom you want when an heir is provided."

"Donald," his mother said, not hiding the shock in her voice.

"It's true! He can do whatever he wants once the line continues on."

"That's what you think I'm talking about?"

"You're spouting on about freedom. Well, son, duty first."

Phillip looked from his father to his mother. Her face reflected the horror that crept through his entire body. He turned and faced the wall. That was better than facing his father. Without warning, the air became thick with tension. He couldn't breathe. When Katherine died, he felt as if he had died, too, but was left to feel the pain of it. Now he knew he had died. Any semblance of being his own man, any chance to make his own way, his own decisions had died that day as well. Silence filled the room, the crackling fire the only sound…that and the miserable beating of his heart.

"It's settled," his father said. "Helena, go ahead and send out the invitations."

His father put a hand on Phillip's shoulder. Phillip jerked away.

"You will one day be grateful for Marianne, as I am everyday grateful for your mother."

Phillip turned and met his father eye to eye. He wondered if the man could detect the anger and the hate radiating from him.

"Grateful," he said, his voice low and menacing. "You are correct. One day my life will be my own. Then I will be grateful." He turned and stormed from the room, his mother calling out to him.

~~*

The hallway was dark except for a few candles that had not been snuffed for the night when Lainey left Charlotte's chambers. She rubbed the back of her neck and yawned as she glanced down the hall. A dim light spilled from Phillip's room. His invitation to join him in the library had followed her around all day like a lost puppy. She knew better than to encourage night meetings, but...same as a lost puppy, Phillip needed someone to care for him. She squared her shoulders and, instead of heading to her room, made her way to the light. At least this time, she was wearing her maid's attire and not her nightdress. She stopped and listened to discover if he might be talking with his ghost. Silence. Peeking around the corner, she peered into an empty room. Surveying the hall and discovering it empty, she proceeded to the main staircase.

Walking down those stairs made her stand a little straighter, walk with her head held a little higher, imagine how it might be to only make grand entrances. At the bottom of the stairs, she looked for anyone who might notice her. With no one in sight, she hurried past Lady Montgomery's office to the library. How her mother would have relished a room such as this one. Tenderness filled her heart, remembering the stories her mother used to share. Tales of pirates, chivalry, knights, all told by memory from books her mother had read as a child. Did anyone in this house appreciate the number of books contained in one room as Lainey did? She doubted it. Well, with the exception of Phillip. But his appreciation seemed centered on the solitude the room offered, not for the wealth of knowledge contained on its shelves.

She approached the door quietly, unsure of what she would find. Glancing inside, a low fire and a small lamp on the far side of the room offered a measure of light. Phillip sat in the same chair where she'd discovered him the night she came for the atlas. He held the top of a glass in his fingertips, his head was bowed, his eyes fixed on a spot on the floor. He took one sip and another from his glass, his expression never changing. How long had he been imbibing? Memories of their first encounter in this room teased her, made her want to turn and flee. Instead, sensing Phillip's distress, she cleared her throat.

In one slow movement, he lifted his head and turned his attention toward the door. "You came."

Lainey stepped into the room. "Sorry to make you wait. Miss Charlotte required extra assistance this evening."

"More giggling and gossiping, I'm sure." His attention returned to the floor.

"No, sir. She was not feeling well…" Lainey doubted he heard her. What did he find so interesting on the carpet?

"Don't call me sir."

"Yes, s…" she cringed. "What should I call you?"

"How about my name?"

"I can do that, Master Phillip."

"No!" He turned toward her with a severe scowl on his face. "My name is Phillip. Call me Phillip. And come into the room. You're hovering at the door like a crow, all dressed in black ready to come scavenge the remains of…"

"Of what?" she asked, trying to keep her expression neutral. Could he detect her concern and fear?

"Of my freedom."

"I'm afraid I don't understand."

"Heaven and earth, come into the room."

Lainey took one hesitant step forward.

Phillip rubbed a hand across his brow. "Completely."

She took a few more steps but stopped well before she thought herself too close. He waved a hand at the chair on the opposite side of the fire. "Sit," he demanded.

She narrowed her eyes. "I may be a servant, *sir*, but I am not an animal to be ordered about with one-word commands."

He opened his mouth as if to respond, then began to laugh. This man was either extremely drunk or he had finally succumbed to his grief and gone quite mad. He laid a hand across his chest, shaking his head. "At this moment, Alaina, you appear completely the mad hen." While Lainey waited, deciding whether to be offended, he continued to laugh until he settled into a chuckle, gathering total control with a sigh—of relief or anguish, Lainey was not sure.

Again, Phillip motioned to the chair. "Please be seated."

Gathering her skirts, she moved toward the chair, sitting at the edge. "Are you feeling all right, sir?"

"Phillip."

She grimaced. Calling him by his given name was so improper. If Mr. Hollingsworth, or worse, Lord or Lady Montgomery heard her use his name she'd be reprimanded at best, dismissed at worst. And yet, she choked it out. "Phillip."

He set the glass on the table next to a carved glass decanter, folded his hands, resting them across his middle as he studied Lainey. The hair on the back of her neck prickled at his perusal. She reached up for her locket, as she waited for him to break the silence.

"Tell me. Do you have occasion to talk with Miss Hilton?" he finally asked.

"I do."

"Does she appear different to you?"

Lainey thought about the young girl. Had she changed since their first meeting? "How so?"

He shrugged. "I don't know. Could be she isn't so enamored on getting married." It sounded more question than an observation. But at least Lainey understood what he was seeking.

"Oh, sir," she said.

"Phillip."

"Phillip." She released a long sigh. "I believe she is as excited to marry as any girl I have ever known."

"Really? She has no reservations?"

"Her only reservation is if she can make you love her."

"Well," he said, as his attention returned to the spot on the floor. "At least she recognizes what she is entering into."

"Yes, sir." She closed her eyes at catching herself using the term. "Yes, I believe she does."

He turned his head in her direction but did not meet her eyes. "Why? Why would she want to marry a man who does not love her?"

"I believe she fancies herself in love with you."

His eyes snapped up to meet Lainey's. "You don't think she loves me?"

"I...I cannot say. She is young. She dreams of being the lady of a great house." Lainey bowed her head. "I don't think she truly understands what it means to be married at all."

"The date has been determined," he said.

Lainey raised her head to find the most defeated man she had ever seen. "That's what you meant by freedom."

His brow furrowed. He took another drink. He was not as inebriated as Lainey had feared. But if he kept at it...

"Do you suppose they make the same arrangements in America?"

"Excuse me?"

"In America, do you think they force their children to marry those they do not love?" He stared off into the room. "I believe I should escape to America." He smiled as if the idea actually held merit. "I could make myself into my own man. I wouldn't be constrained by the rules of society." He met Lainey's wary gaze with a measure of excitement. "You could come, too."

"What?" Her eyes opened wide.

"We could escape together. Ah. But there is the matter of your brother."

"It would be most indecent for you…"

The corner of his mouth pulled into a grin. "Indecent for me? What about you?"

"I'm a servant, sir."

"There you go with that 'sir' again. Please, please call me Phillip. Please give me a moment to be something other than what I am."

"But you are who you are. What would you do in America? How would you earn a living?"

The momentary light in his eyes disappeared. "It doesn't matter."

"It does. You are not used to a life of hardship."

"You don't think I could do it."

"I didn't say that. I…I know what it is to be hungry, to not know where your next meal may come from, to live in situations that make servant's quarters in the lowliest of houses feel palatial. You've not had those experiences. I do not wish them on you."

He didn't answer. Instead, he tossed back the rest of his drink and refilled the glass. The pungent smell of alcohol filled the room. Lainey watched as he stewed about his current predicament, how he might slip out of this knot. Had he really asked her to go to America with him? She allowed herself to be flattered for a moment, to entertain the impossible. The dream faded as quickly as it bloomed. Robert. She must locate Robert. It was more imperative now than it had been before. As much as she had grown to love Montrose, she could not stay. Robert was the key to her new life, her success, her happiness. He always had been.

As if he knew what she was thinking, Phillip broke the silence and asked, "If we cannot locate your brother, what will become of you?"

"I will find him. I have to."

"Why?"

"Why? He's my brother. He's all I have. I'm all he has. We must be together—we need...I need him."

"No." He kicked back another large swallow of whiskey. "No, you don't need him. I appreciate you wanting to locate him, that he's family. But Alaina, you do not need him. You have a place here. Charlotte loves you. She treats you as if you are her equal."

"But I'm not."

"I've seen how you are with the other members of the staff. They love you. They're protecting you; I know they are. They've seen us together." He scoffed. "They notice all that goes on." Phillip leaned forward in his seat, gazing into Lainey's eyes with such intensity that she became mesmerized. "Even if we find your brother, you must stay. I...I need you."

Slowly, as his words and their meaning seeped into her mind, her body, she began to shake her head.

"It's true," he said. "I meant what I said about America."

Lainey bolted to her feet. "That's the drink talking. You should retire for the evening. You are not thinking clearly."

"I am not so gone as to not know what I'm saying."

"So, you understand the ridiculousness of running away with a lady's maid. You would lose all that you have."

"Ah, I understand. Your poverty has made wealth enticing." He sat back in his chair and set his glass on the table.

"Experience has taught me that people do not think clearly when they have been drinking." She nodded toward the glass. "You've had enough that I would be a fool to trust what you say at present."

He rubbed a hand across his eyes. "Someday, Clarkson..." Lainey was relieved to hear him use proper address. "...You must tell me where you gained such knowledge." He lowered his hand and met her gaze. "I suspect your history to be rather enlightening."

That sounded the same as a dismissal. She hoped it was.

Phillip waved his hand. "Go to bed. It is plain you will not indulge me in fantasies. No sense in both of us having a miserable night."

Her heart softened at his words. She sympathized with his plight. But the suggestion of running off to America, and with her no less, was the alcohol talking. Certainly, in the morning he would come to his senses. Headaches had a way of doing that—at least they had for her father.

She offered a small curtsy before moving toward the door. She stopped before walking into the darkened hallway and glanced over her shoulder at the dejected man staring at the floor. "Sir..."

"Phillip," he muttered.

"Marrying for love does not necessarily make for the best marriages."

He turned toward her and laughed; a dark, skeptical sound. "And you have experience with that?"

"Actually, I do. My parents married for love and my father regretted it every day of his life." She lowered her head and slipped into the hallway, half expecting him to chase after her. He didn't.

CHAPTER TWENTY

"The medicine is worse than the disease"
–Francis Bacon

Lainey arrived at the midpoint of the staircase second-guessing her last comment to Phillip. She should leave him with his romantic delusions. He had had an amazing love with Lady Katherine. Who could blame him for wanting that again?

She rounded the banister and started up the stairs to the third floor. A door opened.

"Alaina!" She started at the sound of her name.

Peering over the railing, Lainey saw Marianne standing outside Charlotte's bedchamber, wearing her nightdress, her hair wrapped in muslin strips. Why was Marianne awake and in Charlotte's room? Lainey backtracked down the few steps till she stood again at the staircase landing.

"Thank the heavens I found you." The worry in Marianne's voice was so acute that Lainey's stomach turned at the sound.

The two girls met midway down the hall. "What is the problem?" Lainey asked.

"It's Charlotte. She's dreadfully ill. It all came on so suddenly. I believe she has a fever. She's talking all sorts of nonsense, and her skin is as hot as a poker. I think a doctor should be called."

It only took Lainey a moment to realize she was not going to bed no matter how tired she felt. Just as well. Tending to Charlotte would get her mind off Phillip.

"Go tell Lady Montgomery what you told me. I'll find out what I can do for Miss Charlotte." She sent Marianne off toward Lady Montgomery's room and, wiping her hands down the front of her skirt, headed to Charlotte's room. Marianne had left several lamps burning, leaving the room nearly as bright as noonday. But Marianne had been correct. Charlotte was pale, except for her cheeks which appeared so flushed one would think she'd been in the sun for hours. She let out a barely perceptible moan when Lainey touched her head. Lainey snatched her hand back. When her father was at his sickest, he never felt that hot.

Lainey grabbed a towel from the washstand and dipped it into the pitcher. As she returned to Charlotte's bedside, she turned down the wick on several lamps to make the room easier on the eyes. Lainey sat on the edge of the bed. Charlotte moaned. Lainey dabbed the girl's forehead, cheeks, and neck. A moment later, Lady Montgomery and Marianne rushed into the room. Lainey moved letting Charlotte's mother take the spot near her daughter.

"Oh, my dear girl," Lady Montgomery said as she stroked her daughter's hair.

"Mama?" Charlotte murmured.

Lainey had never heard Charlotte refer to her mother as "Mama." That was nearly as frightening as the girl's appearance. Lady Montgomery extended her hand toward Lainey. Instinctively, she knew what the woman wanted and dipped the hand towel in water, passing it to Lady Montgomery. Lainey stood at the end of the bed, reluctant to move away, and watched the woman dab the cloth across her daughter's head. Lainey reached up and took hold of her locket, remembering her own mother, rocking and singing tenderly to help soothe Lainey when she was ill. Charlotte had her mother to care for her, a blessing Lainey wished for daily. But as an adult, Lainey understood that kind of care differently. An unbreakable bond, a mother's love never left, even in death. Lainey watched on, not in jealousy, but in gratitude for the memories she carried.

Considerable time passed before the doctor arrived. A stout man, with a bald head and spectacles, Lainey instantly didn't trust him. She couldn't say why. Perhaps his brusque manner as he shooed everyone from the room, or Lainey's poor history with doctors led her to the snap dislike. A doctor had arrived hours before her mother passed, and the same happened before her father died. Death followed physicians—at least in Lainey's experience.

When Lainey stepped into the hallway, she found Phillip propped against the opposite wall, his brow furrowed. He looked up as Lainey stepped out of Charlotte's room.

"What's going on?" he asked.

Lainey crossed the hallway to answer, and speaking in hushed tones, relayed what she knew. "When I came upstairs, Miss Marianne called to me, said Charlotte was not well. When I got into the room, Charlotte had a horrible fever. I sent Miss Marianne for your mother immediately. Now we must wait and see what the doctor prescribes."

Phillip wiped a hand across his mouth. "How serious do you think it is?"

"I can't say. She had mentioned some fatigue, but didn't have any symptoms like she does now. This unexpected escalation does not bode well."

He pushed away from the wall and began pacing. "What can I do?"

"I'm not sure there is anything quite yet. But…"

"No one else can die," he said, his voice low and angry.

"Oh, Phillip..." Catching her use of his name too late, she stepped back, eyes wide, and glanced about her surroundings. No one should hear her be so familiar. "Sir...I'm sure that this will pass. She will not die." Lainey hoped her voice sounded more confident than she felt. Charlotte's symptoms resembled the symptoms that Lainey's father experienced before his passing. But Charlotte was young and strong, unlike Lainey's father who had been older, and weakened from years of drinking. Lady Montgomery's appearance in the doorway pulled Lainey from her grim thoughts.

"Alaina. Quick. We need a bloodletting bowl."

Lainey felt her own blood drain from her face. That was exactly how the doctor had treated her father.

"Quickly!" Lady Montgomery said before heading back into the room.

Lainey started down the hallway, then, thinking better of it, turned back to Phillip. Laying her hand on his arm, his eyes held the concern Lainey felt. "You can't let them bleed her," she said just above a whisper. "Please. They did that to my father, and it weakened him so that he never recovered." Then returning to her orders, she ran for the staircase.

~~*

Phillip watched Alaina run down the hall, her words echoing in his ears, her intense gaze vivid in his mind. *He never recovered.* The words awoke dread and fear in the pit of his gut. He could almost smell the coppery blood, the fireplace ash, the excrement that stained the bed linens when Katherine died. He glanced down the hall where Alaina had run and to Charlotte's door and back again.

Before Alaina returned with the bowl, he had to stop this bloodletting.

With his stomach in knots and his faculties compromised by whiskey, he tugged on his waistcoat and marched into Charlotte's room. The fire blazed with uncomfortable heat. His mother sat on the edge of Charlotte's bed. Miss Hilton stood in a corner, a shawl wrapped around her shoulders, twisting the fringed ends around in her hands. Dr. Martin had pulled a blade from his satchel, preparing it to slice open a vein. Bile rose in Phillip's throat. He glanced to Charlotte who lay pale and shivering.

"Miss Hilton, put another blanket on the bed," Phillip ordered. The girl, apparently startled by the authority in his voice, jumped, and went in search of a blanket.

"Phillip," his mother said, "You need not be in here."

"You cannot bleed her." His remarks were directed to the doctor, a repugnant man, whose beard was so unkempt that Phillip wasn't sure the man knew how to use a blade.

"It's for the best," the doctor said. "We need to rid her body of the humors that are infecting her."

"I will not allow it." He wiped at a line of perspiration that crossed his brow.

"Phillip." His mother rose and approached him as if he were a wild animal, her hand extended to soothe him, her voice low and calming. "We need to let the doctor do what is best."

"This is not for the best, Mother." Lainey's words ran through his mind. *Bleeding her will only weaken her. She needs her strength.*

"But Dr. Martin says…"

"I will not allow it."

Dr. Martin stepped close to Phillip taking the same posture as Lady Montgomery. "Sir, I understand your concern." But the man stopped; his brow pulled into a scowl. He leaned closer and took a sniff. Phillip, too late, took a step back. Dr. Martin's lip curled as his head began to shake.

"Your Ladyship, I appreciate your son's concern. But perchance he would not be so anxious about the matter if he had not been imbibing this evening. Please, let me treat the patient as I see fit."

At that moment Lord Montgomery, dressed in nothing more than a night shirt, stepped into the room.

"What in blazes? What's going on in here. It's hotter than Hades. Why is the fire stoked at this time of night?"

"It's Charlotte. She's taken ill," Lady Montgomery explained. "Dr. Martin believes she needs to be bled…"

"To rid her of bad humors," the doctor interrupted.

"Yes…Yes. But Phillip burst in here…"

"Bleeding will only weaken her." Phillip said. "Father, you cannot allow this."

Lainey appeared in the doorway with a bowl. Her face was flushed, and her breathing labored. She looked to Phillip, her eyes full of question.

"Lord Montgomery, I believe your daughter is suffering from the ague. The best treatment is to release the bad humors from her body. I will only make a small incision."

"It will kill her!" Phillip said.

"Phillip!" His mother's voice rang with an odd mixture of sympathy and disapproval. She turned to her husband. "He's been drinking."

"I'm not surprised," his father said with a shake of his head.

Phillip turned to Lainey. "Miss Clarkson…tell them!" The color drained from her face and her eyes grew wide. Phillip snatched the bowl from her hand.

"Good God, Phillip, you're listening to a servant girl?" Lord Montgomery said.

"Tell them," Phillip urged. He tried to control his voice, not bark at her as if she were a dog.

She lowered her head. "My father had a similar illness," she said. Everyone stilled to hear her. "The doctor insisted on bleeding him, but that made him weaker. He was gone by morning." She kept her head down as Lady Montgomery gasped.

Phillip held out a hand to emphasize the girl's story. "See? You cannot bleed her."

"I assure you, your Ladyship...your Lordship, that is a most unusual outcome."

"But it is an outcome?" Lord Montgomery asked.

"It can happen. But I believe you may have the same outcome if I do nothing."

Lord Montgomery wiped a hand across his mouth and pushed his way to his daughter's bedside. He took her hand. "She's burning up," he said to no one in particular.

"Clarkson can stay with her through the night," Phillip said. "She can cool her fever with wet cloths, coax Charlotte to drink...certainly that would be better than bleeding her."

"I never did like this bleeding business," his father muttered. With Charlotte's hand in his, he faced the doctor. Though wearing nothing more than his nightclothes, he still commanded authority. "There will be no bleeding tonight." He glanced in Lainey's direction. "We will ascertain how she fares with her maid's attentions and reassess in daylight."

The doctor sighed. "Sir, I cannot recommend following the advice of a servant girl. What does she know about medicine?"

Lord Montgomery's lips pulled into a straight line. "I guess we will find out," he said. "Thank you for coming, Doctor Martin. While your services are no longer required tonight, it's much too late for you to return home. Lady

Montgomery will show you to a guest room. If you are needed, you will be close and..." he held out a hand in Lainey's direction, "the girl can summon you." He glanced about the room challenging anyone to contradict him. "Now, the rest of you return to your chambers. Charlotte needs her rest."

Phillip held back while his parents and the doctor filed out of the room. Miss Hilton approached Alaina, taking the girl's hands in her own. "Take good care of her," she said, before leaning in and giving her a kiss on each cheek. Phillip's mouth dropped open. He'd been serious earlier in the evening, telling Alaina the whole household was in love with her, but he never expected such a blatant expression of affection from family...or soon to be family.

Before leaving the room, Miss Hilton offered Phillip a small curtsy. He realized in that moment that she wore nothing more than a nightdress and shawl, her hair was tied up in rags and she had the faint scent of lavender about her. What should have tantalized his imagination did nothing. After Miss Hilton left the room, he turned his attention to Alaina, who had taken her seat on the bed next to Charlotte. She wrung out a cloth in a bowl, and dabbed Charlotte's brow, her fingers long, slender, smoother and more elegant than a servant's should be. His sister lay ill and helpless, and he was obsessing over Alaina's hands. Hands that he wished to hold, to feel against his own skin. *Good Lord, help me,* he thought.

Before he said or acted in a manner he'd regret, he abruptly turned and left the room.

CHAPTER TWENTY-ONE

"Death, death; O, amiable lovely death!"
–William Shakespeare

Days later, sitting on the edge of the bed, Lainey spooned another portion of broth to a recovering Charlotte.

"When can I have real food again?" Charlotte asked, sounding the same as a spoiled child.

"When Dr. Martin is convinced you are strong enough," Lainey replied, offering another spoonful.

Charlotte turned her head. "Not another drop."

Lainey leaned back. This wasn't the first time Charlotte had refused to eat. No matter how many times Lainey explained to the girl how she wouldn't regain strength unless she ate, Charlotte had had her fill after only a few sips, insisting she wanted 'real' food. Cook had been kind and included a few noodles in the broth, but Lainey had to admit, a simple broth with a bit of noodles hardly amounted to a meal.

"I'm tired of being in bed. I'm no help to mother. She must be frantic trying to make the arrangements for the wedding." Charlotte leaned slightly in Lainey's direction. "You can't count on Marianne in these matters. She knows nothing about organizing a respectable wedding."

"I doubt your mother has been worrying about the wedding. She's much too concerned about you to fuss with such details."

Slapping her hands on top of the covers, Charlotte's face pulled into the pout of a young child. "I need to get up."

"When you're stron…"

"How's my sweet daughter this morning?" Lord Montgomery said, interrupting Lainey's worthless protest. Both the girls turned to find Lord and Lady Montgomery standing inside the doorway.

Charlotte smiled. "Father. Mother."

"You're sitting up?" Lady Montgomery said.

"Yes. You note, I'm perfectly fine. Will you tell Dr. Martin that I need a real meal…not this, this…" she waved a hand at the bowl in Lainey's hand, "tasteless water."

Lord Montgomery laughed as he walked to Charlotte's bedside. "You seem to have recovered your spirit. That's good news, indeed."

Lainey rose to her feet, stepping aside as Charlotte's parents approached the bedside. She was exhausted. She'd held vigil for two days before Charlotte's fever finally broke. Every day, Dr. Martin wanted to bleed Charlotte, and every day Lord Montgomery instructed Lainey to continue her care. When Charlotte began to recover, instead of allowing Lainey to retire to her own room at night, they had laid blankets on the floor near the fire for her to rest on. The hard floor, the not nearly warm enough banked fire, and the strong musty smell of ash filled Lainey's intermittent dreams with childhood memories. She would wake missing her mother, but happy to find herself in a real home, not the drafty row house she'd lived in as a child.

Lady Montgomery took Lainey's place at the edge of the bed. "Your father will talk to the doctor and determine what can be arranged." She reached up and took Charlotte's chin in her hand.

Every morning, Lady Montgomery had come into the room and followed the exact routine. She'd take Charlotte's chin and inspect her daughter's face, not indicating what she expected to see. But the tenderness between mother and daughter, along with the fitful dreams, left Lainey's chest hollow.

Once satisfied with her daughter's progress, Lady Montgomery smoothed Charlotte's hair, stroking it as one would a cat.

Lord Montgomery joined his wife taking Charlotte's hand in his, her hand dwarfed by her father's. Lainey often thought that Charlotte had no idea how lucky she was. Lainey's father had at one time been tender, but that father disappeared about the same time her mother passed—his grief not unlike Master Phillip's. Lainey smiled. Phillip had been attentive as well over the past few days. While Lainey stood vigil over Charlotte, Phillip had often come into the room with the excuse that he was checking on his sister. No doubt he'd been concerned for Charlotte, but when he lingered and engaged Lainey in conversation, she suspected he had not come simply for his sister's benefit.

At first, the visits unsettled Lainey. Was he going to talk of running off again or spout nonsense about needing her? Instead, unlike the conversation on the night Charlotte took ill, he talked about the estate—with glowing pride—he talked of his horse, an animal to be admired, and he asked questions. What was Lainey's childhood like? What were her favorite toys? Did she play games with her brothers? Did she have a pet? The conversations had been easy and comforting. However, as Charlotte began to recover, he chatted with her only briefly before excusing himself. He hadn't returned since.

"Alaina, I need to speak with you in the hall," Lady Montgomery said. "Donald, stay with Charlotte until I return."

Lainey, a bit confused, followed Lady Montgomery out of the room and into the cooler, darker hallway. The weather had become increasingly gloomy in the past fortnight, with howling winds and the sound of rain against the windows.

Outside Charlotte's door, Lady Montgomery inclined her head toward a settee near the room. She sat and invited Lainey to join her. Lainey wasn't sure what to make of it. But she sat, tall and straight, resting her hands in her lap, a mirror image of the Lady in front of her.

"I must say," Lady Montgomery began, "that when Reverend Porter brought you to our house with that story of Phillip directing him to find you employment, I was most skeptical. You had no references. You did not appear fit enough to work in any respectable house. But Charlotte saw through appearances and insisted that I take you on."

That's not quite how Lainey remembered the event—Charlotte had begged, but Lainey held her peace.

"You have proved yourself not only fit, but invaluable. Since the night Charlotte took ill, I have been advised by many friends that, indeed, bloodletting did not improve their relations' recovery. Many suspected that it hindered. Thank you for speaking up that night, for getting Phillip to stand up for his convictions. I'm not sure how you accomplished that, or how he knew about your father…I'm not going to ask." She shook her head as if to shake off a disturbing thought. "You have proved yourself to be a true friend to Charlotte. I must apologize for my quick judgment and reluctance to take you on. I hope you will not hold it against me."

"No, ma'am." Lainey could scarcely believe the words. Someone of Lady Montgomery's station apologizing to her? She lowered her eyes, smoothed her skirt and fought a smile.

The woman laid a hand over Lainey's. It took every ounce of control she had not to pull away in shock. "I wanted to tell you how grateful I am. How grateful the entire family is for your care over the past few days. You did not leave Charlotte's side. Frequently in the night, I would worry and come to the room, and there you'd be, your head buried in your arms at her bedside, fast asleep. When it comes time for Charlotte to leave us to marry, I will miss having you here. You've been a great help. To Charlotte..." She looked off to her left. "And it appears to Phillip as well." Again, she faced Lainey. "So, thank you. Your service and friendship to Charlotte is most appreciated, particularly since she's being somewhat difficult at present."

"You're most welcome," Lainey said. She had a nearly uncontrollable need to hug the woman. At long last, someone didn't believe the worst of her.

"Now," Lady Montgomery said, patting her hands on her own skirts. "You must be fatigued and ready for a small break, at least. I will sit with Charlotte, demand she eat." The woman offered Lainey a mischievous smile. "And I want you to attend to yourself. Go wash, change your clothes, rest if you need. Charlotte will be in good hands, you may rest assured." She rose to her feet and waved her hands in the direction of the servant's staircase. "Off you go!"

Lainey jumped up and gave the woman a small curtsy. "Thank you, ma'am. I will not be too long."

"Nonsense. Take all the time you require." With that she left Lainey standing in the hall, relieved of all duties—at least for a short while. Having no responsibilities felt strange especially after the days she'd spent caring for Charlotte. But true enough, Charlotte was on the mend. And although she didn't say this to Lady Montgomery, she didn't resent any time she'd spent with Charlotte. The girl really had become a younger sister. Lainey would not abandon people she loved, unlike what her family had done to her. That was unfair, she thought, scolding herself as she made her way to the stairs. Her family had died…that is all but Robert—at least she hoped that that didn't include Robert…so they had not abandoned her, but she did feel forsaken.

Lainey couldn't believe how good it felt to wash and change clothing. She lay on her bed and napped, marveling at how restful a lumpy mattress could be. When she arrived in the kitchen for a bite to eat, Cook was already working on the evening meal for the family, while her assistant cleaned up from dinner. Several staff members remained at the table. The aroma of fresh bread and stew filled the air, reminding Lainey of how hungry she'd become. Jane had brought food to Lainey while she kept vigil at Charlotte's bedside, but being in the dining area listening to the sizzle of meat in the oven, inhaling the tangy smell of green vegetables, and being with her friends made Lainey breathe easier.

"There she is," Jane announced, "Our own nurse in residence. How is Miss Charlotte doing?"

Lainey chuckled. "She's well enough to be complaining. Cook's broth is not enough to satisfy anymore." She sat down next to Jane.

Cook entered the dining hall and dropped a plate of roasted meat, potatoes and carrots in front of Lainey. "She'll take that broth and be glad she can swallow it."

"I'm sure she's grateful," Lainey said. "She's ready for more substantial food is all. And I think she is ready, too. I wonder why doctors are so careful. When a patient is recovering, don't they need the nourishment?"

"Never know what will upset a sick person's constitution," Cook said. "Just as well she takes her time recovering. There will be plenty to do after she's well."

As Lainey ate, she enjoyed Jane's company. After the conversation she'd had with Lady Montgomery, she could almost believe she were part of the family, not part of the staff. Before she returned to Charlotte's room and resuming her duties, she needed a good reminder of her station.

After the delicious meal, Lainey happily returned to Charlotte's room. As she rounded the staircase landing, she heard her name.

"Miss Clarkson." Phillip stood at the second-floor banister as if he'd been waiting for her. She smiled, both surprised and perplexed at how pleased she was to see him. He presented complications. While Charlotte treated her as part of the family, Phillip filled her head with silliness, ideas such as running off to America—that he needed her. Her! What could a wealthy man such as Phillip need from a girl like Lainey? She told herself to forget his words, he had been drinking after all, but she constantly played them over and over in her head. They brought an unexpected warmth, a sense of security. If nothing else, she could count Phillip as a friend.

"Sir," she said, dipping in acknowledgment. "How are you?"

"We need to talk," he said, taking her by the arm and leading her down the hall. At the first open door, he pulled her into a guest suite, one that Lainey had only passed by and never entered. Once inside, Phillip released her arm and took a few steps further into the room.

She wrapped her arms across her belly warding off a chill. The suite had not seen a fire in weeks. And truthfully, Phillip's expression froze her to the core.

"What is it?" she asked.

He bit his lower lip. "I've had some word."

She gulped in a breath and held. "Robert?"

"I can't be certain. But my friend wrote to tell me that he's had word of a merchant ship gone aground near Bermuda. Many on board were…were lost."

She shook her head. "Was it a ship Robert was on?"

"We are not positive. But he was last seen aboard that ship." He paused. "And he hasn't been seen since in Barbados."

"But did he sail on it?" She grabbed at her locket. "Did he?"

"I honestly can't say."

He might not be able to say, but his tone said it all. It was possible.

Robert was gone.

Before she lost composure in front of Phillip, she turned from him, covering her mouth with her hand to muffle the sob that pushed its way up from deep in her soul. Her shoulders dropped as the crushing weight of loss pulled at her heart. As much as she wanted to be noble, she couldn't. Her whole body trembled.

"Alaina." Tenderness filled the word as Phillip laid his hands on her shoulders and, stepping around her, bent to meet her eyes. Shaking her head, she tried to avoid his empathy. Without a word, he wrapped both arms around her, pulling her next to him. With a hand, he guided her head to rest against his chest. He stroked her hair. Lainey couldn't ever remember anyone holding her with such strength and compassion. His arms warm, his stroke soothing.

After a few moments, he led her to a settee near the window. The day had turned glorious, mocking Lainey. Long fingers of sunlight stretched across the green lawn pretending at warmth and peace. Only the bare trees spoke of the chill in the air. Once seated, Phillip continued to hold her, one arm about her shoulder, the other hand rubbing along her wrist. Deep down she knew it improper to allow such affection, but in his arms…

"When Katherine died," he said, his voice lowered, "all I wanted was someone to hold me as she had. I think that's what I missed first. Her touch."

"When my mother passed," Lainey replied, "I tried to crawl into bed with her. I only wanted to lie near her one more time before she grew cold. My father pulled me away. I wanted a chance to say good-bye, to tell her I loved her." Her lip quivered. "I'm not getting the chance to tell Robert either." She turned her head into his shoulder. "I can't stand the thought that he was alone."

Phillip reached into his pocket and pulled out a handkerchief, dabbing at her cheeks. "You will not be alone, Alaina. We are not the same as your brother, but you have embraced us, and we will embrace you. When Mother hears…"

Her head snapped up. "No. No. You must not tell her."

"Why not?"

"I can't say. I don't…I don't want to be viewed with constant pity." She sat up straighter, wiping the remaining tears away. She glanced up at Phillip. "Not even by you. I've been alone before. I will…I can make my way." She stood.

"What are you saying?" Phillip's face reflected a great deal of emotions, but none of it appeared to be pity.

"In the spring, when the weather turns, I will go to London. I will attempt…I will try…"

"I will not have it!" He sprang to his feet, towering over her.

"I can't stay here."

"You can. And you will."

"No. I can't. I can't stay here and watch..." She couldn't stay because she couldn't witness Phillip be husband to Marianne. She lowered her head and took a step back. When did this happen? When did she start to have feelings for him?

"Watch what?"

"I cannot watch you and Charlotte and wish to be part of your family. I am a servant. I will always be a servant. And kind as you and Charlotte are to offer to care for me, I must stand on my own." She shook her head in resolve. "I do not belong here."

She had disappointed him. As stoic as he tried to appear, his eyes betrayed him.

"It may be Charlotte will change your mind before spring."

"Charlotte," she repeated. The thought of the girl filled Lainey with yet another loss. How had her heart been so easily won over? "I must return to her. Your mother was kind enough to give me some time to..." Her breath shuddered. "I cannot leave her any longer. I must go." In three quick strides she was almost to the door, when Phillip grabbed her arm.

"I will not let you leave."

She yanked away from him. "I need to return to your sister."

"That's not what I meant, and you know it."

She dropped into a deep curtsy. "Thank you for all your help, sir. Though the news is unfortunate, I do appreciate your willingness to help me. You are truly the first gentleman I have ever met." She rose and without hesitation made her way out of the door and down the hall toward Charlotte's room.

CHAPTER TWENTY-TWO

"Jealousy is always born together with love"
–Francios, Duc de La Rochefoucauld

Phillip rubbed the back of his neck as he walked into his chambers. The warm fire and the trimmed lamps burned bright enough to make the room feel cozy. A tray set with tea rested on a table near the fire, a plate of scones included. He hoped they were Cook's plain scones with a tureen of honey butter included. He loosened his cravat. He wanted to believe that Alaina had arranged for the treat but that was wishful thinking. More than likely, it was his mother; his heart tempered at the thought.

Slathering a scone with honey butter, he took a bite, and a smooth sweetness filled his mouth. For a moment, he imagined a kiss from Alaina would taste as sweet. Guilt seized his conscience. He gazed at Katherine's portrait on the wall only to envision her standing next to it.

"*You need not feel guilty,*" she said.

"You're only saying that because I want you to."

A smile filled her face, reaching to her eyes. She tilted her head, enough for her dark hair to cascade across her shoulder. "*I say it because it's true. You are no longer beholden to me.*"

For the first time since her death, he wanted that to be true. "If that's so, why do I feel I am?"

"You need to let go, Phillip. It's time for you to love again."

"I will never love, Marianne. I may grow fond of her, more fond than I am presently. I may unexpectedly discover I enjoy her company…but I will never love her."

"Talking to yourself?" Phillip jumped at the sound of his brother's voice. Kenton stood in the doorway, a drink in hand, and fire in his eyes.

"Kenton. I didn't hear you."

"Obviously." Kenton stepped into the room, glancing about as if searching for Phillip's apparition. "I expected better of you, brother."

Phillip's brow furrowed. The gleam in Kenton's eyes, and the combative posture, made Phillip believe his brother had had more than his normal share of the drink. He chuckled quietly—his frequent state, not Kenton's.

"Better in what way?"

"This sham of a marriage you're going along with. I heard you. I hear you. But I expected more."

"You're not making any sense. It's no secret that I do not love Marianne."

Kenton laughed, the evil in the sound concerning. "No, you've made no secret about that. You are not giving her a chance. Marianne is sweet, unspoiled. She's fancied herself in love…"

"Yes. Yes. She believes she's in love with me. The girl does not know me. She's so caught up in her fantasies of marriage she can't hold an intelligent conversation. She prattles on about fashion and…and the latest gossip Charlotte's had to share."

"And what have you given her to talk about? You with delusions of your dead wife."

"I'm going to ignore that comment. It's obvious you've had more than enough to drink this evening."

"Oh, you're one to talk. Tell me Phillip, she cleans up your vomit…is she warming your bed as well?"

Phillip clenched his teeth and growled, "If you are referring to Miss Clarkson…"

"Oh, Miss Clarkson—how proper that sounds."

Phillip stepped away from Kenton, steadying his breath. He did not want to come to blows with his own brother. "Watch what you are accusing…"

Kenton barked out a loud laugh. "I saw you! You can't tell me…"

"Saw me? When? I've never…"

"This afternoon, brother. In the guest suite. I heard voices in rooms that should have been empty, and there the two of you were, wrapped in each other's arms—I can't believe what's become of you."

Phillip dropped into a nearby chair and rubbed his brow. "Kenton, you have no idea what you saw."

"No?" Kenton stepped further into the room, looming over Phillip. "You stroked her hair. I expected any moment for you to pull the pins out…"

"Stop." Phillip jumped to his feet, nearly crashing into his brother. "I am telling you that what you believe you saw is not what happened. I have never acted in a way that would reflect poorly on me or on this family."

Kenton didn't reply, only half rolled his eyes. Phillip had noticed that expression more often than he cared to in his younger brother and bristled with the same reaction—annoyance.

"Confound you, Phillip, Marianne doesn't stand a chance," he said, his tone more subdued than from when he entered the room.

"You know I don't want this marriage."

"Yes, but you get her, don't you?"

The comment confused Phillip. "I get her?"

Kenton, totally defeated, dropped into a chair near the fire. "I must be barmy," he said. "From the day she turned sixteen, I'd been planning on when and where and how I would ask her to be my bride. Instead, I've had to watch you offer a proposal barely worth noting, ignore her at every turn, blaming your wife's death for your inability to love her...and now, now you've taken up with a servant. This will destroy her."

With mouth agape, Phillip slowly sank into the chair across from his brother. "Kenton, I had no idea. Why didn't you talk to father?"

Kenton's eyes rose to meet Phillip's. "Because I am not the heir."

"That doesn't mean—"

"I have nothing to offer her—not at present anyway. I will get an education, afterwards maybe, maybe I could provide a living for her. But that's years from now. In the meantime..." He didn't finish, letting his voice fade into the sound of the crackling fire.

What could he say? Phillip knew how unfair the conditions of inheritance were. "I'm sorry, Kenton. I wish I could change circumstances for you."

The heartbreak he saw in Kenton's eyes, as family tradition collapsed upon them, weighed heavily. He wanted to tell his brother that he'd take care of the girl, try to make her happy, give her a houseful of children to dote upon, but that's not the assurances Kenton desired, nor a promise Phillip could make.

"You'll forgive me if I don't return home often," Kenton said. "I can't watch you treat her with disrespect."

"We are not married yet. Together we can approach Father, tell him of your feelings for the girl."

Kenton shook his head. "While it's nice to think that Father would change his mind, it's improbable. Plus, Mother has already sent the invitations."

"What?" This was news to Phillip. "How can that be? Charlotte's been so ill."

"Your mistress did such a fine job caring for Charlotte that Mother and Mrs. Hollingsworth were able to write out the invitations and send them by post. As of the tenth day of December, you'll once more be a married man. Surprised? Well, you were otherwise occupied."

"Your accusations are misplaced," Phillip insisted. "You're in pain, I understand, but accusing me will not ease it. I know what pain makes of a person."

"If that's so," Kenton said, leaning forward in his chair, "dismiss the girl. Don't leave a hint of scandal for Marianne to hear."

Phillip lowered his head.

Kenton rose to his feet. "Just as I thought. Goodnight, brother."

CHAPTER TWENTY-THREE

"Stolen sweets are always sweeter,
Stolen kisses much completer"
–James Henry

Lainey approached her room, exhausted from her duties and the emptiness that penetrated her bones. Her brother was dead. She was falling in love with a man she could not have. She had no family, no place to call home and no place to go. She remained stuck in a life she could never call her own. All her dreams…gone.

Overcome with emotion, she couldn't open her bedroom door. Instead, she leaned her forehead on the cool wood and let the tears flow. Her shoulders shook. She took great, gasping breaths as hopelessness claimed her. What would become of her?

Afraid of drawing attention to herself, she fumbled with the knob and pushed the door open. She hadn't thought to bring a candle with her, so she stood in the doorway, dim yellow light from the hallway streaming around her, casting a long black shadow on the floor. She stepped into the room and leaned against the wall. Her legs gave out beneath her, and she slid down the wall till she landed on the floor. Burying her face in her hands, she cried. She didn't notice the door drifting in until it bumped her knee. With a shove, she pushed the door closed.

Not sure how long she'd sat there, or how long she'd cried, she eventually grew numb from the hard floor. Taking a deep breath, she pushed herself to her feet and cracked the door open. It allowed enough light for her to locate a candle and matches on the dresser. She struck the match, and then she noticed a crystal decanter half-filled with golden liquid and a glass resting on the stand near her bed.

"What?" she said aloud, right as the flame reached her fingers. She quickly shook the match, and the room became pitch black.

"Ouch!" she cried. Was the whole universe against her?

"Alaina?" A voice came from the hall along with a knock on her door. "Are you okay?"

Before Lainey could answer, Jane poked her head into the room.

"Oh, Jane," Lainey said. "Hold the door for a moment."

She scooped up the box of matches and lit the candle.

"I heard you cry out. What's that?" Jane added, pointing to the decanter on the bed table.

"I was about to find out." Lainey took the few steps to the pitcher and noticed a small note tucked under the glass. She glanced at Jane before unfolding the note, immediately noticing Phillip's signature at the bottom.

"What does it say?" Jane asked. Lainey was about to read the note, when Jane grabbed it from Lainey's hand. Her brow furrowed. "Does that say Phillip?" she asked, pointing to the signature.

"It does."

"Alaina!" Her laugh became brighter, shaking her head all the while. "What have you been up to?"

Lainey snatched the note back. "Nothing." She leaned toward the light trying to make out the brief note. Jane peered over her shoulder.

"What does it say?"

"It says...'The pain is much worse at night.'" Lainey stared at the words.

"What does that mean? What pain?"

Biting her lip, Lainey replied, "I got word today. My brother...he's dead."

Without a word, Jane threw her arms around Lainey and pulled her into a tight hug. Together, they stood there for a long minute.

"I'm so sorry. Did Master Phillip tell you today?"

Lainey nodded.

"What happened to him?"

Lainey drew a shuddering breath. "He was aboard a ship that went down."

Jane laid a hand on the crystal decanter and turned to Lainey. "You definitely need this, but you can't drink alone." Her expression brightened. "Wait a minute. I'm going to get Mary and a couple of mugs from the kitchen. We'll be back and offer tribute to your brother, together." She moved toward the door. "Wait for us, okay?"

"Okay." Realizing she had friends, the weight in her chest lightened.

Left by herself, Lainey sat on the edge of her bed and reread the note. *Pain is much worse at night, Phillip.* He would know. Running a hand across the paper she remembered his embrace from earlier. He'd been so kind, so comforting, as he delivered the bad news.

Phillip, truly, was the best of men. He shouldn't be forced to marry a girl he did not love. Nor should he have to marry a girl who only thinks she loves him. For a small moment, Lainey's heart ached for the brothers—for

Marianne. What was their life going to be after the wedding?

What was *her* life going to be after the wedding? Then again, how could she be jealous, as if she and Phillip could ever be together?

Lainey rose to her feet and paced about the room. Why should Marianne and Kenton be separated? Why should Phillip be saddled with a life he didn't want? A wife he didn't want?

A stab of guilt wedged in Lainey's gut. Though perhaps not a friend, Lainey did care for Marianne. She wrapped her arms about her waist. It wasn't concern for Marianne that grappled at her, but her feelings for Phillip.

She couldn't stay. She needed to leave as soon as possible.

Jane appeared in the doorway holding two battered mugs in her hand. Mary stood behind her, a sad, tender expression in her eyes. She pushed past Jane and wrapped her arms around Lainey. "I'm so sorry, Alaina. How horrible. Drowning must be the worst of ways to die."

"Mary!" Jane chided. "I don't think those are words of comfort." She sat on the one extra chair in the room and held up a mug. "Let the tribute begin!"

Lainey poured each one a portion from the decanter, before joining Mary on the edge of the bed. The three girls stared at each other, not one of them sure what to say.

At last, Jane lifted her mug. "To Lainey's brother…"

"Robert," Lainey said.

"To Robert, may he rest in grand peace with the rest of his family. And from the other side, may he watch over Alaina and help her find joy in her life!"

"To Robert," Mary repeated. The girls touched the rims of the mugs and glass and took a sip.

Lainey's eyes watered as the liquid burned down her throat. "Holy fire of God!"

Jane wiped her mouth with the back of her hand. "Have you not had whiskey before?"

"No." Lainey coughed as she spoke.

"That's why I take little sips," Mary said.

"You can do it that way," Jane said as she took another swig. "But for maximum effect, you need to take it in quickly. Drink up, Alaina!"

Lainey peered into the glass, blinking back more tears, and questioned its effectiveness. Then she remembered her brother. She remembered Phillip marrying Marianne. She had nowhere to go. And with those thoughts, she took a big gulp. This time the burn didn't feel as bad.

"What are you going to do now?" Mary asked. "Since you can't be with your brother, certainly you'll stay with us. Right?"

Lainey shook her head. "I don't know if I can."

"Of course, you can," Jane insisted. "There's no reason for you to go anywhere. Miss Charlotte loves you. We love you. You have a home here. A family."

Tears stung Lainey's eyes, but this time for a different reason. It was true. These people had become family. Charlotte and Marianne felt like sisters, as did Jane and Mary. Everyone on the staff thought well of her, maybe not Mr. and Mrs. Hollingsworth, but all the others. She shared more with Jane and Mary than she did with her brother. He hadn't contacted her in over twelve months. He'd left the navy and didn't tell her. What happened to his promise of being together again, as soon as he made enough money? What of that?! He got himself killed. She downed another swig of whiskey. This time, the burn felt warming, relaxing.

"It's true," Mary said. "Miss Charlotte would be lost without you. Did you tell her about Robert?"

"I didn't. She's been so ill. I didn't want to burden her."

"That's poppycock," Jane said. "She will be sad that you didn't confide in her."

"Miss Marianne has not left. She continues to complain about Master Phillip. I believe she is enough trouble for Miss Charlotte."

"Ahh...Master Phillip," Mary said with a dreamy, faraway expression. "Now that's a man I could love." As she realized what she said her eyes went wide. "I think the whiskey is getting to me."

Jane and Lainey burst into laughter. It felt good to laugh.

"Let us all be truthful," Jane said after downing the last of her mug and insisting on more. "Is there any woman in this house who couldn't love Master Phillip?"

Mary leaned forward, her cheeks pink in the candlelight. "Have you ever wondered?" she giggled. "One time, I accidentally discovered Master Phillip and Lady Katherine, they'd been recently married and had escaped to Cook's pantry. The place where she dries the herbs from the garden? Can't remember why I was there, but I opened the door and they jumped apart as if someone had poked them with a pin. Lady Katherine was flushed and a bit short of breath. Master Phillip had his cravat undone and his shirt unbuttoned."

"What did you do?" Lainey asked.

"What could I do? I let out a little yelp and slammed the door closed. But, oh, I don't think I've ever wished to be another woman more than I did that night. He had a hunger in his eyes as if he would devour her like a tray of Turkish Delight. To have a man gaze at me with such desire? It's what dreams are made of."

Jane laughed. "He does have those lovely, full lips." She turned to Lainey. "Has he kissed you?"

"What? No!" They really have had too much to drink, to be thinking of the Montrose heir in such a scandalous manner. "He's the most perfect of gentlemen."

"What a shame." Jane shook her head. "If he tried, would you kiss him?"

Lainey had never really entertained the idea before—and would not start now. "He wouldn't try."

"I believe that's an evasive answer." Jane lifted her drink to her lips, while giving Lainey a knowing glance over the rim.

Mary shook her head. "The real shame is the ghost he has following him around."

"Honestly, I'd love the chance to help him forget his ghost." Jane raised her mug to toast.

"Jane!" Lainey laughed. "You've had too much to drink."

"Oh, come now, Alaina. You've been having all your private conversations with the man. Certainly, you are not immune to his charms."

"Certainly, I am," she lied.

"You don't think he's the handsomest man around?" Mary asked.

Lainey poured more whiskey in her glass. "I think...I think he is exceptionally handsome. But as you pointed out, Mary, he continues to be very much in love with his deceased wife."

Jane's eyes sparkled with mischief. "You could change that." She shifted forward on her chair. "What do you and Phillip talk about when you're together?"

Memories of Phillip's most recent confession brought heat to Lainey's cheeks. Or it could be the drink. "We talk about family mostly."

"With word of your brother," Mary said, "what did Master Phillip say about your future?"

Lainey focused on her glass. "He said I must stay."

"Well, we are all in agreement," Jane said. "You will stay. Master Phillip has declared it."

"I can't." Lainey chugged down the rest of her whiskey to gasps from Mary and Jane. "I can't see him married to Marianne."

"What did you say?" Jane asked.

Horrified that she'd voiced the thought, Lainey turned toward the wall. "I think I've had enough of this stuff." She frowned at the glass.

"Alaina, are you in love with Master Phillip?" Mary sounded so innocent, so concerned as she asked the question.

"No." She couldn't be. Impossible. Out of the question.

"Forgive me if I don't believe that," Jane said, sounding more sober than she had a right to. "Does he love you?"

"No. He only loves Katherine." Even as she said the words, his words came back to her. *I need you.* They were both doomed to misery.

"Well," Mary said. "You have no family to go to. You have no other job prospects. You must stay. We will help you any we can, won't we Jane?"

Jane held her mug high, time for another toast. Lainey's glass had only a few drops left, but she raised it as well.

"To Alaina," Jane said. "To poor Master Phillip, to Marianne—who if she thinks Master Phillip will give up Katherine's ghost is worse off than the rest of us." Her voice softened, and she added "to sisterhood—because we are sisters."

As they clinked their mugs and glass together, Lainey covered her face to hide another onslaught of tears. She had nowhere to go, and these women were as dear to her as real sisters could ever be. Regardless of her feelings for Phillip, she would not leave them. They would help her find her place, her home, her family.

After the decanter emptied, Mary and Jane decided to retire for the night.

"We're all going to feel this in the morning," Mary said, moving toward the door.

"So we will," Jane conceded. "But we were here for Alaina, and we will suffer together." She chuckled. "And, if needed, use the chamber pots as we clean rooms."

Lainey laughed, as Jane gave her one last hug. Putting her forehead against Lainey's, she whispered, "I'm so sorry about your brother. But I'm not sad that we had this little memoriam."

The lightheartedness Lainey felt quickly gave way to grief. She clung to Jane and prayed that what Mary said earlier would prove true—they would help her survive.

After the girls left, Lainey's room felt chilled and much too quiet. She knew she should get into bed, pull the covers over her head and sleep, but the quiet added to her loneliness. She had a right to be lonely but did not want to think that way. Jane and Mary said they would be her sisters. She eyed the decanter sitting on her dresser.

"Better not leave that here," she said to herself. "Who knows who might accuse me of stealing."

She grabbed a shawl to ward off the greater chill outside her room, tucked the decanter and glass in the crook of her arm, and with a candle in her other hand, headed for the library. She didn't know where the Montgomerys kept their glassware, but she'd seen Phillip with the same items in the library often enough she knew she could leave it there. Mr. Hollingsworth would assume Phillip left the mess—no one would be the wiser. She giggled at the thought. Yes, she'd had too much to drink. She found oddities, such as her mess being blamed on Phillip, amusing, and she could not walk the hall in a straight line. She focused on the staircase ahead and tried to walk without swaying—a most unusual sensation.

Standing at the top of two flights of stairs, gazing down, a moment of fear gripped her. Could she do it? Could she walk down the steps and not fall? There was only one way to know. She let out a long sigh and continued.

At the bottom, she giggled. She had not fallen.

"I'm invincible," she said, standing taller. "Wish I could meet Harold Warrington now. He is a little worm. I would smash him with my shoe." She stomped on an imaginary worm, grinding her foot into the stone floor, and laughed. "Shhh," she whispered, putting a finger to her lips, giggling even more. Phillip knew what he was talking about. Whiskey did make the pain better. She shrugged her shawl back up onto her shoulders, and holding her head high, made her way down the hallway.

Dim light shone from the doorway of the library. Lainey hesitated. Certainly, it was Phillip. Right? Who would be awake at this time of night? Fighting another fit of giggles, she tiptoed to peek inside the doorway. Sure enough, Phillip sat in the chair near the fire, asleep, a book in his lap, a glass on the table next to him. She padded lightly into the room, placing the decanter and glass atop a smaller bookshelf. Afterwards she turned to admire the man in the chair, truthfully the handsomest man she had ever known. She used to think Robert fit that bill, but another peek at Phillip softened her. He had been so kind, so comforting, so sad. She wished she could make him smile. She wished she could ease the pain in his heart. She wished she could give him the freedom he craved. Frowning, she knew she could do none of that. Taking a step closer, she tipped her head from side to side, examining him. He'd removed his coat, draping it across the back of his chair, exposing his shirt. Mary's story came to mind. His cravat was loosened, and his cuffs undone, his sleeves turned up one time. She glanced at the table to find a pair of silver cuff links bearing an Irish knot pattern lying near his glass. His hair lay tousled across his forehead, and his mouth—she smiled—his lips were relaxed, parted enough to tempt her.

Should she? She smiled as she moved another step closer. He was sound asleep. Another step, close enough, if she weren't careful, her skirts would brush against his arm. She licked her lips. A little peck. He would never know. And she would have a memory to treasure when he married another. She stood over him, breathing in, breathing out. She wanted to know what it was to kiss a man she loved, at least once.

Stupid, stupid girl. She'd fallen in love. Yes. One kiss. She leaned over, barely laid a hand upon his cheek and brushed her lips against his. She closed her eyes and pretended he wanted this as much as she did.

Unexpectedly, his hand pressed the back of her head forward and he deepened the kiss. Her eyes popped wide open as she pushed herself back, nearly falling over herself.

"Why did you stop?" he asked.

Slapping a hand over her mouth, she wanted to cry out. What had she done?

"I'm so, so sorry," she blurted, as she turned and ran from the room.

She heard him call her name, but she couldn't stop. She would never drink again. How foolish could she be?

CHAPTER TWENTY-FOUR

"Repentance is not so much regret for the ill we have done,
As fear of the ill that may happen to us in consequence."
–Francios, Duc de la Rochefoucauld

The next morning, Lainey sat on the edge of her bed, head in hands. Her stomach roiled, her head throbbed. And compounding all of that, she ached with embarrassment. How could life be so unfair? Wasn't she supposed to forget what she did while intoxicated? Her father always had.

She rubbed her forehead. What had possessed her? Why had she kissed Phillip? *Master Phillip*, she thought, scolding herself. Familiarity was forbidden—hadn't she told him that herself?

As if a cannon had fired, a knock on the door exploded in her room. She winced.

"Alaina? Are you awake?" Jane's voice carried through the door, the same perky sound she had every morning.

With a groan, Lainey made her way to the door, cracking it open in case Jane held a well-lit lamp.

"Oh my," Jane said. "Should I tell Mrs. Hollingsworth that you're ill? I'm sure she would relieve you of your duties for the day. After all, Mrs. James is about. She could tend to Miss Charlotte."

"How is it you are not ill?" Lainey asked as she pulled the door open wider and leaned on the jamb.

"Not my first time drowning my sorrows, I guess. Mary's a bit piqued today as well." Jane grimaced. "But you...you're more so."

Lainey closed her eyes and wished she could go back to bed. "Maybe if I eat some breakfast."

Jane laughed. "Well, that will either revive you or...send you running to the bushes." The comment made Lainey chuckle. "Should I wait for you?" Jane asked.

"Please. I may need help down the stairs." Lainey closed her door. She made quick work of dressing and pulling her hair back into a bun. Viewing herself in the mirror, she shook her head. Amazingly, she didn't look as bad as she felt. But she wished she could erase the previous evening, not only from her memory, but from existence. She scowled. It was all Phillip's fault! If he hadn't left the decanter in her room. If he hadn't been asleep. If he hadn't filled her head with impossible dreams like running off to America.

None of that helped ease her grief. Her brother was gone, and she had no idea what to do with her life. Closing her eyes, she tried to chase away the memory of bending over to kiss Phillip. She still had to face that humiliation.

Another knock on the door and a call from Jane pulled Lainey from her thoughts. She rubbed her cheeks, straightened her shoulders, and left the room.

✳~✳~✳

Breakfast revived her a bit, and afterwards Lainey helped Mary iron and fold laundry that had been hung to dry overnight. Mary fussed, declaring that Lainey, as a lady's maid, shouldn't be tending to such menial tasks.

Lainey didn't mention she wanted to avoid going upstairs. Phillip might be there. At some point she'd have to answer Charlotte's bell, but until that time, she needn't take unnecessary risks. When the bell did ring, Lainey proceeded with caution, peeking around corners before moving forward and walking softly. She made it to Charlotte's room without being seen.

Lainey helped Charlotte with her typical morning ablutions, helping the girl dress for the morning, and fixing her hair into a simple, but attractive bun. Charlotte had not yet totally recovered from her illness and behaved less enthusiastically than she had been before she became ill. Lainey missed the spirited young girl who pushed limits but suspected that Lord and Lady Montgomery might appreciate the more reserved version of their daughter. And it was a blessing that Charlotte's curiosity had dulled, because Lainey had no heart for conversation.

After she dressed, Charlotte left Lainey alone to straighten the room. She tidied up the bed clothing, put Charlotte's nightdress in a drawer, and lightly dusted the dresser and tables in the room. All the while her mind wandered—to the comfort she found in Philip's embrace, the devastation and loneliness of losing her brother. She stopped at the window and surveyed the manicured grounds. The gray sky matched her mood. Service had been her life for the last six years. Much as she wished for another life, she seemed destined to a life tending to the privileged—but not at Montrose—not after last evening.

Closing her eyes, she cringed and broke into a laugh. Some lessons are learned the hard way. Her mother had often said, "You learn by insight, by observing others, or through your own suffering. It's best to learn from the first of those and avoid the latter." Wasn't that the truth.

Whiskey—the devil's ale, her mother had said. Never again would she put her lips to that wicked drink.

"Miss Clarkson." At the sound of Phillip's voice, she stiffened. "We need to talk."

Her cheeks flooded with warmth. What must he think of her? Without turning, she lowered her head. "You have my sincerest apologies, sir. I don't know what came over me."

"I don't want apologies."

What? What did that mean? She had no one to blame but herself if he dismissed her, but knowing that didn't lessen her fear, her dread, or her total devastation. Working to keep her expression neutral, certain she failed, she slowly turned to address him. She raised her head and squared her shoulders—refusing to cower before him—and waited for whatever would follow.

"We cannot talk here." He glanced in both directions down the hallway. "It would be too easy to be discovered. Are you through tending to Charlotte?"

Lainey blinked. "For the moment."

"Good. Meet me in the conservatory. Wear a wrap, it's cold outside." He turned and walked down the hall.

Lainey stood momentarily frozen in place—what just happened? She glanced about the room as if someone might be there to explain. He didn't dismiss her. He only wanted to talk, or, with her luck, reprimand her. She wouldn't go. She didn't need some privileged gentleman to tell her that her behavior had been inappropriate. She already knew that.

Horrified, the thought possessed her that she'd opened the door to more inappropriate behavior. What if he thought...what if he wanted her to be...his mistress!

She buried her face in her hands. Why had she kissed him? And yet, at the same time, she couldn't deny the pleasure of his lips soft against hers. How he had cupped her head in his hand and deepened the kiss as if he had wanted it, too.

She groaned aloud. "What pail of worms have I tipped?" Swallowing, she ran her hands down her skirt and made toward her room to obtain a wrap.

~~*

Phillip paced across the slate floor of the conservatory. Small beads of sweat gathered near the collar on the back of his shirt. She wasn't coming. He knew he should have closed the door to Charlotte's room and talked with her there. But if they'd been discovered, what a scandal that would create. His mother would have put Alaina out on the street in moments. With the wedding approaching, Lady Montgomery would not allow any hint of impropriety to swirl about the family. His mouth cocked in a crooked grin. The horror on Alaina's face when she had turned around. What had she been thinking he would say to her? He chuckled. What must she be thinking he's going to say now?

"It's not what you think," he said to the air.

A few minutes later, the door of the conservatory unlatched. A rush of cold air swirled about, stirring up an aroma of herbs: oregano, rosemary, peppermint—the fragrant blend of herbs would remind him of this moment for years to come.

Alaina stood immediately inside the door, clutching at her wrap with one hand and her locket with the other— ready for flight. He needed to approach with care. Their eyes met. Fear and uncertainty shone through hers. Not that he could blame her. Her bold behavior, which he knew had been inspired by alcohol, must have her head spinning.

"You need not be afraid." His attempt to comfort her was in vain.

"I must apologize, sir."

"Phillip."

"I don't know what came over me. I should never have presumed to…I've never behaved in such a manner before." Her brow wrinkled like a dried grape.

"Whiskey can do that to a person."

"Yes." She straightened—a slight move, but one Phillip detected and knew it meant defenses were in place. "Whiskey that *you* left in my room."

He grinned. "Well, not me personally. But yes, I sent it. I knew how your night was going to be."

"Your good intentions did not play out as you imagined."

"How do you know?"

She visibly started at his response. "Certainly, your intention was not to…for me to…"

"Miss Clarkson, please…" He laid a hand across his chest. "I thought it a lovely end to a rather dismal day."

"You mock me."

"On the contrary. While your…" he paused, searching for the right word. "Your attentions were a bit of a surprise. I can assure you, they were not unwelcome." His hands, without warning, became clammy, reminding him of the first time he'd asked Katherine to dance. His stomach tied itself in a peculiar knot as he held his breath, waiting for a response.

She pulled her shawl tighter about her shoulders as she took a few tentative steps further into the conservatory. Her expression, one of skepticism and hope, warred across her brow. She walked in a wide circle about him. He kept his eyes lowered but managed to follow her path. He didn't move. And he didn't dare say another word. She eventually stopped a few feet away, directly in front of him.

"Why are you suddenly being so formal, calling me Miss Clarkson?" she asked.

Not what he had expected her to say. But, again, he wasn't sure what he expected. "It's proper to talk to a lady in such terms."

"And when did I become a lady?"

"I've thought of you in that regard for some time."

Her brows drew together in a scowl. "Sir…"

"Phillip."

"I can't call you by your given name when you are calling me by a lady's name."

She had a point. He offered her a small acknowledging bow, acquiescing to protocol.

When he didn't say more, she took a deep breath and continued. "Sir. I am a servant in your father's household."

He shook his head. "We are not going down this path. Yes. You are in my father's employ. And if my father were in the grave, you would actually be in my employ. But I have long since stopped thinking of you in that manner."

"But you can't."

"But I have. And your…attentions…last evening suggest you would wish the arrangement to be different as well."

He broke into a grin when she rolled her eyes. Certainly, a servant would never use that expression in front of their employer—although he was sure she used it frequently out of sight.

"Will you sit with me?" he asked, motioning to a wood and wrought iron bench that sat beneath several larger plantings—plantings that would someday decorate the manor house. He moved toward the bench, hoping she would follow. When he turned, ready to sit, Alaina remained riveted to her original spot. Once more, he motioned to the seat. "Please."

"Are you going to dismiss me?" She tried to sound brave, but her voice wavered.

"No. Why would you think that?"

She scowled. "Are you going to ask me to be your mistress?"

He laughed in shock at the question. "No!" It took him a minute to regain his composure. "Please. Come and sit with me. I simply want to talk to you. I promise, I am not planning anything untoward." He hoped she could hear his sincerity. "I've become rather fond of you." He dropped onto the bench, surprised he'd given voice to such an intimacy. Looking to the ground he continued. "Miss Clarkson, my heart has been..." His eyes misted. What was wrong with him? Swallowing down the unexpected emotion, he went on. "Since Katherine's death, I have only managed to wake every morning because I had a family—my parents, Charlotte, Kenton—who wouldn't let me disappear. I wanted to. I wanted nothing more than to cease to exist. Too much of a coward to act upon it."

She took a step towards him. "That is not cowardice."

He shrugged. "My father deemed it time I fulfill familial duty. I asked Miss Hilton to marry, knowing it was an injustice to her. She deserves better. But now...now I feel I deserve better as well. I will not marry her. I cannot marry her when my heart has been awakened by someone else."

For the first time her expression, her stance, her entire appearance, relaxed. She walked to the bench and took the seat beside him. Shaking her head, she said, "Sir. I appreciate your friendship. But I cannot let you jeopardize your family, your friends, your standing for what can never be." She lowered her eyes, examining her hands.

She spoke the truth, but how could he ignore what his heart yearned for? His eyes rested on the locket that hung about her neck. She wore it faithfully. He'd watched her fidget with it but never asked her. It was a momentary diversion, but one he thought they might need. "Your locket. It's special to you. Tell me about it."

At the mention of the necklace, her hand shot up and grabbed hold of it. In a small voice she said, "It was my mother's. A family heirloom, I believe, although no one ever said so. She wore it day and night. I often saw her when she thought no one was looking, rubbing her fingers over it. I think it reminded her of better times. My father gave it to me a few days before he passed. I wish he'd given it to me sooner. I feel my mother near when I wear it."

"You mentioned one time your parents were from different stations."

"Yes."

"What happened?"

"They were deeply in love. She left her family to be his wife. And all his life he regretted what he took her from. What he could never give her."

"Did your mother regret it?"

She shook her head. "No. At least I don't believe so. But she never talked about her family."

"Are there pictures in the locket?"

"Yes." She looked down and smiled. "An image of my mother and grandmother."

Using a thumbnail, she opened the locket and held it for Phillip to view. He studied the images for a long moment, glancing from the locket to Lainey and back again.

"I see the family resemblance," he said. "I wish I had an image of little Donald. Something to remember him by. His hair was dark, the same as Katherine's. His other features were not so obvious. I often wonder if he would have taken after me." Regret laced his words.

She carefully closed the latch and laid a hand over the locket. He reached out and took her free hand in his. She tensed for a moment, then relaxed, allowing him to be forward with her. He smiled. Maybe she thought it payback for the liberties she'd taken the previous night—whatever her reasons, he wouldn't argue. Her hand was cold, and he wondered if she enjoyed the warmth of his.

"You cannot leave Montrose," he said.

"You cannot make me stay."

He chuckled. "No, I cannot. But," he sighed, "if I could have dreams come true again, I would have you stay...and not as my sister's lady's maid." A bold statement, breaking all the rules of proper behavior. And while he should have been ashamed—his parents would be appalled—he felt nothing but relief at the freedom.

"Dreams," she repeated, her voice wistful. "They are only for sleep. What matters is what happens between sunrise and sunset. That is what makes up our lives. That is what makes us who we are." She turned to him and met his gaze.

Again, she spoke truth, and he knew it. But surely, dreams had a place in a person's life. What was wrong with dreaming of finding love a second time? Why couldn't that be what happened between sunrise and sunset?

"While I can't argue with what you've said, it's a dreary way to fashion a life."

She smiled sadly. "My mother passed when I was twelve. My oldest brother and my father when I was fourteen. And now Robert. I've been in service to the gentry ever since my father passed. I know no other life. I don't perceive a different life in my future—not unless I create it. That is what I meant. Circumstances, as you have said, determine our futures." She sat up a bit taller and pulled her hand from his. "Perhaps I will go to America. With their talk of life, liberty, happiness…certainly there would be a place for me." She rose to her feet. "You have been kind, sir. You offered to help me get to my brother in the Caribbean. Could I be so bold as to impose upon you to a bit more and ask you to help me get to America instead?"

A damp chill moved through him. She would leave. She was determined. He studied her eyes. They held so much emotion. Katherine's had been the same. How could he deny her? But oh, how he wanted her to stay. "If that will make you happy. Perchance we can find someone for you to travel with. Help you get settled. I can make some inquiries."

She curtsied, lingering in the position longer than was customary. "Miss Hilton is indeed lucky to have you. You will ensure her happiness, I am sure."

Phillip rose to his feet. "It is not her happiness I am concerned with."

"Sir, you need to be careful, guard what you say." She lowered her head.

He hooked a finger under her chin, lifting her face to his. Oh, how he wanted to kiss her. Instead, he brushed his thumb along her cheek. He reached down, took her hand and lifted it to his mouth. Her skin against his lips was soft and smelled of rose petals—Charlotte's soap. His eyes rose to hers.

Slowly…ever so slowly, she pulled her hand away. Her eyes were filled with longing—the same longing he felt in his own.

"I should go."

"Stay," he whispered.

She shook her head and hurried toward the door. She stopped only long enough to glance back before bolting.

He could not let her leave. If she insisted on leaving, he would go with her to America. He would be the person she traveled with. He would help her get settled. He would make her his wife. Together they would grab freedom and make it their own.

CHAPTER TWENTY-FIVE

"But now my task is smoothly done:
I can fly, or I can run."
–John Milton

Lainey hadn't been able to concentrate for several days. As she watched Marianne and Charlotte at the piano, her mind kept wandering to the conservatory. The expression in Phillip's eyes as he kissed her hand as if she were his equal—no—more as if she were a princess. She wrapped the favored hand in the other, remembering the warmth of his lips, the heat of his breath brushing lightly across her bare skin. Her hands grew clammy at the mere thought of his touch. She could understand how he could make a woman's dreams come true.

Dreams come true—Ha!—she nearly laughed aloud. Truth was he would marry Miss Hilton. He would start a family with her. He would touch her, kiss her. How would she endure? Even now, her heart ached with the need to catch a glimpse of him about the manor. What would it do to her to stay and be witness to his life with another? With each passing moment she knew…she must leave.

"Did you enjoy that piece, Lainey?" Charlotte stood on the far side of the piano, ready to turn a page for Marianne. "She has improved a great deal, don't you think?"

Lainey's focus shifted to Phillip's sister, working to make sense of the words she spoke. "Oh…yes…very much," Lainey said, hoping her response to be appropriate.

"Do you want to try again?" Charlotte asked Marianne. "Father won't interrupt this time. He's gone into London for a few days."

"Did Phillip go with him?" Marianne asked, saving Lainey from wondering.

"I did not," Phillip said, entering the room. His shoes clipped across the wood floor as he walked toward the piano. Lainey forced herself not to turn and watch his approach. He would notice her growing affection. He would make arguments for her to stay. She could not stay.

"Please continue playing. I did not mean to interrupt."

Charlotte nudged Marianne, who upon Phillip's entry had taken on the appearance of a timid rabbit. She made cursory glances in his direction but couldn't rest her eyes on him for longer than a second. Lainey didn't understand. How could she not want to gaze into his compassionate slate-gray eyes? How could she not admire his regal stature? His confident gait? Lainey sighed.

"Is there…is there a piece you would want me to play?" Marianne's voice carried across the room, despite her reluctance to lift her head when she spoke.

"Surprise me," Phillip said as he sat in the chair next to Lainey. "I enjoy most pieces that Charlotte plays."

"Most?" Charlotte asked, placing hands on hips. "What ones don't you enjoy?"

Phillip shifted in his seat, resting on the arm of the chair, leaning in Lainey's direction. "Those maudlin ones you tend to play. I'd rather hear a tune with a note of promise in it.

Something…happy." He leaned a mite closer until his arm lightly brushed up against Lainey's. She stiffened at the touch. Could Charlotte see what was happening?

"What about Mozart?" Charlotte offered.

"Miss Hilton, you play Mozart?" he asked, not hiding his surprise.

"Not well," she answered, finally looking at the man.

"Nonsense. She's learned to play *The Turkish March* and quite well. Wouldn't you agree, Alaina?"

"Yes," she said, not knowing how well Marianne played any music and too distracted by the warmth of Phillip's arm next to hers to remember.

"Mozart it is," Phillip said, waving a hand to have Marianne begin.

Charlotte helped Marianne discover the piece amidst the pile of music stacked to one side of the keyboard. Lainey didn't move. She should have, she knew that. But the excitement of his arm next to hers felt clandestine. And he smelled of the outdoors, fresh with the scent of pine needles. Should she make conversation? Would Charlotte or Marianne think her impertinent if she did? Unsure, she reached for her locket, worrying the surface with her thumb. Marianne began to play. Lainey recognized the piece—Marianne did play fairly well.

As Charlotte's focus shifted to the music, following so that she might turn a page when needed, Phillip leaned closer.

Without taking his eyes from the performance, he murmured, "She has improved."

"Yes, sir, she has," Lainey replied, also keeping her attention focused straight ahead.

"We have a biography of Amadeus Mozart in the library. Do you think Miss Hilton would want to read it?"

"I cannot say. But it could be a topic that might be of interest to her."

"Would it interest you?"

At that moment, Marianne missed a note and pulled her hands from the keyboard. Her poor hands shook.

"You're doing well," Phillip said. "Please continue." Marianne turned to him, her face lined with worry. This time, she regarded him. At first, her expression reflected her need for his approval. But Lainey saw her eyes narrow and shift between them. For a long moment she studied her fiancé sitting next to Lainey. As if on a spring, her head snapped back to the pages in front of her and she began again to play. Phillip appeared oblivious to the girl's reaction, but Lainey saw it and suspected Marianne didn't approve of what she observed.

"Perhaps you could come to the library, and I could show you the biography," Phillip said once the music again filled the room.

Lainey lowered her head. "That would not be proper."

"Ah, maybe not." Phillip raised a hand to shelter his mouth. "But if you change your mind, I'll be in the library late this evening." He shifted back to the center of his chair to listen to the rest of Marianne's concert. After she finished, Phillip rose to his feet, offered polite applause, and excused himself. As he moved to leave, he clipped the leg of his chair, causing him to lunge forward. He caught himself on the arms of Lainey's chair. Their faces were inches apart. He met her gaze, hesitating long enough for her to notice the hope in his eyes. She shouldn't. She was putting her heart in peril and Marianne seemed more than uneasy. But after hours, she knew she would sneak to the library to get a glimpse of the *Biography of Amadeus Mozart*.

~~*

Lainey stood at the foot of the staircase, gazing down the darkened hallway. She should go back to her room. But she didn't want to disappoint him. She took several tentative steps down the hall, then abruptly turned back toward the stairs and ran halfway up before she stopped herself. With one hand on the railing, her breathing labored, she reconsidered. How many times would she second guess her decision? She wanted to see Phillip. Well, that wasn't all she wanted. She wanted his engagement to Marianne to disappear. She wanted him to consider her to be his wife. She wanted her station in life to be acceptable to him, and to his family so he could realistically marry her. Of course, impossible as all of it may be, it didn't keep her from wishing. She turned about and descended the stairs one more time. At the bottom, she didn't allow herself to stop or think. She pressed on, passing the dining room and the great hall, all the rooms and hallways dark. She should have brought a candle. But there, a little further down the hall, a dim light called to her.

Stopping at the library doorway, she waited. Phillip stood before the floor to ceiling window overlooking the back gardens, his breath leaving a milky film on the glass. Large snowflakes drifted to the ground on the other side in contrast to the room, warm from the brisk fire near Phillip's favorite chair.

He hadn't heard her arrive, too engaged in the snowfall or his own thoughts, Lainey could not tell. She took it as a good sign that he wasn't venting to Katherine, and as an additional sign that she would find him in a pleasant mood.

Biting her lip, she fought the urge to tiptoe into the room, sneak up behind him and wrap her arms about his waist, laying her head gently on his back. He would turn, take her in his arms—kiss her, a forbidden kiss that would have to last them the rest of their lives. When had she developed such fantasies? Her mother would be appalled. Her mother...what would she say to her daughter in a moment such as this? She'd most assuredly advise against it. Lainey lowered her eyes as she considered returning to her room before Phillip knew she had come. An ache of disappointment filled her as she took a step back from the door.

"Miss Clarkson. Alaina," Phillip said.

Too late.

She dipped into a small curtsy. "Sir."

"I was beginning to think you would not come."

"I'm not sure I'm going to stay."

Phillip walked to a nearby bookcase and pulled a volume from the shelf. He flipped through the pages without paying notice to Lainey.

"Is that the Mozart book?" she asked.

"Let me take you to America," he said.

Lainey froze. "What?"

He straightened, set his jaw, and regarded her keenly.

"Let me take you to America," he repeated.

He wasn't drunk this time. In full control of his faculties, he meant what he said.

She shook her head slowly.

"We can go to London, marry there. I can purchase passage to Boston. We can start over. You can start over—pursue some of those dreams you've been neglecting."

"Oh, Phillip." She sank into a straight back chair near the door. Had he noticed she'd barely stepped into the room?

He laid the book on a nearby table and came to her, kneeling in front of her. He probably would have taken her hands, but they were tightly gripping each side of the chair. His hands would be warm, gentle, unlike the solid, rigid edges of her seat.

She met his gaze. His eyes were full of promise and possibilities. But she felt only a deep clutching at her heart—a sense of doom.

"You can't give up everything for me."

"I can! I can. You are worth it."

She shot up from the chair, putting distance between them. "No, Phillip, I am not. I am not worth your family. I am not worth your life of privilege. I am a servant. You would lose all you've ever known. And…someday…you would hate me for it."

He sat back on his heels. "You think I haven't thought of those things?"

"I'm sure you have," she said, her voice reflecting the tenderness and pity she felt for their situation.

"And you don't believe that I think you're worth the sacrifice?"

"You may believe that now, but you won't forever."

Using the chair as leverage, he pushed up to his feet and began pacing about the room. He walked to the fireplace, fiddled with a small statue sitting on the mantle, then once again started about the room, running his hand along the back of chairs, and along tables.

"When I courted Katherine, we often talked of running away. Of going someplace where we weren't confined by station, or money, or family expectations."

"Did you ever discover such a place?"

He scoffed. "America," he said as if she should have assumed the answer. "They were the only people fed up enough with the ways of the Homeland to break from it.

Certainly, they would take in a young couple anxious to make their own life. Isn't that exactly what they did? Fought a war for the exact same ideals?"

"They fought oppression."

"That's what we'd be doing. The oppression of a society that believes people are their station, their class, not their character."

Lainey wrapped her arms tightly around her waist. She wanted to believe him, in his optimism. But her experience in life had taught her such ideas were foolishness.

"We can never escape our birth."

"No!" he said, smacking his hands on a table. "That's exactly the kind of talk that keeps us locked in antiquated ideas."

"Phillip, I am a girl raised in the dregs of London. I have no family. I have nothing to bring to a marriage."

"You have you. That's all I want." He waited for her reply. When she didn't answer, he added, "And I think you want me, too."

She shook her head. "What I want is a dream. It's not the real world."

He tossed his hands in the air. "Is this leading to another lecture on what matters is what happens during daylight?"

"Isn't it? What matters, Phillip, is that you are heir to a wonderful, lovely estate. You are engaged to be married to a sweet, if naïve, young woman..."

"Whom I do not love."

She ignored the comment. "You have responsibilities. Not only to yourself but to your family. To your father and mother. To your sister and brother." When he started to object, she held up her hands to stop him. "Others are affected by your choices. I will not be part of the ruination of your family. They have been too kind to me. For the first time in years, I have a home. Your sister is so kind, so inclusive, she makes me feel I am, in a small way, part of it all. I have Jane and Mary, they are sisters to me. I can't put them in jeopardy for my own selfish reasons. And if you are half the man I think you are, you would not, will not, jeopardize them either."

The room fell quiet. The fire snapped. A wind blew against the window.

"You refuse to even consider what I am offering you," he said, his voice low.

"If I seriously consider it, knowing I can never accept, I will only be torturing myself."

"So, we are to live our lives apart...isn't that torture as well?"

Lainey lowered her head. "There is no good choice for either of us."

Phillip's shoes scuffed on the wood floor as he walked across the room. He reached for the Mozart book, picked it up and handed it out to her.

"Here is the book I told you about, if you wish to read it." The constraints of polite society returned. He stood erect, indifferent, simply offering her a book that might be of interest to her. His declarations of love, marriage, a life together buried where they should be. Lainey surrendered to a sad sigh of relief.

"Thank you, but I don't believe I have time to read at present. A wedding is approaching, and the household is busy preparing. In fact..." She dipped into a curtsey. "I must be returning to my quarters. Much is planned for tomorrow."

He dropped his arm. "Yes, you need your rest."

"Thank you, sir." With one last lingering glimpse, she turned toward the door. Just on the verge of leaving the room, Phillip called to her.

"The offer stands. All you have to do is agree."

She left before she said words she would regret.

CHAPTER TWENTY-SIX

"Every parting gives a foretaste of death;
Every coming together again a foretaste of the resurrection."
–Arthur Schopenhauer

Fortunately for Lainey, she had little time to dwell on her conversation with Phillip. Montrose Manor buzzed with activity. With the wedding a few days away, guests began to arrive. Charlotte spent her time entertaining them and changing dresses constantly depending on the company and the activity. Lainey's head spun trying to keep straight the appropriate attire for garden strolling, riding the grounds, entertaining in the music room, and of course, meals. Charlotte tried to be patient with Lainey's inexperience, teaching her as they went, but emotions were high and Charlotte's normal pleasant, sunny disposition dampened.

Much to Lainey's relief, Miss Hilton had been primarily absent. But that morning all had changed. With the arrival of close friends and family, Marianne and her parents arrived, ready to join the Montgomerys in welcoming visitors and making introductions.

Charlotte insisted that Lainey be a silent, but present witness to new arrivals. Sitting in a corner far from the door, from the fire, and all that made the grand hall feel cozy, Lainey examined her hands as yet another distant member of the Montgomery family arrived. She felt silly sitting in a corner, trying to be inconspicuous. Why Charlotte had been so adamant that Lainey be in attendance puzzled her.

In entertaining guests, Phillip paid her no mind. As it should be. But being as invisible as the furniture sat ill in her stomach and didn't ease her misgivings on how she had left him two nights before. Lainey wished she had some other occupation than to sit and observe—and consider Phillip's proposal. It made for long, lonely hours.

Phillip appeared exceptionally handsome, dressed in a dark cutaway coat with matching trousers, a red brocade waistcoat, and black silk tie. He stood near the fireplace, his hands clasped behind his back. Marianne sat nearby. From what Lainey could detect, they shared little conversation. Phillip concentrated on the guests, offering a slight bow as they came to offer congratulations, and an introduction to Miss Hilton. On another side of the room, Charlotte appeared to be a magnet for the single men in the company. They flocked about her as she twittered and flirted with ease. But Lainey's attention repeatedly returned to Phillip. She kept second guessing her flat refusal of his offer. But how could she allow him to throw his life away? If she loved him, which she truly believed she did, she would never allow him to squander what rightfully belonged to him. But watching him welcome guests into his home, and picturing Marianne as his bride proved more than she could bear.

"Oh, my dearest Phillip."

Lainey's thoughts were interrupted by the new arrival's familiar address. An older woman wrapped her arms around Phillip and took him into a solid embrace while her presumed husband looked on. Phillip's smile was genuine, filled with love and a touch of admiration. Who was she?

"Lady Waller, may I introduce you to Miss Marianne Hilton—my fiancé." Phillip extended his hand toward Marianne. The woman turned and Lainey took notice. "Miss Hilton, may I present to you, Lord and Lady Waller—Katherine's parents." An extraordinary resemblance existed between the portrait in Phillip's room and the woman standing before Miss Hilton. Same smooth chocolate-colored hair, same lovely eyes. Lainey glanced toward Lord Waller—his daughter had inherited his enigmatic smile. Lady Waller graciously extended her hands to Marianne, and helped lift the girl to her feet, examining the woman who would replace her daughter.

"Well, aren't you lovely. Isn't she lovely, Mr. Waller?" She glanced over her shoulder at her husband. He offered a slow, deliberate nod. "Well done, Phillip. Well done." Lady Waller perused Marianne from head to toe.

"It is, indeed, a great pleasure to meet you," Marianne said with a deep curtsy.

"Come, allow these two boring men to droll on about estate affairs." Lady Waller tucked Marianne's hand in the crook of her arm. "Let's go find what refreshment may tempt us." Together, they walked past Lainey on their way to the dining room. Lainey tried to avert her eyes, but as the two women passed, Lady Waller met Lainey's gaze. She stopped for a moment as if she might converse with Lainey, but quickly moved on, chatting amiably with Miss Hilton.

Well, that was curious, Lainey thought. She peeked around the corner, trying to catch where the two women had gone.

"Hal, my good man! You made it!" Phillip's voice drew Lainey's attention back to the parade of people entering the hall. Hal...she'd heard the name before. Yes! Hal! He had helped Phillip discover what happened to Robert. Lainey craned her neck to get a good view of the man.

"How could I miss you ruining your life a second time!" The gentleman in front of Phillip said. He turned enough that Lainey caught his profile. Her stomach rolled. She knew that profile all too well.

Harold. Odious Harold Warrington, with his simpering horse-shaped face.

Her hand shot up and covered her mouth. How could Phillip's beloved friend Hal and Harold Warrington be the same person?

Harold turned to a man standing near, ready to make introductions.

Lainey rose to her feet. "Robert!"

Her brother turned at the sound of his name. Almost everyone in the room turned at Lainey's outburst.

A smile blossomed on Robert's face. He didn't wait to be introduced to Phillip, he started his way across the room, arms open wide. "Lainey!"

Before she could say another word, Robert pulled her into his arms. Lainey wanted to laugh, cry, and scold him all at the same time. Tears spilled onto her cheeks. She pushed herself out of the hug and while crying and laughing, she pushed on his chest. "I thought you were dead!"

"Dead? Where would you get such a notion?"

"Master Montgomery made some inquiries." She glanced toward Phillip and Harold, then turned back to Robert. She grabbed his arms, feeling up and down to make sure he was real. "We received word that you were last seen on a merchant ship that went down in the Atlantic." She focused on his eyes, waiting for an explanation.

"Ah, yes. The *Abernathy*. Shame that was. Lost a profitable cargo. Sugar. Molasses. Rum." He shook his head. "Not to mention the crew. That was utterly a blow."

"You were on that ship."

"No. Well, yes, but only for a short time to collect the manifest. I disembarked before the ship left port."

"Well, well, well," Harold said, stepping up next to Robert, placing a hand on his shoulder. "Your sister."

Lainey worked to ignore the man, instead directing her remarks to her brother. "Why did you not write to me? Tell me where you were, what you were doing?"

"After you left the Bell's I had no address for you. It wasn't till Emma and I returned and met up with…"

"Who's Emma?"

"My wife," he said, as if Lainey should know.

"You're married?"

"Yes," he said. "I married Miss Emma Brown as was. Her father…he owned a shipping company. I met them in Barbados. Mr. Brown, an excellent gentleman, and Mr. Warrington's cousin," he gestured in Harold's direction, "offered me employment after his daughter and I became acquainted. Shortly after we arrived in England I discovered your association with the Warringtons."

"And when was that?"

Robert turned to Harold. "Well, we visited two weeks ago, wasn't it? Emma and I had been previously occupied setting up house and all."

"Small world, isn't it, Clarkson?" Harold said. "Imagine my surprise when I found out that Mr. Clark was your brother."

"Mr. Clark?"

Robert chuckled. "The natives in Barbados got to calling me Clark." He shrugged. "I adopted the name."

"Makes it easier to leave the Navy that way," Harold added.

"You deserted?" she asked.

Before he answered, Phillip appeared on Robert's other side. "Miss Clarkson, is this your brother?"

She curtsied, and with eyes lowered, answered. "Yes, Sir. Master Montgomery, may I present to you, my brother Robert Clarkson…uh, Clark. Robert this is—"

"Yes, yes, we've met." Robert extended his hand. With a lukewarm smile, Phillip shook hands. He turned to Harold.

"Warrington, by golly, you've come through again—as you always do."

Harold smirked. "Did you doubt me?"

"With your last correspondence—I thought for sure this one time you had failed."

"I detest failure." Harold turned to Lainey. "As does Clarkson here."

Lainey was ready to turn and flee when Charlotte appeared. "Is there something amiss?" She asked, coming to stand next to Lainey.

"No, ma'am," Lainey replied, grateful for the young lady's timely arrival. "Happy news. Miss Charlotte Montgomery, may I present my brother, Robert Clark."

Robert had the decency to bow as he was introduced.

Charlotte's face lit in a jubilant smile. "Your brother! Alaina! This is the most amazing of news!" She turned to Robert. "You are not dead."

An uneasy laugh passed through the circle as Robert acknowledged he was most certainly alive.

"Miss Charlotte, may I be excused to have a few moments with my brother?"

"Yes! Yes!" She leaned over and gave Lainey a hug. "If I should need you, I'll send for you." She took Phillip by the arm, shaking it slightly. "Phillip, isn't this delightful? Alaina and her brother reunited?"

"It is. It is very…very fortunate." His tone lacked his sister's enthusiasm. Lainey could only guess as to what he must be thinking.

"Come, Robert, let us go catch up." Her brother lifted his arm to escort her from the room. Before walking away, she glanced back to Phillip. He was not hiding his emotions very well. Concern etched his forehead, and apprehension filled his eyes. She'd have to deal with him later. Presently, she needed to speak with her brother. As much as she tried to tamp down her growing excitement and relief, she couldn't. Robert's sudden resurrection was perfect timing. She had a family. She had a way to leave Montrose. She would not have to witness Phillip's marriage, or wrestle with his offer. God had provided her an alternative. Robert.

~~*

They stepped into the garden room which had been lit for entertainment but remained empty. The vigorous fire in the grate warmed the room. Decorated for the wedding and holiday, pine boughs added a crisp, clean scent to the air, hinting at a new start for Lainey. Once in the room, and away from any prying eyes, she turned to Robert, throwing her arms about his neck.

"It's been forever since I've seen you." She squeezed him before letting him go and stepping back to get a better view. He was the handsome brother she remembered, if a little weathered. That's what would happen out on the sea.

"I cannot get over how you have grown," he said, walking in a circle around her, measuring her from head to toe. "You have grown more beautiful than mother, if that is possible."

Lainey pressed her hands to her cheeks. "You must tell me all about your adventures. The few letters I received piqued my imagination." She moved toward a settee, motioning for Robert to join her. "I planned to come and join you."

Robert sat next to her, taking her hand. "It is best you did not. After I left the navy—"

"Did you really desert?" If that were true, he would not be safe anywhere in England.

He chuckled softly. "I did not. But my leaving was not under the best of circumstances. Let us leave it at that."

"But why? What happened?"

"Really, Lainey. I count those days as incredibly dark. If it had not been for Emma...well, there was Emma. That's all that matters." The tone of his voice, the distant gaze in his eyes told her Robert was no longer only a brother. He was a husband, and his wife held all his allegiance. That's as it should be. Why did it unsettle her?

She examined her hands. "How did you meet Emma?"

"I rescued her dog."

"What?"

His expression filled with affection. "She was on the dock, just arrived with her father. She had this little dog, cute as a button. I saw them the moment they stepped off the boat. Her dog slipped his leash and lost traction, slipped right off the pier. I heard Emma's cries and jumped in."

"In all your clothes?"

"Haha...yes, not one of my brighter ideas. But I succeeded in saving I little Wobford. Emma was so grateful she insisted on repaying my kindness. She invited me to dinner. There I met her father who offered me a position with the Brown and Burrows shipping company. Said he admired a man who would come to a lady's aid. I accepted. Shortly afterwards, I proposed marriage to Emma, and she agreed. We were married and have come back to England to establish residence in Liverpool. I left her there for this trip. She's with child. I didn't want to jeopardize her health."

"Child? Oh, Robert. How magnificent. I cannot wait to meet her."

"Yes. Well, you have a nice situation here, no?"

"I suppose. And you sound as if you are in a prosperous situation."

He lowered his head. "I believe that Emma and I have a bright future in front of us." He raised his head, meeting Lainey eye to eye. "And now that I know you are well situated, I will rest easier."

She licked her lips. "Actually Robert, now that you are here, I was hoping...well wishing...that I might go home with you. I won't be a bother. I can help with the housekeeping and the new baby. It would be temporary...only until I find my way." She studied her hands. "I'm a bit lost at present regarding my future. I need a place to go, a place where I can figure out what to do. I've entertained the idea that I could open a shop and make a success of it with my sewing skills. Liverpool would work nicely." As she considered it, Liverpool could be an exceptional location. "I mean, with the port, it would be easy to import fabrics from all around the world." Her spirits brightened at the idea. But as soon as she saw Robert's expression her hopes withered like autumn leaves on the ground. His frown spoke volumes.

He released a heavy sigh. "Why would you want to leave here?" He waved a hand, taking in the room. "You're a lady's maid...that's only a step under governess. How could you hope for more?"

Lainey sat back, dismayed. "Hope for more? Why shouldn't I hope for more? Why should I settle for service when I have skills that could provide my own way?"

"Dear, Lainey." He laid a hand on top of hers. "Do you recognize how challenging it would be to establish yourself as a seamstress? There are shops on every corner in Liverpool. Your talents are nothing exceptional, nothing that would make you stand out."

"Okay, that might be true. But certainly, I could obtain other employment. I could get a job in one of those shops. How long were you planning to stay at Montrose? I could tell Miss Charlotte that I am leaving with you. She will understand. She knows I've been searching for you."

His mouth twitched as if he were fighting to keep words closed tightly within.

"What is it, Robert?"

"I don't think that will be possible."

"Why not?"

"Well, first of all, I'm leaving this very evening. I promised Emma I would not be gone long, and with this unexpected trip to come see you, I've been gone longer than I anticipated. I only came to discern that you were well. And look at you! You look marvelous." He smiled. "Montrose has treated you well."

"I could leave this evening. I have very little."

He wagged his head back and forth. "Lainey, you don't understand. You wouldn't fit in."

"What do you mean I wouldn't fit in? Fit in where?"

"My home is not in any way similar to what we grew up in."

"I should hope not."

"I have all the servants I need."

She tipped her head to the side, trying to comprehend his meaning. "But I am your sister," she said in a measured tone.

"I don't have a sister."

Immediately she rose to her feet. "What do you mean you don't have a sister? I'm standing right here." She held her arms out.

"Emma knows nothing of you. The Browns believe I am alone in the world. What will they think if I tell them I lied, that I have a sister—a sister in service no less?" Before Lainey could respond, he continued. "They took me under their wing. Made me my own man."

She moved to the window where she could see his reflection instead of facing him. He slowly rose to his feet. "I am to inherit Mr. Brown's shares in the company. He has no sons...except for me. I will not jeopardize that future—not even for you."

She turned on him. "You should not have come. It would have been better to believe you were dead."

"Lainey, come now..." He took a step closer.

"Do you not remember the times I cared for you? Do you not remember the meals I fixed for you, the clothes I mended? Do you not remember how I diverted Father's anger from you when you lost one job after another? I took care of you, and you somehow act as if it were the other way around."

"I don't remember it the way you do. Could it be your privilege here has skewed your memories."

"Privilege! Privilege!? Oh, dear brother...while you were off adventuring with the navy, saving little dogs from imaginary sharks, denying your family, I was scrubbing floors, emptying chamber pots, cleaning up after the privileged. I had to fight off the advances of disgusting men like your friend, Mr. Warrington."

"Yes, yes," he said, "When Mr. Warrington realized who you were, he told me all about that event. How could you? You stole jewelry from his sister, and when he confronted you about the crime, you attacked him? He was certain he would be scarred. It is by the grace of God he is not."

Any hope Lainey had at making a new life of her own became nothing but a stick thrown on the fire that warmed the room. Her brother believed lies. He denied her existence. She wasn't of any more worth to him than one of those sticks.

"I believe it is time for you to leave." She squared her shoulders. "Someday, *Mr. Clark*, we will meet again. But unlike you, I *will* condescend to acknowledge you. I *will* claim our relation. But do not expect more than that."

She could now only hope that Phillip would get her to America, where she would make her mark in the world. She dipped into a perfunctory curtsy and stormed from the room.

Tears that Lainey held at bay in front of Robert now tumbled down her cheeks. As quickly as she could, she made her way to the servant's staircase, dodging her way about lest anyone notice her in such a state. Her whole body ached at Robert's betrayal. What an ungrateful, selfish prig he had become. To think of all the times she had cared for him, almost as a mum to him! She washed his clothes. Cooked his meals. How could he never find it in his heart to mention her to his bride and her family? How self-seeking could he be?

Hurrying to get to her room, Lainey rounded the landing on the second floor and ran straight into a woman. The lady grabbed Lainey by the arms, steadying them both. Mortified, Lainey took a quick step back, wiping at her cheeks and offering an apologetic curtsy all in one motion.

"Pardon me, ma'am. I wasn't watching." She remained in the curtsy, hoping for leniency from the stranger.

"No, no. It was my fault. I'm afraid I'm a bit turned around. I've forgotten how large this home is."

Realizing she was not going to be reprimanded, Lainey wiped any telltale tears from her face and straightened up.

"Oh," the woman said, "You're the young girl I saw in the great room. Charlotte's maid, someone said."

"Yes, ma'am."

"Are you all right. Have you've been crying?"

"I'm fine, ma'am."

The woman waved a hand toward the family bedrooms. "I was looking for Mr. Phillip's room. I long to view my daughter's portrait. The one he has is by far the finest there is."

"It is a lovely portrait," Lainey agreed, again noticing the family resemblance—the large dark copper-colored eyes, the shining chocolate hair.

"It is, isn't it." The lady smiled. "There is so much of my daughter's personality in that portrait. I wanted to gaze upon it and remember." Her smile turned sad. "But here I am...lost."

"I can show you where it is." Lainey extended an arm to direct the woman, but the lady's attention became fixed on Lainey, right below her chin.

"Your necklace...it's lovely. Do you mind?" She reached out not waiting for Lainey to give permission.

An odd request. No one ever paid much attention to Lainey's locket. Only Phillip had ever asked to see it. And while she didn't really want to let the woman that close, she had been kind and Lainey didn't know how to say "no."

"Of course."

The woman held the locket and opened it for inspection. "This is a lovely Celtic design, is it not?"

"Yes, Ma'am."

"Where did you get it?" She snapped the locket shut but did not release it.

"It was my mother's. My father gave it to me before he passed."

"What's your name, dear?" The woman gently laid the locket against Lainey's dress. She could feel the warmth of it through the thin fabric.

"Alaina. Alaina Clarkson."

"I am Lady Waller. Lady Katherine Montgomery's mother. But you must have already deduced that."

Lainey dipped into a small curtsey. "Yes, ma'am."

"Where is your mother now?"

"My mother passed when I was twelve years old." Lainey swallowed. Somehow mentioning her mother brought back the awful conversation she'd had with Robert. The traitor. Lainey blinked back a fresh round of tears—this time not sure if they were tears of anger or hurt.

"You must miss her." Lady Waller reached out and wiped a tear from Lainey's cheek. Lainey took a tentative step back.

"Yes, ma'am."

"What was her name?"

"Rebecca." This was the strangest conversation Lainey had ever had with the gentry. And she didn't really know if she could trust this woman. She seemed kind enough. She appeared genuinely interested. But Lainey had run into that sort before. Before she knew it, she would be stabbed in the back.

The woman nodded. She turned and gazed down the long, open hallway that led to the family's rooms. "You said you could show me to young Mr. Montgomery's room?"

Lainey curtsied. "Yes, ma'am." She walked down the hallway, Lady Waller a few steps behind her. "His chambers are on the right, the door that's open. You can see light coming from the windows."

"Thank you, my dear. I really am anxious to view the portrait. You've been most kind."

"It was my pleasure, your ladyship."

With a wan smile, the woman turned and walked to Phillip's room, without glancing back before she entered. The encounter had proved a momentary distraction for Lainey. The sting of Robert's conversation had worn off a bit. She glanced at the clock standing in the hall. Time had come for Charlotte to change for dinner. Best for Lainey to return to her duties. She wiped her hands across her face one more time, dried them off on her skirts, and with a deep sigh, she headed toward Charlotte's chambers to select her a gown for the meal.

CHAPTER TWENTY-SEVEN

*"This is the night that either makes me
Or fordoes me quite"*
–William Shakespeare

From her perch at the window in Charlotte's room, Lainey saw Robert say goodbye to both Phillip and Harold. Good riddance. With any luck, he'd never have another good night's sleep. He didn't deserve one. She clutched at the collar of her blouse, the thought making her ache. What was worse? Thinking her brother dead, or his acting as if she were? She let out a sad sigh and turned from the window. Charlotte's room was a mess. The girls, Charlotte and Marianne, had bustled into the room with barely thirty minutes to prepare for the evening meal. Lainey had helped them both change into evening dress, put their hair up with jeweled pins, and freshened their makeup. At the end of the whirlwind of activity, Charlotte gave Lainey a hug.

"You're a marvel," she'd said, then took Marianne by the arm and together they hurried from the room.

Lainey smiled. The hug reminded her that she did have a home, a family. People were fond of her. Some would be sad to see her leave. Lainey picked up a chemise, giving it a quick snap to remove wrinkles. She'd learned a lot since arriving at Montrose a few short months ago. She hadn't batted an eye when it came time to redo the ladies' hair. A skill she had no experience with when she arrived. And makeup? There wasn't much to adding a bit of rouge to their cheeks and painting their lips a luscious rosy red. Except...except when she thought about Phillip kissing Marianne's luscious red lips. Lainey grabbed Marianne's dress from off the bed. Not as fine as Miss Charlotte's clothing, but it was a far cry, with silk and lace and delicate buttons, from Lainey's black wool skirt and cotton blouse. Holding Marianne's day dress up, Lainey stood in front of the framed mirror that adorned the corner of Charlotte's room. How would it feel to wear a dress made of such fine fabric, in such rich colors? The maroon in the dress made Lainey's amber colored eyes deepen in color—burning embers, she thought. But was it the color of the dress or the events of the day that gave her eyes the tormented color. If she wore dresses such as this, would Robert have been so quick to distance himself from her? Would he have considered her beneath his new family? If she had her own shop, she could make dresses this fine, or finer. Men like Robert wouldn't be able to so quickly dismiss her.

The door banging on the wall behind her made Lainey jump. She turned, expecting to find Miss Marianne or Miss Charlotte in the doorway needing some assistance. But it was neither. Lainey let the dress fall from before her. Harold Warrington leaned against the door jamb, his expression his usual glib smile.

Lainey worked to keep her expression neutral. She didn't want to reveal her deep need to flee. "Mr. Warrington. Is there something I can help you with?"

His mouth crooked up in the corner. "Your brother left without you." His comment held no sympathy.

"Yes, sir." How she hated having to address the man in polite terms. "He was expected at home."

"Were you surprised to discover he was married, and heir to a fortune?"

"I could not be happier for him."

"Imagine my surprise when I learned that Mr. Clark was indeed your brother. And that all this time, I'd been searching for the brother of an insignificant trollop! Phillip was not forthcoming in his motive for discovering the location of Robert Clark."

Picking up Marianne's dress, Lainey moved to the bed, retrieving a silk covered hanger that had been tossed aside earlier. Trying to act casually, she worked at hanging the dress. "Master Phillip has been kind in assisting me."

"You should have told me you wanted to locate your brother. I would have happily accommodated your request."

"Until I left Harlsburg Manor, I did not know I wanted to find him." She took the dress into the large walk-in closet. Her first mistake. When she turned to leave, Harold was in the doorway.

"And for Phillip's favor...what favors are you giving in return?"

Her bottom lip quivered. "Mr. Montgomery is a gentleman. He would not assume to take advantage of a woman in a quest to locate her family."

Harold snickered. "Mr. Montgomery is a man. He's not granting favors for free."

Lainey took a step back. "You are mistaken. Mr. Montgomery has required nothing from me, nor have I offered anything."

"Really." Harold's eyes lit with malice. "Well, I am not so philanthropic. I do require compensation for my efforts."

With each deliberate step he took in her direction, Lainey's heart beat harder and faster. She scanned the small dressing area for a way to protect herself. She'd fought him off once, she could do it again. "Keep your distance," she said, hoping the words would carry some power. Instead, her voice wobbled, her fear evident by the evil smile that widened on Harold's mouth. If the devil had a face, it would match that of Harold Warrington. She took one step back for each step he took forward until she bumped up into a wall. How could she get out of this? Her eyes darted about as he drew closer.

"The Montgomery family will not take kindly to assaults upon their staff. You'll be sent from the house." Ready to strike him with one hand, she used the other to search the nearby area for a weapon.

He laughed. "Wait until I tell them about the thief they brought into their home." Within inches of her, and before she had time to react, he grabbed her by both wrists, lifting and pinning them against the wall. He leaned his body into hers. She turned her face wanting to avoid the sickening smell of whiskey on his breath. "Your brother was appalled at your behavior. Never expected that of you. Imagine what the Montgomerys will think. Proper Lady Montgomery exposing her home and family to such trash." He leaned in, kissing her neck, dragging his tongue along her jaw toward her mouth. She fought back the urge to vomit.

Struggling to get her hands free, she turned her face further away and pressed back on the wall. "Please, let…"

"Are you begging for me now?" He moved quickly, planting his mouth over hers. She gagged, then acted on the only idea she could think of. She stomped her foot atop his boot. The move caught him by surprise, ending the kiss. He moved enough to free her leg, and when he did, she brought her knee up between his legs with all the might she possessed. She watched in horrified satisfaction as he doubled over and dropped to his knees.

She scrabbled past him, barely escaping as he reached out to grab her skirt. "Slut," he cursed.

Stepping out from the closet, Lainey was shocked to find Charlotte standing in the doorway. "Miss Charlotte." Lainey glanced about the room and its upheaval. "Are you already turning in?"

"No," she replied, a confused muted expression on her face. "I came up to..." Before she finished her thought, her eyes grew wide, her mouth dropping open. "Mr. Warrington?"

Not totally recovered, he propped himself on the closet frame. "Miss Charlotte. Sorry to upset you, but I believe I've been put upon by your maid. I need to speak with Lady Montgomery." His movements were not nearly as smooth as they'd been before, but he handled walking past Lainey and bumping her harshly with his shoulder as he exited the room.

Charlotte watched him leave. She turned back to Lainey, her eyes and mouth open in awe. "Alaina, what have you been doing?"

~~*

At last, the day ended. Standing next to Miss Hilton, Phillip choked out the word "fiancé" with each introduction, an ordeal Phillip could barely tolerate. The darkness outside reflected exactly how he felt. Grabbing a glass and decanter, he moved to his favorite chair near the fire. He poured a healthy portion of whiskey, stoked the fire, and took his seat. He slung back a drink and released a long sigh.

Alaina had sat in the parlor's corner nearly the entire time...that was until her brother appeared. The light in her eyes at the sight of him had been Phillip's only joy the entire day. Good old Hal, bringing Robert Clarkson to Montrose. Despite his ways, Hal had proven to be a good friend. Phillip smiled.

"I think that's the first pleasant expression I've seen on your face all day." Hal walked into the room and immediately took the seat opposite Phillip near the fire. "Most of the day you acted as if you were drinking vinegar. If I were Miss Hilton, I'd be having second thoughts about hitching my horse to your carriage."

"If you were Miss Hilton, you would be less jaded to the idea of marriage."

"Not true. If I were Miss Hilton, I would embrace the role of mistress. I'd find a handsome, wealthy ne'er-do-well—"

"Such as yourself." Phillip took another drink.

Hal raised a hand to his chest and bowed. "As I was saying, find such a man and live off his assets while enjoying the freedom to live life on my own terms." He smiled. "I'll take her off your hands. She is not hard to look at."

Phillip chuckled. "I may not love her, but I cannot condemn her to a life with you."

"You really underestimate how well I treat my mistresses, Phillip. I cannot comprehend why we remain friends."

"You amuse me."

"Ha! Tis true, I am sure." Hal leaned forward. "In all seriousness, my friend. You are doomed to marriage, to be sure, but you do not have to be unhappy. Take a mistress, all the best in society do."

Phillip rose from his chair to retrieve his friend a glass. Hal never disappointed him. The man was consistently straightforward and loose in his morals. He never understood what Phillip had with Katherine, why Phillip couldn't settle for a loveless marriage even with a mistress.

"You do recognize that true gentlemen love their mistresses," Hal said. Phillip poured him a drink. "I'm not totally dismissing your romantic notions."

"No," Phillip said. "Simply dismissing everything decent in gentlemen."

Hal tossed back a slug of the whiskey and laughed. "Decency is in the eye of the beholder."

Phillip returned to his chair, stretching his legs out long before him, and loosening his cravat. Memories of Alaina's unexpected kiss tugged at his heart. If only she hadn't run away.

"So, what will you do?" Hal asked, bringing Phillip out of thought.

"About what?"

"This marriage? Being this unhappy, you certainly cannot go through with it."

"I have no choice."

"Bah! There are always choices. If I can't persuade you to take on a 'friend'—does that term sit better on your pallet?"

"Not really."

"You must find a way out. I cannot bear to know you are so unhappily yoked. As much as your marriage to Katherine saddened me, that you would saddle yourself with a wife, not that Katherine wasn't a lovely wife, I will admit that I'd never seen you happier or more content. You deserve at least a similar situation."

"I thought about America."

Hal, in mid-sip, sputtered. "What? America? That's a bit drastic don't you think?"

Phillip shrugged. "It sounded a viable alternative to marrying Miss Hilton. Before you brought Miss Clarkson's brother—thank you for that, by the way—I thought I might escort her to America. Help her establish herself there." Phillip stared into his cup, swishing the contents about. "But she will not allow it."

"Really. That's a bit of a surprise."

Hal's voice had lost its usual merriment. When Phillip looked to his friend to detect what brought about such a change, he found Hal staring at him with…what? Was that disgust in his eyes? In his slightly turned up nose?

"Why? What's the matter?"

Hal stared at his drink, and after a moment took a long swig. "I wish you had told me that your favor was on behalf of Clarkson."

"You know her?"

Hal met Phillip's gaze. "The little chit didn't tell you she worked at Harlsburg Manor?"

"No."

Hal studied Phillip for a long moment. Slowly, his head began to shake. "You haven't developed some sympathies for the trollop."

"Don't talk about her like that."

Hal threw himself back in his chair. "Oh Phillip! You can't be serious. She's a servant. She's the kind you take as a mistress and there's no obligation to set them up. She's beneath you. Even her brother has deserted her."

"What? Why?"

"There are things you don't know. Things about her time at Harlsburg. I wouldn't be a good friend if I did not warn you."

As the story unfolded, Phillip found it challenging to believe Hal was talking about the same girl. And yet…some of that behavior he'd seen firsthand and dismissed. Or had he simply been bamboozled by a clever girl who could spin a sad yarn. No. He knew her. She was nothing like the person Hal described. She must have changed. Unless. Unless her refusal to have Phillip accompany her to America was more in keeping with the girl Hal described, and Phillip was simply being duped. Believing that she loved him. Believing that she wouldn't allow him to travel with her because she truly cared about his well-being, his future as much as her own. Was he so lost in grief that he couldn't detect a woman playing him for his wealth? Hal's words rang in his head, but his heart would not let go…in the same way it refused to let go of Katherine.

~~*

The night was long, longer than Lainey could remember. The expression on Charlotte's face when Harold had walked out of the closet haunted her dreams. Nothing had been said, but as Lainey helped Charlotte dress for bed, the girl kept throwing furtive glances at Lainey. No matter how friendly and inclusive Charlotte had been, Harold Warrington ruined it. He reminded Charlotte there was no room in her life for Lainey as anything more than a servant. An ache left Lainey feeling cheated, small, and most especially—alone.

She was no longer safe. Harold would spin his lies with just the right amount of truth to make Lady Montgomery believe Lainey unfit to serve at Montrose. And it could be she was. She had let herself become too comfortable, duped into believing she was more than a servant.

With every creak of a floorboard, every moan of wind, she'd awakened sure that someone had come to get her—to take her to meet her fate. By the time the household started to stir, Lainey was exhausted—physically and emotionally. How would she face the day? History would certainly repeat itself, when she'd stand before the lady of the house and answer for crimes never committed.

Throwing back a blanket and placing her feet on the cold floor reminded her that winter had arrived. Not only would she face the humiliation of dismissal but be turned out in the cold with no prospects. Her brother wouldn't assist her—the coward. It seemed at every turn, her life spiraled into a pit too deep to escape.

As she dressed, she rehearsed possible explanations. Would anyone really believe her if she told the truth? If she ratted on Harold Warrington, calling him a scoundrel? Of course, as a servant, she wouldn't be given any credibility. The same thing happened when Charlotte had been ill. If she had suggested that Lady Montgomery not allow the doctor to bleed Charlotte, no one would have listened. Who knows what kind of shape the girl would be in, presently. She knew she had to have Phillip make the suggestion.

Phillip.

He would not abandon her. He offered to sail off to America with her. Willing to give up this house, these lands, all of it for her. Could it be she was not alone? Could it be she had one friend she could count on?

As the morning wore on, and nothing materialized, Lainey became more guarded. She had expected to be called into Lady Montgomery's quarters at first light. Now it was past the midday meal, and not a word had been said. Charlotte chatted all through her dressing, but there had been a distance that had not been there before. Lainey told herself that her relationship with Charlotte would recover after Harold left. Jane and Mary had not behaved any differently, but perhaps they knew nothing of the night before.

It was just like Harold to spring on her—part of his game. Bringing Robert here—fed full of lies. Together they had probably laughed, and all the while, Harold planned his treachery. At Harlsburg, the odious man had planned and schemed to get her dismissed. No doubt hoping she would grovel for mercy at his feet, offering whatever he desired in order to stay. She had shown him.

In the music room, Charlotte helped prepare Marianne for a small recital to help show off her improved talents. As Lainey hurried down the hallway to join them, preoccupied by the endless loop of injustices and how to avenge them, Mr. Hollingsworth stepped out of the library.

"Clarkson."

Lainey had already passed the door, but at the sound of her name, she slowed her step. Deep in her gut, a hole opened allowing all hope and courage to drain away. Hollow, and with a shiver, she turned.

"Mr. Hollingsworth." She curtsied.

"Lady Montgomery wishes to see you in the library."

Lainey's lower lip quivered. "Yes, sir. Of course, sir. I was on my way to help Miss Charlotte. May I inform her of my delay?"

"I will send someone to tell Miss Charlotte that you are in conversation with her mother."

"Of course. Thank you, sir." With head lowered, Lainey retraced the few steps to the library. The sound of each footfall rang in her ears, the echo of every time her life had failed her. No one would come to her defense now. Well, except maybe Phillip. But she had seen no sign of him.

As she entered the room that she'd spent so much time in with Phillip, the sheer number of people gathered surprised her. She scanned the room. Mrs. Hollingsworth, joined by her husband, stood at attention in a far corner. Lady Montgomery sat in a chair near the fire. Mrs. Hilton sat across from her. Harold, across the room, stood next to a bookshelf, his arm casually propped up on a shelf, a drink in hand. Kenton slouched in another armchair, as if the business at hand bored him. And Phillip. He stood with his hands clasped behind his back, gazing out the window. Lainey tried not to focus on him, but he appeared to be the only ally in the room. Glancing from him to Lady Montgomery and back, Lainey squared her shoulders and readied herself for the onslaught.

"Miss Clarkson," Lady Montgomery began, "I've been given some rather shocking information regarding you." The woman paused as if Lainey should make some kind of reply. Without knowing the accusation, she remained silent. "I acted against my better judgement taking in an employee without references. The good Reverend sounded so pleased with your help at the rectory, and after Charlotte's pleading, I accepted you into our household. If I had known that you had come from Harlsburg and the reason for your lack of references, you would never have been allowed to ingratiate yourself as you have." She raised a handkerchief to the corner of her eye as if dabbing a tear. "You held such promise, so attentive to Charlotte when she became ill. And dear Charlotte, why, you've worked your deviousness upon her and now she's especially attached. She will be devastated when she hears of your treachery."

Lainey glanced about the room. Treachery? What lies had Harold conjured up this time? He only smirked at her. Phillip remained focused on the view outside of the house.

"I could not believe it when Master Harold told me of your shenanigans at Harlsburg. How you pursued him, trying to set yourself up with a wealthy benefactor. And when he wouldn't give in to your seductions, you stooped to stealing jewels from Miss Lucinda. And now…now you have tried to take advantage of our poor Phillip in the same manner."

"That's not true," Lainey burst out, taking a step forward. She glanced at Phillip, whose head was lowered.

"Miss Marianne saw it. She's a clever girl. She told her mother a day ago that she thought you had ensnared Phillip with your wiles. And after a lengthy conversation with Master Phillip this morning, he has confessed to plans of leaving Miss Marianne behind and taking you to America. How could you betray our trust in such a way? To bring ruin on our family?"

She would not cry. She would not give Harold the satisfaction. Instead, she turned her attentions to Phillip. His refusal to face her screamed of his betrayal. How could he? As her eyes bore into him, she wished he would turn around. Wished he would face her. All his proclamations of love, all his tenderness was what? A ruse? Had his friendship with Harold overshadowed his professed love?

Plainly, she was being dismissed. In fact, as Lady Montgomery spoke the words, Lainey was too enraged to hear any of it. She refused to walk away quietly. She refused to let Harold Warrington have the last laugh. And she would not let Phillip desert her as every other man had in her life. Without thinking of decorum, she crossed the room and stood in front of Harold.

She didn't know if he saw it in her eyes, or discerned the determination of her step, but when she stopped in front of him, he straightened, leaving his drink on the bookshelf. She didn't care how tall he was. She didn't care that everyone in the room believed him to be a man of honor. She knew differently and this was her chance to say so.

With rage and indignation leading her, she reached up and smacked him across his smug face. The sound of it, a cannonball passing through the threshold of the mansion.

"You," she said. "You loathsome creature. You are the devil himself with your lies and twisted truths." From the corner of her eye, she saw Phillip turn.

"You go about trying to take advantage of women—" she turned back to Lady Montgomery. "Did he tell you that? Did he tell you how many times I had to fight off his advances? And when I'd done it one too many times, he made sure I was dismissed without references." She whipped around to Harold, pushing his shoulder. He fell into the bookshelf. "Did he tell you how he cornered me in Miss Charlotte's closet last night, again trying to satisfy his devilish lusts?"

She moved into the middle of the room. Kenton, who had nearly dozed off while his mother prattled on, sat erect and attentive, like everyone else, stunned into silence.

"I have done nothing—nothing—to deserve such vicious tales to be told about me. All I am guilty of is trying to earn a living, trying to locate my family, which you..." she pointed her finger at Harold. "...you turned against me." Your day will come. Someday, someone will treat you as you have treated me and who knows how many other innocent young women. May your heart be ripped out and fed to wild dogs, because you yourself are lower than a dog."

Her eyes met Phillip's and for the first time since entering the room, she felt the bitter sting of tears. She couldn't uncover words to say to him. His betrayal hurt most of all. How could he corroborate Harold's lies? Her mouth trembled. She shook her head.

"I will go pack my belongings." She turned and stormed from the room.

CHAPTER TWENTY-EIGHT

"We know how to speak many falsehoods which resemble real things, but we know, when we will, how to speak true things."
–Hesiod

Lainey fled into the hallway, her heart broken, tears streaming down her cheeks. Was there no one who she could count on? No one who in the end wouldn't abandon her? Jane. Mary. They would stand by her. But what good could they do her now? As she continued down the hallway toward the servant's staircase, she slowed her pace, taking in all that she had learned to love about Montrose Manor. The uneven feel of the slate floor beneath her feet. The sweet smell of honey and polish. The chill in the hall, except when she passed a room where a fire blazed.

She stopped at the foot of the turned staircase. One side led upward, the other down to the kitchen and servant's dining. The faint hint of roast and parsnips and potatoes wafted from below, along with the murmur of kitchen staff and others. Her lip quivered. She would miss Cook's pastries. She would miss the chatter and gossip among the other servants. She would miss Mr. Hollingsworth's stern rebukes, although she found the thought absurd. This place had become home. And now she was being banished. She had no home. No family anymore.

"Alaina!"

Lainey turned to the sound of her name, startled to find Lady Waller approaching.

"My dear, you are crying. What has happened?"

Lainey worked her mouth as she tried to form words that wouldn't land her in uncontrollable tears.

"I'm…I'm afraid." She wiped at her cheeks and squared her shoulders. She would not let anyone see her humiliation. "I believe I have to leave Montrose Manor."

"Why?"

Couldn't the woman leave well enough alone? What was it to her if Lainey left?

"I cannot work where I am not trusted." And that was true. If the Montgomery family didn't trust her, she would never be comfortable. If Lady Montgomery came at that exact moment and apologized, Lainey would invariably anticipate another accusation to surface and resurrect past insinuations.

Lady Waller tilted her head and perused Lainey for a long moment. "I suspect you feel you have been unjustly treated."

"It is not a perception, your Ladyship."

Again, Lady Waller examined Lainey, this time from head to toe. "Yes," she said. "You are very much like her—your mother would never bend to injustice."

"Excuse me?"

"Come, I want to have a talk with you." She took Lainey gently by the arm. "Do you know of a place where we might have some privacy?"

Lainey knew she was staring at the woman, and that was most improper. But what could this woman have to say...why did she talk as if she knew her mother? Lainey blinked.

"I believe there is no one in the morning room this time of day."

"Perfect. I know where that is."

With a smile, she led Lainey down the hall and into one of Lainey's favorite rooms. The bayed windows stretched from floor to ceiling, revealing the lawn and a part of the gardens covered with a light layer of frost. Lainey shivered. The fire had been banked, making the room chillier than usual.

"Please, sit," Lady Waller said as she pulled a chair away from the table. Pulling up another chair, she sat across from Lainey. "I thought you might want to see this." She reached into her pocket and pulled out a pendant on a silver chain. No. It wasn't a pendant. It was a locket. Lainey reached up, taking hold of her own.

"Here." Lady Waller placed the locket in Lainey's free hand letting the chain drop from the edge.

Lainey's eyes widened. "This is exactly like mine."

"Yes, it is. Open it."

With trembling hands, Lainey popped the locket open. Her mouth opened. "How did you...where did you?" She raised her eyes to Lady Waller's. The woman had a knowing smile and a sparkle in her expression.

Pointing to one of the photographs, Lady Waller said, "This is a likeness of me, when I was eighteen years old, right before I married Lord Waller. This." She pointed to the other picture. "This is my sister, Rebecca. Rebecca Mary Drake. When she was seventeen, my father arranged a marriage for her with a Mr. Andrew Frum. He was the second son of a baron, a reasonably attractive man, but Becca did not love him. She'd fallen for a young stable hand, also a handsome young man, but one whom our father would never approve of. His name was William, William Clarkson."

Lainey slowly sank back into her chair. "Are you telling me...?"

"I believe, dear, that you are my niece."

Lainey glanced down at the open locket in her hand and the likeness of her mother. She was younger than Lainey remembered. But it was definitely her mother. She laid a hand across her lower neck as her breathing became erratic.

"Did they tell you the story?" Lady Waller asked.

"No, not really," Lainey said with a shake of her head. "My father mentioned he was not suited to her, he was beneath her. But they loved each other and married against family wishes." She lowered her head. "He told me he regretted it, because he could never provide her the life she deserved."

Lady Waller reached out, laying a gentle hand on Lainey's wrist. "I knew your father. William. He was a good man. He had a pure heart. I'm sure that he did feel inadequate at times. But he loved Becca, and she loved him." She pulled her hand back. "But as you say, they married without family permission. They went to Scotland to do it. Father was furious beyond reason. He removed Becca from his will. She received no dowry. And he forbade us to talk of her. He removed all of her pictures. I never knew where he stored them. And I was devastated."

Lainey sat up straighter to listen to the rest of the story.

Lady Waller smiled sadly. "Becca was my only sister. We were close. For a time, I was angry with her as well. Mad that she took off as she did, never confiding in me. I came to realize that she did that for my protection. Father would have sent me off to a convent." She laughed. "And we're not Catholic!"

Lainey broke into a laugh as well. But this time fighting tears, for a different reason. She blinked rapidly. "We're family," she whispered.

Lady Waller's eyes filled with moisture. "We are." She paused before taking Lainey by both hands. "And…since you feel you must leave Montrose, I wish to offer to take you home with us."

"What?"

"My sister's daughter needs to be treated as the young lady she is. I want you to come live with Lord Waller and me. We've discussed this. He is quite in agreement."

Lainey was speechless. How had this happened? Could it be true? She had a family to go home to? A family she didn't know. But a family, nonetheless. Robert crossed her mind, and she wanted to laugh. What would he think when he found out their true heritage?

"Oh," Lainey said, remembering that she had been dismissed and ordered to leave immediately. "I'm afraid that…well, I wasn't completely honest earlier. I didn't decide to leave Montrose. I was dismissed. On false charges I assure you," she added quickly. "I must leave now. I was on my way to collect my belongings when you found me. I have nowhere to stay until the wedding is over."

"I see." Lady Waller gazed about the room. "I guess I will have to offer my apologies, and we will leave immediately as well. I'm sure that Lady Montgomery will understand. Phillip might be distressed at our leaving. But I'm not sure I really wanted to witness this wedding as it is. Phillip does not give the impression that he is at all enamored with the girl. I suspect Lord Montgomery has put some pressure on the boy and he is marrying out of duty. What say you?"

Lainey smiled. "I say you are a perceptive woman."

~~*

Phillip swallowed. What had he done? Alaina had turned to him, he saw it, he saw the anguish in her eyes, and he had said nothing. He had let her walk out without so much as a sympathetic nod. What a coward he was! He let Hal turn him against her…Hal who he knew to be a womanizer and cad of the worst kind.

He glanced about the room. It was in chaos. Mr. and Mrs. Hollingsworth had slipped from the room shortly after Alaina left. Kenton was laughing. Laughing! What was that about? Phillip's mother and Mrs. Hilton were discussing Alaina's accusations toward Hal, loudly talking of the girl's hysteria and delusions.

"She's definitely given to fits. It's good that you are rid of her," Mrs. Hilton said. "One can't be too careful in whom they employ."

Hal had the decency to keep his head low, but Phillip noticed a subtle smirk across his friend's face.

Charlotte burst into the room, scanned it quickly, as she approached her mother. "What have you done?"

"Now Charlotte, you don't realize…"

"You're sending Alaina away?"

"It's for the best."

"She's my maid. I should have a say in whether she is dismissed."

"You're too young to deal with such delicate matters. For your brother's sake…"

Charlotte turned on Phillip. "Why couldn't you leave her alone? She was my maid. If you'd just marry Marianne, this wouldn't have happened."

"Charlotte," Lady Montgomery scolded. "Your brother is not at fault. Clarkson was playing tricks on poor Phillip."

"Please don't call me that," Phillip said, but not loud enough for anyone to pay attention.

"She took advantage of your poor brother's grief-stricken heart all to secure a wealthy benefactor. She tried to lure him to America!" She raised a hand to her heart as if Phillip had barely escaped the worst of fates.

"Mother," Phillip said sternly, "That is not…"

"If it weren't for dear Harold enlightening me to what was happening, it might have been too late," Lady Montgomery said, ignoring Phillip's attempt to speak.

"She's my maid!" Charlotte stomped her foot.

"Charlotte. That's enough. What's done is done and we're all better off for it."

"Are we?" Phillip said.

A light knock came on the door and Lady Waller walked into the room. For the first time since Alaina had walked out, the room fell into silence. The fire popped. The wind rattled a window. Phillip released a defeated sigh.

"Excuse me," Lady Waller said. "I hope I wasn't too presumptuous in entering without permission. There was so much chatter going on, I wasn't sure my knock was heard."

"Oh my, Lady Waller," Phillip's mother said, rising to her feet and welcoming the unexpected guest with open arms. "We've had a bit of a trying morning. But having you here, and the upcoming wedding, reminds me of all we have been blessed with."

The women joined hands and kissed each other's cheeks. Phillip watched, amazed at how quickly his mother could regain composure when a guest entered a room. With everyone returning to respectable behavior, now would be the time for him to speak his peace.

"I hope you will understand," Lady Waller said, "But I must offer my apologies. Lord Waller and I will not be able to stay for the wedding."

Phillip took a step forward. "You're not?"

"Oh, dear Phillip," she said. "I'm so sorry. But we have a family matter to take care of."

"Certainly, it can wait one more day," Lady Montgomery said. "The wedding is to be tomorrow."

"I'm afraid it cannot. You see…" the woman gazed about the room, meeting each person eye to eye, landing lastly on Harold. "The most unusual incident has occurred. I have discovered, here in your home, my long-lost niece."

"What?" Lady Montgomery raised a hand to her mouth.

"And it appears she has nowhere to stay, so we must take her home—immediately."

While everyone in the room appeared stunned, confused, Phillip's mind spun. Her eyes. The connection he felt with her from the beginning. Alaina. Alaina was the long-lost niece. Katherine's cousin.

"I don't understand," Lady Montgomery said. "Your niece? Here in my home?"

"Yes," Lady Waller said. "And I believe she has been dealt with unfairly." She turned a pointed gaze to Harold—the disgust Phillip felt for his friend reflected in her expression.

He saw the moment his mother put the pieces together. "Oh dear," she said.

"So, as you can understand, we need to depart this afternoon. Thank you so much for your hospitality. I'm sorry that we cannot stay, but given the circumstances, I am sure you appreciate our reason for leaving."

"Yes, yes of course."

"What? What's going on?" Charlotte asked.

"Your maid," Kenton said.

"What about her?"

"Alaina is Lady Waller's niece," Phillip said. He didn't know whether to be thrilled or to be mortified.

"Really?" Charlotte said. "How did she end up being a maid?"

Lady Waller smiled and patted Charlotte on the arm. "I will one day explain that to you. But for now, I need to take Alaina home. I'm so sorry to deprive you of her company. She says you have been a good friend."

Tears welled in Charlotte's eyes. "She's been the best maid I've ever had."

"In all seventeen years of your life," Kenton snickered.

"She doesn't deserve to be a maid, Charlotte," Phillip said. "Don't you understand that? She's Katherine's cousin." His eyes met with Lady Waller. "She should be treated as such."

Lady Waller agreed. "She should. Now if you'll please excuse me, I need to arrange for our departure."

"Please inform me if there is anything you need," Phillip's mother said, giving the woman another kiss on the cheek.

"Well, that's a surprise," Hal said under his breath as Lady Waller left the room.

Phillip turned on him. "I think you should leave as well. I don't believe you're suitable company to be around my sister."

"Phillip!" his mother exclaimed as he hurried after Lady Waller.

The woman was well down the hallway when Phillip exited the library. He called to her, and she stopped and turned.

A tender smile spread across her lips.

Phillip hurried down the hall to meet up with her. She reached out and took his hands. "Dear, dear Phillip. I have no words to express how sorry I am that I cannot stay and share this occasion with you."

"Take care of her." His voice came out strangled.

Sympathy and concern crossed Lady Waller's face in an instant. Raising a hand, she laid it on his cheek. The tenderness and warmth were more than he could handle.

"I'm afraid I have abandoned her as have all the others," he said. "Will you tell her I'm sorry?"

"Phillip." Her voice became stern, but the admiration in her eyes softened the tone. "Do not marry a woman you do not love. Katherine would never want that for you."

He took a step back, lowering his head. "Nor would she want me to dishonor my family."

"Pash." Hearing the expression from his mother-in-law took Phillip aback. "There is duty to family, Phillip, and there is duty to yourself. You cannot have one without the other."

Phillip smiled. "*This above all to thine own self be true.*"

"Your father would be proud, quoting the Bard." She broke into a bright smile. "I think you should have a conversation with Alaina before we depart. I also think that your parents might be concerned about such a conversation. Meet us at the carriage before we leave. You can say what you need to then." She patted his cheek, lovingly. "You are a good man. We share in our losses. Let us also rejoice in our discoveries."

Phillip took her hand and kissed the top. The scent of roses filled his nostrils, bringing Katherine to mind. She smelled of roses. Alaina smelled of Charlotte's soaps and hair tonics. But soon Alaina, too, would use scented soaps and have soft hands. He would miss seeing the transformation. But he would rejoice in her new family, her new standing, her new life.

With a bow and a curtsey, the two parted ways. How Phillip wished he could go with the Wallers.

CHAPTER TWENTY-NINE

"But, at our parting, we will be, as when we innocently met"
–Ben Jonson

Lainey held a letter of Robert's in each hand. Should she keep them? After all that had happened in the last few days, her head spun. She'd discovered Robert alive but drastically changed. She found out that her mother was a member of the gentry, and while that shouldn't have been a surprise, that she was a cousin to Phillip's Katherine stunned her. But there had been no more opportune moment to discover the relation than as she was leaving Montrose. At least now she had a home to go to, she wasn't being turned out in the cold with nowhere to turn. As if to remind her, a low whistle floated down the hall as the wind blew. A storm must be coming in, to have such winds.

While holding the letters, she weighed and ultimately decided to keep them. Robert's behavior was despicable, but if he could change one way so quickly, it stood to reason he could change back to the brother she knew just as swiftly.

As she dropped the letters in a threadbare satchel Mrs. Hollingsworth had scrounged up for her, a sound at the door caught her attention. Jane, wide-eyed and out of breath stood in the open doorway. Mary joined her a moment later.

"Is it true?" Mary asked as soon as she arrived.

"Depends on what you're inquiring about." Lainey snapped the bag closed.

"You're leaving us?" Jane said.

Lainey had tried to keep that prospect from her mind, instead concentrating on her new life. But seeing Jane and Mary, her friends, her sisters, standing crestfallen in her doorway laced her departure with sadness. She really didn't want to think about the people she'd be leaving behind. Charlotte. Jane. Mary. Phillip. Ah, Phillip—she sighed. She didn't know whether to be angry at the man, or heartbroken—for him and for her.

"I am," Lainey answered. "Appears one way or the other I am leaving today."

"So, it is true," Mary said, stepping into the room.

"That I'm leaving? Yes. That is true."

Lainey sat on the edge of her bed, Mary joining her. Jane stayed fixed in the doorway.

Mary took both of Lainey's hands in hers. "I'm so happy for you."

"Happy!? Where will you go? What will you do? I can't believe Lady Montgomery would believe Harold Warrington over you! She liked you! I could tell."

Mary began to laugh.

Jane placed her hands on her hips. "What's so amusing? Are you not concerned, Mary? What kind of friend are you?"

"Jane, you haven't heard the whole story," Lainey said, patting the bed for Jane to come and sit as well. With a furrowed brow, Jane sat next to Lainey. Before she could explain, Jane threw her arms around Lainey in a crushing hug.

"Jane. Jane. All is well, I promise you." Lainey told Jane and Mary all the details of Lady Waller's discovery. "I can barely believe it myself," Lainey said. "My mother never said a word about her family. I thought she might be embarrassed by them. But now," she peered down at her hands, "I think it was too painful for her to talk about them. Lady Waller made it sound as if they were close sisters." Tears sprang into Lainey's eyes. "Oh…I will miss the two of you. You have become so dear to me. And now…I have no idea when or if we shall meet with each other again."

Jane sprang to her feet. "You remember us," she said. "When you need a lady's maid or a housekeeper. Mary and I would fill in nicely." She dipped into a curtsey.

"And which of you would fill what position?"

"I'll be the maid," Jane said. "I think I'm more suited to that. Mary can be your housekeeper—she's good at those sorts of tasks."

"Who says?" Mary also rose to her feet.

Lainey beheld her friends. "Thank you for welcoming me as you did. This has been the best house I've worked in. I'm sad to leave. But…well…given all that's happened, I'm also not sad to leave."

"I can't believe how poorly they were going to treat you. All because of Master Warrington. I think I shall add salt to his tea this afternoon," Mary said.

Lainey stood, opening her arms to her friends. As they embraced, the scent of wood smoke emanated from Mary, fresh linens from Jane, while a lump formed in Lainey's throat. Would she discover such friends in her new life? Would society accept her? If she didn't have to leave, she would stay if only to be with these friends.

As they broke apart, all three girls wiped a tear or two from their cheeks, then laughed.

"We should get back downstairs," Jane said, taking Mary by the arm. "Write to us, won't you, Alaina?"

"I will. I promise." As the two girls walked arm and arm from Lainey's quarters, she swallowed. Exchanging farewells was never easy, but the uncertainty of Lainey's new life made this parting particularly difficult. She inhaled deeply, and with feigned confidence, picked up her bag, and without a backward glance, walked from her room.

She descended solemnly down the stairs, reminding herself that this departure proved a positive development. Far from being dismissed, she gained a new beginning, a new family, a new home. Why did it feel so awful?

Lainey kept her head down until she reached the main floor. On any other day, she would continue one more flight down to the kitchen. There she would be overcome with the scents of the evening meal. Roasted meat, sweet potatoes, apple tarts. Jane and Mary, Henry and Charles seated about the table, gossiping over what they'd seen or heard that day. Lately, the gossip centered mostly on Phillip, and whether he would actually go through with the wedding. Lainey assured them he would. Phillip was honorable...until he wasn't. Until today. She swallowed down the sharp pain his behavior caused her.

As she stepped from the last stair, a hand reached out and took her bag.

"Allow me," Henry said, relieving her of the burden. "A lady should never carry her own bag." His smile warmed Lainey from head to toe.

"I'm not really a *lady*," she protested.

"From what I hear you are. And..." he leaned closer, "I've always thought you behaved better than some ladies I've known."

Lainey broke into a bright smile.

"I will miss having you downstairs with us," he said, as he stretched out an arm, leading Lainey toward the front of the house.

It was strange having Henry serve her as he would Charlotte, or Lady Montgomery. It was strange to think of leaving the manor through the front entrance, a door she'd only walked through one time. But strangest of all was the reception line waiting for her. Lord and Lady Waller, dressed in heavy coats, stood with Lord and Lady Montgomery. To their right, Miss Charlotte waited, bouncing ever-so-slightly waiting for Lainey to appear. Next to her, Kenton and Phillip stood, hands clasped behind their backs, both carrying the same severe expression.

"Ah, there's our girl," Lady Waller exclaimed as Lainey approached. The woman turned to Lady Montgomery. "I cannot express enough gratitude for your hospitality, Helena. I deeply regret that we cannot stay."

"It is for the best," Lord Montgomery said, cutting off any chance his wife might utter something inappropriate. Or offensive? Or kind? Lainey wasn't sure. Instead, Lady Montgomery gave Lady Waller a hug, kissing her on both cheeks.

"Do come another time," she said.

"Of course," Lady Waller replied.

Lainey's new-found aunt and uncle exchanged handshakes with Lord Montgomery. Afterwards Lady Waller turned toward Lainey.

"Come, child. We need to go. It is a long ride."

"Yes, ma'am," Lainey said, confused on how she should address the woman.

Lady Montgomery took Lainey's hand in hers, patting it gently. "How fortunate that you should find family. You showed yourself to be wise and kind, and I must offer apologies regarding the conversation we had this morning.

I appreciate your candor. Master Warrington's offensive behavior has been discovered because of your courage. We thank you for that."

At that moment, Lainey wished she could exhibit another bout of courage, but she didn't sense her candor had impressed anyone. Master Warrington had once more tried to ruin the goodness Lainey had found. If it hadn't been for the unexpected discovery of her heritage, Lainey would be leaving this house on extremely different terms.

"Thank you, Lady Montgomery," she said, stuffing down her anger. "It pleases me to think that you find me courageous. I did not think I would leave this house with such kind thoughts. But thanks to Lady Waller," Lainey glanced to her aunt and smiled, "for helping me discover that I have a family." She dipped into a small curtsey.

"Yes, yes," Lord Montgomery said, taking Lainey's hand giving it a good shake. The gesture surprised and puzzled Lainey.

Next, she stepped in front of Charlotte. A lump formed in her throat as she curtsied before her mistress. Charlotte's lip quivered. Then unexpectedly, Charlotte launched herself at Lainey, pulling her into a tight hug.

"I am going to miss you so much," she said into Lainey's neck. Charlotte pushed herself back, resting her hands on Lainey's shoulders. "You must write to me. Will you? Will you write to me? Tell me all about your new life?"

Lainey laughed. "I will. I will write to you."

"And perhaps we can meet up in London. We can both have our coming out at the same time. Wouldn't that be delightful?"

"Don't be ridiculous, Charlotte," her mother said. "Miss Clarkson is not of an age to have a coming out."

"I will write to you, and someday soon we can have tea," Lainey said. This had to be the strangest moment of her life.

Never did she envision herself having tea with the gentry. But here she was, now, part of society. How had this happened?

Kenton offered a slight bow. "May you find great joy and happiness."

"Thank you," she said just above a whisper.

Turning to Phillip, she straightened her shoulders, determined to meet him eye to eye. Let him know the pain she'd experienced early that day.

"Miss Clarkson," he said, also giving her a slight bow.

"Master Montgomery." She didn't bother to curtsey. "My sincerest congratulations on your wedding." She didn't wait another moment. Lady Waller stood near with an arm extended to assist Lainey out the door and to the carriage. She took her aunt's extended arm, and with head held high she walked out the front entrance to Montrose Manor. The chilled air hit fast. She pulled her frayed coat tightly across her shoulders.

A footman, whose name she would have to learn, opened the door to the carriage and helped Lady Waller climb in. As Lainey took his hand, ready to climb in herself, someone touched her shoulder.

"Lady Waller," Phillip said. "May I take your charge for a short walk before you leave?"

Lainey had not turned to his touch, nor to his voice. Her eyes fixed on the woman in the coach. Her aunt smiled knowingly.

"Phillip, if you must. But a short walk, please. We really do have some distance to cover."

"Of course, ma'am." Phillip offered Lady Waller a brief bow. He extended his arm to Lainey. "Miss Clarkson?"

She peeked into the carriage, in some respects asking for permission—in others hoping for an escape. Her aunt smiled and dipped her head. Lainey sighed, turned, and walked away. Phillip scrambled to catch her up.

~~*

Phillip was and wasn't startled by Alaina's quick departure. He didn't blame her for being angry at him. He must apologize, and he wouldn't let her leave the manor without doing so.

She'd pulled her coat tight around her, whether to protect her from the cold or from him, Phillip could not tell. She needed a better coat and he hoped Lady Waller would arrange for that immediately. He envied Alaina. She was going off to Katherine's home. She would dwell under the loving guidance of Lady Waller, saved from the life of service she'd been subjected to. He could scarcely believe she was Katherine's cousin. Truthfully, she'd exhibited her true blood line all along.

She paced ahead more quickly. Clasping his hands behind his back, he lengthened his stride. The walled garden came into view, the perfect spot to talk with her. She would pass it in moments if he didn't hurry. Jogging to catch up, he startled her by taking her arm and leading her through the gate.

She yanked her arm away. "I am not your servant anymore. You cannot manhandle me."

The fire in her eyes didn't deter him but only endeared her more to his heart.

"I could not let you leave without apologizing."

She walked further into the garden, leaving more space than he desired between them. Turning to face him, Phillip thought for sure that she would chastise him for his reprehensible behavior earlier in the day. She made no reply.

"I should have come to your defense," he said.

She crossed her arms and lifted her chin a bit. *Yes*, he thought, *her true heritage is manifesting.*

"I ask…" he took a few hesitant steps toward her. He expected her to bolt any second. "No, I plead for your forgiveness."

His words hung in the frosty air.

Her mouth twitched. She was ready to speak, he simply had to have the patience to wait her out.

"Just like that," she finally said.

Not what he had expected. "I am not sure what you mean."

"Because you said the words, I should forgive you?"

He blinked. "Because I mean the words."

"And you didn't mean your silence this morning?"

"Oh, Alaina…" his shoulders dropped, and he took several steps forward. She took as many steps back. "My behavior this morning was abominable. I should have spoken up."

"But you told your mother that I was trying to lure you away from your family so you could take me to America."

"That is not what I said. That is how she interpreted my report. Can we sit?" He motioned toward a stone bench, one where they had sat together before.

"I prefer to stand. Lord and Lady Waller are waiting for me. I must not detain them much longer."

Phillip sighed. "My mother spoke to Warrington before she spoke to me. I tried to explain my feelings toward Miss Hilton. I told her that I entertained the idea of running away with you to America to keep from entering this marriage. I also told her about Kenton's feelings for the girl. All she heard was that I was willing to go with you to America. Nothing else mattered."

Alaina stood her ground not responding. She wanted him to grovel.

"Alaina, truly…I should…" And it came to him. He knew what he had to say. He lowered his eyes. "I was fooled by

Warrington as well. He told me how you had stolen the tiara…and I knew…"

"I didn't steal it. He planted it. Did he tell you that?"

"No." Phillip raised his eyes to hers. "But when I confronted him about his behavior toward you, he admitted that he tried to…well, that he…"

"Should I applaud his sudden truthfulness?"

"No!" Phillip moved toward her and this time she didn't retreat. "He is a scoundrel. I've known that about him since college. But I never suspected that he already knew you. Or that he had tried…apparently several times…to make inappropriate advances toward you." He paused. "And in my house! If I'd suspected…well, I might have taken matters into my own hands."

Her mouth twitched for a moment before she broke into a laugh.

"Would you have challenged him to a duel?"

"Would that surprise you?"

"Most assuredly."

"I don't know whether to be offended by your doubt in me or not."

"No offense is intended. But you must admit…the thought of you challenging anyone to anything more violent than a game of whist is an entertaining thought."

He smiled. "I suppose."

"I only ever stole an apple…in which you so kindly rescued me. And I only did that…"

"No need to explain. It was the best moment of chivalry I've ever experienced."

"Seems your chivalry has limits." She squared her shoulders, her previous defensiveness returning.

"What do you mean?" He asked, half afraid.

"Where was your chivalry in your mother's court? I was tried and convicted with no one…not anyone, including you to come to my defense. It was your idea to go to America. Did you offer that? No! Your silence was as condemning as Mr. Warrington's words."

Phillip hung his head.

"I felt as if I were the woman taken in adultery. Everyone circled around me, ready to throw stones. No one there to defend me, except God alone. And He did. He appeared in the form of Lady Waller. She believed me. If she had been in the room, she would have defended me. But you…" her voice tempered. And if Phillip wasn't mistaken, there was trembling as she continued. "You, who claim to care about me, should have stood up for me."

He took a step closer. "You are right. I will forever regret my cowardice." He held out his hand toward her. "I love you, Alaina Clarkson. There. I've said it. And it is true. I am not inebriated. I know exactly the words I am speaking. I am in love with you, and if I were not engaged to another, would marry you."

She scoffed. "Marry me…a servant."

"The situation is different now," he said. "You are no longer considered beneath me."

She let out an incredulous laugh. "No? I'm not so sure your parents would agree. I've served in your household these past months. In their eyes, regardless of who my mother was, I will forever be a servant."

"You are more than what society has made of you."

Now it was her turn to lower her head. Her foot scuffed at the ground, but her shoulders relaxed, and her breathing eased.

"Please forgive me, Alaina. I will never, ever abandon you again."

"You cannot say that. Your allegiances will belong to another."

"That doesn't matter. Say you forgive me, and no matter what, I will come whenever you need me."

"Given time, I suppose I will forgive you. Even miss you," she added, her voice a breath above a whisper.

"As I will you." He took a step closer.

"I hope you will find happiness with Miss Hilton." She didn't sound convincing, at least he hoped she wasn't trying to be.

"In light of my feelings, and Kenton's, I don't know how this marriage can go forward."

She nodded and raised her eyes to his. He was caught by the familiarity of those eyes that always reminded him of Katherine. But as he gazed into her eyes, he saw only Alaina. Only the woman he loved.

He took another step closer—close enough now that he could sweep her into his arms if he wished.

"Sir…"

"Call me Phillip!" he said.

She smiled sadly. "Phillip. You are engaged to another. I am leaving, which will be a blessing for both of us."

"How can you say that?"

"Because it would be torture to see you married to another." She paused. "And I will not be a mistress to anyone."

"You think I would take you as a mistress when I want you for a wife?"

"You flatter me. I wouldn't know how to be your wife. And…I need to get to know my new family. I need to learn where I fit in."

"*Parting is such sweet sorrow*," he whispered.

"Pardon?"

"Take no mind. I think Shakespeare knew very little about love."

"Thank you. Thank you for saving me that day in the market. Thank you for helping me to locate my brother."

"That didn't turn out so well."

"No. But still you tried to help me." She bowed her head as if what she had to say next proved too difficult for her to say to his face. "And thank you for giving me a home, a family of sorts and…" He saw her swallow as she lifted her head to him. "Thank you for loving me." Tears welled in her eyes.

"Before you go," he asked, "May I inquire of your feelings for me? Might you also love me?"

"At the risk of being imprudent…" her lips quivered. "I believe I do."

He reached up to touch her cheek. She flinched. But surprisingly without warning, took his hand, and gently raised it to her cheek. As his eyes misted with tears, he pulled her into his arms and pressed a kiss to her lips.

~~*

Lainey closed her eyes and melted into Phillip's kiss. This wasn't a drunken kiss. This wasn't a lover's kiss. This was goodbye. As she relished the warmth of his arms, the tenderness of his lips, she knew the end was near. Tears formed beneath her lashes.

As the kiss ended, he held her tighter. She was as reluctant as he to let go, to make this final parting. But she knew Lord and Lady Waller waited for her. From the way he held her, tight and close, she understood on some level he did need her, as he'd said. She was a lifeline—a way to move forward, a way past his grief. He trembled ever-so-slightly in her arms. She needed to be the strong one. She had to let go. Steeling herself, she slowly pushed herself from his arms. The sudden chill was unbearable. The heartbreak in his eyes, in her whole being, was more than she could bear. Any moment, she would lose all her resolve and stay.

"I must go," she whispered, refusing to meet his gaze.

He took a step back, his shoulders sagging, his arms hanging limp at his side.

Lainey swallowed, mustering every ounce of courage she had. When she knew she had control, she spoke. "May you find joy in your new life," she said. "I will think of you often." With one hand, she clutched the collar of her coat closed, with the other she grabbed up her skirts. Pushing past Phillip before he could stop her, she fled out of the garden.

EPILOGUE

*"There is only one happiness in life,
To love and be loved."*
–George Sand

Six Months Later

With the third outing this week, Lainey had tired. The past few months had been a whirlwind in assuming her place as a member of the Waller family. When she'd been introduced to her maternal grandmother, aged and hard of hearing, the woman wept openly at meeting the granddaughter she never knew existed.

Lainey had faced an accelerated course in etiquette, fashion, and the decorum expected of a daughter of the gentry. Now and then she longed for the upper floor of Montrose Manor and time to relax with Jane and Mary, giggling over family gossip and Mr. Hollingsworth's grotesque expressions when he became agitated. At present, the memory made her smile.

The Wallers treated Lainey better than she could have ever imagined. She heard story after story of her mother and aunt, their shared hopes and dreams. Her mother became more alive in the last months than Lainey ever thought possible.

But with the onset of spring, the outings became a burden. It was necessary, Aunt Elizabeth, now affectionately called Aunt Beth, told Lainey. She had to be introduced into society, but the introductions never included her past. She was simply the daughter of Lady Waller's sister who had passed, with nothing said about how many years ago, or how Lainey, raised in the squalors of London, had worked as a servant in the homes of the gentry, people like those she was meeting. She smiled, carried on trivial conversation, and missed her old life.

At a garden party with the Minnick family—longtime friends of the Wallers, and pillars in London society, a footman held out his hand to assist Lainey as she exited the coach. The hardest adjustment to her new life had been having servants herself. She often told Aunt Beth that she could mend her own clothing, dress herself—although with some of the new fashions, she appreciated someone to help her lace up a corset—and she could brush her own hair at the end of day. Being ignored, she quickly quit complaining about all the attention and simply tried to be courteous to the staff. In return, a loyalty and fondness had developed between her and the servants that Uncle George often frowned upon.

The Minnick family owned a grand estate five miles from the Waller home. Aunt Beth had assured Lainey that Lady Minnick was excited, if not a bit too curious to meet Lainey, as was the Minnick's second son, Thomas. To ensure the introduction went well, Aunt Beth had ordered Lainey a new silk dress. Lainey felt as if she were royalty in the cream-colored gown with its inlaid lace bodice and embroidered green vine with pink flowers. The wide skirts and multiple petticoats pleasantly swished about her legs when she walked toward the front door. She fought a childish urge to spin in a circle to see how far the skirts would flare.

The door opened on their approach, where the Minnick's butler greeted them. Although he bore no resemblance to Mr. Hollingsworth, his manner reminded Lainey of the man. Too often she found herself remembering and comparing all other estates to that of Montrose.

They were led through a grand hall to the back of the home and a large balcony that overlooked vast lands owned by the host family. Lord and Lady Minnick stood immediately outside the door and smiled as Lainey's aunt and uncle approached.

"Lady Waller, how wonderful to see you again," Lady Minnick said, opening her arms for a faux hug and an air kiss aimed at both cheeks.

"Lovely day for a gathering," Uncle George said.

Lainey lowered her head and grinned. Yes, talk about the weather if other polite conversation failed.

"Lady Minnick, may I introduce you to my niece, Miss Alaina Clarkson," Aunt Beth said. Lainey stepped forward and offered a small, but conciliatory curtsey.

"Ah, Miss Clarkson, I have heard so much about you. How extraordinary that you've been able to come and stay with your aunt and uncle."

"Yes, ma'am. I have been blessed, indeed."

"So sorry to hear about your poor mother. I knew her as a girl and thought most highly of her."

"Thank you, Lady Minnick. If it's not too much trouble, at your convenience, I would love to hear about your time with her."

"Of course, dear. We must have you and your aunt over for tea one afternoon and I can tell you how much I admired her." Lady Minnick laid a hand on Lainey's arm as she surveyed the grounds. "I am anxious for you to meet my son, Thomas. He's about your age and would be a good connection for you about town. Where is that silly young man?" She leaned toward Lainey. "Often, I think he purposely avoids me."

"When you are constantly trying to introduce him to eligible females, I wonder why you are surprised?" Lord Minnick said, offering a wink to Lainey.

Aunt Beth took Lainey by the arm. "We will certainly watch for Thomas and introduce Miss Clarkson when the moment arises. We mustn't keep you from your other guests."

"No, no, of course not," Lady Minnick said. "Please, help yourself to the refreshments and enjoy this beautiful day." She swept her arm heavenward as if she had ordered the weather specifically for this occasion.

As Aunt Beth led Lainey away, Uncle George muttered, "Why must they hold these parties in the middle of the afternoon when it's not sociable to imbibe, and hotter than blazes standing out in the sun. Elizabeth, did you bring a parasol for shade?"

"I'll locate a comfortable spot under a tree. First, I must find Thomas and introduce Alaina to him."

"Forgive me for not accompanying you on your quest. I truly believe young people need to be left to their own devices. If Mr. Minnick finds Alaina attractive, he will beg for an introduction. You need not worry." Uncle George turned to Alaina. "And you will discover the introduction less taxing." With that, he tipped his hat and went in search of other gentlemen, where Lainey knew he would imbibe and smoke his pipe as well.

True to her word, Aunt Beth found a lovely spot under a large oak tree where several other women were seated. Lainey's aunt knew all the women and made quick introductions, too quick for Lainey to remember their names. She had learned quickly that using *ma'am* and *your ladyship* worked as well as knowing proper names.

She also knew her conversation would be limited. Aunt Beth had given Lainey strict instructions on their first outing to never discuss her past life. Instead, she circulated the story that Lainey's mother had recently died, and how, when the Waller's received word of the event had immediately sent for Lainey. If anyone knew the story behind her mother's infamous elopement, Lainey received instruction to simply agree and redirect the conversation to a topic less personal…such as the weather.

The shade proved pleasant, as did most of the conversation. There was talk of new babies and engagements and the scandalous behavior of someone's child at the last ball. Lainey smiled and made small talk when needed, but otherwise her attention drifted toward the grounds. The Minnick estate was grand, with several large oak trees, sculpted topiaries, and Lainey noticed several gardens paths. She longed to walk amongst the flowers and shrubberies and have a moment away from the clamor.

"Oh, look!" One woman said, catching Lainey from her daydream. "It appears Mr. Thomas Minnick is approaching."

Aunt Beth leaned close to Lainey. "It appears your uncle was correct."

Lainey glanced in the direction the woman had indicated and saw the silhouette of two men approaching, the sun behind them blinding a clear view. She lowered her head not wanting to appear too anxious to meet the young master. Truth was, she dreaded it.

Before long, four pleated pant legs came into her view and stopped in front of Aunt Beth.

"Lady Waller, welcome."

Lainey caught sight of the young man bending over and leaving a kiss on her aunt's glove. She tensed, readying herself for an introduction she didn't want.

"I believe you've met my friend."

"Mr. Montgomery."

Lainey's head shot up as her aunt rose and accepted Phillip's embrace. They exchanged a few moments of pleasantry. After the brief conversation, Aunt Beth extended an arm toward Lainey.

"Gentleman, may I present my niece, Miss Alaina Clarkson." In that moment Lainey realized she could not let on to an acquaintance with Phillip. She couldn't risk anyone asking how they were acquainted.

"Miss Clarkson, this is Mr. Thomas Minnick, and Mr. Phillip Montgomery."

Both the men turned toward her and bowed. She inclined her head ever so slightly. Phillip appeared more agreeable than she remembered. For one, he was sober. She nearly laughed at the thought but caught herself in time. He wore a light silk cravat. His frockcoat was open, revealing a buttoned waistcoat with a chain draped across it. He appeared brighter—happier than she ever remembered.

Marriage must agree with him. The thought left a sour taste in her mouth. It wasn't that she didn't want him to be happy. She did. But she thought it would take longer for Miss Hilton, er...the new Lady Montgomery to bring him joy.

She frowned. She should be more gracious.

"Miss Clarkson," Thomas said. "My mother will be glad to hear we have actually met."

"It is my pleasure, sir." She inclined her head briefly. She watched Phillip work to keep his expression composed. She couldn't imagine what he found so amusing.

Unexpectedly, a footman appeared at Thomas' side, handing him a note atop a silver charger. Mr. Minnick took the note and after perusing it for a moment, said, "Please excuse me. A guest is ready to leave, and I've not yet had the opportunity to speak with him." He turned directly to Lainey. "Miss Clarkson, please allow me to return and show you around the grounds. The gardens are beautiful this time of year."

"Of course," she said. He bowed and walked toward the manor house. Her gaze shifted to Phillip, who smiled, mostly to himself. With a glint in his eye, he turned to Lady Waller.

"Lady Waller, would you permit me to take your charge on a short walk about the gardens?" He leaned a little closer. "I know these grounds as well as my friend, Mr. Minnick. And the young lady here," he held his hand out toward Lainey, "appears to be a young woman who appreciates fine gardens."

Aunt Beth smiled. "Why, Mr. Montgomery, do I notice a bit of competition for the lady's attention?" She laid a gentle hand atop Lainey's as the other women in the group tittered about the young men's advances.

"They say, your ladyship, early birds catch the worm."

Aunt Beth and the other women snickered at his response.

Lainey cocked her head. He must only wish to inquire about Lainey's life in a private setting. And she, too, wished for a chance to speak to Phillip, but what would she learn? Was he happy? Had marriage released him from his father's heavy hand and granted him the freedom he desired? Was a child expected? On the other hand, maybe she didn't want to hear about his newfound life.

Aunt Beth squeezed her hand, and in her eyes, Lainey saw encouragement. After a small hesitation, she offered an imperceptible nod. This could be the last time they would have a moment alone.

Smiling, Aunt Beth said. "I believe you are correct, Mr. Montgomery. Miss Clarkson loves a fine garden. And…" she turned to Lainey, "I think my niece would much enjoy getting away from our stuffy conversation." She laid a gloved hand on Lainey's shoulder. "Isn't that right, my dear?"

"Yes, ma'am. Thank you."

Phillip offered a grateful bow and held his arm out to Lainey. She rose from her chair, wrapped her hand about his forearm, amazed that she could touch him in such a sociably acceptable manner. Together they walked toward the nearest garden path.

Hyacinth and lilac filled the air. Lainey took a deep breath, releasing it slowly—not only to enjoy the wonderful fragrance, but to calm her sudden onset of nerves.

"I cannot tell you what a pleasure it is to be with you," Phillip said after they were out of earshot from Lady Waller and her company.

Lainey dropped her hand from his arm and moved sideways to put a respectable amount of distance between them. After all, he was a married man.

"Likewise," she said, unable to really look at him as she desired.

"Have you adjusted well to your new life?" He made no attempt to close the distance, instead clasping his hands behind his back as they walked.

"I believe so. Lord and Lady Waller have been incredibly kind to me." She laughed. "I've met more relatives than I knew existed."

"And how are you getting along with Katherine's sister, Miss Louisa?"

"She is most entertaining." Lainey smiled thinking about the girl who was similar in age to Charlotte. "I believe she will marry soon."

"Will she? I hope it is a good match."

"She's smitten with the young man, if that's what you're asking."

"I'm happy to hear that. Miss Louisa was regularly underfoot when I courted Katherine."

"I think you will find her much grown now."

"I would think so."

They walked in companionable silence for a time. Lainey stopped occasionally to inspect a budding rosebush, or to tug on the branch of a flowering fruit tree.

"They have lovely gardens here," she said absently.

"They do."

A small pond appeared, thick with lily pads and surrounded by pines and trees flowering in new, golden leaves. A breeze whispered through the branches carrying the scent of newly sprouted pine boughs. Lainey paused to take in the sight. Sunlight filtered through the trees, warm on her arm and shoulder. Everything around her suggested tranquility.

"Speaking of sisters, Charlotte misses you a great deal and is sad that she has not heard from you," Phillip remarked as he came to stand beside her.

"Please give her my apologies. Lady Waller has kept me busy with social engagements. I barely have time to myself." That was only a half truth. She missed Montrose enough as it was. She didn't need any reminders remotely related to the estate. Even more so, Lainey worried that any correspondence with Charlotte would be filled with tales of Phillip and Marianne. She didn't want to think about that presently...or ever. She looked up at Phillip, surprised to find him gazing at her. "Please assure her that I will write soon. How is Miss Charlotte? I do so miss her."

"I thought you might. And she is well. She has taken on a house maid to be her new lady's maid. Her name is…" he scowled as he tried to come up with the name. "Jane, I believe. I assume you know her."

"I do. Jane is a delightful person. She will serve Charlotte faithfully."

"Our father is still trying to arrange a marriage with Sir Markhall. But so far, nothing official has come of it."

"Ah, poor Charlotte. I know she does not wish to marry the man."

"No, she doesn't. Which reminds me," he said as he reached inside his frock coat and pulled out an envelope. "I have this for you."

"What is that?"

He handed her a letter. "I believe it is from your brother."

"Oh." Lainey snatched her hand back. "I'm not sure I'm ready to correspond with him."

"I expected as much. But here, take the letter anyway. Read it at your convenience and respond as you feel appropriate. I understand from Hal, Mr. Warrington, that your brother was astonished to learn of your mother's relation to the Wallers."

"I imagine so. And I won't be surprised to learn that he wishes to come visit me to make their acquaintance. I never imagined…well, that he was so self-centered. Our mother would be undoubtedly disappointed with his behavior."

"But not yours." Certainly, he meant that as a compliment, but she wondered. Her mother would have wanted her children to get along, for Lainey to be more forgiving. She sighed heavily. Maybe someday.

Phillip surveyed the pond. "I understand that Lady Minnick was anxious for you to meet Mr. Minnick."

"I was under that impression as well." Lainey's shoulders slumped. "I don't know how young members of society stand all the parental matchmaking that goes on. Or in my case, my aunt's matchmaking."

"I'm sure she is only looking out for your interests. Being without parents to care for you, I'm sure Lady Waller only wishes for you to marry well so you are taken care of. My feelings are similar. I am certain she worries about what you have already suffered and wants to alleviate all she can."

"Well, that is kind of her…and you, but I have no intention of marrying."

"And why is that?"

She took a deep breath and released it slowly as she thought of how to answer his question. She'd decided as soon as she entered society.

"Look," Phillip said before she could answer. He pointed down the path. "There's a bench. Shall we sit?"

Without waiting for her reply, he began walking. Momentarily caught off guard, Lainey hurried to catch him up. He waited for her at the marble bench, only taking a seat next to her after she had pulled her skirts to the side and seated herself.

Sitting next to him, Lainey felt the press of his leg against her skirts—a welcoming and distracting sensation.

"So," he said, "Tell me why you have no intention of marrying?"

Her nose crinkled. "I'm not sure you will appreciate this."

"Try me."

"My aunt and uncle have been gracious to me. So kind. So giving. They have made sure that I have all I could need or want. I have clothes. I have shelter and food, they provide music lessons for me. They treat me as their daughter. But what they cannot do is erase my past. And as I say that, I really don't want them to. My past, the way I grew up in the heart of London with parents who struggled to provide, who worked their fingers to the bone to make a home for me and my brothers. That's part of who I am."

"Of course it is."

"And more so, the time I spent in service tending to the needs of ladies that I'm now on equal terms with—I cannot reveal. Yet, that time also made me who I am." She let out a heavy sigh. "If I am to marry well, I can reveal none of my past life. I can't talk about being a ragamuffin on the streets of London, or a chambermaid, or a lady's maid. I'm expected to invent some kind of life that I never lived." She stared up into Phillip's eyes. "I can't ever reveal who I truly am, because if I do, I am not considered worthy to be in my husband's social circle. I would rather live as a seamstress or a governess and be myself, than to marry well and pretend to be someone I'm not."

"I don't think Lady Waller would want you to pretend to be someone else either."

"Aunt Beth," Lainey said, her heart filling with tenderness for the woman. "She is as good and kind as a woman can be. But she's the one who warned me of telling anyone of my background. She recognizes I will be shunned from any good society. So, they may introduce me to as many worthy young men as they desire." She shook her head. "But I will never accept any of them."

"Any man worthy of you, Miss Clarkson, would surely accept you as you are."

"I believe you think too highly of your sex. I have met few who would do so…and they are already spoken for."

All the talk of societal pressure dampened the joy Lainey had experienced in Phillip's company. And as much as she wanted to sit and spend more time with Phillip, she was keenly aware of appearances. She had to be. Before she carefully made sure that she never stepped out of her station. Now she had to observe the rules of propriety. She was alone with a man—a married man. It would not bode well for them to be discovered in a secluded area alone. She would be marked as wanton, he as a scoundrel.

She stood. "I believe we should continue on. I wouldn't want word to get back to Lady Montgomery of a secret rendezvous. I have learned that people of property have little to do but misinterpret and gossip about people they know so little of."

Phillip laughed. "Lady Waller has been teaching you well. But I assure you, no such assumptions will be made."

"No?" Lainey took a step sideways, crossed her arms ready to paint the unfortunate rumors that would spread. "A young girl of marriageable age, consorting with a married man in secluded places."

Phillip laughed harder. "First of all, we are not consorting. Secondly," he paused and searched her eyes. "I am not a married man."

Lainey stood frozen in place, her mind racing at his words. "I…I don't understand."

Phillip rose from the bench, standing in front of her. He reached out and took both her hands in his, the warmth she felt was familiar and frightening in the same moment.

"I am not married. After you left, Miss Hilton and I had a lengthy conversation." He chuckled. "The first real conversation we have had since my proposal." His brow wrinkled. "Did I ever tell you what a fiasco that was?"

"No," she said, her voice not much more than a whisper.

"A story for another day. Anyway, we were candid with each other. I told her point blank, that I did not love her. That I did not know if I ever could. She cried a little, but admitted that because of her childhood infatuation with me, she had made me into someone that she didn't recognize when we spent time together. She felt more comfortable with Kenton, and thought she actually fancied him more than me.

"I pretended to be clueless to the idea, and certainly did not reveal Kenton's feelings for her. In the end, she proposed we call off the wedding. My father was not pleased. But when I promised to step up into the role he wanted for me, working relentlessly to be a leader around the estate, and less the wounded, crazed, grieving husband, he acquiesced."

"How did I not hear about this?"

"That's a good question. The way gossip spreads over the countryside, I thought for sure you knew."

"I did not." Was this the reason he had changed so much? Because he had his freedom, not only from a marriage he did not want, but also from his grief? "No more conversations with Lady Katherine?" she asked.

"No more conversations with Lady Katherine...well, almost. I will occasionally visit her grave and talk to her. But I found I'd rather have a real person to converse with...someone who will have a different opinion, or insight. I want a real relationship. Alaina..."

"Stop." She held up both hands as if to push him away.

"Alaina, I know who you are. You wouldn't have to hide your past from me."

"Ah, Phillip, not from you...but from everyone else. I cannot leave who I am behind."

"Everyone of importance knows, Alaina. They all love you. They would welcome you."

She lowered her head and began fiddling with the fabric of her skirt. "Not your father. Not your mother. They will think you married beneath you. The staff will think I married too far above me. I don't want to live that way."

"Will you not consider it?"

She gazed up into his pleading eyes. She had decided months ago that life proved difficult enough without inviting others to judge you, without purposefully walking into difficult situations. And she knew...what Phillip proposed would be difficult at best.

"I told you. I have planned my future, and marriage is not part of it."

Releasing her hands, he took a step back.

"I'll forever be your friend," she said, hoping to ease his disappointment.

It didn't. He lowered his head, but not before Lainey saw his furrowed brow and the pain in his eyes. Silence hung between them like a heavy fog. Strange how that didn't keep birds from singing or the occasional croak of a frog from breaking the stillness. It amazed Lainey how the world moved on. The sun rose and the sun would set. Hopes and expectations come, and later they change and morph into dreams scarcely recognizable. Now that she could dream of marrying this man—she knew it would not answer his longings for a stable quiet life. Nor would she ever be comfortable living half in his world, and half in the one she made for herself. She was doing what was best. Wasn't she?

Phillip sighed, and without comment, held out his arm. Lainey swallowed. The end had come, and her heart ached at the thought of it. She reached out and laced her hand through the crook of his elbow and, in silence, they walked back out in the open and into society.

When they broke through the garden entrance, Lainey saw her aunt and uncle standing ahead near a reflecting pool at the rear of the manor house. Phillip must have noticed them as well. He led Lainey in their direction.

Aunt Beth smiled at their approach, her admiration for both evident. Coming to Lady Waller's side, Lainey let go of Phillip's arm, and in that small movement the reality of their separation became real. Suddenly she saw herself sitting in a dark, dank room of a shop deep in the heart of London, her fingers numb from needle pricks, her hands rough from washing and pressing fabrics for wealthy women who couldn't sew a straight seam for themselves. Her neck ached as if she had been sitting under poor lamplight, hunched over a woman's garment, one who would never have to leave someone she loved because she was deemed unworthy by society. Loneliness seeped into her skin. She blinked, trying to force the vision away. It left, but in its wake, she saw herself surrounded by children...not her children, but children unruly and spoiled, pampered children never taught basic manners. She was dressed in black, as if in mourning...and she was, mourning a life of love, laughter, and children of her own. Bile rose in her throat as she saw how it would be caring for other women's children. Marked as a spinster and a recipient of constant pity because she chose not to marry. This is what lay ahead of her.. She was choosing to be lonely. She glanced between her aunt and Phillip, seeing them but not hearing a word they spoke to each other.

She cocked her head to the side, noticing the resemblance between Aunt Beth and her own mother. Her mother who had turned her back on society. Her mother who went against the wishes of her family to be with the man she loved. Her mother who lived with the hardship of her choices—not choices made of fear, but of love. Memories of sitting at her mother's feet learning to stitch a hem, standing at a table that wobbled as her mother taught her to knead a loaf of bread. The expression in her mother's eyes pierced Lainey with love down to her very core. Without thinking, Lainey reached out and laid her hand on Phillip's arm to steady herself.

His voice, which Lainey realized had been filling in the background of her thoughts, stopped. He turned to her. She raised her eyes to his and there it was…love that blossomed and spread through her from head to toe. Not his love for her, but hers for him. This is what her mother had felt for her father.

Phillip met her gaze, studying her for a long moment. His mouth cocked up at the corner slightly, enough that she knew he felt it, too. He turned to Lainey's aunt and uncle.

"Lord Waller, I desire your permission to call upon Miss Clarkson."

Lady Waller smiled.

Lord Waller, after at first appearing a bit puzzled, said, "Of course, my good man. Nothing would delight us more."

Phillip turned to Lainey, a sly grin across his mouth. "Miss Clarkson?"

For the first time she looked into his eyes and truly felt worthy, not because of her relation to Lady Waller, and not because she had a dowry or a fancy dress. Loving Phillip made her worthy. The same as her father had been worthy of marrying her mother—because she loved him. Perhaps nothing would become of a relationship with Phillip. Perhaps a few months from now, she would decide to go to America after all. But she owed it to herself to find out where this would lead. She smiled and offered the gentleman at her side a slight curtsy. She lifted her face to his, to the sun, perchance to a new life, and said, "I would be most honored to have you call, Mr. Montgomery. You see me as I see you. And yet, I believe we have more to discover, possibly, much more."

THE END

Acknowledgements

My path to becoming an author started late in life. Without the support of my wonderful husband, Doug, it never would have happened at all. I will be forever grateful. Between Sunrise and Sunset exists because of the wonderful staff and cohorts I had at Seton Hill University. A special shoutout to Paul 'Goat' Allen, my mentor, Therese Stadul, Anne Chambers Lynch, and Rosanna Capellutti, the best critique partners ever. Thanks to my daughter Sarah Talley Porter, for her comments and edits. Also, a special thanks to the team at Black Rose Writing for their wonderful support and care through the publishing process. The writing community is truly one of most inclusive and encouraging groups of people to ever exist.

About the Author

A. R. Talley lives with her husband in northeast Ohio with its wet springs, warm summers, and beautiful autumns. She doesn't talk about winter. She has an MFA in Writing Popular Fiction from Seton Hill University and has won several first chapter awards at the Storymakers Writers Conference. When not conjuring new characters and storylines, she enjoys playing with one or more of her 12 grandchildren, reading, watching movies, playing piano, cooking, and flower gardening. If asked, her favorite vacation is a Caribbean cruise, preferably one with coconut ranger cookies.

Note from A. R. Talley

Word-of-mouth is crucial for any author to succeed. If you enjoyed *Between Sunrise and Sunset*, please leave a review online—anywhere you are able. Even if it's just a sentence or two. It would make all the difference and would be very much appreciated.

Thanks!
A. R. Talley

We hope you enjoyed reading this title from:

www.blackrosewriting.com

Subscribe to our mailing list – *The Rosevine* – and receive **FREE** books, daily deals, and stay current with news about
upcoming releases and our hottest authors.
Scan the QR code below to sign up.

Already a subscriber? Please accept a sincere thank you for being a fan of Black Rose Writing authors.

View other Black Rose Writing titles at
www.blackrosewriting.com/books and use promo code
PRINT to receive a **20% discount** when purchasing.